com
ADVANTAGE

COPYRIGHT

Competitive Advantage

Published by Author AK Landow, LLC

ISBN: 978-1-962575-29-4

Edited and Proofread By: Chrisandra's Corrections

Cover Design & Illustration By: K.B. Designs

Formatted with Vellum

DEDICATION

To all the women out there who defend, protect, and uplift other women. It's easy to stand on the shoulders of others. It's much harder to let them stand on yours.

"I'm all about empowering other women. I'm about helping my teammates be their best selves. I'm all about being my best self. And I just feel like that if we can do that together, then great things are gonna happen. I'm gonna let her be the star that she is, and she totally deserves it…I'll be there to support her."
~Sophie Cunningham
(My inspiration for Kennedy Jeffries)

#8 KENNEDY JEFFRIES

#11 PALMER PAYNE

#18 LAYLA LADRÓN

#22 SULLEY O'SHEA

#44 SHAY WALKER

MEET THE BEAVERS

MEET THE CAMELS

CAMELS

#6 PRESLEY LADRÓN

#19 VANCE MCCAFFREY

#30 CHAMP WILLIAMSON

#88 DAYLEN HUMBLECUT

#97 BEAU FUDD

PROLOGUE

DAYLEN

"Sir, would you like some headphones?" the friendly stewardess innocently asks me on our private jet to Las Vegas.

I smile at her and answer, "Absolutely, but how did you know my name was Phones?"

The guys all snort in laughter, but the stewardess and the rest of the women seem unamused. Frankly, I think I'm the funniest guy on the planet.

There's one person who most definitely disagrees. Kennedy *fucking* Jeffries. Kennedy is the dark-haired, green-eyed, over-six-foot stunner who plays for the Beavers, the new women's basketball team in Philadelphia. I met her about ten months ago, and it was…hate at first sight for both of us.

Kennedy is the exact opposite of what I want in a woman. I consider myself a happy man who looks for the good in life. I'm the glass-half-full guy. I enjoy being goofy and having fun. I prefer women who share the same sentiment. Those who don't take everything and everyone so damn seriously.

Kennedy, on the other hand, is the poster child for a glass-half-empty woman. She sucks the joy out of everything and everyone. I despise her and everything she stands for with her snarky demeanor and snotty designer clothes.

The first words she ever spoke to me were along the lines of me checking off multiple items on her red flag list. It's not a theoretical list. She actually maintains a stupid catalog of things she considers red flags on her phone. Things she hates about men. Who does that? Who searches for the negative in people all the time?

Kennedy Jeffries does.

Unfortunately, I can't seem to avoid spending time with her. First, our friend and placekicker, Presley Ladrón, is married to Kennedy's friend and teammate, Layla Ladrón. Second, my best friend, Vance McCaffrey, is in love with Kennedy's teammate and close friend, Sulley O'Shea.

Vance and I were both drafted to the Philly Camels nearly a decade ago, and we just clicked right from the beginning. I'm the tight end, and he's the quarterback. Our on-field chemistry is what players dream of. It's like we're in each other's heads at times. It's not any different off the field.

Vance is a country boy from Bumfuck, Montana. He's a little grumpy at times, but it's a façade he uses to mask his pain. He's had a rough road over the past few years, but I know, more than most, that he's one of the best men I've ever met. Appreciating the burden he carries, I do my best to keep things light and make him smile. To the world, we may look like a mismatch, but with the possible exception of my father and sister, I trust Vance more than anyone else.

Every March for the past several years, we've gone to Las Vegas for the NCAA basketball tournament. It's a huge sports weekend where we watch the games, gamble, drink, dance, and party until we pass out. The wives and girlfriends (WAGs) of the Camels, specifically Layla, arrange it all. We rent a few floors of suites at a nice hotel, enjoy beautiful meals, and party until the wee hours of the morning. It's a blast. This year, Layla invited her teammates to join us, and, unfortunately, that includes Kennedy.

Did I mention that Kennedy also happens to be my coach's daughter? Yep, the princess is practically wrapped in layers of bright yellow caution tape.

Kennedy stares at me in disgust as she narrows her eyes at my off-handed comment to the stewardess. "You look like the last guy a lesbian sleeps with before deciding to come out."

Everyone but me laughs at her joke while she smiles in satisfaction before turning to where Beavers' player Shay Walker and her girlfriend, Alyssa Doyle, are sitting. "Am I right, ladies?"

Alyssa nods and sarcastically quips, "Yep, the last guy I slept with before coming out was a six-foot-six, two-hundred-and-fifty-pound white dude." She runs her hands down her extremely petite body. "'Cause I could totally take a man that size," she adds tongue-in-cheek.

"Two hundred sixty-five," I correct. "And let's just say I'm...*proportionate.*" I wiggle my eyebrows up and down suggestively.

Kennedy snorts in disgust. "Ugh. *Proportionate* men don't have to talk about it."

"Is that one of your red flags?" I snap.

"Men who feel the need to talk about how well-endowed they are? Yep," she pops the P. "You better believe it is. In fact, I noticed your tattoo of a girl's name when you lifted your luggage earlier. That's one of my top red flags. What woman wants to see the name of another woman on a man?" She makes a look of contempt. "You're so basic."

Vance begins to interrupt on my behalf, but I hold up my hand and shake my head to silence him. Fuck Kennedy. I don't owe her any explanations.

I stand, needing to get away from her vitriol. "I'm going to tap the kidney."

She rolls her eyes as she often does when I mention going

to the bathroom. I tend to find new and creative ways to tell people I need to relieve myself. I used to do it sporadically, but knowing how much it bothers Kennedy only drives me to do so more often.

She stares at me. "You know what happens when your bottom lip and top lip push together?"

"What?" I ask.

"You shut the fuck up. Stop announcing it every damn time you go to the bathroom. No one cares," she snarls. "It's disgusting, just like everything about you."

Fuck. This is going to be a long trip.

FIFTEEN HOURS LATER

Kennedy and I crash into my room with our lips locked. It's the middle of the night, and we've been partying for hours.

First, I had to watch this crazy bitch prance around all afternoon in a gold bikini that left *nothing* to the imagination. A freakin' gold bikini. *Star Wars* kick-started that fantasy for every man in America. Any man is lying if he says he hasn't dreamed about fucking a sexy woman in a gold bikini. I hated myself for the fact that my dick was hard all day watching her walk around the pool like she owned the place.

When it came time for our evening activities, she strutted into the lobby in a teeny tiny red dress I couldn't take my eyes off of. It looked like she was seconds away from having a lip slip. Yep, those lips.

We've all had a lot to drink. The last few hours are spotty for me. I'm not sure I remember everything that's gone on, and I truly hate this woman, but the urge to fuck her is stronger than anything else right now. Judging by her hands roaming all over my body, she seems to be feeling the same.

I'm in the process of enjoying the taste of the pink vodka drink on her tongue when she bites my lip. Hard.

I think she drew blood, and my cock oozes in excitement. I rock my hips into her so she can feel what she's doing to me.

"You're a freak," she spits out as she rubs her hand up and down my length.

"Takes one to know one," I bite back as I pinch her nipple through her flimsy dress.

"Ow, you dick." She squeezes my cock harder, to a near-painful level. "Do it again."

I look into her eyes. We've both had a lot to drink, but she appears to be aware of what's going on. I have a brief moment of thinking maybe this isn't right, but, as if reading my mind, she grabs me by the shirt with both hands and says, "I know what I'm doing," before she rips it open, causing the buttons to scatter all over the room. "I'm not too drunk to fuck, so fuck me, you big gorilla."

"Maybe I can fuck the raging bitch out of you."

She smiles as her teeth scrape along my jawline until her lips suction on my neck like she's hoping to draw blood again. I know I'll hate myself in the morning, but I'm too worked up and too drunk to care right now.

I push her shoulders away, giving me room to roughly lift her dress over her head, leaving her in a red lace bra and matching thong. She does a little twirl for me. "You like what you see? All men do," she announces with complete and total confidence.

I might hate this woman, but there's no denying she's beautiful. Long, muscular legs, shapely hips, and huge tits. What's not to like? *Besides the personality.*

Refusing to let her know what's going through my head, I shrug, acting unaffected. "Meh. You're okay. Good enough to fuck while I'm drunk. Not sober."

She narrows her eyes at me before nodding her head to the obvious tent in my shorts. "Your body says otherwise. I bet your cock is leaking for me right now. Your tip is dripping with the need to slip into my overly wet and extremely tight pussy."

She's not wrong. Resisting the urge to squeeze myself in relief, I suggest, "Why don't you find out for yourself, sugar lips?"

Without hesitation, she unbuckles my belt, unfastens the button on my shorts, and pulls down my zipper. My shorts fall to the floor on their own. I think I smoothly kick them away along with my shoes, but it might be a little clumsy given my state.

Her soft fingertips trace the muscles of my stomach, causing shivers to run down my body, before they enter the waistband of my boxer briefs. She slowly pulls them down, staring unashamedly at my cock. She mumbles, "I guess you weren't wrong today. You're very...*proportionate*." She swipes her thumb across my tip. "And leaking for me, just like I knew you would be."

I can't help but reach for her. With a simple twist of my fingers, her bra falls away, and I take in her tits for the first time. Oh hell, they're even better than I imagined, and I've imagined them a lot in the past ten months. They're full, with rosy nipples begging for my mouth. I'm going to mark those suckers up.

She circles her thumb all over my pre-ejaculate and then brings the evidence to her mouth and sucks on it. "Hmm, it sure tastes like you like what you see."

The need to fuck is at an all-time high. I clumsily reach for her, but she avoids me and squats down. She grabs for her purse before opening it and pulling out a roll of what must be ten condoms. I guess she's not too drunk to think about safe sex.

She tosses them on the bed before bending over seductively and slowly removing her panties, putting on a bit of a show for me. She's sexy and she knows it. I hate her for being so damn attractive.

Her eyes fill with lust as she rakes them up and down my body. "Buckle up. You're about to get it good, big boy."

She attempts to shove me onto the bed, but I don't budge. She's a tall, strong, muscular woman, but I'm still bigger and stronger. I grab her like she weighs nothing and toss her violently through the air and onto the bed. She lets out a loud squeal.

"God yes," she moans when she lands. "I like being manhandled. Don't take it easy on me. I don't believe in safe words."

"No problem, Cruella."

She smirks at the name I've called her quite a few times since we met, then crooks her finger at me. "Bring Cruella the puppy."

"I'm no puppy," I shout as I jump on top of her until I'm on all fours. "I'm the big dog. Ruff, ruff," I bark into her chest.

She lets out a laugh as she wraps her legs and arms around me. My lips immediately move to suck one of her tits into my mouth. She thrusts her pussy over my dick repeatedly. I love an aggressive woman. She's so damn hot.

"Fuck me, Neanderthal," she orders.

"Stop talking. You're ruining it for me. I'm trying to pretend you're someone else."

She giggles as she agrees, "Me too. I'm thinking of Chris Hemsworth."

"That wimp? Thor has nothing on me," I declare as I shove three of my thick fingers from my right hand inside her.

She screams out, "Yes. Harder. Deeper."

I thrust them in and out of her at an animalistic pace while my mouth continues to devour her breasts. Her fingernails scrape across my back in a way that I know I'll be marked.

I go to grab her throat with my left hand, but for the first time, I notice my hand is bandaged. What the hell did I do to myself? Am I injured?

My thoughts are interrupted by her thrashing and vocally begging to be fucked.

Before I know it, the condom is on, and I thrust inside her like I want to kill her. Crazy lady loves it and pleads for it faster and harder.

At some point, I can hear screams coming from Vance's bedroom in our suite. They're rivaling Kennedy's, and she doesn't like being outdone. It becomes a contest between the women.

All I know is we go at it like animals. She claws every inch of my back and ass along the way, only serving to spur me on.

I WAKE in the morning feeling somewhere between death and a great night because my head is pounding but my dick is wonderfully sore. I get flashes of the evening, mostly involving fucking. Who did I fuck? I remember it being hot as hell and lasting for hours, but I can't see the face.

I quickly turn, but no one is on the other side of the king-sized bed. Looking around, I notice several condom wrappers strewn about the room. At least I practiced safe sex. Crisis averted.

When I reach over to the other side of the bed, it's still warm. I wonder if the woman is in the bathroom. Looking that way, I realize she's not. I suppose she left.

Oh well. It's easier this way and certainly better than the alternative. I hate it when they're all clingy in the morning.

Reaching for the pillow, I smell it and shoot straight up. Oh fuck, I know that scent. Suddenly, things come into focus. It's like someone has adjusted the camera lens in my brain. Oh god, I had sex with Kennedy. I must have been really drunk to go there.

As I begin to move my body, my back experiences shooting, burning pain. What the hell?

Getting out of bed, I stand in front of the mirror and turn so I can see my back. Scratch marks are everywhere. That crazy bitch marked me, though a small smirk finds my face when I remember leaving marks of my own all over her tits. There will be no prancing around in a tiny bikini for her today.

I go to run the fingers of my left hand over my battle wounds when I realize my fingers are bandaged. I have a vague recollection of seeing the bandage while we were having sex, but no memory of it being put on or any kind of injury.

I slowly unravel the white gauze, noticing one of my fingers is swollen and raw. It feels like a cheese grater has been rubbing against it. Did I burn myself?

As the finger is fully revealed, my eyes nearly bug out of my head. My ring finger has the word Kennedy written around it. Please, God, let this be the product of a Sharpie joke from one of the guys.

I run to the bathroom and begin to scrub my finger with soap and water. It hurts like a motherfucker. Worst of all, it's not coming off. This is a damn tattoo. A real one. My heart feels like it's pounding out of my chest. Why in the world would I get her name tattooed on my finger like it's a ring?

A ring. More memories flood my mind. No, no, no. It can't be.

I run back into the bedroom and locate my pants from last night on the floor. Emptying the pockets, I retrieve a folded piece of paper.

I quickly unfold it and let out an audible gasp as I begin reading.

Oh. My. God. I married Kennedy *fucking* Jeffries last night.

ONE

TEN MONTHS AGO

KENNEDY

The shrilling sound of my ringtone wakes me from a peaceful slumber in the luxurious comfort of my silky, high-thread-count sheets. I try to reach for my phone, but there's a meaty arm holding me in place. Did I let this guy sleep over? I never do that. Hmm, I must have passed out after we had sex, and he decided to stick around.

I rack my brain trying to remember his name. Gary? No. Greg? No. Oh right, Geoff with a G. He made a whole annoying thing about it being spelled G-E-O-F-F and not J-E-F-F.

When I saw it spelled with a G when he messaged me on Tinder yesterday, I should have known he'd be the clingy type and sleep over. At least he was a decent lay.

I quietly extricate myself from his hold and slip out of bed naked before grabbing my phone and heading out into my living room. I look down at the phone and realize it's the owner of my team. Shit. What does Prescott Wellington want?

I accept the call and do my best to act cheery when I'm anything but. "Good morning, Mr. Wellington." Ugh. I sound like the angels in *Charlie's Angels*.

In his raspy, near-death, old-man voice, he responds, "Good morning, Kennedy. Do you have a minute?"

"Of course." I roll my eyes as I look out the window of my New York City apartment and see a billboard of the most annoying basketball player in existence.

Tonight is the WNBA draft. I know he's going to ask me to babysit whoever we select. Ugh. Rookies. Fucking useless. At least we have the fifth pick, so I know I won't have to play with the most over-hyped player in league history, Sullivan O'Shea. The media-greedy bitch has practically hijacked the league, and she hasn't even been drafted yet. Yet here she is, on a billboard for our league already. God, I hate her.

I pull the phone from my ear when he loudly clears the disgusting phlegm from his throat. Good lord, he should be on some sort of breathing machine.

"Kennedy," he wheezes, "there's no easy way to say this, so I'm just going to shoot straight."

"Ooookay."

"As you know, there's an expansion team this year." The Philly Beavers. "We're only allowed to protect five players from our current roster. The rest are subject to being scooped up by the Beavers."

Everyone knows this, but I'm one of the best players on my team. In the league. Surely they protected me. It never even occurred to me that they wouldn't.

He continues, "After careful internal conversations with the general manager and coaching staff, we decided not to protect you and—"

"Are you fucking kidding me?" I interrupt. "I've led the team in rebounding all three years I've been here. I led the league in double-doubles last year. I'm a goddamn all-star."

He exhales another audible wheezing breath. "Kennedy, it's

not about your numbers or your performance. You're obviously valuable to the team in that regard. It's your…camaraderie with your teammates and general demeanor that are problematic for us. You've been suspended by the league seven times in three years for your dirty play. Your teammates have been in my office countless times asking that we trade you. Put simply, you're a cancer in the locker room. We've reached our boiling point. When we made the decision not to protect you, Philly immediately grabbed your contract."

"No!" I shout. "Not Philly. I refuse to live in Philadelphia ever again."

"It's your hometown, Kennedy. Where your family lives. I was hoping this would be welcome."

Panic rises to my chest. "It's not. I promise to do better. Please let me stay. I love New York City. This is my home. Give me one more chance," I desperately plead.

He clears his throat. "I'm sorry, sweetie. We can't keep you."

"What about a trade to a different city? *Any* other city."

He's quiet for a brief moment before admitting, "I tried, but we weren't able to find an appropriate fit. It's already a done deal. Philly owns your contract now. I'm truly sorry, Kennedy. Use this as an opportunity to reinvent yourself. If you embrace it, it could be a fresh start for you," he says in a hopeful voice.

Fresh start? Fuck him and everyone on the damn team and staff. "Screw you, Prescott Wellington the Fifth and your fucking pretentious name. You'll regret this, asshole."

I end the call before he can respond. My mind is spinning. I hate Philly. The prospect of living in the same town as my family again is beyond unappealing. There's a reason I went to college in California. To get as far away from them as possible.

The rage in my body is overflowing when my phone pings with a text notification from an unknown number.

Unknown: Hi, Kennedy. This is Reagan Daulton. I'm the new owner of the Philly Beavers. We're excited to have you on our team. As I'm sure you might assume, we're drafting Sulley O'Shea tonight as the first overall pick in the WNBA draft. She's in New York for the draft. I'd like for you to meet her and some of your other teammates tonight at nine. I need you to come thirty minutes early so we can talk privately before the others arrive.

Oh crap. Sulley O'Shea. She's going to be my teammate. I wonder if life smokes a cigarette after it fucks me.

The media worships the ground that princess walks on. They refer to her as a phenom. This is such bullshit. This whole team is going to be about her. What a nightmare.

Me: Sorry. It's late notice. I'm out of town.

Unknown: No, you're not. I have eyes and ears everywhere. You'd be remiss not to remember that. Let me be clear, you WILL be there tonight. You WILL arrive thirty minutes early. I'll send you the address later. I look forward to seeing you then.

Who does this bitch think she is? I'll arrive if and when I want to.

I walk back into the bedroom and notice G-E-O-F-F. Oh shit, I'm not dealing with morning-after nonsense. I grab all of Geoff's clothes from the ground and throw them at him. He startles awake and gives me a sleepy smile as his eyes take in my naked body. "Come back to bed, baby. Let's go for another round."

Baby? We just met. I'm adding that to the list of red flags I keep on my phone. Men who call you *baby* just after you meet… or ever. Gross.

I narrow my eyes at him. "I'm not your baby, and I have a

busy day. I'm getting in the shower. Don't be here when I get out. Lose my number while you're at it."

I ARRIVE at the address Reagan gave me just before nine. I didn't show up extra early like she asked. I'm not in the mood for a lecture, and this bitch needs to know she can't boss me around. She should be happy I showed up at all.

The hostess escorts me to a private room in the back, where I get my first glimpse of my future teammates, all sitting around a table. First, I notice Shay Walker. She's a veteran forward from the team out of LA and is very good. I can't believe they didn't protect her. That's odd. She's tall, with dark skin and eyes. We've thrown a couple of elbows at each other throughout the years, but I'm not unhappy to see her here. She's a good addition to the team. Ironically, her girlfriend went to the same college as me. I don't know her well, but I've met her a few times and never had a problem with her.

Next, I notice Layla Ladrón. She's been in the league a little longer than me. She played for the team out of Miami. I know she recently had a baby and is married to a football player from Philly. I suppose it makes sense that she'd be willing to move there.

My eyes then find Palmer Payne. She's new to the league. I don't know much about her, but I watched the draft today and knew she was selected by the Beavers in the second round. She's a curvy, extremely tall center with mousy, frizzy brown hair. She wears goggles—fucking goggles—when she plays. Who does that?

She's wearing regular glasses now, and I can see her eyes better. They're unique. Almost purple. If I were her, I wouldn't cover those eyes. They're her best attribute.

Reagan stands, looking irritated, but musters a fake smile

while holding out her hand. "How kind of you to join us," she says with a bit of an edge. "I'm Reagan Daulton. You can call me Reagan."

She's extremely attractive—like model attractive—with blonde hair and blue eyes. I can't imagine she's more than thirty-five. Wow. She's tall by conventional standards, but not around this genetically gifted group of women. She's wearing a pink power suit. Her wavy hair and makeup are perfect. She exudes wealth and sophistication.

I shake her hand in return as I try to size her up. "Sorry I'm late." I give an over-exaggerated smile. "I was *super* busy restarting the dryer so I don't have to fold my clean clothes."

Her lip twitches with amusement, and she nods. "It's safe to say we all do that at times."

We sit, and Reagan begins. "Ladies, I'm thrilled that we got the opportunity to sign all of you to our team. With this group of talent, I know we'll be competitive in the league from day one. I'll get into this more when Sulley arrives, which should be in a few minutes, but I want to say something before she gets here. Sulley is from a small town. She's suffered some real trauma in her life. I know she garners a lot of media attention, but she doesn't ask for it."

I scoff. "The hell she doesn't."

Reagan turns to me. "She doesn't. When you meet her, you'll see her for the humble woman she is. You can't find one sound-bite where she comes off as arrogant because she's not. I wouldn't have drafted her if I thought she was going to be problematic."

"You picked up Kennedy's contract," Shay mumbles.

I snap my head at her. "Screw you, wannabe celesbian."

Reagan holds up her hands. "Ladies, enough. Everyone is getting a fresh start." She stares at me. "Some are on shorter leashes than others, but everyone has a chance to start anew. I'm asking you all to come into this with an open mind." She pauses briefly as she steeples her fingers. "I have two sisters, one older and one younger. Between them, my mother, and my aunt, I've been surrounded by strong women my whole life. Having a girl tribe you can count on makes each individual stronger. You all have two options. Go at it alone or become a tribe. I personally suggest you spend some time together. Try becoming friends. After I introduce Sulley, I'm going to leave, but my tab will remain open. Order drinks. Hang out. Talk. Throw out all preconceived notions and simply get to know each other."

Before she can continue, Queen Sullivan O'Shea walks into the room. I expected a cocky demeanor, but she looks like a deer in headlights. She's outwardly nervous and dressed like she hit up the clearance rack at Walmart.

She waves a shaky hand and mutters, "Hel…hello everyone," as she cautiously takes in the various faces in the room.

Reagan introduces the group to her. Sulley appears wide-eyed. If I didn't know better, I'd think she was starstruck by the group in here.

After Reagan runs through a few things, she leaves, again encouraging us all to stay and enjoy food and drinks on her.

I turn to Sulley. "Well, Queen Sullivan O'Shea. We were all dragged here kicking and screaming to roll out the red carpet for you. I imagine we'll be doing that all season. How lucky for us. What is it that the queen would like to talk about?"

Sulley physically deflates at my snarkiness. I thought she'd have a stronger constitution.

We make idle chitchat for a bit. Sulley keeps telling me over and over that her friends call her Sulley, so I call her Sullivan for the rest of the night just to piss her off and let her know we're not friends and never will be.

THE NEXT DAY I'm home, reluctantly packing up my apartment, when my doorbell and phone ring simultaneously. I glance at my phone. It's my mother. She and my father have been blowing up my phone since the news of me coming to Philly broke. Fuck me, they're going to be all up in my business now that I'll be living in the same town as them. I don't have the energy to deal with them. I'm still managing my emotions over this move.

I walk over to my door and open it to see Reagan standing there in a different designer power suit. I'd love to see her closet one day. It's probably like a scene out of a movie with rows and rows of high-end clothes. It probably rotates on a smart wheel as she decides what to wear each morning.

She looks pissed, and without waiting to be invited inside, she stomps past me. "Please come in," I say sarcastically while I close the door and follow her as she marches into my living room with clear intent.

With a tight jaw, she points to my sofa and commands, "Sit. Now."

I give her an exaggerated fake smile. "Thank you for inviting me to sit down in my own home. Do you want to make me a pot of coffee while you're at it? Maybe an espresso? Easy on the foam, please."

She exhales a frustrated breath as we both sit across from one another like adversaries. "Kennedy, are you aware of your reputation in the league?"

"For being a badass, amazingly talented player? Yep."

She shakes her head. "No. There's no denying your talent. It's there. It's your attitude that's a big *fucking* problem. Did you know that Prescott Wellington shopped you to every team in the league? Every. Single. Team. He knows you have family issues and didn't want to end up in Philly. He cared enough about you to try to find you another home and was practically giving you away to other teams for nothing, yet no one took him up on it. It's not about your talent, it's about you."

I shrug, acting unaffected even though hearing that cuts deep. "What do you want from me? If I were a man, we wouldn't even be having this conversation. I'd be praised for having confident charisma. But because I'm a woman, I'm a bitch? A problem? Fuck everyone and their double standards."

She surprises me by nodding and saying, "Frankly, I agree with that statement, but the fact remains you're not a man. For better or worse, we play by a different set of rules, and that giant chip on your shoulder does nothing for you. I'm the CEO of a Fortune 500 company. You don't think I have to deal with sexist shit like this too? Double standards are the regular course of business for me. I eat them for breakfast every morning…in my mansion…that I paid for. All before I get into my two-hundred-thousand-dollar car…that I also paid for. And then I make my way to the biggest skyscraper in Philly…that I own. To the top floor…because that's where my corner office is. The office of the CEO of one of the biggest, most successful companies in the world…that I run."

I roll my eyes at her dramatics. "Congratulations. Good. For. You, Madam CEO. What do you want from me?"

She leans back on the sofa. "I'm a *very* good judge of character. You don't get to be in my position without learning how to read people. I think there's a smart woman behind all your abrasiveness. I think there's a way to channel your tough-girl exterior into something that works *for* you, not *against* you. If I were you, instead of feeding into certain dialogue, I'd flip the script. It's not too late for you to change the way people view you."

I exhale an audible breath. "Again, what is it that you want from me? Spit it out in English."

She sits upright. "First, I want you to cut your shit with me. I see through it. This bravado you've got going for you is likely masking some other crap in your life. I'm guessing it has to do with your family."

I ball my fists until my nails cut into my palms. "Screw you. I don't owe you an explanation of my family dynamics."

She nods. "Agreed. But I'm the only one giving you what's likely your last shot at making a true name for yourself in this league. If I waive you, no one will pick you up. That's a guarantee. You should learn to play nicely in the sandbox with me. If you're as smart as I think you are, you'll realize you still control the dialogue. You still control your future. You're in a unique situation right now. Like it or not, Sulley O'Shea is a phenomenon. She's unlike anything this league has ever experienced before, bringing in millions of new fans every damn day. Our games are already sold out for the season. Not just our home games. Our away games too. Every single one is sold out because people want to see her play. And it happened in less than twenty-four hours since we drafted her yesterday."

I can't mask my shock. I don't think I've ever played a professional game in a stadium that's been more than half full. Sold out? Every game? I have no words for that.

She gives me a knowing smile. "Yep. Unreal. Like I said, she's a phenom. A superstar never seen before in women's sports. But she's wet behind the ears, Kennedy. Innocent through and through. Sulley is a good kid. She's very unaffected and unaware. Instead of working *against* her, work *with* her. Be her friend. She could use a guide in this new, scary world. She's originally from a small town. She went to a college five minutes from that town and has never lived in a big city. You saw how she was dressed last night. Maybe start there. Help her find some new, more appropriate cosmopolitan clothing. She's going to be photographed. I want her to look good, and if I were you, I'd want to be the person photographed next to her. Star power tends to rub off on those close by."

I cross my arms. "I'm not a fashion consultant; I'm a basketball player."

She runs her finger over her bottom lip. "No, you're not a fashion consultant, but you have real style. You're always dressed well and made up perfectly. You put time and thought into your appearance. It matters to you. You're a beautiful, smart, talented woman. There's *so* much untapped potential with you. If I were you, I'd embrace what Sulley can do for you and your career." She reaches into her purse and fishes around for a moment before emerging with a black American Express credit card. Handing it to me, she says, "After you move to Philly, call her and take her shopping. Take Palmer and a few other teammates too. The two of them are living together. They could both use your sense of style, and it will be an olive branch. A way for you all to bond."

I raise an eyebrow. "You're giving me uninhibited use of your Black Card?" I know black American Express cards are invitation-only and given to very few people in the world. It's a billionaires' club with no spending limits.

She stands and runs her hands down her suit before holding up a single finger. "One day. You can use it for one day as long as you're with Sulley and Palmer."

I smile as I rub my hands together. "Ooh, this is going to put a dent in that big bank account of yours."

She returns my smile with a genuine one of her own. "Do your worst, Kennedy Jeffries."

Game on, Reagan Daulton. Game on.

TWO

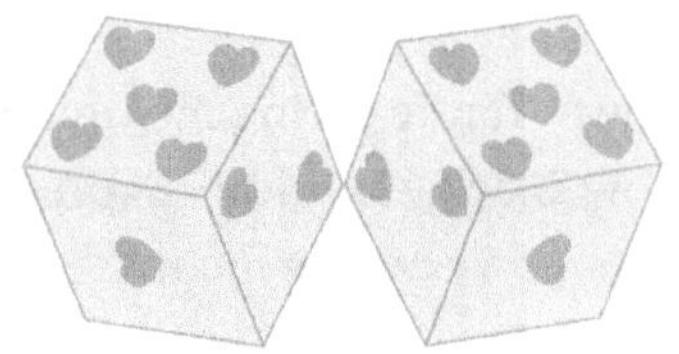

DAYLEN

I walk into my house at eight in the morning, wearing the same clothes I left in last night. I can hear the loud thumping of BJ's feet padding across my large, marble-floored foyer to greet me before she leaps into my waiting arms. I squeeze my favorite being on the planet into a tight embrace. "I missed you too, sweet girl."

Bark.

"Is my precious angel hungry?"

Bark. Bark.

BJ is my Doberman Pinscher. Her name is short for Blackjackie. I originally named her Blackjack when I thought she was a male dog as a puppy. Admittedly, it took me a full week to figure out I had a female dog. The guys love to rib me about it, but BJ is the love of my life. I can't imagine being without her. We have a special bond that no one understands.

I scratch behind her ear and, in a playful voice, tell her, "I'm sorry Daddy didn't come home last night. I met a blonde who could suck a golf ball through a garden hose, and she wanted to suck on Daddy's garden hose all night."

Bark.

I sigh at her obvious hurt. "I know you hate all women, and I'm aware that breakfast is late, but I'll make you a big serving today."

She turns her head away and gives me the silent treatment. Spoiled brat.

I sigh. "Fine, I'll make extra bacon too."

Bark. Bark.

I rub my nose against her wet one. "I knew you'd understand. Let's see what Chef Benny has for us in the refrigerator."

Chef Benny is my house manager, for lack of a better term. It's not as pretentious as it sounds. Benny was drafted out of college by the Camels a few years ago. In his very first game, he suffered a career-ending knee injury. It was heartbreaking and only made worse by the fact that his fiancée was pregnant at the time. Rookie contracts aren't very big. While the team took care of him for another two years, he was struggling to make ends meet. It coincided with my getting BJ and buying a big house in the suburbs. He happens to be an amazing cook, a gifted handyman, and a hard-working guy. I offered him a job where he helps around the house, does my grocery shopping, meal preps for me at times, and stays with BJ when we're on road trips. I overcompensate him, and I'm completely okay with that. I know how fortunate I am to make the kind of money I do. With one unlucky twist of fate, I could easily have been in Benny's shoes.

BJ and I take in the contents of my always-full refrigerator. With my bestie next to me, I cook her favorite breakfast. She prefers French toast and bacon in the morning, just like her daddy.

While I'm at the stove, I pull up my sister's contact information on my phone. Jagger is technically my half-sister, given that we have different mothers, but there's nothing half about our relationship. Even though we only lived together for her first two years of life, we're very close. She lives with my dad and his wife in Maryland. They're about two hours away from me, and I do my best to see them as much as possible. I can't believe Jagger will leave for college in a little over two years.

She answers right away. "Hey, D."

"Hey, Jag. Any juicy gossip for me? What's the latest on Wysteria Lane?"

She giggles at my *Desperate Housewives* reference. "Same old shit. My mom wore a thong to the neighborhood pool party barbecue yesterday. Half the men nearly stroked out."

I chuckle at Ashleigh Humblecut's antics. My mother passed away when I was a little boy. Years later, my father met and married Ashleigh, twenty-five years his junior, putting her at only eight years older than me. Besides a little Botox, lip fillers, and a breast augmentation, Ashleigh's body gives Pilates a good name. And she *loves* to show it off *all* the time. She's a bit ditzy, but, fortunately, Jagger got my father's brains. She's super smart.

Unfortunately, Jagger received every ounce of good looks from my dad and Ashleigh, getting the best of both of them. She's grown up a ton in the past year and, much to my chagrin, is garnering a lot of attention from the inferior sex.

"Sis, your mom is one of a kind."

"Yep, *bro*. Sometimes I think half the guys who ask me out only do so to see her prance around in her tight clothing."

I scoff. "Are you nuts? You're gorgeous. I don't want you coming to my games anymore. I know the guys on my team are going to bust my balls about you."

She lets out a laugh. "Ha! I wouldn't mind an intro to your new guy, Reece Sanders."

I curl my lips in disgust. "Ugh. He's a douchebag." He's a rookie on our team. He acts weird around our gay teammate, Champ Williamson, and none of us care for that kind of behavior. Champ is a star running back who was traded to the Camels this off-season. He's an awesome guy and has fit right in with our group. Reece, on the other hand, is universally disliked for his disgusting bigotry and unappealing immaturity.

"What about Beau Fudd?" she coos. "His muscles are so hot. There are countless TikToks about his big thighs."

I growl. "While I love Beau like a brother, he's *way* too old for you."

She lets out a loud laugh. "Ha! I'm just fucking with you. They're all too old. There's one guy at school I like, and he seems to like me too. His name is Will."

"What's his address?" I practically yell. "I need to do a background check and pay him a visit."

She giggles again, which is always music to my ears. "Oh stop it." I wasn't joking. "Are you coming home soon? I miss you, bro."

And this right here is why I couldn't accept the huge contract that was offered to me from the team out of Arizona. My contract with the Camels ended recently, and Arizona offered me big-time, life-changing money. More than I could ever spend. But I didn't want to be a flight away from my family. A car drive where I can go home for dinner on any given night was my priority. I won't miss big events in Jagger's life. She's going to have proms, graduations, and other things that I want to be at. Initially, the Camels wouldn't match Arizona's offer, but my agent and friend, Tanner Montgomery, negotiated like a boss and eventually got them to. I will play the rest of my career here in Philly.

"We have a bunch of off-season training coming up," I answer, "but I'll shoot home for dinner one night soon."

"Cool. Oh, you'll love this one. I told my mom that WTF means, *wow that's fantastic*." She starts laughing. "Now she uses WTF inappropriately all the time."

"Oh my god, that's classic. I can't wait to hear her use it."

"My friends think she's nuts."

"She *is* a little nuts."

"Facts. Hey, I gotta go to school. Love you, D."

"Love you too, Jag."

While BJ and I are sitting at my table eating breakfast, Vance walks in and stops short when he takes in the scene before him. "You've gotta be fucking kidding me. BJ sits at the damn table with you?"

I shrug like it's totally normal for a hundred-pound dog to be sitting like a human in a chair at my kitchen table. "Where else would she eat?"

"On the fucking floor, like every other dog in the world."

I gasp. "That's uncivilized."

He briefly closes his eyes. "*You're* uncivilized. I can't believe you won't let women even step foot in your house but you let your dog eat at the table."

I sigh. "I don't let women in because BJ hates them and attacks them...and I don't like for them to know where I live."

I used to bring women home. BJ flipped her shit. I don't think she likes the prospect of me having another woman in my life, taking my attention away from her, though she does love Jagger. Maybe BJ smells the gold-digger in all of them. BJ went so far as to bite one of them, which is when I put her in training. Even female delivery women set her off. And several of the women I used to bring home kept showing up after I had clearly blown them off. It's easier to go to their places and for them not to know where I live.

Honestly, I sleep around a lot. I suppose when the time comes that I'm serious with a woman, I'll have to reconsider my ways, but as of now, I'm having fun and have no plans to settle down. Would I love to be a father? Yes. Am I ready to be devoted to one woman? No. The former will have to wait until I am.

Vance makes himself a plate of French toast and bacon, as he often does. I love that my best friend feels comfortable enough to walk into my house and take food. He has the code to my front door, just as I do for his.

He sits down at the table and points his fork at BJ. "Keep your paws to yourself. This is *my* food, beast."

"BJ would never steal your food." I wink at BJ before commanding, "Still." She knows that means to sit in her seat until she's dismissed. I smile at my angel. "You're such a good girl. You and Daddy will watch *Cobra Kai* in bed together tonight."

She lets out a howl of joy while Vance rolls his eyes at my love for that show. Best. Show. Ever.

I cast a pointed look at Vance. "How are you managing?"

The Philly Beavers drafted Sulley O'Shea last night. Vance and Sulley grew up in the same small town. Vance was best friends with her older brother. He was killed in the line of duty, and there was a shitstorm that ensued afterward, causing a huge rift between Vance and Sulley's family. He was freaking out during the draft when he realized she'd be moving to Philly. Our teammate Presley's wife is now on the Beavers too, so Vance running into Sulley is inevitable. I don't think he's seen her in five years, and I know he's internally flipping out over the entire situation.

He looks at me with pain written all over his face as he runs his fingers through his overgrown brown hair. "Honestly, I'm shitting bricks."

I wince. "That sounds painful. I shit out an entire intact burrito once, and that was rough. Bricks sound even worse."

He cracks a small smile. "You're a dope."

"I know. Speaking of giant shits, I'm gonna walk my girl while you finish breakfast. Then we can head to the gym."

"Why do you need to walk her? You have a doggie door."

I give him a look of disbelief. "It's our special quality time every day. While the doggie door affords me a little freedom, my best girl still expects some QT with Daddy. It will be a short walk, I promise. Don't worry, I already ate my celery while I was cooking."

He rolls his eyes even though he knows my thoughts on

eating a daily dose of celery, which Chef Benny always keeps on hand.

VANCE RAISES an eyebrow from the bench where he's lifting a heavily weighted bar in our team gym. "Does that crap really work?" he asks.

I nod as I sit back in the leg press machine with a huge smirk on my face. "Every. Damn. Time."

Coach Jeffries walks into the oversized gym. Coach is in his mid-to-late forties. He's got dark, wavy hair and a beard. Both have a smattering of grey. He works out with us almost every day and can likely outlift half the guys on the team. He's been my coach since my rookie year, and, despite his sometimes-weird personality, I love him like a second father.

He got divorced a few years ago. Even though he doesn't lack the attention of women, I don't think he indulges much. I've tried to push him on that front, but he's reluctant for some unknown reason.

He has a daughter who plays professional basketball for a team out of New York City. In all the years he's coached me, I've never once met her. I've heard they have a strained relationship, though he never talks about it. His son, Pierce, is seventeen. He's a good kid who grew up hanging out in our locker room.

Coach immediately asks, "What works every damn time?"

I wiggle my eyebrows. "Every first kiss with a woman. I break it up before they can and tell them it was a solid B+. They get so flustered and competitive that they beg for another chance to show me they're an A. It's always aggressive and turns into much more than kissing…if ya know what I mean." I wink at him.

Coach narrows his eyes at me. "You know, Humblecut, I've

always assumed the thing that would eventually break me is having to constantly enter my email address and password into my television via the remote control, but it might end up being your dating stories."

I chuckle, but he shakes his head. "Women aren't objects to toy with, Humblecut. You should be looking for the right woman, not the right-now woman. Don't you believe in monogamy?"

I twist my lips. "Of course I do. I've got a table made out of it at home."

Vance and Beau spit in laughter. I snap my head toward Beau. He doesn't normally laugh at my silly jokes.

My teammate and close friend, Beau Fudd, is a walking contradiction. The guy must be at least six feet eight inches and weigh well over three hundred pounds, all of which is muscle. He wears his dirty-blond hair super short, unlike me—I have a different hairstyle every week since my hair grows freakishly fast. People assume he's a meathead, but he's the exact opposite. He's a genius. A genuine 150 IQ genius with multiple degrees, currently working toward his PhD.

"I can't believe you laughed at my joke."

He raises an eyebrow. "I laugh at clever jokes, not ridiculous ones. That was clever. Unlike the other day when you asked *what do you call a deaf gynecologist?*"

I smile. "A lip reader. I think it's brilliant," I proudly declare.

Beau shakes his head. "No, that's ridiculous. I prefer thought-provoking comments. You can make sexual innuendos yet still be thought-provoking. They're not mutually exclusive. Like, did you know orgasms dump oxytocin into a woman's brain, which is why they become more attached and cuddlier after an orgasm? If you want a woman addicted to you, do your job as a man, and she'll be all yours."

I twist my lips. "So if I don't want a woman to get attached,

I shouldn't make her come? Hmm, that *is* thought-provoking, Fudd."

He scowls at me but eventually turns his attention to Coach. "Coach, I saw on the news this morning that your daughter is going to be playing for the Beavers. You must be excited."

Coach nods. "We're thrilled to have Kennedy come home. She's not big on visits. I'd love to get to see her more often." His face lights up. "She's such a talented athlete. Better than any of you knuckleheads. She's great at everything. I'm hoping to get her to join my pickleball league. No one will expect her to be as good as she is. That's the story of her life. Always underestimated."

Vance and I exchange bemused glances. Coach loves that old-man sport of pickleball. He plays all the time. He's tried to get us to play on a few occasions, but we always make excuses. We feel like it's one step from retirement. When I'm eighty and can't move anymore, I'll learn to play that so-called sport.

"I didn't know Kennedy got traded to the Beavers," I admit. "I look forward to finally meeting her."

Coach narrows his eyes at me. "Stay away from my daughter."

I chuckle as I hold my hands up in defeat. "No ill intentions, I promise."

I turn to Presley. "You happy to have your girl playing in town? I heard the good news."

Our placekicker smiles widely. "Estoy tan feliz. I'm so damn happy to have my girl home all summer. The dual residency has wreaked havoc on our relationship. Now that we have the baby, it will be so much better this way. I feel like a huge amount of stress has been lifted from my shoulders."

I give him a genuine smile. Presley is a good man who loves his wife, even though they bicker at times. "That's awesome, buddy."

He nods. "Yep, we're having a celebratory dinner tonight."

"Where are you going?"

"I'm not sure yet." He winks. "Let me give you a pro marriage hack. Never ask your wife where she wants to eat."

"Why?"

"She'll get pissed that you can't read her mind as to what she wants. What I do say is, *guess where I'm taking you?* And whatever she says is where we go. It makes me look like the most attentive husband."

I chuckle. "That's kind of genius. And good advice. My dad gave me great advice recently. He said if it flies, fucks, or floats, it's easier to rent it."

Vance and Presley snort in laughter, but Coach looks at me with pure venom and mouths, "Stay away from my daughter."

Beau rolls his eyes at my antics and tells Presley, "You should take her to that new place that opened on South Street. It's very good. They have a high-protein section of the menu."

Coach scoffs. "South Street? Parking is horrible down there. I'm at an age where not finding parking is reason enough to go home."

I let out a laugh. Coach makes fun of his age all the time. In fact, he loves to talk about Gen X and how different they are than us.

Presley smiles. "Like I said, my wife is picking the restaurant; she just doesn't know it yet."

THREE

KENNEDY

I tug on Sulley's oversized, unflattering college T-shirt. "Every woman should always look her best. When you feel iconic, you *are* iconic. Time to slay, queen."

I'm doing my best to be nice, so she agrees to go shopping. I can't use Reagan's Black Card if Sulley doesn't come with me, and I refuse to miss out on this amazing opportunity.

She sighs as she plops down on the sofa of her new apartment. "Ugh, I'm exhausted from the move. I just want to chill this afternoon before we go out tonight. And I hate shopping." She makes a look of disgust.

I don't think she and I could possibly be more opposite.

I look up and down her Hanes sweatpants and T-shirt-clad body. "It shows. Don't you want to look hot tonight? It's your first night out in Philly," I note as I plead with her to go shopping with me.

Layla arranged for us all to go out with her husband and his teammates. I have mixed feelings about hanging out with any of the guys my father coaches, but Reagan laid down the law, and I'm trying to 'play nice in the sandbox.' Plus, I don't have any friends or regular hookups here. Sitting at home at night is very unappealing. At least I know the Camels players will get us VIP access to every hot club in the city.

She points toward her pathetic excuse of a closet. "I'm sure I can find something to wear tonight in there."

I gasp. "Your closet is tiny, and it's not even full. I would need ten closets if mine were that size. And I looked through it. Trust me, you don't have anything to wear to this club. It's bougie."

Fortunately, the apartment I found in Philly has huge closets. My kitchen may be tiny, but who cares about that? I don't cook anyway.

She scrunches her nose as she takes in my designer jeans, fashionable T-shirt, and pumps. "How much money do you spend on clothes?"

I straighten my shoulders and proudly announce, "It's an investment. I'm investing in my fabulousness."

She waves her hand dismissively. "I *genuinely* appreciate you asking, but I'm going to pass. I'm trying to save money to buy a house. I can't afford to spend a lot on frivolous things like clothing. I'm an old T-shirt, baggy jeans, and sneakers kind of girl."

I pull out the Black Card from my purse and hold it up. "Reagan is treating. For *all* of us." I look at Palmer. "You too."

Palmer's eyes widen. "No, no, no. I hate shopping. They never have things for women my size."

I shake my head. "Don't worry. I know where to go for tall women. I have to shop at those stores too." I'm not as tall as Palmer, but I'm unconventionally tall. I can't shop everywhere.

Her shoulders fall. "It's not my height that's problematic. It's because I'm fa—"

"Fabulous," I interrupt, not letting her get away with a pity party. I hate seeing how insecure she is. Is she bigger than most? Yes. Does she have potential with a little bit of encouragement and finesse? Absolutely. Her eyes are honestly the most beautiful I've ever seen. I've never met anyone with purple eyes like hers.

I continue, "I'm not taking no for an answer. We've all been moving for the past few days, sweating and eating crappy pizza like animals. Tonight is a big night for us. We deserve to get a little spoiled by our billionaire boss." Plus, I have a few expensive pairs of shoes I've been eyeing for months and will gladly let Reagan pay for.

Sulley shakes her head. "I don't think I'd feel comfortable using her card."

I roll my eyes. "All our games are sold out because of you. We're the first franchise in league history to sell out every single game before the season even starts. She's making a shit ton of money off you."

She looks down shyly, like she either doesn't believe the truth of what I just said or is uncomfortable being thought of as the reason for the team selling out. She really does hate being the center of attention and doesn't appreciate that she's the face of this team and the league. I'm starting to think maybe I've misjudged her a bit.

I sit down next to her and look her in the eyes. "Know your worth, Sulley." It's the first time I've called her Sulley and not Sullivan. I see a small smile form on her face as I continue, "Spoil yourself. Get used to receiving nice things so you'll never accept anyone in your life who gives you the bare minimum. I *really* want to do this for you." And I mean it.

She sighs. "Fine, I'll go, but only if we can include Layla and Shay too."

I stand and pick up my Prada purse before moving the strap over my shoulder. "Already done. And Shay's girlfriend is also coming. I've met Alyssa. You'll like her. They're meeting us on Walnut Street in thirty minutes. Now pull down your sweatpants."

"What?" Her eyes just about bug out of her head. "Why?"

"Pull down your pants. I want to see if we need to shop for lingerie too."

She bites her lip nervously. "I like cotton. It's comfortable."

I sigh. "I thought as much. No man wants to feel granny panties when he slips his hand up your dress."

Palmer snorts a laugh, and I look at her. "You too, girlfriend." I twirl my finger in the air and loudly announce, "New lingerie for everyone."

Palmer's expression turns horrified.

OKAY. I can admit we had an absolute blast today. You couldn't possibly find six more different women, yet we all laughed our way through the afternoon. Alyssa is hilarious. Her lesbian jokes had me in stitches. I love self-deprecating humor with some edge to it, and Alyssa has it in spades. She and Shay are kind of adorable together. They're probably the most functional couple I've ever been around. It's like they're best friends and lovers, unlike any dynamic I've ever seen. My parents barely tolerated each other when I was growing up. I'm still not sure why they got married.

I'm at Palmer and Sulley's apartment helping them get ready for tonight. They have no clue how to use all the high-end makeup I bought them today, so I have to teach them. Palmer is still reluctant, but Sulley seems to be embracing her new look. She keeps staring at her big blue eyes that I've managed to make appear even bigger. It's like she didn't realize how attractive she is. It's endearing. Dammit, I want to hate her, but she's making it kind of hard.

I'm showing her how to enhance her natural beauty while she's telling us about her boyfriend, Shane. They've been dating for over a year, and he's playing professional basketball in Europe. When players aren't quite good enough for the NBA but are still good, they often play overseas.

I internet stalked him. He appears to be a bit of a media whore, but I'm being a good girl and keeping my opinions to myself. Sulley isn't acting like those annoying girls who think they're in love at a young age. She seems to enjoy his company when they're together but is equally happy that he lives so far away because she has so much going on and doesn't have time for a boyfriend who requires daily attention.

She just hired an agent, Tanner Montgomery. He's one of the biggest sports agents in the world. She's lucky to have a guy like him. I don't garner many endorsement offers. I have a small-potatoes attorney who reviews my contracts and the limited handful of offers I get, but I don't have an agent like her. I would love the opportunities she has to make more money. We're paid very little in our league.

I take in Sulley wearing her new thousand-dollar brown leather pants and red sequined top, feeling very proud of our *Pretty Woman*-esque shopping spree today. She's beaming. I know she's never worn anything this nice or sexy before. I'm surprisingly happy I'm the one who made her feel this way.

Putting the final touches on my own lipstick, I check myself out in the mirror. I'm in a short, tight, black silk skirt with a silver glittery tube top, all courtesy of Mrs. Daulton. My toned, tan stomach is on full display, as are my shoulders. I have my stylish ponytail in place, as I often do. It's almost always up, not in a messy, soccer practice way, but in a high-fashion way with two carefully placed wavy tendrils hanging down on the sides of my face. I'm rocking cherry-red lipstick and eye makeup that makes my green eyes pop. After my height and generous bust, my eyes are usually the first thing men notice about me. They're a piercing shade of green, exactly like my father's. The one good thing I got from him.

Well, that and my athleticism. My father was a star quarter-back in professional football throughout most of my childhood. He began his career in New York, where I was born, but by the time my brother, Pierce, came around, he had signed with Philly. Even though I was young, I was livid about the move. I loved New York and vowed to move back there as soon as I could but went to college in California to get as far away from my family as possible.

Everything in my life growing up revolved around his career. Everyone knew me as Jett Jeffries' daughter. Guys tried to use me to meet my father. Girls wanted to come over to my house to salivate over him. I never knew who liked me for me and not for my famous father.

They all thought I was so lucky to be his daughter. I wasn't. He was never home. He rarely showed up at school events. He rarely saw me play ball. When I was in high school, he retired. I assumed it would mean he'd start spending more time with us and attending my games, but that's not what happened. The Camels offered him the head coaching position, and he became *obsessed* with it. He left before five in the morning to review game tape and didn't come home until we were all asleep. We never had family dinners like a normal family. My so-called friends thought it was cool that the famous Jett Jeffries was my father, but it wasn't cool at all. It was only made worse by the fact that he's considered attractive. He feeds into that dialogue with shirtless, thirst-trap workout videos. It's so self-serving. I'm not sure why he needs the validation.

Our small handful of conversations were limited to him pushing me to play college basketball. Being athletic was basically the only thing we had in common, so it's the only thing he would ever talk to me about. He's never taken the time to otherwise get to know his own daughter. By the time I was back on the East Coast playing professional ball, he started to reach out to me all the time. Too little, too late, Jett Jeffries.

My mother got caught up in the money and her social life. She made being a fashionable WAG her whole personality. She may be the most selfish person I know. Whereas most mothers would revel in their daughter being as successful as I was, she resented all the accolades I received.

She's much shorter than me, with blonde hair and brown eyes, and she always hated how much attention I garnered for my height and good looks. I think her sense of style might be the only thing I got from her. For a reason I've never told another soul, I hate her and will never have her as part of my life again.

My brother and I were raised mostly by nannies. My parents rarely exchanged a single pleasantry with one another. I never once saw them be loving and affectionate. It felt like an arrangement. I guess years of their sham of a marriage finally took its toll, because when I was in college they got divorced. It didn't affect my life since I was no longer home, but I'm guessing it impacted my little brother. I feel bad he was left alone in the trenches, but it's been easier for me to disassociate with all of them.

Pierce is going into his senior year of high school. I know he's a good quarterback on the school's football team, but I don't think he plans to play in college. At least I haven't seen any announcements on his social media suggesting anything of the sort. It's not like I'm otherwise in the loop. The fact is, I don't know much about him. I have a tinge of regret about that. Perhaps now that I'm living here, I'll consider reaching out to him, but I just don't want anything to do with my parents. I've ignored her texts and his emails over the past few days since news broke that I'm playing for Philly.

My phone buzzes with an email notification. Shit. Another email from my father. He only emails or calls, never texts, because he doesn't live in the twenty-first century. Last I saw him, he was still using a flip phone, and that was last year. I didn't think they even produced those anymore.

I open the email:

Hey Marshmallow,

There's a pickleball tournament coming up. Mixed doubles. Registration just opened. Any interest?

Dad

Marshmallow was a nickname he used to call me when I was a little girl. I roll my eyes at his attempt to connect, but there's no denying he knows the way to my heart. Competition. I love pickleball. I love that the older men assume because of the way I look I can't play, and then I kick their asses. It's the one and only thing I've ever done with my father.

I'm certainly not responding now, but maybe I will in a few days. I wouldn't mind playing. We'll see how things go.

I take in Palmer's bare face and drab clothing, imploring her to let me help, but she refuses. I had to force-buy her a few things today, but it wasn't much. She was super shy in the dressing rooms. Sulley pleads with me to leave Palmer alone about it. I'm trying to help, but I guess you can't help someone who won't help themselves.

A little while later, we're in an Uber on the way to the club. Sulley smirks at me. "Please tell me one more red flag on your list."

When we all met the other night, it was awkwardly silent, so I suggested an icebreaker game of each of us giving a few of their red flags when it comes to the opposite sex. For some unknown reason, they all got the biggest kick out of it. I have hundreds of them listed on my phone. I don't know why everyone doesn't have that. It reminds me of things I *don't* want in a man.

I pull out my phone. "Hmm, I already told you a few of my top ones, like men who use Androids, men who take selfies, and men who know every word to the rap verse from 'Waterfalls' by TLC." I keep scrolling. "I added Sulley's disgust for men who wear sandals and Layla's distaste for men who wear necklaces because I agree with those. Ooh," I perk up, "here's a good one. Men who order fruity drinks." I make a look of disgust. "It's so…unmanly."

Sulley and Palmer giggle uncontrollably. They really are wildly amused by my red flags list.

"One more," Sulley begs. "Please. They're so funny."

I roll my eyes but scroll through my list again until I find a good one. I look back up at them with a smirk. "Men who have pictures of themselves in front of their cars. It's even worse if it's a selfie. Such a douchebag thing to do." In a deep voice, I mock, "Oh, look how cool my car is. I'm a big man with a manly car." I roll my eyes. "Losers."

Sulley breaks into hysterics. "Oh my god. Hilarious. I never would have thought of that one, but it's true."

I stare at Sulley and Palmer in awe as they continue to giggle like schoolgirls about my list throughout the entire Uber ride. Then they discuss groceries for the week and how they will equally divide household chores. They even chat about how much they miss their moms and how they talk to them every single day. These two may be the purest, most Hallmark-like, unaffected women I've ever met. I don't think I've ever known anyone like them, and I'm honestly not sure they're going to survive life in a big city. There are so many people who will take advantage of them. For a reason I can't explain, I feel protective of their innocence and don't want anything bad to happen to them.

We walk into Club Liberty, and I look around. I used to sneak in here while I was in high school, but it looks like it's been renovated and is so much nicer than it used to be. It's wall-to-wall people. Drinks are flowing, the music is pumping, and the dance floor is jammed with bodies.

Layla materializes out of nowhere and is immediately right in our faces. She's clearly already had a few drinks and is practically bouncing up and down. God, overly cheery people annoy me.

She introduces us to her husband, Presley, and then they practically make out in front of us. Ugh, I hate people who are all loved up like that. It's usually bullshit. A façade masking some underlying resentment. I bet they'll be divorced within five years.

He's cute, with brown hair, chocolate-brown eyes, and olive

skin. He's shorter than her though. I don't know that I could be with a man shorter than me. She jokingly refers to him as her short king, and he doesn't seem to mind at all.

He then invites us to their private booth, which is on the roped-off VIP balcony overlooking the dance floor. Now he's speaking my language.

We make our way up the stairs and to the booth. I see four men standing as we approach. I've never met any of them in person, but I know who they are. Vance McCaffrey is the golden boy who succeeded my father as the Camels' quarterback. Creepily enough, he looks like my father, with dark hair, green eyes, and a bit of an ever-present scowl on his face.

I also notice Beau Fudd. Good lord, he's even bigger than he looks on television. He's a defensive lineman with shaven, dirty blond hair and muscles that have muscles. He looks like the Incredible Hulk.

Next to him is Champ Williamson. He's a sexy, mocha-skinned running back with a badass bleached mohawk. He's a little shorter than the rest of the guys, but he matches their muscles. I wish I wasn't taller than him because he's gorgeous. By far the sexiest man here. I'm immediately attracted to him. Screw the height, I'm taking that guy home with me. Yummy.

Finally, my eyes find Daylen Humblecut. He's the tight end who comes across as a giant goofball known for touchdown dances and playing to the cameras. Ugh, I hate immature men who don't take anything seriously. The blond hair on his head and his face is unruly. He's wearing wrinkled clothing that looks like he picked it up off the floor before he left the house. There's nothing more unattractive than an unkempt man who takes no pride in his appearance. I work hard on mine and expect the same of the inferior sex.

My disgust for the beast before me is broken up by the awkward as fuck way Vance and Sulley interact. "Do you two know each other?" I ask.

Sulley looks like a deer in headlights, but Vance gives me a small nod and answers, "Sulley and I are from the same hometown."

What? I didn't realize that.

Daylen waves for the waiter and orders drinks for everyone, including a strawberry daiquiri for himself. I can't help but laugh. I just told the girls how much I dislike men who order fruity drinks.

"What's so funny?" he asks.

I take in his entire ridiculous appearance and answer, "We were recently having a few conversations about red flags and, to be honest, you check a lot of those boxes."

His head jerks back in obvious shock. "Like what?"

I do my best to hide my bemused smirk. "You're wearing sandals and a necklace." I nod toward his phone on the table. "And your cell phone is an Android." I say Android like it's a bad word because nothing fucks up a group chat like the dumbass who uses an Android.

He goes into a whole thing about me being petty and a negative person. No shit.

He then goes on to boast about his conquests. I make a note to add that to my red flag list. This guy might very well encompass every red flag I've ever imagined. He's beyond unappealing. I can't believe any woman would fall for him. Yes, he's mainstream attractive and a giant of a man, but everything else about him is so…unsexy.

What's with his facial hair? He can't even shave properly. Women could never get away with being so improperly groomed.

I narrow my eyes at this disgusting, unhygienic beast. "I feel like your birth certificate is an apology from the condom factory."

He has a smug look on his face. "Sugar lips, I'm so well-equipped that when I was born, I got a girth certificate."

What. A. Douchebag.

Our drinks arrive and there's more conversation, but I can't focus on anything other than the fact that Daylen Humblecut may be the most annoying man in existence. He loves to be the center of attention, constantly saying outrageous, immature things. He even stands and finds some perverted way to loudly announce he's going to the bathroom. I don't think this man has fully evolved. He's like a caveman.

Fortunately, he and Vance disappear like schoolgirls running to gossip in the bathroom. While I'd love to turn my attention to Champ, I instead turn to Sulley and see her looking like a deer in headlights. She's pale, and her skin looks clammy. There's something about Vance that clearly upset her. I squeeze her arm as I lean over and whisper, "Are you okay?"

She nods, but I can tell she's not managing very well. She almost looks scared. I think she's physically shaking.

With their attention elsewhere, everyone else at the table starts laughing. I must have missed the punchline. Layla kisses Presley's cheek. "This is why I married you, mi amor. You're so funny."

He nuzzles his nose into her. "I thought you married me because I'm good in bed?"

She smiles at him. "See, you're funny."

Everyone laughs again except Sulley. She's practically frozen in place. What am I missing? What happened between her and Vance?

I gently wrap my fingers around her arm, hoping to distract her from whatever is bothering her. "Let's go dance."

I want to dance with Champ, but I think Sulley is in desperate need of a distraction. My hitting on Champ will have to wait.

She nervously fidgets with her shirt. "I'm...I'm not a very good dancer."

I wink at her. "It's a good thing I am." I stand and announce to the table, "We're heading down to the dance floor if anyone would like to join us." I stare hopefully at Champ, and he smiles.

Good lord, he has perfect features. That face will look damn good buried between my legs in a few hours.

Champ, Layla, and Presley like that idea, and they decide to join us. Ooh, maybe I can help Sulley and grind up on Champ all at the same time.

Our group walks down the stairs toward the overly crowded dance floor. As we find our groove, I can see Sulley begin to relax. With her close by my side, I wrap my arm around Champ from behind and begin to sway my hips to the beat of the music. He joins me in my movements. He's got great rhythm, but he never turns around to grind himself onto me. That's a first. Usually a man immediately does that when I touch them from behind. All men ever want is contact with their dicks.

Champ eventually drifts away into the sea of people, but I don't give chase. Kennedy Jeffries chases no man.

Sulley and I dance without a care in the world until I feel a masculine presence pressing up against me from behind. My lips curl in amusement. They always come back for me.

I'm about to turn around to wrap my arms around Champ when an unfamiliar voice tickles my eardrums. "You got a man?"

Crap, it's not Champ dancing with me. I turn around and find a guy who has no chance with a woman like me. I stare him straight in the eyes and calmly say, "I am one."

His smirk immediately disappears, and he turns as white as a ghost before spinning on his heels and running away. Sulley spits out in laughter. "Oh my god, that was amazing. And genius."

I have a huge grin on my face. "Always works. Every single time. Easiest way to get the wrong guys to leave you alone."

We continue dirty dancing with each other. I'm happy to see her uneasiness from earlier nowhere in sight.

At some point, Vance and Daylen approach us. Before I realize what's happening, Daylen grabs me by the waist like I weigh nothing and carries me away from Sulley. I pound my fists against his rock-solid body. "Let me go, you animal."

"Stop fighting," he growls. "You're like one of those annoying flies that pesters you throughout a meal."

I continue pounding my fists until he finally sets me down on the other side of the dance floor. I shove his chest. "What's your fucking problem? Don't ever touch me without invitation again, you buffoon."

He rolls his eyes. "Trust me, I have no interest in touching you. Nasty bitch isn't exactly my cup of tea."

Screw this guy. "I drink coffee, asshole. Seriously, what the fuck is wrong with you? What was that about?"

"Vance needs to chat with Sulley. I was giving them privacy."

I push him again. "You're still too close to me. You smell like bologna." He doesn't. He happens to smell better than I would have thought, but I won't give him the satisfaction.

"Is that another red flag of yours?" he spits out.

"It's not a red flag. *No* woman likes a man who smells like processed, cured meat, you idiot."

He makes a look of disgust. "It takes a lot for me to dislike another person, but I think I might actually hate you. You're so... mean and miserable."

I cross my arms. "Let me put on my glasses so I can see if I give a fuck." I place pretend glasses on my face. "Nope, I don't."

His eyes take me in, but not in the way I'm accustomed to men looking at me. "I see you, Kennedy Jeffries. I see the kind of woman you are. I'd bet Vance's dick that you were one of those girls who never had any friends because you're such a horrible person. I'm guessing there was no goodbye party for you when you left New York. More like a party when the Wicked Witch of the West left town. Usually, red carpets are used to welcome people. I bet there was one rolled out when you *left* the city."

"Says the man in sandals who feels compelled to announce it when he goes to the bathroom," I immediately reply, not letting him know how much his words sting me.

He sighs. "How do you sleep at night knowing people don't like you?"

I immediately respond, "With no underwear, in case they want to kiss my ass."

He cracks a small, lopsided smile. "That one was funny."

I roll my eyes. "So thrilled to have amused you." I look toward Vance and Sulley. It seems like they're fighting. Nodding their way, I ask, "What happened with them? Obviously they have history, and not the good kind."

He shrugs. "Not my business to discuss, especially with you."

"Thanks for being so helpful, Mr. Perfect," I announce with a sarcastic tone.

He flashes me a huge grin. "Ah, you like perfection. Shocking. I don't mind perfect women. Did you know that the most perfect woman in history is Ms. Pac-Man?"

"Because she has no brain?" I ask. "Just like you probably prefer women."

He shakes his head. "No. It's because for twenty-five cents, she'll just open wide and keep swallowing until she dies. You should try it."

I stare at him in disbelief. If there were a poster of a man who encompasses all that I despise in men, it's this one. I don't think I've ever disliked anyone more, and that's saying a lot because I dislike most people.

I shake my head. "I need to go find a real man." I look around until my eyes find Champ dancing in a group of people. I point his way. "Like him. He's gorgeous, sexy, and," I look him up and down, "he doesn't dress like his mother wasn't home to dress him for elementary school."

Daylen's jaw tics for a few moments before he relaxes. "You should hit on Champ. I'm sure he could *never* resist a woman like you."

"Thank you for the permission. I think I will. Maybe I'll take him home and fuck him tonight."

Daylen fails miserably at biting back a smile. "Good luck with that, Maleficent."

What the hell? Does he honestly think I can't get Champ if I want to? Screw Daylen. I'm *definitely* fucking Champ tonight, and I'll send this ogre the photos to prove it.

Suddenly I hear Sulley shouting at Vance and then see her run away in tears. "What did your asshole friend do to her?"

He shakes his head. "Nothing. Vance is the best man I know."

I shove him in the chest and mumble, "You're clueless," before I leave and run after Sulley.

FOUR

KENNEDY

Last night was intense. Sulley was inconsolable. I felt terrible for her. Palmer and I took her home and let her cry herself to sleep. We decided it wouldn't be right to leave her alone, so we borrowed some clothing and invited ourselves to stay over. We didn't ask any questions, though we were curious as hell. We just slept in her bed with her, holding her until she eventually fell asleep.

When she woke in the morning, she told us the truth about her long, crazy history with Vance. They grew up together in Montana. He used to be her brother Finn's best friend, but Vance betrayed him just before Finn died in the line of duty. Vance has been shunned by their hometown because of everything that went down. He can't even show his face there. It's one of the most heartbreaking stories I've ever heard.

Palmer and I sat in stunned silence before vowing to support her as best we can. I meant it. This poor woman has been through so much. More than I ever realized. I remember Reagan referencing some trauma in Sulley's life, but I had no idea just how bad it was. I can't believe I was so wrong about her. All my preconceived notions have officially been thrown out the window.

Sulley is still very damaged by the loss of her brother, even though he's been gone for over five years. It gives me a huge pang of guilt over how much I've abandoned my own brother. On my way home from Sulley's, I decided to text him and invite him to lunch. Much to my surprise, he responded immediately and seemed very welcome to it.

I'm on my way to meet him now. I'm nervous as hell. I can't remember the last time we were alone together. I visit very infrequently. In fact, I don't think I've had a meal alone with my brother since I was in high school, which would have made him ten years old. He's seventeen now. I can't believe he'll be headed off to college in a year. I have no clue where he wants to go or what he wants to study. Why have I abandoned him? Nothing that happened was his fault. I doubt he even knows about it.

I arrive at the trendy, downtown restaurant on Rittenhouse Square right on time. I offered to drive out to the suburbs, but he wanted to come into town. I suppose he has his license now. It's hard for me to believe he drives. I still think of him as a little boy with a huge smile who never wanted anything from me but a little attention. Something I rarely gave him. Hearing Sulley's heartbreaking story has me up in my feels and full of regret over how unfairly I've treated Pierce.

When I walk in, I see him standing at a table and realize he's no longer a little boy. He's a man. Though not nearly as tall as our father, about my height at a little over six feet, he's a handsome man. Whereas I resemble our father, he resembles our mother with blond hair and brown eyes. He gives me that always-present, familiar smile and holds open his arms for a hug. "Kennedy, I'm so stoked you called. Mom and Dad are gonna be so jelly that I get to hang with you."

Holy shit, his voice got deep. It's weird to hear him like this.

I tentatively hug him in return while he squeezes me like he's genuinely happy to see me. I admit, "I don't care much about them, but I'm happy to see you. I'm sorry I haven't reached out until now."

He pulls away and shrugs in a totally unaffected manner. "It's chill. I'm happy to see you too. I'm super stoked that you're back in town. Dad got us Beavers' season tickets on the floor so we can come to every home game. I can't wait to watch you play in person all the time instead of on TV. I love how tough you play, especially that triple-double against Dallas last year when you had thirty-two rebounds, eleven points, and twelve assists."

"You watch my games?" I ask in surprise.

He jerks back a bit with a stunned look on his face. "Of course. My sister is a fucking star. Dad and I *never* miss a game. It's kind of our thing. He had a huge theater installed in his house just so we can watch them on the big screen with surround sound."

I lift a skeptical eyebrow. "I doubt that's why he did it. I'm sure it's to watch game tape."

Pierce shakes his head. "No way. He's obsessed with watching you play. He knows all your stats like the back of his hand. He tells everyone about you all the time. Watching you play is legit his favorite thing to do. Mom comes over sometimes and watches with us. Dad's constantly reminding her that you were always destined for greatness."

I plop into my seat in a bit of shock. I can't contain my surprise at this bit of information. "They watch it, like, together?" I ask. "In the same room?"

He chuckles. "Of course. Their divorce wasn't ugly. They're totally chill. Rooster—he's my best friend—his parents' divorce was chopped. They can't even be in the same room as each other. Mom and Dad aren't like that at all. They sit together at all my football games. Rooster's parents won't even sit on the same set of bleachers, let alone next to each other." He swallows nervously. "I was thinking maybe you could come to a game or two of mine this fall. My senior night is in October. Your season will be over by then. It would be sweet if my superstar sister was there." He scratches his head. "You've never seen me play, and this will be it for me. I'm not playing ball in college."

"Why not?" I ask. "I'm sure Dad is pissed." He lives for the glory. He probably hates that his only son isn't following in his footsteps and playing football in college.

He twists his lips. "Nah, just the opposite. Dad was the one against me playing. He told me to just go to college and have fun without worrying about the pressures of playing ball."

Huh?

Pierce lets out a laugh. "You look surprised, bruh."

I lean back in my chair, purposefully ignoring his ridiculous teen lingo. "I am. I assumed he'd push you to be a star like him."

He shakes his head. "Nope. Not at all. He said he could tell it wasn't my passion and that I'd grow to hate it. He said he just wants me to do what makes me happy, and he doesn't think football does." Pierce leans forward a bit toward me and places his elbows on the table. "You know what? He was right. As soon as that decision was made, it was like a huge weight was lifted from my shoulders. I guess I felt the burden of being Jett Jeffries' son my whole life, and once that was gone, I felt great. Dad knew it. He's the best. It took Mom a little longer to come to terms with it, but eventually she was on board too."

I can only shake my head. "I'm sorry, are we talking about Ginny and Jett Jeffries?"

He smirks. "Yep. Dude, I don't know what went down with you all, but it would be fly if you could get along. It's kind of a big year for me. I want you around." His face turns more serious. "You're the only sister I've got. I want us to be…friends. I want to get to know you. I want you to get to know me."

I fiddle nervously with my menu. I wasn't planning on getting this deep with him, really only wanting to catch up and maybe *start* to form a relationship.

In an attempt to redirect the conversation, I ask, "Do you know where you want to go to school?"

He shrugs. "Somewhere close to home. I don't want to go far, especially now that you're living and playing in town." He smiles hopefully, and I feel like the biggest asshole on the planet. This kid, my brother, just wants a relationship with me, and I've ignored him for years. *Years.*

He starts talking about how much he loves science and wants to be a doctor, but my stomach is flip-flopping. From his sweet demeanor to his longing for a relationship with me and his description of our parents, this has all taken me off guard.

The waitress finally approaches, and we place our orders. I do my best to let my walls down a bit, and we talk like friends for the rest of the meal. I'm realizing he's not a little kid anymore, despite his use of certain words I'm not sure I know the meaning of. He's just a sweet young man who is aching for some attention from his big sister. The age gap suddenly feels much less than when we were younger.

One thing is clear. He doesn't have any clue what happened, and he definitely didn't experience the same fucked up childhood as me. I see no signs of damage other than wanting his sister in his life. It's like we have two different sets of parents. His were attentive while mine were anything but. I have no idea what to make of it all.

I leave lunch feeling completely off kilter and in need of someone to talk to. Daylen *fucking* Humblecut's words from last night about me not having any friends are rattling around in my head. He wasn't wrong. I don't have a lot of friends. I've known my new teammates for less than a week, and I'm already closer to them than I was with any of my New York teammates.

I vow to make continued efforts to form real friendships with these women. None of them have been anything but kind and welcoming to me.

I don't want to burden Sulley with my family drama. It seems wrong to talk to her about my sibling when she's so messed up from losing her own.

I'm not the kind of girl who has ever talked about personal things with other women, but desperate times call for desperate measures. I decide to go to Shay and Alyssa's apartment. Alyssa and I hit it off right away when we went shopping. Having a bit of a shared history helped.

When I knock on the front door, Alyssa opens it. Alyssa Doyle is tiny. She must be at least fourteen inches shorter than Layla. She's very attractive, with wavy brown hair and honey-brown eyes. I think she's of Filipino descent. She's got a sarcastic, fun personality. We hit it off right away.

She gives me a sly smile as she opens the door. "Ooh, Black Widow. To what do we owe the pleasure?"

I bite back my smile. "I came up with a genius idea that I wanted to run by my Chief Lesbian Officer. It's a pill for depressed lesbians. It's called Trycoxagain."

She holds her stomach as she leans forward and lets out a huge laugh. "Holy shit. I haven't heard that one. Hysterical." Waving her hand, she says, "Come in. Step into your CLO's office."

I walk inside and look around. They have a nice, homey apartment. Whereas a lot of people my age have Ikea-furnished apartments, this one looks like it's a bit higher end.

Alyssa does well. She's a sales manager at an online payment service company. She can work mostly from home, so moving across the country for Shay wasn't a big deal for her.

She turns her head back toward me as we enter her living room. "Shay is showering. She'll be out in a minute. I was procrastinating working out. Your visit gives me an excuse not to go to the gym."

I shake my head. "If a CEO can run a billion-dollar company, raise three kids, cheat on his wife, and bring his side piece to a Coldplay concert, you can find time for a thirty-minute workout."

She scrunches her face as we both sit on their sofa. "When you put it like that, it's hard to argue."

I smirk at her while she stares at me from her seated position with a bit of skepticism on her face. "What's up? You don't strike me as the random-drop-by type. Is something on your mind?"

"Hmm, I suppose. I was up last night wondering why there's D in fridge when there's no D in refrigerator."

She giggles. "Excellent point. Anything else? You're not a mindless chitchat kind of girl." She gives me a knowing look.

I fidget nervously with the bottom of my shirt. "I…umm… just had lunch with my brother."

"O…kay. Seems normal."

"That's the thing. It's not normal for me. I have a strained relationship with my family. My parents. I don't talk to or see any of them very much. Because of that, I've never been close to my little brother. I'm feeling guilty about being a shitty sister. He very clearly wants to build a relationship with me."

"How do you feel about it?" she asks.

I appreciate that she's not asking me why I have a strained relationship with my parents. I'm not ready to talk about that with her.

I chew on my lower lip. "I think for the first time I might want that. I just don't have any interest in spending time with my parents, especially my mom."

"Then don't. How old is your brother?"

"Seventeen."

"He's old enough that you guys can spend time together outside of your parents."

I nod my head as I absorb her words. She's right. I can do that. "It just makes me nervous. I can't be around my mother. I *won't* be around her."

Before Alyssa can respond, Shay walks into the living room with wet hair and stops short when she sees me. "Kennedy? What are you doing here?"

Alyssa answers before I can. "She just stopped by to tell me lesbians only shop at Sports Authority because they hate Dick's."

I can't help but let out a laugh while Alyssa winks at me.

"Nah, I just needed some family advice. Alyssa helped me. Thank you."

Shay smiles lovingly at Alyssa. "She's a good listener." She looks back at me as she sits down next to Alyssa with a long sigh. "Sulley is different than what I expected. Don't you think?"

I nod. "Absolutely. I've been thinking the exact same thing. I had some preconceived notions that were completely off base."

"Me too," Shay agrees. "But she's more like a brand-new puppy with her excitement and naivety."

I let out a laugh. "True. That's exactly what she's like."

Her face turns a bit more serious. "You know some of the bitches in this league are going to be rough with her, both on and off the court." She gives me a small smile. "My best guess is part of Reagan signing you was to protect her investment in Sulley."

I consider her words as I admit, "Reagan told me to tone *down* my behavior."

She bites back a smile. "Good luck with that. She's a smart lady. There's no toning down Kennedy Jeffries, but, frankly, I think you're exactly what this team needs. You're a great player, Kennedy. We need you on the boards, but we're also going to need you to make sure Sulley doesn't get pushed around. Like it or not, you're her protector."

We chat a bit more about the team and what we think about each player, as well as our coaches, Coach Lakshmi and Coach Carroll, who we all like. I leave feeling a bit better than when I arrived.

I want to do my best to build a relationship with Pierce. He's basically the only family I have. Whether I was happy to come here or not, this is a chance for me to have at least a little family in my life.

As for my team, Shay is right. Sulley is going to get brutalized by the women in this league. It's already started in the press. Hell, if I were playing against her, I'd be doing the same. Reagan's smart. She knows my style of play. Maybe she signed me to stand up for a naïve, young girl who may not be capable of standing up for herself. Maybe that's my role on this team.

FIVE

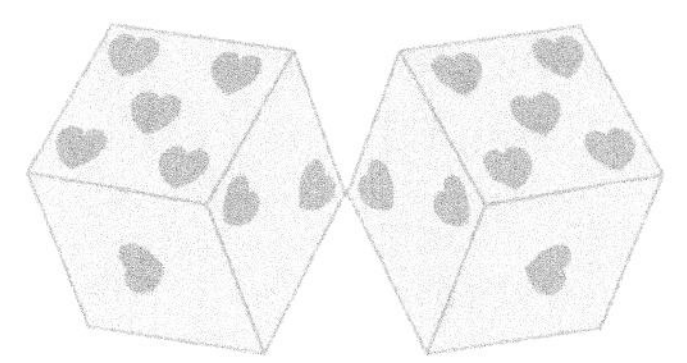

DAYLEN

"If you want the easiest way to build testosterone," Beau says matter-of-factly, "you should just watch porn and eat oysters."

Beau is obsessed with the science of working out and it all being based on increased levels of testosterone. He believes that the higher your testosterone, the more muscle you can build. I can't argue with the results. The guy is a Mack truck. I've never met a person with more muscle than Beau Fudd. It doesn't hurt that he's hard working and extremely disciplined.

He's always finding new and creative ways to increase our testosterone levels. Hell, he had us all sunbathe naked last week because direct sunlight on your balls is supposed to increase testosterone production. And like the dutiful followers we are, nearly the entire team participated. Most people are familiar with the term *blue balls,* but the entire Camels team is now well-acquainted with *red balls,* as in sunburn. Those were a few rough days for all of us. I had Chef Benny at every drug store in southeastern Pennsylvania buying them out of aloe vera.

"Porn, I understand, but oysters?" I make a look of disgust. "Who's the person who looked at an oyster and said, this smelly, snotty substance would make a delicious and expensive delicacy?"

He shrugs. "I don't know the answer to that, but I do know that oysters have a ton of zinc, which is a mineral that helps with natural testosterone production."

I twist my lips. "Hmm, I'd rather eat ass. That's my favorite delicacy."

Beau raises an eyebrow. "It's a bit less hygienic than oysters."

I shrug. "If we're not supposed to eat ass, why is it between two buns?"

I see Beau trying to fight his smile as we sit in the stadium chatting, waiting for the Beavers' game to start. We went to their home opener the other day. It was a blast. The atmosphere in the stadium was electric. The fans are excited to have this new team in town, and the level of play was incredible. These women are amazing and so damn fun to watch.

Between Presley wanting to support Layla and Vance being obsessed with Sulley—though he pretends otherwise—I have a feeling we'll be attending a lot of these games.

Our seats are on the floor, close to the action. Coach, Pierce, and his ex-wife have seats directly across from us on the floor. I give Coach an overenthusiastic wave, and he rolls his eyes. I love fucking with him. He pretends to be annoyed, but I know he loves me deep down. Well, I'm ninety-nine percent sure he loves me.

My agent, Tanner Montgomery, walks toward me with his daughter, Harper. She's fucking adorable. I think she's around eight years old but has the vocabulary of a Rhodes Scholar. I don't understand half of what comes out of the kid's mouth. She's always happy and excited. For some reason, she's drawn to me, always running to me when she sees me. I love it. I love kids.

I truly can't wait to have my own one day. I've seen many guys on the team become fathers. They're always so nervous about it. Not me. If I had the right woman, I'd want an army of kids right now. It's finding the right woman that's proven problematic.

I take in Tanner as he approaches in his always-present business suit. He's in his forties, with dark hair and a dark beard, both getting grayer by the year. He says it's because of me, but I know he's joking. I'm not a difficult client. I'm thankful for all he's done for me, including negotiating my amazing new contract, which will set me up for life. He's not only my agent, he's one of my best friends.

When I came out of college, I was solicited by agent after agent. My mind was spinning, but there was something special about Tanner. He didn't bullshit me. He told me my rookie contract wasn't going to be life-changing money. That teams were a little cautious about drafting me because of my party-boy reputation. I would have to prove myself for a few years before earning that big payday. All the other agents promised big money right away. There was something about Tanner's honesty and integrity that drew me to him. He was a straight shooter then, and he's the same now.

He used to live and work in New York City, but after his divorce five years ago, when his ex-wife wanted to move to Philly, he relocated his entire sports management company because he didn't want Harper to have to travel all the time between Philly and New York City. He's a great agent, but more importantly, he's a great father and a great man.

I see his ex-wife, Fallon, walking in with them. She's a blonde-haired, blue-eyed smoke show. She's only a few years older than me. If she wasn't his ex-wife, I'd happily ask her out. Their marriage always felt a little robotic to me. It wasn't like my parents' playful, loving marriage. My parents were marriage goals.

Tanner and Fallon have a good relationship and very peacefully co-parent Harper, as evidenced by the fact that they seem to be coming to these basketball games together.

Harper sprints toward me and leaps onto my lap. Throwing her little arms around my neck, she screams, "Uncle Daylen! I'm elated to see you again."

I chuckle at her word choice, as I often do. "I'm a lucky man to get to see the prettiest girl on the planet twice in one week."

She pulls her head away and unexpectedly frowns.

"What's wrong, sweetie?"

She crosses her arms. "Daddy said people should be most excited for my mind, not my looks."

I see Tanner smirking, and I nod. "You're right. I'm very excited to be in the company of such a smart young lady."

She gives me a toothless smile while Vance plops down next to me and mumbles, "It doesn't happen often, Harper. He doesn't spend time with *any* smart women. Ever."

I subtly flip him the bird before looking down at Harper's new Beavers jersey, noticing number eight on the front. Rolling my eyes, I ask, "Why did you switch from Sulley's jersey to Kennedy's?" At the home opener, she was wearing Sulley's number twenty-two jersey, as was nearly every little girl in the stadium.

Her little face lights up. "I told you. I like how tough Kennedy is. She's my new favorite player."

At their last game, I learned quickly that Kennedy is a rough and tough player. She battles hard for rebounds and appears to have taken on the role of protector against all the opposing players who seem to want to push around Sulley, the new star of the league.

The players on other teams aren't too kind to Sulley. I don't understand it. The league is on an upward trajectory in large part due to her star power. They should be celebrating her. Thanking her. Instead, they shove her when refs aren't looking and badmouth her in interviews.

Women. I'll never understand them.

They eventually begin announcing the starting lineup. Everyone gave Sulley a standing ovation at the last game, but I'm noticing tonight that Kennedy is receiving a lot more cheering than she did at their first game. I guess I'm not the only one noticing her protective vibe. The fans seem to be seeing and liking it.

"WHEN I'M DATING SOMEONE," Kennedy annoyingly announces in our booth at a club a few hours later, "I change their name in my phone to three hearts. Whenever they make a mistake, I remove one. When there's none left, it's over. I won't waste my time on a man who doesn't give me what I need."

Staring at her in disbelief, I think to myself that she may be the most high-maintenance woman in existence.

I roll my eyes at her ridiculous statement. "You know what's a bigger waste of time? Someone who obviously plays games like you. Playing hard to get is so cliché."

She narrows her eyes at me. "I don't *play* hard to get. I *am* hard to get."

She looks me up and down as if just now noticing my attire. "What the hell are you wearing?"

I take in my colorful Hawaiian shirt with a repeating pattern of Vance's face. "I'm supporting my bestie. You should understand that more than most."

Kennedy practically tackled a player who shoved Sulley tonight. She was ejected from the game for doing so, but the hometown fans gave her a standing ovation on her way back to the locker room. The problem was, without Kennedy on the boards, they couldn't get a single rebound. I would never admit this to her, but she's extremely valuable to the team. She's not flashy like Sulley, dropping three-pointer after three-pointer, but her contributions are undeniable, and they couldn't win without her.

She sighs. "Why did I get stuck sitting next to you…again?"

"Getting stuck in bad situations is the worst. My penis got stuck in a zipper yesterday," I offer. "That's the last time I'm zipping up someone's dress."

She shakes her head. "I feel like I'm in Oz and you're all the characters in one. No brain, no heart, and no courage."

I nod toward Champ, who's walking toward us along with Layla and Presley. "There's your *crush*. Go fangirl over him, Cruella."

She narrows her eyes at me. "Why don't you think I can get him?"

I raise an amused eyebrow. "You think you're such hot shit, and you're not. You're right, I don't think you can get him." I inwardly laugh. She's got no clue he's gay. I'm gonna fuck with her as long as I can over this.

She scowls as she crosses her arms. "Why don't you put your money where your mouth is, bigshot?"

I nod enthusiastically. "Happily." I run my fingers through my facial hair. "Hmm, what can we wager? If you can't get him to come home with you, I get to join one of your postgame interviews, saying and doing whatever the hell I want."

"Home with me tonight?" she asks.

I shrug. "No. I'm a reasonable man. Let's say by the end of August, right before my season starts. That gives you the rest of the summer to work your so-called *magic*." I air quote the word magic. "I don't think your ugly ass can get him," I taunt.

Okay, she's not ugly. She's fucking hot…on the outside. With great tits. *It's the inside I hate.*

She narrows her eyes at me. "And if I win?"

I pop a fried pickle into my mouth and purposefully chew with my mouth open because she mentioned it as another red flag of hers. "You can join my first postgame interview, also saying and doing whatever you please. It will be seen by millions more than yours. Great PR for you. I imagine it will help your image."

Her green eyes light up. She likes that. "He doesn't have a girlfriend, does he? It doesn't count if he does."

I hold up my right hand. "Scout's honor. I swear on my life he doesn't have a girlfriend."

"And you can't interfere by saying something to him about this bet."

I nod. "Agreed. I honestly don't think you can seal the deal with him. You're not as hot as you think you are," I lie.

Steam practically shoots from her ears as she holds out her hand. "Deal. No limits. The winner can say and do anything they want."

I smile as I happily shake her hand in return just before Champ, Layla, and Presley reach the table. Presley shakes his head in exasperation. "Sorry we're late. When a woman says five minutes, it's more like five minutes left in a game and both teams have all their timeouts."

I look his sexy wife up and down in her tiny dress. Knowing she's a little insecure about the last few pounds of baby weight, I want to make her feel good about herself. I let out a loud whistle. "Wow. Totally worth the wait. Are you a Beaver, because *dam*..."

Layla giggles, but Kennedy snorts in annoyance. "You truly have a way with words. Shakespeare walked so you could run. Good lord, I hate your sense of humor."

I bring my index finger to my pursed lips. "Shhh." I look up. "We need to see if flying fucks fall from the sky."

I stand, needing to get away from Kennedy's vitriol for a few minutes. "I'm going to drain the dragon. I'll stop by the bar and grab a round afterward. Anyone want anything?"

Kennedy glares at me. She hates my bathroom references. "I'll take a drink. Watch out for the woman running the cash register. She was a real bitch earlier."

"Were you at self-checkout?" I ask.

She gives me the finger before saying, "I'll have a Cosmo. Make it a double since you're buying. Not too much cranberry juice. I prefer it to be a lighter shade of pink."

I wink at her. "So do I, sweetheart."

Her lips curl in disgust. "You just ruined it for me. Make it an espresso martini."

I shrug. "Don't worry, I like the brown parts of a woman's body too. Brown puckered rosebuds are a personal favorite."

She pinches the bridge of her nose while I inwardly smile as I walk away. I think fucking with Kennedy Jeffries is about to become my new favorite hobby.

KENNEDY

I mentally run through every single thing I said and did last night as I sit in the receptionist area of Reagan's office waiting for her to see me. Champ seems so unaffected by my advances. I've never had a man react this way to me. What the hell am I doing wrong? It's not like he was talking to other women. He was chilling at our table the whole night. He talked to a few men, but no women. Have I lost my mojo? It's like Philadelphia is my kryptonite. This fucking city is cockblocking me.

I was summoned to Reagan's office this morning. I imagine I'm about to get yelled at for getting ejected from our game last night. The player on the other team had her hands, elbows, and hips all over Sulley for the entire game. It was bullshit. That woman had a hard takedown coming to her, and I was the one to serve it up.

The middle-aged receptionist with neon pink glasses looks up from her desk without an expression as she points toward Reagan's closed office door. "Mrs. Daulton will see you now."

I exhale a long breath as I build up the courage to face the tongue-lashing I'm about to get. Standing on wobbly legs, I make my way to her door and slowly open it. I see her sitting at a desk that might be bigger than my car, and her office is definitely bigger than my apartment. It's got a living room, a small kitchen, and a small play area that is filled with kids' toys.

Reagan is in yet another designer outfit. This one is green. There's another blonde, in an equally impressive power pantsuit, sitting in a chair on the other side of her desk. She resembles Reagan and has a canned drink in her hand.

Reagan motions her head toward the woman. "This is my cousin, Jade. She works here and wanted to meet you."

Jade, who must be around my age, gives me a big smile. "Ahh, the black widow of professional basketball. I've been dying to meet you."

I hate the nickname I've been called for years, but I don't let on. I simply nod as I pull a similar can from my purse. "It looks like we have the same taste in energy drinks."

It's a drink called Pussy Juice, and I don't really drink it. I just find it amusing and keep it in my purse at all times to be busted out when needed for entertainment value. I don't think I've ever met anyone else who has heard of it, let alone drinks it. It's not like you can buy it in a regular store.

Reagan lets out a laugh. "You've met your match, Jade."

Jade's smile turns mischievous. I like her immediately. "It looks like I have a new bestie. Come in." She waves her hand. "Have a seat."

I stand still as I look at Reagan. "Is that what I'm here for? A bestie sleepover?" I ask sarcastically.

Reagan rolls her eyes. "No, smartass." She points to the chair next to Jade. "Have a seat. We need to talk."

I sigh as I sit. "Look, I'm sorry about getting ejected. That player was out of line all night. She had it coming."

Jade scoffs. "Pft. Totally had it coming. Good for you for doing what every Beavers fan wanted to do all night. Hell, I almost stormed the court and tackled that bitch myself."

Huh? I look at Reagan in question, and she nods. "Agreed. She had it coming. I have no problem with how you acted. We can't have you doing that every game because it was fatal to our team to lose you, but when a player is being handsy like that, I'm okay with you protecting your teammate. We can't allow Sulley to get manhandled like that in every damn game. Did you not notice the standing ovation you received from the crowd on your way out?"

I feel like I'm being trapped. Licking my lips nervously, I admit, "I did," while I consider Shay's words from her apartment. Is that why I'm here? To be Sulley's protector?

She smiles as she picks up a small piece of paper from her desk. "People liked it so much that you had a very generous offer come in shortly after the game ended."

"Offer…for what?"

She gives me an amused look, like she's trying to bite back a smile. She then loses the battle, and they both start giggling. "What's so funny?" I ask. "What's the offer?"

She clears her throat. "Have you heard of FC2?"

I shake my head. "No."

She and Jade exchange bemused glances before Reagan's eyes once again meet mine. "It's a female condom. Get it? Female protector, just like you." She and Jade break into a fit of giggles.

I cross my arms. "Is this a joke? Did you bring me all the way down here just to fuck with me?"

With the laughter not quite subsiding, she shakes her head and hands me the piece of paper she's been holding. "This is their offer. Does that look like a joke to you?"

I take the small Post-it from her hand, and my jaw nearly drops. It's about the same amount as my basketball salary for the entire year. I've never had an opportunity like this.

"W…what do they want me to do?"

"Promote their product. Appear in a few print ads. I imagine it doesn't hurt that you're attractive. I told you if you played nice in the sandbox with Sulley her star power would rub off and good things would happen."

"I don't have to, like, really use the product, do I?" I ask.

They both begin hysterically laughing again. Reagan shakes her head and wheezes, "No, of course not. Fuck, that's funny though."

Jade nods. "You should have told her yes."

I stand and cross my arms in annoyance. "I think I'm done amusing you two for the day."

Reagan is still laughing as I walk toward the door. She shouts out, "The phone number is on there. Call them, Jenna Jameson."

The sounds of her and Jade howling in laughter ring through the office as I make my way to the elevator bank. I can't help the small smile that finds my lips. Maybe it's not Gatorade or some giant cosmetics company, but this is my first big endorsement offer. This could very well be my big break.

I begin my long walk home feeling pretty good about myself. While the product isn't ideal, I've got to start somewhere, and this is a big payday for me. The biggest of my career.

I wonder if I should try to get an agent. I'm not big enough for someone like Tanner Montgomery to take on, but I need to find someone. Maybe I should talk to my father. I've successfully avoided my parents at our two home games so far, but I know I can't avoid them forever. He keeps emailing me, and she keeps texting and calling me. While I won't entertain returning her messages, maybe I should reach out to him. It's so annoying that he doesn't text.

On my way home, I'm stopped by three people asking for photos and my autograph. That's most definitely not normal for me. It's kind of exciting to be recognized like this.

Without bothering to go inside my apartment, I head straight to the garage and get my car. I've never been to my father's post-divorce bachelor pad, but I know the address.

Making my way out to the suburbs, I realize he lives only a few miles from my mother's house. She kept my childhood home. Perhaps she'll move when Pierce graduates in less than a year. Who knows? Who cares?

The one thing I did notice at our first two games is that my mother has developed a little plastic surgery habit. She barely looks like herself, but I try not to stare too much or get too close. She was attractive. Not in a super sexy way, but still attractive and always dressed extremely well. I'm not sure why she messed with her face. She's only in her mid-forties.

I pull into his driveway and look around. It's a traditional Main Line house with old stone and stucco. It's not what I was expecting. For some reason, I didn't think it would be so… domestic looking. I was imagining a modern bachelor pad with naked women prancing around on the front lawn.

Okay, maybe not naked women, but something that says the Hugh Hefner of the East lives here.

I step out of the car and take a deep breath. Wiping my clammy hands on my shirt, I make my way to his front door and ring the traditional doorbell. I'm sure he's the only house in the neighborhood without a Ring doorbell or a similar device. There's no way my dad's tech-savvy enough to operate a camera security system.

The door opens, and he stands there with a rare smile on his face. He breathes, "Kennedy, I'm so happy you're here." I think I even see tears well up in his eyes as he motions for me to walk inside. "Come in, come in. Please."

He steps aside, and I walk in. I look around. The inside is as domestic as the outside. No leopard rugs or stripper poles to be found. No black leather couches or giant speakers. "Your new house is…nice. It looks like Martha Stewart decorated it, not Ron Jeremy, like I expected."

He chuckles. "Thanks…I think. I asked your mom to decorate it. I don't know how to do this kind of stuff. It's been a couple of years since I moved here. It feels like home."

"Mom decorated *your* house? The person you divorced?"

He chuckles. "Yep. You know I'm clueless with decoration

crap. She loves that kind of shit. I wanted it to be like her house so Pierce felt comfortable whenever he stayed over. We had a formal fifty-fifty agreement at first, but he's almost eighteen. Now he sleeps wherever he wants." He mumbles, "He definitely won't be sleeping here tonight."

"Why?" I ask.

My father scratches his fingers through his scruff, which I'm noticing for the first time has a little gray to it. "Well, I told him he's no longer allowed to come home at three in the morning like he did last night. He replied that I don't understand what it's like to be him. I said, *you're right, buddy. I've never cried tears over a Wi-Fi outage while wearing three-hundred-dollar sneakers I didn't pay for.*"

I can't help but giggle. That's such a my-father thing to say.

He gives me a small smile. "Yep, he didn't care for that too much. Stormed out of here." He exhales a long breath. "This generation..."

I roll my eyes. Here we go. I'm about to hear how much harder Gen X had it.

"Anyway," he interrupts himself, "I'm happy you're here. Is everything okay?"

"Can we sit? I need to ask your advice on something."

His face lights up like it's Christmas morning. "Of course." He points toward the big glass doors covering the entire back side of the house. "Let's go sit by the pool. I love it out there. It's my favorite part of the house. I spend all my time back there in nice weather."

"There aren't any, like, Playboy bunnies in the pool, are there?"

He lets out a loud laugh. "Umm, negative. Never even met one."

"Really?" It's shocking. I half expected him to open the door with a maroon velvet robe and a pipe, surrounded by women half his age.

He offers me a drink, but I decline. We then walk through to the backyard pool area. I understand why it's his favorite place here. It's stunningly luxurious out here. The pool is huge and unconventionally shaped. There's a rock structure with a waterfall and a slide cut into it. It's rounded out by a beautiful summer kitchen, complete with a bar that has an oversized television sitting behind it. There are multiple chaise lounges that look new and comfortable.

"Pierce must love this," I say as we both sit in oversized chairs with cushions.

Dad sighs. "I think you're right. When I'm on road trips, he's supposed to stay with your mom, but when I come home, I always find beer cans and those girlie canned vodka drinks. High Boom or whatever they call it."

I smile at his naivety. "High Noon."

He points at me. "Yep, that's it."

I rub the high-end fabric of the luxurious chair. "This is really nice, Dad."

He shrugs. "Better than the deathtrap lawn chairs I grew up with. Those things would eat you alive. But I survived, as did my entire generation, all without seven-*thousand*-thread-count fabric in our lives."

I bite back my smile while he fidgets nervously. "Your season has started off well," he offers. "That girl had it coming last night."

I nod. "She did. That's why I'm here."

"Did you get fined by the team? The league? Do you need me to cover it?" He reaches for his wallet as if its contents would actually cover the cost if I were levied with a fine for my behavior.

I lift an eyebrow. "Have I asked you for any money since the day I left for college?"

He shakes his head. "No, but I'm always happy to help. Whatever you need."

"Noted and appreciated, but it's unnecessary." I lick my lips nervously. "I just left Reagan Daulton's office."

He nods. "I hear she's a hard ass."

I twist my lips. "Yes and no. She's a force to be reckoned with, but I think she's well-intended and very smart. She's made me a few promises, and today she delivered on one of them. I was offered a big endorsement opportunity. The biggest financial offer I've ever had. I think I might need a real agent. Can you help me find one?"

His face lights up. "That's great, sweetie. What company did it come from?"

I wince. "It's…umm…female prophylactics."

He pinches his eyebrows together. "I have no idea what that means."

"It's better you don't know. Can you help me find someone? I know it's not enough for big agents like Leo or Tanner Montgomery, but I'm sure some smaller agents would be willing to take me on with a contract like this one in the queue."

Leo Anderson is my dad's longtime agent and friend. He's nearly as big as Tanner, way too big for me.

"I'm happy to call Leo. He'd do me a favor and take you on as a client."

I shake my head. "I don't want to be at the bottom of the food chain. I'd rather have someone a little smaller who I matter to. Does that make sense?"

He nods. "Of course it does. That's smart. I should have a few names for you. Let me grab my Rolodex."

He runs inside and returns a few moments later with an actual rotating card apparatus. I can't help but start laughing. "Oh my god, Dad, I can't believe you still use a Rolodex. You can store all that information on your phone."

He pulls his phone out of his pocket. His flip phone. That has the antenna taped on with gray electrical tape. Yep, an actual antenna.

"Right, you still use that antique product. Why don't you upgrade?"

"I don't trust a phone without real buttons. Hell, I still drive a car that has an ashtray in the armrest."

I gasp. "No you don't."

He smiles. "I don't, but I had you believing it for a second."

I let out a small laugh. He's trying so hard right now. It's kind of sweet.

He places reading glasses I didn't know he wore on his face as he begins rolling through his contacts, one at a time. Half the index cards are torn or stained. He eventually pulls out the one he's obviously looking for but scrunches his face. "Crap, I spilled coffee on this one. I can't see all the numbers. Let me call your mom. She'll have Ray's number."

Ray Delgado. That makes sense. My father used him at the beginning of his career. He runs a small agency, but he's a good guy from what I remember, and he represents several lesser-known athletes. He stayed friendly with my dad after my father moved to Leo's bigger agency.

He opens—yes, opens—his phone and begins dialing before placing it to his ear. "Hey, Gin. Can I get Ray's number? I spilled coffee on my copy."

I can't hear what she's saying. He listens for a second before responding. "Kennedy needs it."

And then, "Yes, she stopped by."

After another pause, he says, "I'll tell her. Can I get the number, Gin?"

He pulls out a golf pencil stuffed into the Rolodex and begins writing on the stained card.

"Thanks, hun. Yep, I'll tell her. I said I would."

He closes his phone and holds up the card. "Here's Ray's number. And your mom wants you to stop by the house after you leave here."

I scoff. "Fuck. No. Not happening."

"Ken, we're your family. Let us in. Don't act like this."

"For complaints about the product, please see the manufacturer." I stand. "This was a mistake. I shouldn't have come here."

I begin to turn away, but he grabs my arm. "Stop. I'm sorry. I promise not to pressure you. I'm happy you came to me." He places the card in my hand. "Call Ray. He can help."

I give him a small nod and mumble, "Thanks."

He visibly swallows. "Did you get my email about the pickleball tournament? It's after your season ends."

I sigh. "I did. Let me think about it."

"Okay, Marshmallow. Anytime you want to practice, just let me know. Anytime at all. I'm always here for you. Whenever you need me."

Except for my entire childhood. I think it, but I don't bother to say it aloud. It won't change anything.

SIX

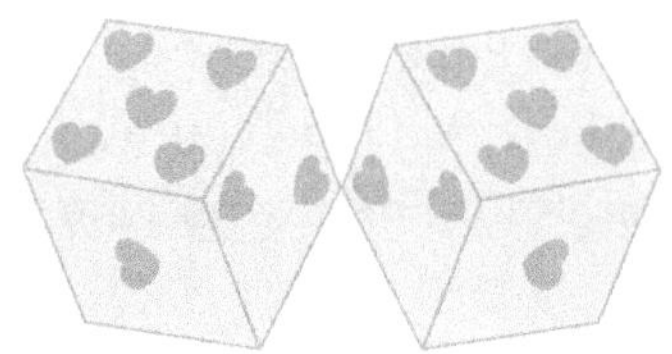

DAYLEN

"What's the difference between Iron Man and Iron Woman?" I ask at the poker table while examining the hand I was dealt.

Tanner raises a thick, dark eyebrow as he blows out a plume of cigar smoke. "What?"

I answer, "One's a superhero and one's a command."

All the guys start laughing.

Monthly poker games in Tanner's mancave have become a tradition among my closest group of friends, who all happen to be Tanner's clients. Vance is always here, along with three professional baseball players from the Philly Cougars. Layton Lancaster recently retired, but he was the face of the Cougars for over a decade. Trey DePaul is their third baseman who's happily married with a baby son. Cruz "Cheetah" Gonzales is their speedy center fielder, who's dating professional softball player Kamryn Hart.

To say that Kam is my dream girl would be an understatement. She's smart, sexy, talented, funny as hell, sassy as sin, and just plain perfect. Unfortunately, Cheetah met her first, so

I immediately backed off. I would never interfere in my friends' relationships, but he found himself a rare gem among a sea of unremarkable stones.

Her twin sister, Bailey, also a professional softball player, moonlights as Tanner's nanny. She's much more subdued than Kam, and I'm pretty sure Tanner is in love with her. They've been secretly fucking for nearly a year, but Tanner refuses to talk about it, and we don't pry.

Layton is married to one of their teammates, Arizona Abbott. They eloped last year but are having a big reception this fall during our bye week. It was cool of them to do it then, enabling Vance and me to attend.

The Cougars had a day game today, and the WAGs are having themselves a girlie night, so it was the perfect night for us to have our monthly game, which gets hard to schedule at times. I love this group of men like the brothers I never had and truly cherish this time of busting balls, good food, good drinks, and lots of laughs.

Our season starts this week, and things are about to get crazy for us. It's been a fun summer. We've spent a lot of time with the Beavers players. Besides Kennedy, I like all of them very much. Sulley and Vance seem to have achieved a level of peaceful co-existence. I know he has a crush on her, but he refuses to talk about it.

Tomorrow is the Beavers' last game before our season begins, which means Kennedy is about to lose our bet, and I'll join her postgame interview. Watching her try to win over Champ all summer has been a riot.

I can't imagine Kennedy normally gets turned down by men, so this rejection must be rattling her. I'm sure men usually fall at her feet. As much as I dislike her, her body is ridiculous, and no *straight* man could possibly be immune to it. She has the best tits. I had a wet dream thinking of what they might look and feel like the other night. I woke up disgusted with myself, but it happened. I think it's because

I'm always being subjected to watching them bounce. Be it on the dance floor or the stadium floor, she's always moving around, and they're bouncing. It's hypnotizing.

Women's tits are the reason I know God has a sense of humor. He creates the most perfect, squishy stress reliever in existence, but then he puts it on the one thing that causes the most stress.

Kennedy has mostly given up on Champ. He obviously pays her no attention, but watching her swing and miss has become my favorite pastime. She tries not to be obvious in front of everyone, but because I know what she's trying to do, I keep a careful eye on her. And I know exactly what I'm going to say and do on camera tomorrow night to embarrass the shit out of her. We agreed to no limits, and I'm going to smash it out of the park.

Layton smirks at my Iron Woman comment. "You better not tell that joke in front of the girls. You'll get your balls fried for it."

Vance's trademark scowl momentarily disappears. "Daylen gets his balls fried all the time by Kennedy Jeffries. It's a fucking riot. She hands him his ass on a daily basis. They're gonna hate fuck one of these days. I just hope they both survive the encounter."

I purse my lips. "I will *never* touch that bitch. She and her fucking red flags drive me nuts. I was wearing white jeans the other night, and she told me that's on her red flag list. What's wrong with white jeans?"

Cheetah scrunches his face. "They're kinda girlie. I don't like them for men either. I think chicks can be both green and red flags at the same time. If you grab her by the throat and she smiles, you know right then and there she's both. She'll definitely be a problem," he wiggles his eyebrows up and down, "but you'll have *a lot* of fun along the way."

Trey bites back his smile. "As the longest tenured married man here, let me give you some advice." He winks at us. "Hold her hand in public, hold her throat in private, but smack her ass everywhere."

Words to live by.

TONIGHT IS THE NIGHT. Kennedy keeps glancing my way during her team's warm-ups. For the first time ever, she appears nervous. Fuck, this is going to be fun.

I purposefully wore white jeans, a Hawaiian shirt, sandals, and I capped it all off with a giant gold chain that would put Mr. T to shame. I even managed to find the biggest, fruitiest drink they have in the arena. I've got that in one hand and my Android in the other. I've messed my hair up as much as possible and shaved my face in an uneven manner, all knowing how much she hates an *unkempt* man. I think I've got nearly every red flag she mentioned working for me tonight.

The game hasn't started yet, and I see Coach walking across the floor toward our seats. I nod at him. "Hey, Coach. You didn't have to walk your old ass all the way over here. If you missed me, I would have come to you."

He narrows his eyes at me. "Humblecut, believe it or not, I'm okay walking twenty feet. I come from a generation that had no remote controls. When I was a kid and we wanted to change the channel, I had to fucking get off my lazy ass and walk over to the TV to change it. And we only had four stations. And the reception sucked. And I had to stand next to the TV sometimes just so it would work because I was a human antenna."

"Must be your magnetic personality," I deadpan. "What brings you over, Coach?"

He looks me up and down. "Why are you dressed like the mentally slow guy from *The Hangover*?"

Vance, Presley, and Beau, all seated around me, burst out

laughing. Vance agrees, "Holy shit, that's exactly who you look like. All you need is a man-purse to complete the outfit."

I proudly pull my new purchase, another of Kennedy's red flags, from under my chair and hold it up. "I love my man purse. By the way, it's called a satchel. I can't believe more men don't carry them. So much better than having keys, condoms, and a wallet in my pocket. I can also fit way more condoms in this, keeping my options open and plentiful for the evening."

Coach scowls at me. "Something ain't right with you, Humblecut."

I nod. "My father would agree." I turn to Vance. "Speaking of my father, the fam is coming to the game tomorrow. Want to have dinner with us afterward?"

His face lights up as he nods before Coach retreats to his seat. Vance is amused by my silly, fun family. His coming home with me for dinners and holidays is commonplace. Since he's had some drama in his hometown, it's difficult for him to go home.

The game finally gets underway. Layla is playing particularly well tonight, with a ton of rebounds and points. I lean over to Presley. "Layla looks great."

He raises an unamused eyebrow. "You lookin' at my wife's ass, D?"

I start to get defensive. "No, of course not. That's not what I meant. I just—"

"Why not?" he interrupts. "She has the best ass."

I chuckle. "Agreed."

"But I didn't marry her only for looks. I married her for her personality. I just didn't realize at the time that it came with a variety pack."

I laugh again as we continue to watch the game. The other team is suffocating Sulley tonight, though they're playing clean with solid defense, not the normal cheap shots Sulley endures. She's currently being double-teamed but manages to pass the ball to Kennedy, who pops the three. Kennedy is having a career night.

I look up at the board and realize she has a triple-double. That's amazing and not easy to do, especially for Kennedy, who's primarily used as a rebounder and for her excellent defensive and picking skills.

No less than ten times, she's looked my way with worry written all over her annoyingly pretty face. It's because if she's one of the better players in the game, they'll interview her. She knows what will happen if she's interviewed tonight.

I'm sitting back in my seat with the biggest grin I've ever had in my life. I can't wait to fuck with her.

The game finally comes to an end, and the fans begin to file out. Not me. I sit back and wait patiently for my big moment.

She's given earphones, and one of the broadcasters stands next to her with a microphone. The cameraman is in front of them as they prepare to begin her post-game interview.

She turns her head and gives me one last pleading glance as if to say *don't do this.*

It's just Vance and me. Presley is with Layla, and Beau left at halftime to get his beauty sleep.

Kennedy's back is to me now, and she's a few minutes into answering questions. I stand and slowly make my way to her. While she's mid-sentence, I grab her around the waist and dip her. She screeches when my lips meet hers for a long, juicy, passionate-yet-closed-mouth kiss. I was originally planning tongue, but the thought of kissing her like that turns my stomach. I don't need tongue to get my point across.

Her eyes widen to a size I didn't know possible. I pull her back up and break the kiss. Looking straight into the camera, I grin widely and say, "Don't I have the best sister ever?"

MY VIDEO with Kennedy played on a loop on television and social media last night for hours until they finally realized it was a joke. That we're not, in fact, brother and sister. She tried to correct things in front of the camera right away, but the interviewer and cameraman got out of there faster than Ashlee Simpson when she was busted lip-synching on Saturday Night Live.

The hours of humiliation Kennedy suffered fed my soul. I fell into the most peaceful slumber last night, with a bigger smile than I usually have after sex.

She vowed her revenge, to which I responded, "Bring it, sugar tits." She equally did not care for that new nickname.

She made a whole big thing about having to disinfect her mouth. Blah blah blah. So unoriginal. She's going to have to up her game to get one over on me.

We're in the locker room just before our game. Coach is motivating us with his pregame speech. "Does anyone have any questions?"

I raise my hand. "I do."

He pinches the bridge of his nose. "God help me. What is it, Humblecut?"

"What do you call identical boobs?"

I hear a few snickers from the guys.

I smile and answer, "Iden*tit*ies."

The guys bust out laughing, but Coach stares daggers at me. He has been doing it all day since the Kennedy kissing thing. I had to explain that it was a joke due to a bet she lost to me. I spared him the terms, but I think he understood why I did it. I explained to him and assured him in no uncertain terms that there never has been and never will be anything between Kennedy and me.

KENNEDY

"Isn't it weird that it's socially acceptable to put someone's genitals in your mouth, but if you eat a potato chip off the floor, you're gross?" I declare to Sulley and Palmer as Reagan scolds her son for picking up a potato chip off the floor and popping it into his mouth.

We're sitting on the other side of her suite at the Camels' game, but we watched it all go down as the little devil sneakily grabbed the chip and quickly gobbled it down. Not surprisingly, Reagan didn't miss it. She misses nothing.

They both giggle. Sulley answers, "I suppose that's true. It's been a few months since I've had genitals in my mouth. I wouldn't mind that right about now."

"When are you seeing Shane again?" I ask.

"Next month in Italy."

"Right. You should have an open relationship and join Tinder. It's so much better. The guy I was with last night was fire."

Palmer's eyes widen. "Last night? With all the shit surrounding Daylen's declaration?" She smiles softly. "You have to admit, it was funny."

"It was *not* funny. It was a mess. For hours. I needed something to take the edge off. I got this big, tattooed, muscular dude to come over and take care of business. Like five times. Otherwise, I would have murdered that Neanderthal in his ridiculous white jeans."

The corners of Sulley's mouth turn up slightly. "Are you sure it isn't that white-jeaned muscular man you wanted in your bed last night?"

My mouth hangs open in both astonishment and disgust. "I'd rather never have an orgasm again than allow that human fungus into my bed."

"Hmm," is all she responds while she and Palmer share a glance.

The game gets underway. Daylen has a long catch for a touchdown, and during his celebration he does a fake dip and kiss like he did to me last night. He then looks up at our booth and makes a heart sign with his hands. Our eyes meet. I kiss my middle finger and blow it at him.

The fucker laughs while my rage boils over.

I don't know when, and I don't know how, but I'm going to get him back someday.

SEVEN

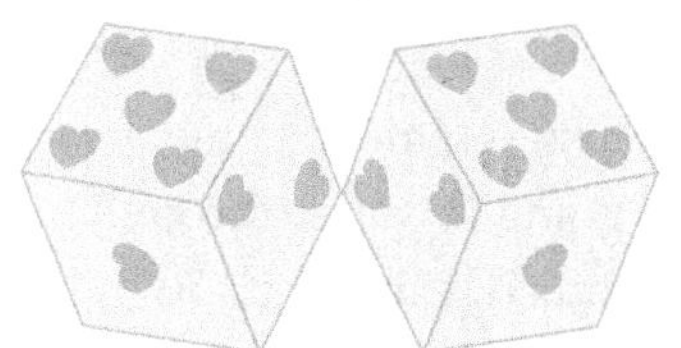

KENNEDY

Our season ended a few weeks ago. We made the playoffs, which is great for a first-year franchise, but we got eliminated quickly. I think this team could be very good. I'm committed to a rigorous off-season workout to get myself into the best shape possible.

Sulley is off doing a photo shoot in Italy, after which she's going to spend some time with her unworthy boyfriend and then go home to Montana through the holidays. I can't believe I'm going to admit this, but I'll miss her. She's become a good friend and a sounding board for me. She's always so level-headed. I need that in my life.

We just got off a call, where she had to talk me off the ledge. I've been on the fence about going to Pierce's senior night football game. I've managed to live in Philly for over four months without having to spend any time with my mother and minimal time with my father. I played pickleball with him once, and I'm playing with him in a tournament today. His pickleball friends are actually kind of funny.

Pierce and I have met for a handful of meals, and I talked to him after a few of my games while managing to avoid my parents.

Sulley thinks I'll regret it if I don't go to his final senior year home game. The last time she saw her brother was at her high school basketball senior night. He surprised her and flew in from his deployment overseas for a short visit. It meant everything to her.

Pierce has been begging me to come. It obviously means a lot to him. I think I'm going to suffer through a few hours with my mother and go. I'm on edge about it, but Sulley was able to calm me down by helping me see the big picture.

I walk into Dad's pickleball club, and his friend David Debois, who I met the last time we played, is standing at the entrance. I high-five him. "How's it hanging, Double Dees?"

The man, who must be in his mid-sixties, smiles at me. "Pretty low, Triple Dees."

I smile at his new nickname for me.

Here's what I've learned about the senior men in the pickleball community. They're fucking perverts who also happen to think they're the funniest human beings alive. They also have a wiseass comment for everything. Every little thing. And most of those comments are sexual in nature. They're funny as hell, and I honestly had the best time when I played with them a few weeks ago. My father doesn't join in on their shenanigans though. Instead, he rolls his eyes, but I can tell he has a lot of affection for them.

While, of course, they get off on playing with the famous Jett Jeffries, they seem to genuinely like my dad. Though always a fierce competitor, he's a bit more relaxed when he plays than I'm accustomed to seeing him. I think it's his form of escapism.

I walk over to the bench where my father is sitting. He raises an unamused eyebrow as he takes in my outfit. "Don't you think that skirt is a little short?"

I smile innocently. "As long as you can't see my dick, it's fine."

He exhales a long breath. "Can we remember that I'm your father and we should have boundaries in how we talk to each other?" He looks around. "You're going to give these old guys a coronary."

I shrug as I place my paddle on the bench and remove my sweatshirt, leaving me in only a sports bra on top. He gives me a disapproving scowl. Beginning to stretch my legs and arms, I state, "Whatever it takes to win, Dad."

He stretches his right arm across his body. "We're both all-American athletes. We have zero chance of losing today."

I giggle. He's not wrong. We're going to wipe the floor with these guys.

As I'm leaning over, stretching my hamstrings, I notice his iPhone sitting by his bag. I gasp. "Did you get a new phone? One from this century?"

He nods. "I did, and it's confusing me. Your brother won't help." He picks it up and holds it out for me. "Please show me the basics. I can't figure out how to dial. There are no numbers or buttons. How can you dial a phone without numbers and buttons?"

I bite back my smile. "It's a touchscreen. Haven't you ever had an iPad or anything along those lines?"

He runs his fingers through his thick, dark, wavy hair. "Nope." His eyes meet mine. "Please. A two-minute drill. That's all I need."

I take his phone from him and turn it on. "What's the passcode?"

"The salesman helped set it up for me. It's 0-2-2-9."

I lift my head and swallow hard. "My birthday?"

He nods. "The day I became a father. That's my passcode for everything. It's also the code to my front door. You're always welcome. No need to knock or ring the doorbell. Just come inside. Anytime. All the time," he begins rambling. "Whenever. Bring friends. The pool is closed now, but you're always welcome to use it when it's open in the summer."

I don't acknowledge any of that as I pull up his small handful of apps. There's one that sticks out right away. I look up at him again. "You're on a dating app?"

His eyes widen in horror. "Oh…umm…I was just trying it. A…friend recommended it."

"I'm surprised. I'm sure you don't have issues meeting women."

He licks his lips nervously as he admits, "I haven't dated since your mom. I plan to wait until your brother graduates. I don't want to confuse him." He fidgets with the bottom of his shirt. He's acting like a teenager caught in the act. "Just toying with the app. I'm sure nothing will come of it. I want to learn how to use it before really putting myself out there."

What the hell? It's not like I would ever admit this out loud, but my father is an objectively handsome man. He also happens to be a former superstar athlete with a muscular physique and a very full bank account. Does he not realize what a commodity he is? If he's not looking for skanks, why does he post all those TikTok videos of himself working out? Something doesn't add up.

And then it occurs to me. There's no way he has TikTok, or any social media for that matter. He didn't even have a real phone until now. I quickly scroll through his apps. Sure enough, no TikTok. No other social media. The dating app is the only non-factory setting app on the phone.

I look back up at him again. "How have you been posting all those workout videos if you don't have TikTok?"

He pinches his eyebrows together. "What workout videos?"

"The ones that have been a mainstay on #SilverFoxTok for two years."

"What's a hashbrown silver fox tock?" he asks innocently.

Before I can inquire further, David walks over to us. "Andy Tucker withdrew. I guess he's *tuckered* out." David chuckles to himself. "Will you two warm up with me?"

I nod. "Sure, Double Dees. Do you have a ball?"

He smirks. "I have two, but they're both old."

I snort out a laugh. "Double Dees, you're a degenerate."

He throws his shoulders back as he stands tall. "Proud of it."

I GUESS I will add Dink and Drink Club champion to my resume. My dad and I wiped the floor with our competition. I barely broke a sweat. I then agreed to a short lunch with him while I showed him how to use his phone. He was sketchy as hell about his dating app, but I gave him the tutorial he wanted and desperately needed.

I'm now walking into my brother's game wearing his team's sweatshirt. My father gave me one when I was with him and told me how much it means that I'm coming tonight. I reminded him that it's for Pierce and only Pierce.

He said player announcements would begin at seven, but they'd be there by six if I wanted to come early to hang out. Fat fucking chance of that happening.

At one minute before seven, I walk into the stadium and see all the parents lined up on the sideline with their sons. As I get closer, I notice one female player. That's cool. There's a new professional women's football league, so I guess women playing in high school will start happening more and more often. That didn't exist when I was in high school. Too bad. I have a rocket of an arm. I could have been the quarterback.

Seeing my mother feels like a punch to the gut. Of course she had her hair blown out. Her face is covered in makeup for a damn high school football game. She's probably prowling for men here.

Maybe this was a mistake. I turn to leave but hear Pierce shout, "Kennedy!"

I exhale a long breath before slowly and begrudgingly turning around. He's running toward me. He looks so grown up in his football uniform with eye black on his face. His blond hair is messy from the helmet. But it's the enormous grin on his face that clutches my heart. He's so damn happy I'm here.

Suck it up for him, Kennedy. You can do anything for a few hours. Even hang out with the Wicked Witch of Philly.

He crashes into me and wraps his arms around me, lifting and then twirling me around. "Ahhh, you came. I'm so happy," he shouts with pure glee.

He places me down, and I see tears welling in his eyes as they meet mine. He croaks out, "Thank you. This means everything."

Fuck, now I've got tears in my eyes. I never cry.

He grabs my hand and brings me over toward our parents, as well as all the other seniors lined up. My father mouths, "Thank you," as I approach. I don't know what my mother does because I avoid eye contact with her.

I feel her grab my arm, but quickly pull away and grit out, "Don't. I'm here for him."

"But Ken—"

I finally look at her. I've done my best not to glance her way at my games and have avoided her like the plague afterward. While I noticed she looked different, this is the first time I've seen her up close in a long while. She has truly ruined her once-good looks with plastic surgery. She's got fillers everywhere. Her lips appear as though she was stung by ten bees. She's very obviously had work done on her eyes. She basically looks like Catwoman. I don't know why she'd do this to her face.

"I. Said. Don't," I practically spit. I give her a look to suggest she not make a scene because I will turn around and leave.

She has the fucking nerve to appear teary eyed. Or maybe she just can't blink properly with all the work she's had done to her face.

She pinches her giant, fake lips together but doesn't otherwise say a word. Pierce seems blissfully unaware. He's beaming as the man with the microphone begins talking about the seniors.

My parents are now on either side of Pierce. Picking the lesser of two evils, I stand on the other side of my father.

We gradually move to the front of the line. The man on the microphone starts talking about Pierce's accomplishments. Holy crap, he's super smart. He has a ton of academic awards. It sounds like he's a science genius. When they get to his athletic accomplishments, they're a bit more limited, but when they get to his personal statement about what shaped him, my mind is blown.

The man talks about how Pierce mentioned how lucky he was to grow up with one of the biggest athletic superstars in the country. All eyes in the stands find my father, whose own eyes briefly turn to mine before the corners of his mouth raise ever so slightly.

The man continues, "In his personal statement, Pierce wrote, *'While some people get to watch their idols on television, I was fortunate to live with mine. I learned what hard work and determination can achieve. What perseverance looks like. And lucky for me, I now get to see her play more often. My sister, Kennedy, is my idol.'*"

What? He grew up with a Hall of Fame father and *I'm* his idol?

My father's smile grows. He knew what Pierce wrote beforehand. He leans over and whispers, "Like I said, thanks for being here. He worships you."

Pierce throws four touchdowns and runs for another. He's quite obviously the best player on the field. At some point, I turn to my dad and ask, "Why isn't he playing in college? He's *really* good."

He briefly tucks his lips under his teeth as if choosing his words carefully before tapping the left side of his chest. "Heart. Football isn't in his heart. He enjoys it like a hobby, but it's not the air he breathes. I think he felt pressure to do so because of me, not because it's what he truly wanted. He's obviously got some talent, but he's not like you, Kennedy. You have this extra quality about you, and you have since you were a little girl. It's an inner fire that you either have or you don't. You had it. You still have it. He doesn't. He loves science. He wants to be a doctor. You and I both know how hard it is to balance being a student and an athlete at a high level. He shouldn't have to sacrifice what he truly wants because he's my son and feels like he *has* to follow a certain path." He twists his lips. "Does that make sense?"

I nod. I could never have been on the pre-med track with my basketball schedule in college. "Pierce told me you're the one who encouraged him not to play in college."

"That's right. Because I just want what's best for him. For both of you."

"But you always pushed me." Playing basketball was the only thing he and I *ever* discussed growing up.

He exhales a long breath. "If it was too much, I'm sorry. You were born to be a star, Kennedy. Sometimes your attit…strong convictions got in the way. I did what I thought was best, but I'm not perfect." He smirks. "I suppose I'm mellowing in my old age."

When the game is over, Pierce runs over to me and gives me the game ball he was awarded by his coach. He then proudly introduces me to all his friends.

I'm so caught up in my emotions that I somehow manage to offer his best friend, Rooster, an internship with me. He wants to go into sports management, and Pierce begged me to take him on and show him the ropes. I wasn't really in a position to deny my brother anything tonight. He said Rooster also happens to be a tech genius if I have any needs in that regard.

EIGHT

DAYLEN

"What in the actual fuck?" I roar.

Vance, Cheetah, Trey, and Layton are practically on the floor, hyperventilating with laughter.

We're all in tuxedos at Arizona and Layton's wedding reception, though at this point in the evening, our jackets are off, our bow ties are loosened, and our sleeves are rolled up. We've been drinking and dancing all night. It's been a blast celebrating the very-much-in-love couple. Layton was a bigger playboy than I am for *many* years. But he fell fast and hard for Arizona. She's already pregnant with their first child.

I can't imagine there are more than a few songs left before we bid adieu to the happy couple, and they head to the airport for their honeymoon. We were all at the bar doing one last round of shots when Kam held up her phone for us to see. With a huge smile on her face, she announced, "I have Google alerts set for all of you. This just popped up for you, D."

I shrugged. "I'm fucking famous. I have shit written about me all the time. What's the big deal?"

She tried to bite back her smile as she said, "You might want to take a look at this one."

With my friends all looking over my shoulder, I grabbed the phone and was horrified by what I found.

It's a text that is made to look like it was sent by me, even though it wasn't. That's my damn telephone number online for the world to see. Whoever posted this knows my cell phone number. The text is of a damn dick. A teeny tiny dick with my number and the Camels logo tattooed on it. And it doesn't look fake. It looks fucking real, like I have a small dick with a tattoo and sent this to someone.

Kam smirks. "I didn't know you had a... tattooed dick, D. Hopefully the images appear smaller than they are in real life, right?" She winks at me.

Everyone is still laughing. "Who in the world would do this to m—" And then it hits me. Kennedy *fucking* Jeffries. That ruthless bitch did this. I know it.

Suddenly the Electric Slide begins playing. Kam's eyes widen. "Ooh, I love this song. Did you all know that it's rumored to be about a vibrator?"

Everyone just stares at her. "Yep." She starts singing the words to the song. "You can't see it. It's electric. You gotta feel it. It's electric. Oooh, it's shocking. It's electric."

They all start laughing again before heading back to the dance floor to do all the well-known moves to the song. Not me. I'm walking out of the room to call the most horrific woman to ever walk this planet.

I click on her number, and it rings once before I'm sent to voicemail. That cunt isn't bothering to pick up.

I call at least five more times, all with the same result. I'm not leaving some ranting voicemail that she'll probably post on social media. I'm smart enough for that.

I text her.

Me: Pick up the damn phone.

Black Flag: No hablo inglés.

Me: I'm calling again. Pick up or I'll tell your father you fucked half the team.

Black Flag: I don't care. Tell him that made-up story. Doesn't bother me if he thinks I got gang banged by the whole damn city. What's he going to do, spank me?

And my traitorous dick twitches at the notion of spanking her. I look down at it, moving from limp to a semi. What the fuck is wrong with my dick? I think she broke his will. I tug on my hair. Ahh. This woman is infuriating.

I try calling her again, but this time she picks up right away, cackling. "I thought I might hear from you, scarecrow. How's the wedding?" she asks innocently.

"Don't *how's the wedding* me, you evil witch. This is way overstepping," I scream into the phone.

She scoffs. "Pft. Overstepping? Overstepping is kissing me on national television and then announcing that we're siblings. Newsflash, I don't get paid millions of dollars like you. I nearly lost my biggest endorsement deal thanks to your antics. You fucked with my image and my livelihood. That, asshole, is overstepping."

Hmm, I never thought about it that way. I'm starting to feel bad until I remember what she just did. "You know where I am, Cruella? At a wedding. Something you'll never have because no one in their right mind will ever want to spend their life with you. You're such a ruthless bitch."

"Thank you."

"It wasn't a compliment."

"I disagree. I read that every time you're a bitch, it adds a year to your life. I'm immortal, motherfucker. Have a good night doing damage control. Toodaloo," she sings before ending the call.

Shit. She's right. I need damage control. I can't have this misinformation out there. I will fucking go full Monty if I have to in order to prove what my manhood looks like.

I need a plan. Tanner. I have to find him. Last I saw my agent about an hour ago, he was grinding up against Bailey on the dance floor. So much for their relationship being a secret.

By the time I head back into the reception room, it's nearly empty except for Cheetah and Kam. They're doing a choreographed dirty dancing routine on the dance floor to a sensual Latin song. They're all alone except for the band, like it's a private party just for the two of them.

I couldn't take my eyes off Kam tonight. She's wearing a tight, strapless, royal-blue bridesmaid dress that has a high slit up the side where her long, defined legs keep making an appearance. I can't believe that asshole met the perfect woman before I had the chance to.

My mother and father used to dance all the time. It's one of the few memories I have of them as a couple.

Kam and Cheetah smile, laugh, and kiss. They look so in love. I adore Cheetah, and I'm happy for him, but I've never been more jealous of another man than I am right now.

I LET OUT a loud laugh at the Thanksgiving table. My dad is the funniest man I know.

Hank Humblecutt is big like me, but he now also has a giant tummy hanging over his belt. While he's never been as fit as me, I don't think I've seen him this heavy since my mother passed.

I was six years old when they told me her cancer had returned. A cancer I never knew she had the first time around. It was ovarian, and apparently the first bout was the reason they never had another baby after me.

I was young, but it felt like she went from a beautiful, vibrant woman to bedridden in a matter of days. I know it was over the course of a few months, but it felt quicker to me.

My father took a leave of absence from his job as a federal judge to care for her and me those last few months. He was always positive around me. Always had a smile and a joke. But when he thought I was asleep at night, I'd see him alone in the kitchen crying. My heart broke for him. I did my best to stay out of trouble, which happened with regularity prior to her getting sick. I wanted him to have one less thing to be sad about. One less thing to worry about.

Alone was how he remained for many years after she passed. It was him and me. The big Humblecut boys. The dynamic duo. He did everything for me. Of course I longed for my mother, but I never felt like I missed anything, thanks to my dad. He drove me to school and sports, came to every school function, read to me at night, practiced football with me, made me dinner, and even made cookies a few times for school bake sales.

He worked and was a father. That was it. He had no social life. I never once saw him date until one day when I was about fourteen. He brought home a sexy blonde in tight clothing who had just graduated from college. I swear I thought she was a hooker he bought me for my birthday. Never in a million years did I think she was for him.

Despite their quarter-of-a-century age gap, Ashleigh looked at him like he hung all the stars in the sky and laughed at everything that came out of his mouth. I'm not sure she understood half the jokes—she's not the sharpest tool in the shed—but she was always smiling around him. More importantly, he was always smiling around her.

I wanted to hate her; I really did. But she made him so damn happy. The sparkle was back in his blue eyes, one I'm not sure I realized had been missing for so long until it returned.

She was always kind to me, even when my father wasn't around. Within weeks, she moved in and was doing the stereotypical "mom things" like driving me to practices and cooking dinner. She happens to be a great cook. I think he paid for culinary school for her, among a few other dead-end career endeavors she had.

A year later, they were married. She got pregnant with Jagger about five minutes after that. I remember my father sitting me down and having a conversation with me saying I was the joy of his life, and he had always hoped to expand our family. This was his last chance to do so.

I was sixteen when my little sister was born, but I immediately loved her and felt protective of her. My friends complained about their bratty little sisters, but not me. Ever. I adore my sister. I'm thankful my dad found Ashleigh for both his happiness and for giving me my amazing sister.

Ashleigh always wanted me to call her mom, but I refused to do so. It's not about the fact that she's not my real mother. It's more about how it's a little embarrassing to call a woman mom when she's younger than some of the women I've slept with. It's weird, and I refuse, but she has never stopped trying, even though I'm thirty-two.

It's Thanksgiving, and we don't have a game until Monday night. Sometimes we play on Thanksgiving but not this year. Vance came home with me, as he often does. His family runs a farm in Montana, and they travel infrequently. He tries to get them to visit, but they hate leaving their farm.

So he took the two-hour ride with me to my father's house in suburban Maryland. It's a nice upper-middle-class neighborhood, even though all the houses look the exact same. It's not the house we had when my mother was alive. My dad sold that pretty quickly after she died. He said it was too hard for him to live there without her.

Jagger mentioned a few weeks ago that her on-again, off-again boyfriend, Will, is coming by for dessert. Vance and I scared the shit out of him this summer when we felt he was jerking her around. Apparently, he's been very attentive since. I'll be the judge of that little droopy-jeans punk who's undeserving of my sister.

"That's a good one, Dad," I bellow as I calm down from his latest hilarious joke.

"Actually," he responds, "your sister came up with that one."

I turn to her. "You really did get the best of everyone, Jag." I shake my head in disbelief. "I can't believe we're less than two years away from you going to college. Where does the time go? I feel like I was rocking you to sleep just yesterday."

She used to fit right on my giant forearm. Sometimes neither Ashleigh nor my dad could get her to go to sleep. She wanted her big brother. I would rock her while I'd both sing and rap "Waterfalls" to her, the greatest song ever created.

"Any thoughts on where you want to go to college?" Vance asks her.

She tucks her blonde, curly hair behind her ear and nods nervously. "Um, yes. I was thinking I might like to go to a school in Philly."

I jerk my head up. I didn't know that. "You would?"

She gives me a small smile. "We only lived together for my first two years, and I don't remember them. We haven't lived in the same state since. I thought it would be cool to live near you. We can meet for dinners and stuff like that," she says hopefully.

I can't contain the huge grin on my face. "I would *love* that. Holy crap. This is the best news."

BJ barks from her spot on the floor next to my chair. I add, "BJ is excited to have Aunt Jagger around too."

Jagger smiles as she rubs behind BJ's ear, and BJ sighs in contentment. "Cool. Maybe we'll visit sometime soon, and I'll look at a few of the schools. I was also thinking maybe this spring you could come to one of my softball games. I think I'm getting pretty good. My coach thinks I might be able to play in college, but I'm not sure I'm good enough for that."

My father nods enthusiastically. "She's downplaying it. She's a superstar, like you were. This will be a big year for her." He smiles at Jagger. "I'll bet you anything that you get a few college offers to play ball, if that's what you want to do. The Humblecut athletic genes run strong in this one." He winks at Ashleigh. "She certainly didn't get them from her *mama*." He wiggles his eyebrows up and down. "Speaking of *yo mama…*"

I perk up immediately while Jagger moans in malcontent. "Noooooo. Don't go there on Thanksgiving. Pleeeeaaase," she begs.

I don't remember exactly how it happened, but shortly after my mother passed, my father and I began trading *yo mama* jokes as a way to cope with the pain. It was his way of making me smile and started off innocently, but it's morphed throughout the years into something much dirtier and has become a bit of a contest between my father and me. We trade jokes back and forth until one of us breaks and laughs, which is almost always me. Vance gets a kick out of it, so Dad always goes out of his way to do it when Vance is around. Jagger hates it. Ashleigh giggles through most of it, as she does for just about everything else.

My father sets his fork down on his plate and looks at me with a bit of intensity. "Yo mama is so dumb, when she was driving to Disneyland, she saw a sign that read *Disneyland Left*, so she went home."

Vance lets out a laugh, and Ashleigh giggles uncontrollably, but I remain stoic and respond, "Yo mama is so stupid, she was told her password needed eight characters, so she typed *Snow White and the Seven Dwarfs*."

I actually see my father's nostril twitch. It's hard to get him to break, but he's damn close right now. Once again, Vance and Ashleigh laugh. Even Jagger snickers at that one.

Dad eventually regains control before staring at me in the eyes and saying, "Yo mama is like a vacuum cleaner. She sucks, she blows, and she gets laid in the closet."

I spit out laughing, as does everyone except Jagger. She rolls her eyes, per usual. I love hearing my father laugh. It's loud and makes the house feel like it's shaking. I'm told I have the same laugh, but I don't think it's quite at his level. His always feels like home to me.

Ashleigh giggles at everything he says, whether it's funny or not. I'm never sure if she understands half of what he says, but she always appears amused. She pats his hand and smiles. "WTF, honey."

Jagger and I share bemused looks as I remember she told me that Ashleigh thinks WTF means, *wow, that's fantastic.*

I love my family. When I get married, I want one just like it.

NINE

KENNEDY

I hand Alyssa a case of champagne as I walk through their apartment door. "Thanks for having me." I bend down to kiss her cheek. "Happy New Year to my favorite pillow princess," I joke. I know she's the more dominant one in their relationship.

I've spent a lot of time with Alyssa and Shay in the past few weeks. Everyone else went home to their respective families, but they stayed in town and adopted me as a would-be family member.

She smiles up at me with amusement. "I'm no pillow princess. I'm a dommy mommy. If you remember, my nickname in college was *the vagilante.*" She flicks her tongue, complete with a piercing, suggestively.

I burst out laughing. "I did *not* know that, but I like the name. I wouldn't mind a man with that nickname. I might as well date a woman. Every man I've ever dated is nothing but a little bitch." I sigh. "Life would be so much easier if I were into women."

She smirks. "It sure would. And Happy New Year to you too. Thanks for bringing all the champagne."

"No biggie. I sent Booster out for it today." I let out a laugh. "He's only eighteen. It was a fucking riot watching him sweat it out at the liquor store. He's so uptight. I love forcing him to do things that make him uncomfortable. Last week I made him give me a pedicure."

She raises an unamused eyebrow. "I can't believe you have an intern. I *really* can't believe some of the shit you make him do."

I smile. "I know. It's the best. He does my laundry, irons, cleans, makes my bed in the morning, and basically runs all the errands I can possibly think of. He's also our towel boy at the off-season workouts. He does every little thing I ask of him without a single complaint. It's amazing."

"It's indentured servitude," she responds.

"Pft. It's a resume builder for him. Booster wanted the job. He loves the attention. I think he has a crush on me. It's cute. It's like having a dog without the hassles of walking him."

"Isn't his name Rooster, not Booster?" she asks.

"Yes, but I don't like Rooster. It's lame, and he's super short. Booster is more fitting. That's what I call him, and I'm the boss. Can't argue with the boss."

She rolls her eyes. "You're one of a kind. Come in. Everyone is hanging out in the living room."

We're all having dinner and drinks at Alyssa and Shay's apartment before going out to celebrate New Year's Eve at a karaoke bar. I'm so excited to let loose and have a good time.

It's a Wednesday, and I guess my dad gave the guys tomorrow off because they're primed to party. The Camels are having a great season and have locked in the two-seed for the playoffs. Their last game this upcoming weekend is meaningless for their playoff seeding, so I imagine most of the starters won't play more than a quarter or two.

Everyone from our usual gang is here except Sulley. We haven't seen her since she left for Italy in October. She'll be back at some point in January. I've missed her, but we talk on the phone all the time. She's been a good sounding board for me regarding my family issues, gently encouraging me to make amends.

Despite spending Christmas Eve with Alyssa and Shay, I begrudgingly spent Christmas morning with my family. My father hosted. Unfortunately, my mother attended, but I mostly ignored her. The tensest moment, however, didn't come from her. It came from an anonymous gift left for me under my father's tree. None of my family members seemed to have been in the know as to what it was and who it was from. At some point, my father wanted to call in the bomb squad, but when I saw a red flag sticking out of it, I knew who it was from.

I asked my father if Daylen had stopped by during the week. He said yes, and he couldn't figure out why.

I knew why.

I contemplated whether or not to open it up in front of my family, but curiosity got the better of me.

I should have waited.

I opened a huge box of what must have been a thousand of the FC2 female prophylactics. The ads came out last month, and I was hoping no one saw them. I certainly didn't tell anyone about it. Of course Daylen saw it. It probably appeared on a porn site he watches. Dirty fucker.

I thought my father was going to die of embarrassment. My brother turned a bright shade of red. I didn't bother to take in my mother's reaction. I'm not sure she can react anyway with her skin so damn tight.

All things considered, Daylen's retaliation could have been worse. I generously brought a gift for him tonight to thank him for his.

I take a few sniffs as I walk through the apartment and ask Alyssa, "Why does it smell like Fireball in here? Are you guys doing shots?"

She shakes her head. "No, you alcoholic, it's a cinnamon candle."

I let out a laugh. "Whoops. Is Champ here?" I ask hopefully. I haven't fully given up on him. We've been hanging out for well over six months now, and I've never once seen him leave with a woman. I can't figure him out. Maybe he's shy.

She turns her head and blinks several times. "You *do* know he's gay, right?"

"What?" I practically screech as I stop in my tracks.

"Champ is into men."

My mouth opens and closes several times. I'm in shock. I had no idea, but I know a certain someone who definitely did. A lightbulb goes off in my head. That's why he was so confident I couldn't seal the deal. That's why he agreed to that bet. God, I despise him, and I truly hate that he pulled one over on me. I owe him.

I enter the living room to the sounds of loud laughter. "What's so funny?" I ask.

Daylen smirks in his loud, neon, obnoxious New Year's sweater paired with jeans that look like they came from The Gap. "I'm a funny guy, and I told a funny joke. Is having a sense of humor a red flag of yours?"

I roll my eyes. "A bad one like yours certainly is. What sixteen-year-old boy joke did you tell them?"

"What's a porn star's favorite drink?" he asks.

I cross my arms. "What?"

"7UP in cider," he answers while laughing at his own joke.

I sigh. "You're an idiot. Speaking of people who could never be porn stars, I brought you a holiday gift to thank you for the one you kindly left for me…in front of my family."

"How…thoughtful," he tentatively says as he stares at my chest when I remove my jacket. "Are your tits getting bigger?"

"They're filled with rage just for you."

He nods. "I had a wet dream about you last night. A different kind of wet. I pissed myself laughing when you fell off a cliff."

I ignore his stupid joke and stare at his sweater. "The eighties called. They want their sweater back."

He gives me the finger before motioning his head toward my expensive fur jacket. "Do you know how many animals had to die to make that pretentious jacket?"

I shrug. "Probably the same amount I fucked to afford it," I quip back while smiling innocently as I hand him the box from my jacket pocket.

His eyes rake over me skeptically, but he takes it from me. "I'll hold off thanking you until I see it."

He opens it, and all the guys start laughing when it's revealed. It's an exact replica of the tiny dick I was able to get Booster to make appear authentic online. The one with Daylen's number and the Camels logo.

Daylen rolls his eyes. "You suck. You have no idea what you're talking about. Did you know my penis used to be in the Guinness Book of World Records?" He pauses for several beats before continuing, "But the librarian asked me to take it out."

The guys all spit in laughter, but I exhale a long breath. "You're such a joke."

"Want to hear a joke about my penis? Never mind, it's too long."

"Want to hear a joke about my pussy?" I immediately clap back. "Never mind, you'll *never* get it."

Vance shakes his head and mumbles, "I wish you two would fuck and get it over with."

I'm about to tackle Vance for even considering that when Palmer throws her arm around me. "Hey. I've missed you."

She's been home in Texas for the past few weeks. She only just got back into town today.

I return her embrace. "I missed you too." I take in her appearance. She's wearing something we bought during our shopping spree. A purple, figure-hugging dress. This is the first time I've seen her in any of the clothes we bought that day. "You look great."

She smiles shyly. "You don't think it's too much?"

I shake my head. "No way. I'm telling you, purple is your color. Your eyes look vibrant."

As I look more closely, I realize she also attempted a bit more makeup than is normal for her. She didn't do a great job, but I can fix this.

I grab her hand. "Come to the bathroom with me."

Ten minutes later, we emerge with my latest masterpiece on my arm. Beau's face when he sees my work is priceless. I know she's been crushing on him, but now I'm starting to wonder if he returns the sentiment. I'm not sure Palmer can handle a beast of a man like Beau Fudd, but crazier things have happened.

We sit around eating the sushi platters and other food Shay and Alyssa provided while toasting with full glasses of champagne. It's fun having a group of friends like this.

We chat a bit about the Camels' season. The guys are excited about it. We're all planning to go to their first playoff game in two weeks.

We also talk a bit about our upcoming trip to Vegas in March for the NCAA basketball tournament. It's a huge sports and party weekend in Vegas. Apparently, the Camels and the WAGs go every year and have a blast.

Layla invited our group to join in on the fun, and I can't wait. It's something I've always wanted to do, but it's expensive and I've never been able to do so.

Layla has planned everything from the swanky suites to the private jet taking us all out there. All I have to do is show up in my fabulous clothing. That's something I can handle.

Daylen's obnoxious meter is off the charts tonight. The more he drinks, the more unbearable and cruder he gets. Every little thing he says bothers me. I dislike most people, but none as much as him.

DAYLEN

"Lesbian first dates are a minimum of six hours. I've had several as long as twelve."

I look at Alyssa in disbelief in our booth at the karaoke bar as we get ready to celebrate the New Year. "What in the world could you possibly have to talk about for that long?"

"Don't mind him," Kennedy interrupts. "He doesn't have enough words in his vocabulary to talk to anyone for six minutes, let alone six hours."

Why? Why do I spend time with this woman? There is nothing redeeming about her except her tits, which happen to look spectacular this evening. She's in some sort of plunging, gold, sparkly shirt that looks like it was wrapped around her from behind. It's barely holding those boulders. If I pull the strings in the front, her tits will pop out. I've contemplated doing so multiple times since she took off that over-the-top fur coat. This woman thinks she's royalty.

Why, God? Why would you put the best tits in the world on the worst woman? It's the greatest travesty I've ever heard of... besides war, violence, famine, and homelessness.

Speaking of Kennedy, she's knocking them back tonight in a way I've never seen from her. She's getting sloppy, and it's not even midnight yet. She's been talking to some preppy douchebag all night. At least she's not fawning all over Champ anymore. Maybe she finally figured out he's not into women. Watching her fail at trying to win him over all those months was extremely satisfying.

For some unknown reason, she's been particularly salty to me tonight. Maybe it's the booze. It figures she'd be a nasty drunk. She's mean when sober, why not drunk too?

"Next up," the MC announces, "we have Richard Dickgrabber." He looks around. "Richard, are you still here?"

Vance elbows me. "I can't believe you still use that name."

Richard Dickgrabber is the real name of one of my father's

childhood friends. And he goes by Dick. Dick Dickgrabber. What were his parents thinking?

I've been using it as my fake name on everything my whole life, from restaurant reservations to hotel reservations, and even my fake ID before I was of age.

I chuckle. "Time for good old Dick to sing. I bet you know what song I chose."

He shakes his head at me in exasperation. "God help us all."

I stand and walk to the stage, grabbing the microphone. Speaking into it, I wink at Vance and say, "This one is for the sexiest quarterback in the world."

I begin to sing "Waterfalls" by TLC, the greatest song in existence. Vance knows I play it on repeat in my car. I've been working with BJ on the lyrics. I think she's starting to get the melody.

As soon as I get to the rap verse, I proudly belt out all the lyrics without even having to look at the screen. For some reason, the girls at our table start laughing hysterically. Like falling on the floor type of laughter. I don't know why.

I finish to a loud sea of applause from the crowd. I take a little bow. Man, I crushed it. My accompanying dance moves were on the mark tonight.

There's a cute blonde in the corner making googly eyes at me. I'm going to play it cool a little longer, but then I'll make my way over to her.

I walk back to our table, feeling like a million bucks. That song is my happy place. I have so many great memories of it.

I'm surprised to see the girls are all still laughing. I clearly missed the joke. "What's so funny?" I ask.

Unable to speak because she's cackling so damn loud and hard, Kennedy hands me her phone. I notice that it's open to her notes app. Her damn catalogue of red flags. "Why are you showing this to me? I already know this obnoxious list exists."

She sputters, "Look at item four."

I scroll down to the fourth of what must be two hundred. Sure enough, it reads, *men who know every word to the rap verse of "Waterfalls" by TLC.*

"What?" I ask, feeling slightly offended and very surprised. "Why is this a red flag?"

"It's...girlie and nerdy," she croons in her whiny, annoying voice.

I narrow my eyes at her. "Do you even know what the song is about? It's about making good decisions in life. About staying away from the pitfalls. It's deep shit."

Her laughter only grows louder. "Don't throw a mantrum, manchild."

I ball my fists. I usually only choke women with their consent, but this bitch is really asking for it.

She goes on and on about what a tool I am for knowing all the words. I'm feeling a level of anger I've never before experienced. I'm such a happy guy, and this woman makes me so damn unhappy.

I turn and head back up onto the stage. After whispering into the MC's ear and handing him money to move me to the front of the line, he hands me the microphone again, and a new song begins to play. I calmly begin to sing the lyrics.

I keep going until I get to the chorus, at which point I jump off the stage and walk over to the table. I look directly at Kennedy and yell-sing, "So let me spell it out, A-B-C-D-E, F-U and your mom and your sister and your job."

TEN

KENNEDY

I wake in the familiar, silky confines of my bed on New Year's Day, feeling like a skunk died in my mouth and an eighteen-wheeler ran over my head. Ugh.

With every ounce of energy I have, I turn my head to see if the man I came home with is still here. I hope not. I'm not in the mood for morning-after fake pleasantries. Just fuck me hard, knock me around a little bit, and then leave me alone.

I have zero recollection of who it was, but I remember a man carrying me and placing me on my bed last night, so it must have happened.

The other side of the bed doesn't look like anyone even sat on it, let alone slept in it. Hmm. That's odd. Did I not get laid? Damnit. I wanted to ring in the New Year with a bang.

Flashes of last night begin to hit me. I remember Daylen pushing some guy away from me and then carrying me out of the karaoke bar. No way. I must be misremembering.

I pull back the blankets and take in my wardrobe. I'm in my top from last night with just my panties on the bottom. My jeans are nowhere to be found. Oh god, I hope I didn't throw them out the Uber window. I did that a few times in New York.

It's rare that I have sex with a top on. My tits are usually the first thing men want to see on my body.

With Herculean effort, I turn my head back around and look at my night table. There are two glasses of water and a bottle of Advil sitting on top. My eyes move down to the floor, and I notice a trash can full of puke next to me. This is too thoughtful for a man. One of the girls must have taken care of me. A waft of the puke stench invades my nostrils. Oh cheez, it stinks. I need to dispose of that.

I slowly and gingerly make my way to my bathroom and pour out the contents of the trash can before rinsing it out until the odor is gone. I then strip and get into the shower, letting the hot water pour all over my achy body. Why did I drink so much? We started too early, that's why. Such a rookie New Year's Eve mistake. Very unlike me. Daylen was pissing me off so much, I needed to do something to numb the pain and drown out his annoyingly loud laugh. It's like he has no sense of normal social boundaries.

After showering and a good ten minutes of brushing every square inch of my teeth with half a tube of toothpaste, I start to feel slightly human again. A loud rumbling in my belly alerts me to the fact that I need something in it to soak up the booze.

I slip into my short, red silk robe and walk out of my bedroom toward my kitchen, stopping short when I see a giant male figure sleeping on my couch.

I have no clue who it could be. Maybe I had sex with this guy, and then he passed out on the couch on his way out? Seems plausible given my state.

As I approach the large figure, I notice it's Daylen sleeping on his back. What in the fuck is he doing here? Oh god, I hope I didn't fuck him. No, I would never, and neither would he. He hates me as much as I hate him. There must be some other explanation.

I notice his ugly sweater and cheap, out-of-style jeans on the floor. If that motherfucker is naked on my sofa, I will burn it with him strapped to it.

Walking closer to him, I inwardly laugh as I take in my small throw blanket over him. It covers exactly two inches of his enormous body. He's in an *I Heart the Jonas Brothers* T-shirt and neon pink boxer briefs with his hand shoved down the front holding onto his dick. Why do guys do that in their sleep? Are they jerking off or trying to protect it? I've always wondered.

I think I prefer him sleeping. I can inwardly admit he's a very attractive man, but then he opens his mouth and all the attractiveness vanishes. One of my few memories from last night was him singing a medley of *fuck you* songs to me. It started with "abcdefu" by Gayle and ended with "Fuck You" by Lily Allen.

I wonder what set him into the bout of insanity. Even on our worst day, I've never seen him that pissed off at me. He was like a raging bull, and all the animosity was directed at innocent me.

I may have waved the red flag in front of the bull a bit, but he was asking for it.

I don't want to touch him. He's probably disease riddled. Grabbing a pillow, I gently hit his chest. The giant doesn't budge.

I do it again a little harder. Nothing.

I then smack him as hard as I can. Again, nothing. Maybe he's dead.

This time, I wind up and whack him right in the face. He smiles and moans, "Do it again, baby. That makes me so hard."

Now he's fully stroking himself. Fucking freak.

I reach over and grab his nipple through his shirt before twisting it hard.

"Umm, hmm. Just like that, baby."

Is this guy for real? Is he fucking with me right now?

I lean over and wave my hand in front of his face to see if he flinches, but before I know what's happening, he grabs me around the waist, throws me onto the sofa, turns us so I'm under him, and then pushes his large, hard erection between my legs.

Did I mention that I'm not wearing panties? And his dick is now well above his boxer briefs. *Several* inches.

I let out a shriek, which is immediately muffled by his lips taking mine. He's heavy. I've never had a man this big on top of me. I'm rendered completely immobile except for my one arm hanging off the sofa.

I'd like to say I stop him right away, but I haven't gotten laid in two whole weeks, so I let it go on for a solid ten seconds before I reach for the remote control, lift it high in the air, and then bring it down hard, shoving it right into his ass.

He lets out a loud yelp before his eyes pop open, and he breaks the kiss. When he sees me, he practically levitates off me in a way I would never have thought a man his size capable of. He stumbles backward until he trips ten feet away from me, landing on my floor with a loud thud that likely wakes everyone in the building.

I let out a laugh. "Ha. Holy shit, that reaction was amazing."

He reaches around and rubs his ass. "What was that?"

"My remote control. You were groping me without invitation. Don't mess with a bull if you can't handle the horns…up your ass." I giggle as I sit up while making sure my lady bits are all covered by my small robe.

I nod my head toward him. "You want to put the stallion back in the corral, killer? It's grossing me out."

He looks down at his dick, which is actually kind of impressive, sticking way up and over his boxer briefs. His eyes widen while he quickly tucks it back into the confines of his ridiculous boxer briefs that I'm now noticing also have an image of a hot dog covering the crotch.

He runs his fingers through his messy hair. "What the fuck happened?"

"Umm, why don't you tell me? Why are you here? In my home." I look down at his briefs. "And why are you still hard?"

"Why are you looking?" he snaps back before exhaling a long breath. "I'm here because you were a mess, and your friends weren't much better. You puked more than I weigh. I was afraid you'd choke to death or wet the bed, so I stuck around and kept checking on you throughout the night. You're welcome, wench."

"I used to get in trouble for wetting the bed as a child. Now I get called a good girl."

He barks out a laugh. "You're truly one of a kind."

I cross my arms. "Did you cockblock me? I remember dancing with a hottie, and we were talking about getting out of there. Why isn't he here instead of you?"

He narrows his eyes at me. "Oh, you mean *Brock*?" He says his name like it tastes bitter on his tongue. "The guy who turned you and kissed you while his friends dropped something into your drink? He's likely in the hospital with a broken nose, along with his two buddies. I'll probably get sued, but please allow me to apologize for cockblocking you from a certain gang rape," he says with a heavy dose of sarcasm.

My face immediately falls, and my hand covers my mouth. "What?" I breathe. "They put something in my drink?" I'm usually super conscious about that kind of stuff, but I was pretty trashed, so it's plausible.

He nods. "I was coming out of the bathroom, getting ready to leave with a blonde hottie of my own, when I happened to see it all go down. I just started swinging at them. Mayhem ensued. More than half our group had already left. Your remaining friends were too messed up to take care of you, so I carried your heavy ass home. I couldn't even get a cab or Uber because you were vomiting more fluids than I've ever seen emitted from a human being."

My entire body begins shaking as tears form in my eyes just thinking about what almost happened to me. He stands and walks over before plopping next to me and pulling me close with one arm. "Don't cry. I hate when women cry." He covers my mouth. "Before you say it, no, women don't cry after having sex with me. I know you were thinking that."

I let out a small giggle through my tears, appreciating his attempt to make me laugh in light of the heaviness of what he told me. "I'll give you a day off. You earned it," I mumble into his hand.

He nods as he removes said hand and looks at me. "I'm glad I was there. I might hate you," he winks, "but no woman deserves that." He chews his lower lip nervously. "Do you maybe want me to call someone before I head out? Someone you can talk to about what almost happened to you. I'm sure it's a lot to process."

I shake my head. "No, I'll be okay. Thanks though." I fidget with my robe, feeling bad about how I treated him last night and this morning. "Can I make you breakfast? It's the least I can do after what you did for me."

He twists his lips. "Hmm, I do love breakfast. Can we make it quick? I should get home to feed my dog."

I immediately smile. "You have a dog?"

He nods as he stands and begins to dress. "Yep. BJ. The light of my life."

I raise an eyebrow. "BJ? Are you for real?"

He smirks. "It stands for Blackjackie. Get your head out of the gutter, Jeffries."

"What kind of dog is she?" I ask.

"A Doberman. I adore her. I sort of bought my house in the 'burbs so she'd have more room to run around. My best girl requires a lot of exercise."

"I love dogs, but my father's ex-wife is allergic to them, so we never had one."

He pinches his eyebrows together. "Ex-wife? Was he married to someone else besides your mom? How did I not know that?"

I shake my head. "No, that's how I refer to my biological mother. I don't speak to her at all, and I certainly don't refer to her as my mother. It's a long story I'm not interested in sharing. I prefer to call her my father's ex-wife or by her first name." I let out a breath as I stand. "Let me get breakfast started. Are eggs okay? It's all I have and the only thing I'm capable of cooking. I make a mean cup of coffee though, if you're interested."

He nods. "Sounds good." He points toward my bathroom. "I'm going to pop the cork while you're cooking if you don't mind."

I pinch the bridge of my nose. Not now, Kennedy. Don't give him shit for his crudeness in announcing his bathroom visit. Just smile and walk away.

He stares at me, waiting for a comment, but none comes. Not today. Not after what he did for me.

Ten minutes later, he's laughing in my kitchen. "You weren't joking. The entire contents of your kitchen are eggs, milk, coffee, and vodka. And you don't even have a set of pots and pans. Only one frying pan."

I nod as I stand at the stove. "Yes, for the eggs. Like I said, it's the only thing I make. Why would I need all that other stuff if I don't use it? Do *you* cook?"

He nods. "I do, for me and BJ. She prefers human food. I have a guy, Chef Benny, who does my shopping and some meal prep for me. He stays with BJ when I travel. But I do the actual cooking myself. It's soothing. I kind of like taking care of my dog."

I start to judge the fact that he has someone like Chef Benny, but then I remember that I have an intern. Booster would probably meal prep and cook for me if I asked.

I turn to him and ask, "How do you take your coffee?"

He shrugs and deadpans, "Usually in a cup."

Stay quiet, Kennedy. He did something incredibly kind for you. It's no small feat, but I do manage to control my snark.

I plate the eggs and pour the coffee before we sit at the small kitchen table. He looks ridiculous in my tiny kitchen at my tiny table made for two. He must need extra-big doorways and high ceilings in his house. I'm pretty sure he's judging the kitchen right now.

"I know this kitchen sucks," I say, "but this apartment has great closet space, and I value that over a kitchen. I can't afford a place with both."

"Right, for all your designer clothes," he says as he rolls his eyes. He then takes an obscenely large bite of his eggs and swallows before looking at me. "Can I ask you a question without getting a bitchy response? It's a real question."

"You can," I respond.

"Why do you hate 'Waterfalls'? It's such a feel-good song."

I smile. "I don't hate the song, per se, I just think it's weird when a man knows every word to the rap verse. I happened to have told the girls that a man knowing the words is on my red flag list. That's why we were laughing. We weren't laughing at you, just the coincidental situation. What are the chances of you singing that exact song I told them about?"

"Hmm," he moans as he looks at me skeptically. "Why is it weird to know the words to a once-very-popular song?"

I shrug. "I don't know. I haven't put that much thought into it. Why do you like the song so much?" I challenge.

A small smile finds his face. "My mom died when I was a little kid. I was only six. It's not like I have a million memories of her, but one I do have is of her and my dad singing that song together, smiling and laughing. I remember it as if it were yesterday. They had a whole dancing bit to it. After she passed, my dad told me what the song is about. Not chasing waterfalls is a euphemism for not succumbing to temptations like drugs and other dangerous or unhealthy activities. To make smart decisions in life." He lifts his eyes and then brings them back to me, conveying uncharacteristic softness and sadness. "It's not like my mom had time to teach me many lessons, so I take that one to heart. And my parents loved to smile and laugh throughout life. Even after she passed, my dad always made me laugh. Still does. I don't know," he says introspectively, "that song just means happiness to me. Choosing to make good decisions and be happy in life. That's how I like to live. It's how I honor her."

I nod in understanding. "Sorry if I offended you. I didn't mean to."

"No biggie." He stands. "I'm heading out. Thanks for breakfast." He places his dish in the sink before looking at me with an uncharacteristically sheepish look on his face. "I'm sorry if the TV interview incident messed up your endorsements." He walks toward me and holds out his pinkie for me to take. "How about we agree to keep the fighting clean moving forward?"

I take his pinkie in mine and give it the proverbial handshake. "Agreed. And sorry about the dick pic." I give him a small smile. "At least I now know firsthand that it isn't true."

He lets out an overly loud laugh. I think my kitchen light fixture shakes from it.

Still holding his pinkie, I twist it a bit, and he grimaces. "Ow, what the fuck?"

"That's for lying about Champ being straight."

He chuckles. "I didn't lie. I didn't say he *wasn't* gay. You assumed. Watching you hit on him for months was too damn funny though. You were so frustrated. I bet you've never been rejected like that in your life."

I smile. "Ooh, did you just admit that I'm hot?"

"When you don't talk, yes. Unfortunately, you talk."

"Back at you, big guy."

I walk him to the door, looking up at him as I open it. Grabbing his bulging bicep gently, I say, "Thanks for what you did for me, Daylen. Sincerely. I don't know that I can ever repay you for stepping in the way you did and then taking care of me."

The corner of his mouth raises slightly. "Your tit popped out of your robe earlier. That was payment enough."

I punch his arm and mumble, "Asshole."

He chuckles. "Don't go soft on me, Sea Witch. I said to keep the fighting clean moving forward, not that I wanted to stop fighting with you."

I bite back my smile. "Don't worry. I'll still bring it."

He nods. "So will I."

ELEVEN

DAYLEN

"Sex isn't math, D," Beau calmly says to me as he squats an ungodly amount of weight in our team gym without barely breaking a sweat. I've never seen a physically stronger human being in my life, and I could probably lift a car. In fact, one blocked me in a few years ago, and I did, in fact, lift it out of my way.

I drop my feet down to the floor from the pull-up bar and cross my sweaty, workout-fatigued arms while glaring at him intensely, fighting the slowly rising corners of my mouth. "Sex *is* math, Beau. Add a bed, subtract the clothes, divide her legs, and then pray you don't multiply."

The guys all break out into laughter, even Beau.

Champ, who's next to me, mumbles, "At least I don't have to worry about multiplication when I have sex."

I smile widely. Champ used to be very tight-lipped about his sexuality, but he's been more open within our small group over the past few weeks. It makes me so happy that he's comfortable with us. He's only been with the team for a year, but I feel like I've known him so much longer. He's quickly become a good friend.

I throw my arm around him. "Holy crap, you're right. Maybe I should switch things up. You available tonight?" I wiggle my eyebrows suggestively. "I'm looking not to multiply."

He chuckles. "You're not my type."

I gasp. "What? Why not? I'm a hottie." I turn my body so I can check out my own ass and show it to him at the same time. "Does my milkshake not bring all the boys to the yard?"

He shrugs. "I'm sorry, D, but I don't like blonds."

I touch my overgrown hair, which is in desperate need of a haircut. "What if I dye my hair? I love it, but I'd do it for you as a grand romantic gesture."

He rolls his eyes. "I know you prefer a bubbly partner, clearly not *my* style. So I'm not your type either...and I have a dick. Also not your type. You're a vagina man, through and through."

"Hmm. I suppose that's true." I rub his bleached-blond mohawk. "If it makes you feel better, know I prefer blondes, so if I liked men, you'd be *my* type."

"You sure about that?" he asks with a thick tone of suggestiveness.

"What does that mean?" I probe.

"It means I think you like a certain brunette."

"Who?" I genuinely have no clue who he's referring to. I went home with another sexy blonde just the other night.

He smiles as he condescendingly pats my chest. "There's a fine line between love and hate, D. And hate sex..." he bites his lips and shivers, "hmm, there's nothing better."

Is he referring to Kennedy? It's been about ten weeks since New Year's Eve. For the first two, she was uncomfortably civil to me. It was bizarrely off-putting, so I decided to poke the bear back to life. I kept saying things I knew would bother her until one comment finally tipped her over the edge. I told her one set of women's lips is for arguing while the other set is for apologizing. As soon as I said it, she fell right back into her natural state of raging bitch where we've happily remained for the past two months.

I even lost another bet to her, but the stakes were clean and fun, as we pinkie swore they would be. She now gets to pick my walk-in outfit for our first game of the season later this year.

Gameday walk-in outfits have become sort of a thing over the past few years. We get photographed walking into the stadium and then judged by social media for what we wear. I love to wear wacky clothes, so I don't care what she chooses. Maybe a fun pimp outfit, complete with a fur coat, floppy hat, and a pimp stick. Or, knowing Kennedy, she'll probably just want me in something fashionable since I never wear nice, designer clothing, and it drives her nuts. Whatever she chooses, it will be funny, I have no doubt.

I scoff at Champ's comment. "I will *never* have sex with—"

"Who won't you have sex with?" Coach asks as he walks into the gym.

It's probably not a good idea to mention sex with his daughter, even though I'm discussing *not* having sex with her.

"Vance," I answer. "I'll never have sex with him."

Vance gives me the finger from the free weight area. "What's wrong with me?"

"You're too broody for me. I like them bubbly."

"You like them stupid," Vance mumbles.

"Oh, well then, maybe I *am* interested in you."

Once again, I'm gifted with his middle finger, and I can't help but chuckle.

Coach shakes his head. "I feel like other teams discuss football in their weight rooms, but every damn time I walk in here, you're talking about anything *but* football."

I shake my head. "We were discussing math, but before that, we were chatting about Vegas. You should come this year, Coach."

"Pass. Vegas is for the young. You all have fun without me. Not too much though. Stay out of trouble," he commands in a warning tone.

"Okay, *Dad*. Any other advice?"

"Print out your boarding pass the night before so you don't forget it in the morning."

I let out a laugh. "We're flying private, but even if we weren't, no one prints boarding passes anymore. Save the environment and all that jazz. You can download your boarding pass to your phone without killing planet Earth."

"Hmm," he growls. "I don't trust that virtual wallet thingy on my phone. My generation still prints boarding passes because we all suffered error messages at two in the morning when we lost term papers and had to start them over from scratch five hours before they were due."

I let out a laugh. I love Coach's Gen-Xisms.

He glares at me. "I'm being dead serious."

A few hours later, I'm out back throwing BJ her favorite ball. I hate the thought of leaving her for four days so I'm giving her as much attention tonight as I can.

My doorbell rings. It must be Chef Benny. He obviously has the code, but he had texted a few hours ago that he was going shopping for items needed for my house. His hands must be full, and he's in need of help.

I walk toward the door and open it without looking to confirm who it is. It's an Amazon delivery woman. A cute one.

Before I have the chance to react, BJ leaps past me and knocks her to the ground, growling on top of her. Ohmigod, she's about to bite the woman.

I quickly shout, "Release," at BJ, at which point she lifts her mouth from the near bite of this woman's neck. BJ doesn't, however, otherwise move. The poor woman is whimpering.

I then command, "Bed," and BJ retreats into the house. She should be heading to her downstairs bed in my living room right now.

I crouch down. "I'm so sorry, sweetheart. I thought you were someone else. Are you okay?"

She blinks her pretty blue eyes a few times. Her cherry red lips are spread, but no words come out of them. I think she's in shock.

In the sweetest voice, she eventually answers, "I...I...I think so."

I offer her my hand, and she takes it with her small, soft one, offering me a sweet smile when her eyes meet mine and then move up and down my body. "Would you like to come inside, beautiful?" I ask.

She nods as if on autopilot with her eyes transfixed on me. "I would."

KENNEDY

"Yesterday I learned the average woman sleeps with eight men in her lifetime," I announce. "Yesterday I also learned that I'm a huge whore."

Sulley, Palmer, Shay, and Alyssa all laugh hysterically in the back of the car while Booster moans in annoyance from behind the wheel. "Queen Jeffries," the name I force him to call me, "just a reminder that your brother is my best friend, and I don't love hearing that stuff about you."

"Booster," I snap from the front passenger seat, "the help is supposed to be invisible. Stop listening if you don't like what I'm saying. Just drive the car and look pretty."

He nods nervously as he grips the steering wheel tightly. "Sorry, Queen."

"Booster, why are we going this way?" I ask with annoyance. "We're going to hit traffic."

"With all due respect, Queen, it's five in the morning. I don't think there will be traffic on the way to the airport at this hour. I woke up at this time yesterday to study the traffic patterns and confirmed this is the best route at this precise time of day."

We're on our way to the airport to fly out to Las Vegas for the long weekend. We're getting the full red-carpet treatment from the private plane to the fancy suites and the VIP experience at all the big-name clubs. I can't wait.

"Valid point," I admit. "Men who take time to consider traffic patterns ahead of time are a huge green flag for me, Booster. Congratulations."

He smiles. "That's a relief, Queen," he says without a single amount of edge to his tone.

Sulley claps her hands in excitement. "Ooh, give us another red flag, *Queen*."

I roll my eyes. She's *obsessed* with the red flags. It's become a whole team thing now. It's probably our number one locker room conversation at this point and a mainstay on our team text chain. The good news is that I've learned a few new red flags I didn't know I had.

I pull out my phone and scroll through my catalog. "Hmm. Men who use the phrase *teehee*." I twist my lips in disgust. "So lame."

Sulley giggles. "I get that. It's girlie."

"Oh," I offer, "men who wear socks with the equally appalling sandals. It's two red flags in one."

Palmer, whose red flags almost always revolve around food, says, "I recently discovered I don't like men who are picky eaters. Be a man and eat the damn food as the chef prepares it. Don't be a Karen or a Chad about every little thing, ordering things on the side and demanding variations." She says it with a sparkle in her eyes. She knows how much her red flags about her food amuse us.

Sulley shakes her head. "Always with the food, Palmer. There's a hidden kink in there, I know it."

Alyssa interrupts, "Lesbians also have food red flags, but they're different from straight people's food red flags. Women who don't like sushi are a huge red flag for us." She wiggles her eyebrows up and down, and we all laugh.

Twenty minutes later, we walk into the airport, and I notice a luggage store in the terminal. I turn to the girls. "Why is there always a shop selling luggage at the airport? Who's going on vacation, carrying armfuls of clothing, saying, *I'll pack when we get to the airport*?"

Sulley shrugs. "That's a good point. Maybe it's for people who break their luggage."

I shake my head. "No way. Are there really enough people who break their luggage to necessitate an entire store dedicated to it at the airport?"

They all laugh like I'm the funniest person on the planet. I'm not sure I've ever had teammates who are as amused by my often-off-putting sense of humor as this group. We've known each other for less than a year, but they're already the best friends I've ever had. They accept me for me, and I've truly never had friends who have done that before. I don't think I realized how much I needed it until I had it.

Sulley leans over to my ear. "Don't forget that your brother's birthday is next week. You're going to get him those shoes he wants, right?"

Fucking expensive shoes. "Maybe something a little less extravagant is in order."

She crosses her arms in obvious disapproval. Always pushing. She's a pain in my ass.

I look back and yell, "Hurry up, Booster," taking my frustrations out on my intern as he struggles to carry all our luggage through the airport.

He momentarily drops the bags to adjust the crotch of his

tight gray sweatpants. "I'm doing my best, Queen. It's umm…a little hot in here."

Sulley gives me a bemused expression as she whispers, "I can't believe you make him wear those sweatpants that are purposely a size too small."

I shrug. "I told you before, it's payback for decades of men forcing women in their employment to wear small, uncomfortable clothing."

I'm *always* forcing him to wear clothing that is too small for him. Shorts, pants, T-shirts, sweatshirts. All of them. It wildly amuses me to see him struggle. Do men think women enjoy wearing short skirts, tight midriff-bearing shirts, and high heels to serve food and alcohol for an eight-hour shift? Hell no. It's time for men to suffer too.

She whispers back, "He's a nice guy, he works for you for free, and he actually works hard at it. Give him a break now and then."

I roll my eyes. "Oh, please. He loves the attention. When has a woman as hot as me ever given him the time of day?"

She smiles as she shakes her head in exasperation.

"If he were so miserable, he would quit," I add.

She raises her eyebrows like she's scolding me, and now I feel bad. Crap, I'll do something nice for the little shit.

We get to the plane and wait at the bottom of the steps while Booster loads everything for us. God, I love having him around. When he's finished, I turn to him. "Enjoy your weekend off… after you pick up my dry cleaning."

He nods. "Yes, Queen. It's already on our shared calendar. I'm on top of it."

I hand him a credit card. "Oh, and can you please buy my brother those Alexander McQueen sneakers he's been wanting for his birthday next week? The ones my parents refuse to buy him because of the cost."

I hear a squeal of excitement from Sulley while Booster grins widely. "Oh wow," he exclaims. "He's going to freak out. He's been dying for those and was so bummed when your parents told him no. He and I were salivating over them in a store window just the other day."

I feel an elbow from Sulley before she clears her throat. I look at her, and she nods. She's like a damn angel on my shoulder, always pushing me to make the "right" decision. I've traditionally preferred to listen to the devil on the other shoulder, but Sulley's voice has become louder over the past year. I'm dangerously close to becoming a nice person.

Exhaling a long breath, I point at the card. "Get a pair for yourself too. Consider it your bonus for doing such a great job for me over the past few months."

His face lights up like it's the greatest news he's ever received. "Are you for realz right now?"

"As *realz* as tits on a bull," I respond.

He looks at me in confusion, not remotely understanding my joke. I shove him. "Just go get the sneakers for both of you. Enjoy them. Don't do something stupid like walking in mud with them on the first day."

He bounces up and down like a little girl. "Thank you, Queen. Have a great trip. I'll be right here waiting to pick you up on Sunday with the Chinese takeout you requested."

I pat him on the head. "Good boy. Don't forget the chow mein."

He nods, and then we finally ascend the steps onto the plane. Sulley throws her arm around me. "Didn't that feel good?"

I scowl at her, knowing how much that just cost me. "You now have to buy me drinks tonight. Actually, for the whole weekend," I mumble.

She giggles. "Deal. Totally worth it to see how excited he was."

"Hmm, tell that to my declining credit."

We walk onto the plane and two women in pilots' uniforms greet us. "Welcome," the younger one says. "I'm Alana." She points to the middle-aged woman next to her. "Jean and I will be your pilots today. The skies are blue and clear. It should be an easy ride. Sit back and enjoy."

"Ooh," I respond, "women pilots. It's not a cockpit on this airplane. It's a clitpit."

The older woman spits her water, but my girls all laugh. They're such a good audience for me.

As we walk further into the plane, I see Daylen placing his bag into the overhead bin. His wrinkled T-shirt raises slightly, revealing his toned abs. He's so solid, and he's got one of those paths of dirty blond hair from his belly button that disappears into his jeans. It's kind of hot.

I shake my head in disbelief of where my mind went. Where did that come from?

I then notice a rose tattoo on the side of his abdomen with the name Rose written under it. Ugh, men with tattoos of women's names on their bodies. That's certainly a mainstay on my red flag list. I've honestly never met a man who encompasses more of my red flags than Daylen Humblecut.

I swear I did my best to be nicer to him after the New Year's Eve incident. I was truly appreciative of what he did and bit my tongue at his ridiculousness for weeks. But it's like he hated me being nice to him, and he went out of his way to be extra douchey to me. By the end of January, we were back to our verbal sparring where we belong, as if New Year's Eve never happened.

I look at him. "Speaking of men who probably can't find a clit, good morning, Daylen," I say in an over-the-top fake cheery voice.

He narrows his eyes at me. "You're so damn negative. Can't you ever just walk into a room and say something nice to me?"

I cross my arms. "I'm not here to build you up, Hannibal Lecter. If you're broken, you're a project, and I'm not Home Depot."

He exhales a long breath. "Who brought her?"

"I did," Layla happily sings as she throws her arms around

me. "And I'm so happy she's here. We're going to have the best time," she squeals as she kisses my cheek.

I look around and take in my surroundings. Holy shit, private planes are like floating houses. "This is really nice, Layla. Thank you," I express to her sincerely.

She smiles. "My absolute pleasure. Get ready for the most memorable weekend of your life, girlfriend."

I rub my hands together with excitement. "I'm ready."

After takeoff, everyone crowds around the big table and begins drinking. I hang back for a moment. It's not even eight in the morning, and it's going to be a long day. I need to pace myself so I don't have a repeat performance of New Year's Eve. That night scared the shit out of me. I've barely had more than an occasional glass of wine since.

I know I should probably talk to someone about that night, but I'm kind of embarrassed by my naivety and equally embarrassed that Daylen was the one who saved me.

I've had more than a handful of nightmares of what could have happened if Daylen hadn't noticed what was being done to my drink. Despite our return to verbal jabs, I've softened on him. How could I not after what he did? He may be an annoying Neanderthal without an ounce of sexual appeal, but he's a good guy. Okay, maybe he's a little more appealing than he used to be, but obviously I'll never go there.

I notice one of the flight attendants flirting with him as she offers him a drink. He's got her laughing, along with everyone else in earshot. I remember what he said about choosing happiness every day. He's definitely one cheery motherfucker who gets off on making everyone around him laugh and smile. While I find it irritating, I suppose there are worse things a man could be.

And then I consider my earlier thoughts of having a group of friends who laugh at my over-the-top jokes. I suppose I enjoy making people laugh too. That might be the only thing we have in common.

Sulley walks off to chat with an older couple hitching a ride with us. I think she said they're Reagan's mother and stepfather. I should probably also say hello at some point.

I step into her spot around the big table. Beau is telling everyone his beliefs on how testosterone helps build muscle and how increasing cholesterol intake plays an important role in that. Sometimes I don't understand half of what comes out of Beau's mouth. He's freakishly smart.

He looks at the guys. "I can't believe you all don't drink Boner Shakes."

What? Now he has my attention.

He continues. "Trust me. It helps build muscle. The added benefit is it will be the best and biggest boner of your life. Guaranteed."

I smile. "We know from those *anonymous* online photos that Daylen could use help in that department."

Daylen narrows his eyes at me, and I can't help but laugh. Okay, so it's just the opposite. I didn't see much of his dick, but I saw enough to know it's not small, not small at all. I may have had a dream or two about the handful of seconds it was rubbing through me. I don't think he realizes it happened, but it did. It figures the only remotely attractive thing about the man would be something that's covered most of the time.

Beau continues, "All you need is four eggs, a scoop of vanilla protein powder, and water. You shake it up in the evening and then drink it. Overnight, the uptick in cholesterol will trigger an increase in testosterone production. You'll feel like the Incredible Hulk during your morning workout, lifting weights you never imagined possible. You'll have the added effect of the boner. But it's the egg, powder, and water that make the magic. That is what you call a Boner Shake."

"Huh?" Sulley interrupts as she rejoins the circle. "What in the world did I miss?"

Layla, who was apparently taking notes, gives Sulley a summary of the Boner Shake recipe. Like me, she's much more focused on the larger erection than on the muscle-building effects of it.

Daylen then makes a series of crude jokes. I swear, every time I think something nice about him, it's like he knows and says something stupidly annoying.

TWELVE

KENNEDY

When we land, a giant party bus is waiting for our big crew, and we're driven to our hotel. As we pull into the fountain-lined driveway, Sulley, Palmer, and I look at the stunning structure. It's so glamorous.

We walk into what must be the biggest hotel lobby I've ever been in. It's opulence on the most extreme levels, complete with more fountains, marble, dancers, and grand, elegant chandeliers.

There's a man in a suit waiting for us, so we don't have to wait in the regular check-in line. Layla has planned this to a tee. We all get our room keycards, and she's got a spreadsheet of who is in which suite.

We head up the elevators and get our first look at our lavish suite. It's incredible. I've never had a room like this. It's like being in a movie.

Our suite has two large bedrooms with an enormous living room, kitchen, and bar between them. The kitchen is stocked with food, and the bar is overflowing with alcohol. Staying anything close to sober this weekend won't be easy.

The wraparound balcony overlooks the entire Vegas strip.

We're all taking it in with both wide-eyed disbelief and anticipation. You've never seen five more excited women in your life.

Everything is high-end, from the Brazilian rosewood flooring to the high-thread-count sheets. Each bedroom has a large en suite bathroom, complete with an oversized rain shower and jacuzzi tub suitable for ten people.

We decide to give Shay and Alyssa one bedroom while Sulley, Palmer, and I share the other. Shay and Alyssa are most deserving of some privacy from the rest of us. I joke to Palmer and Sulley that if my bra is hanging on the doorknob of our bedroom, they shouldn't come inside.

Sulley makes a look of disgust and tells Palmer they'll share one of the beds while I'll get the other for myself.

We wash up and then spend the next few hours at one of the hotel's massive sports bars. I allow myself one drink but am still a little trigger-shy and don't accept drinks from the several strange men who offer them to me.

Every single basketball game is being played on the hundreds of televisions spread all over the walls of the bar. It's like basketball porn, and we're eating up every second of it.

After a few morning games, we decide to watch the late afternoon games from the rooftop pools at a different hotel. Apparently, the pools are set up like stadium seating, and there's a huge screen with all the games playing. Layla arranged it so that one of the pools is roped off for our party. It's fun to be a rockstar, even if only for one weekend.

I'm in my nicest gold bikini. Admittedly, I look sexy as sin. The top barely covers my nipples, and my breasts are big and spilling out of it. The thong bottoms show off my firm ass. My legs are super long, so I'm killing it in this thing. I have every man at the pool drooling over me. I'm offered twenty drinks before I even make my way across the patio, but I won't be accepting a drink from anyone except the bartender.

I look over at Palmer to check on her. She was super self-conscious about wearing a bathing suit. We bought them at a store the other day, and she made a whole production about showing herself in it. We couldn't get her to come out of the dressing room for twenty minutes.

She seems comfortable now as she and Beau are sitting together while they talk and laugh. I know she has a crush on him, but I'm noticing more and more lately that it might not be one-sided. Go Palmer.

I'm sitting at the bar now, waiting for my drink, ignoring the man trying to talk to me while I take in Daylen in his ridiculous swim trunks, complete with a cock in the middle. Cock as in the adult male chicken. He's such a tool, but he has an amazing body, the best one here. His arms are shredded, complete with thick forearms and huge biceps. He's got a broad, muscular chest with the same dirty blond hair that sits on his head. He has a respectable haircut right now, which isn't usually the case. It looks freshly cut. His abs are so perfect that if you saw them in a photo, you'd think they were photoshopped. Naturally, his bathing suit is ridiculously short, so I can see his thighs. They're as thick as tree trunks.

I find myself staring at his tattoo. I wonder who Rose is. An ex-girlfriend who broke his heart? Is that why he's a manwhore? Or did something happen to fuck up his ability to have a real relationship, like what happened to me so many years ago? I have a bizarre and unwelcome pang of jealousy that her name is permanently printed on his body.

I look up at the guy trying to hit on me. A few months ago, I would have been into him, but I haven't been with anyone since before New Year's Eve. It wasn't a conscious decision. I just haven't been into the whole casual sex with a stranger thing. My current feelings of uneasiness around men might run a little deeper than I'm allowing myself to believe.

I offer him a small smile when he asks me to go to the hot tub with him. "Sorry, maybe another time. I'm here to hang out with my friends."

He smirks, revealing dimples I'm sure many women drool

over. "Come on, baby," he grabs my arm, "let's find somewhere quiet to talk."

I pull my arm away and grit out, "Dude, it's not happening. Don't call me baby and don't touch me again." I try to stand to get away from him, but he boxes me in with his arms.

As if I didn't just ask him not to touch me, he reaches for me again. Before his hand makes contact, Daylen appears from out of nowhere and grabs his wrist. "The lady said no. How it works is that when a woman tells you no, you move on. Fuck off, asshole."

The guy's eyes widen at the six-foot-five mass of muscle glaring down at him with a venomous look I haven't ever seen on Daylen's face until now.

"Wow, Daylen Humblecut. Sorry, man. I didn't realize she's your girl."

I open my mouth to correct him, but Daylen shifts his glare from the dickhead to me as if to say *why bother*.

I uncharacteristically remain tight-lipped while Daylen shifts his eyes back to the man and then gives him a little shove. "Yes, she's my girl, so buzz off."

The moron grins. "She's sexy as fuck, man. Congrats." He holds up his hand for Daylen to high-five, but Daylen doesn't budge. He just stares at him like he's about to pummel him.

The man *finally* gets the hint and walks away.

I look up at Daylen. "I don't need you to protect me. I can handle myself."

He shakes his head in obvious frustration. "A simple *thank you* would suffice."

I eat a bit of humble pie, and my voice cracks a bit as I croak out, "Thank you."

His face immediately softens, and he rubs my arm. Why is his touch suddenly so comforting to me? "Are you okay?" he asks. "Have you been with anyone since New Year's? I haven't seen you go home with anyone in months, and it used to be the regular course of business for you."

"Are you keeping track of my sexual partners?" I snap in annoyance. Who the fuck is he to keep tabs on my sex life?

He exhales a long breath. "I don't know why I bother." He starts to turn away but then looks back at me. "You haven't told any of the girls, have you?"

I shake my head.

"You should. I think it will help."

I smirk. "Looking to help me get laid, Dr. Humblecut?"

"No, looking to be a decent human being. You should try it sometime."

I DID my best to flirt with every man at the pool all afternoon to prove to Daylen *and myself* that I'm fine. I could feel his eyes on me the whole time. For a reason I will never understand, I liked it. I liked that he was watching over me. It made me feel safe.

We're now getting dressed to go out for the evening. Palmer is letting me do her hair and makeup. We're at the vanity in the bathroom as I put on the final touches for her. Sulley gasps as she walks in. "Oh my god, Palmer, you look amazing."

Palmer's face lights up. She likes how she looks too, with the makeup on point and her adorable dress that we bought last year together.

I nod. "How fucking amazing are her eyes? I swear I've never seen anyone with this shade. I bet you used to get accused of wearing colored contact lenses when you were a kid."

Palmer's face falls a bit. "All the damn time. People can be so cruel."

Sulley and I exchange knowing glances in the mirror. No one gets more online hate than Palmer. It's tempered down since last season ended, but I'm fearful it will start up again as the new season approaches.

Sulley looks me up and down. "You look amazing too. Wow,

that dress. And those shoes. Holy crap. I don't think I could walk in those."

I'm wearing a very short, tight red halter dress with a plunging neckline. A little gift to myself after the PC2 check came in this fall. My matching red, strappy Ferragamo shoes and lacy undergarments are all courtesy of Reagan's Black Card last summer. My hair is up, a little looser than I normally wear it, but I'm very excited about my overall look. I've been dying to have somewhere to wear this dress, and a night out in Vegas seems like the perfect choice.

Sulley is also dressed to kill. In fact, all the girls are. Everyone has stepped up their fashion game. I'd like to think I had some small hand in making that happen.

Layla joins the five of us for a champagne celebratory toast. I look around at my beautiful friends. "We clean up pretty good, ladies. Not bad for a bunch of jocks."

They all agree as we toast. I let the citrusy, flavorful bubbles slide easily down my throat as I vow to have a good time tonight. It's been far too long.

We make our way downstairs to meet the guys. They're all dressed stylishly except you know who. Daylen Humblecut. He's wearing cargo shorts, sandals with socks, and a black T-shirt that reads *Walking Red Flag*. He's capped it off with a giant —and I mean giant—gold necklace.

The girls all break into hysterics when they see him. His eyes move up and down my body. I think he's about to say something complimentary, but instead he says, "Is that dress short enough, Peppermint Patty? I guess we're about to find out if the curtains match the drapes."

I cross my arms and happily reply, "There is no carpet. Only floor tiling."

His lips twitch with amusement while the other guys all laugh. I roll my eyes. "Your outfit is ridiculous. Are you going to change? You're not seriously wearing that all night, are you?"

He shrugs. "I wore it just for you. And I will *never* change."

FOR THE FIRST time in months, I'm finally letting loose. It feels good. I still won't accept drinks from strange men, but I've been getting them from the bartender and knocking them back all night. We're on the dance floor at a club, dancing and singing. Sulley and Palmer have let loose in a way I'm unaccustomed to from them.

Sulley and Vance keep exchanging longing glances, though they keep their distance. I lean over and whisper-yell, "Are you fucking him?"

Her eyes widen. "What? No. Of course not."

Hmm. I'm not sure I believe her. The iciness between them from last summer has thawed significantly since her return to Philly from the holidays. I know he was in their hometown at the same time. Something definitely happened between them.

Even Palmer is shaking her ass tonight. Beau is standing at a nearby high-top table, homed in on her, taking it all in. He hasn't moved his eyes from her body since we met up hours ago. His gaze is intense and obvious. I don't think he bothers to acknowledge the hordes of women who try to talk to him.

Women are also all over both Vance and Daylen, but while Vance pushes them away, Daylen basks in the adoration. What's wrong with these women? Don't they see what he's wearing? Why is it annoying me so much?

A few more hours and several drinks later, we're all wasted. I've never seen Daylen this drunk. He's talking to the bartender while a skanky woman is trying to stick her hands down his pants. I think he's too drunk to notice.

In my own inebriated state, I decide I should rescue him from unwanted advances like he rescued me. In a bit of a stumbling, zigzag pattern, I make my way toward them and grab the girl's arm. "Hands off, hooker."

She snarls, "Fuck off, bitch. I'm taking him home tonight."

I shove her and stand in front of him to protect him from this overly aggressive, vicious woman. Before I realize it, I cross my arms and yell out, "He's my husband. Stay away."

The woman's chin drops before she scurries away. Daylen bursts out laughing. "Hooker?" He cackles like it's the funniest word he's ever heard. "What do a hooker and Walmart have in common?" He pauses for a few seconds of silence because I have no idea what they have in common. He continues, "Everyone makes fun of them, but when you're in one at four in the morning, everyone loves them."

He then bends over while his louder-than-reasonable laugh intensifies. For some bizarre reason, I decide it's the funniest thing he's ever said and join in on the laughter.

He throws his arms around me. "Well, wifey, what can I get you to drink?" He runs his nose through my hair. "Fuck, the smell of my wife makes me hard. I'd know that scent anywhere."

I reach over to feel the truth of his statement. His dick is hardening. And I decide that it's a good idea to keep rubbing and rubbing and rubbing.

He moans. "God damn, that feels good, wifey. Did I tell you how hot you look tonight? I'm gonna fuck those tits later."

My panties flood at the thought. Suddenly I can't manage to remove my hands from his hard body as I move them over every inch of him, wanting to explore his masculine, defined body. He's so sexy. Was he always this sexy? It must have just started tonight. Yep, that's it. Just started. Like spontaneous hotness.

He grabs my ass and pulls me flush with him before his lips crash to mine. He tastes like the lame-ass fruity drinks he's been downing all night, but it's kind of nice. Usually men taste like whiskey or scotch after a night out, but Daylen tastes like… strawberries. Yummy. Why have I been against this for so long?

Wait, his tongue is in my mouth. Oh my god, my tongue is in his mouth. Before I know it, we're swallowing each other whole as we make out at the bar. My body ignites in a way it hasn't in several months.

I don't recognize my own voice when I mumble into his mouth, "Bend me over and fuck me on this bar, Neanderthal."

A throat clearing ends our make-out session. We both turn to the bartender, who says, "You two can't have sex in here. Why don't you head out for the night and find a more private place to have a good time?" He hands us each the same drinks we've been drinking all night, Daylen's girlie one, complete with fruit and an umbrella, and my espresso martini. "These are on the house, kids. Just leave before the bouncers get involved."

Daylen smiles. "Free drinks. Wow, you're the bestest, man." He looks down at his drink, blanketed with an umbrella and fruit, and slurs, "Can I have two more umbrellas? Don't open them though."

The bartender sighs. "Sure thing. After that, you need to leave."

He retrieves the two closed umbrellas and then hands them to Daylen. Daylen removes the small rubber bands keeping the umbrellas closed. Taking my left hand, he slides one of the rubber bands onto my ring finger. "My wife needs a ring." He slides the other rubber band onto his ring finger. "I need one too. Now it's official," he smiles widely.

For some reason, I decide this is a brilliant idea and hold it up into the light as if the light will shine off it like a diamond. I'm mesmerized by its elastic-y beauty.

We each grab our free drink, link arms, and happily stumble our way to the exit door of the club, full of laughs and good cheer.

The club is a few blocks from our hotel. We took a party bus here, but it seems to be gone, so we decide to walk. As we do so, we're both wildly amused by me leaving red lipstick kiss marks all over his neck. I inhale him while doing so. Ooh, he smells good. Has he always smelled this yummy?

About a block from the club, we pass a small wedding chapel with Elvis sitting out front, belting a few tunes. In his best Elvis impression, he looks at us and sings, "You two can't help falling in love. How about a little jailhouse rock?" He shakes his hips and does a little hip twist.

Daylen and I think it's the funniest thing that has ever been said or seen. We're practically on the ground laughing.

I ask, "Is your real name Elvis?" He doesn't look like the real Elvis. I think he's Indian, but maybe Elvis was Indian and I didn't realize it.

Without breaking his Elvis character, he answers, "That's my stage name, sugar pie. My real name is Pinky Punnathanathukunnele."

Daylen and I really lose it this time. We fall onto the sidewalk in a fit of hysterics. It's the funniest name we've ever heard in our lives. We keep trying to repeat it over and over without any success.

Elvis/Pinky starts singing the words to "All Shook Up" followed by "Love Me Tender." He's even got a microphone, though I don't think it's connected to a speaker. None that I can hear.

As if it's just occurring to Daylen where we are, he gasps. "Oh my god, this is a sign. Let's make it official, wifey." He proudly shows Elvis/Pinky his ring finger. "This rubber band ring is getting tight. We need real ones. Do you have those?"

Elivis/Pinky nods. "Sure do, my hunk of burning love. We've got all kinds of wedding packages. Come inside, love birds. We'll get you two married in no time."

My face falls. "I can't get married without a veil." I go on and on about not being able to properly get married without a veil. I make no mention of a dress, friends, or family, just the veil. I don't know why I'm fixated on it, but I am.

I'm now standing again on the sidewalk, but Daylen is still on the ground. He gets on his knees in front of me and runs his hands up my bare thighs. I shiver at his touch and the erotic movement. "Your hands are so big, hubby." They're huge. I never realized how big Daylen's hands are, and the thought is making my nipples harden.

He nods as they move up and then under my dress. I stand there and let it happen because nothing has ever felt better in my entire life.

His fingers brush over my long-neglected pussy, and I gulp. I don't care where we are, I just want those thick fingers inside me as soon as possible. Please let him pull my panties to the side and push a finger into me. I've had dicks in me smaller than those fingers. I know I could orgasm from it, and I desperately need a non-self-induced orgasm. It's been far too long.

Before I realize what's happening, he's pulling my red lace thong down my legs. I watch, transfixed by the move, wondering what he intends to do next. His dick inside me is what I'm hoping for.

"Lift your feet, wifey," he breathes as if he's as turned on as I am.

I lift one at a time until my thong is in his hand. He brings it to his nose and inhales deeply. It's so hot. If I were still wearing the panties, they'd be flooded. There's now a waterfall of slickness between my thighs.

After a few more inhales, he hands them back to me. "You can use this as your veil."

Why didn't I think of that? It's genius. It matches my dress perfectly. I find myself wondering if other brides use their panties as veils too. It makes sense that they would, right?

After placing it in my hair, we walk inside the chapel. It's got a disco ball hanging that is hypnotizing me. There are several rows of wooden pews with pretty flowers. They might be plastic, but they look beautiful.

We learn you get a free pizza when you buy a wedding, which we're extremely excited about because it's been seven hours since dinner and we're famished. After paying for the upgraded package—my husband-to-be is very good to me—we make our way to the altar.

With our drinks still in hand, Elvis/Pinky begins the service. Daylen stares at me the whole time. When it's his turn to repeat after Elvis/Pinky, he goes off script. "You have the prettiest eyes. They're the first thing I noticed about you. I was lost in them until you opened your mouth and ruined it. But your eyes never fail to stir something in me."

"If you think they're pretty now, wait until you see them while I'm on my knees looking up at you with my ponytail wrapped around your hand."

"Fuuuck," he moans as he adjusts himself. His eyes widen as if something has just occurred to him. "Did you know that a blowjob is the only job in the world you can't use on your resume despite years of experience and number of references? But don't worry," he slurs, "I'm like Maxwell House. Good to the last drop."

I giggle at my hysterical husband before responding, "Good to know. You should know that Yelp just rated me the best place to eat out."

He pumps his fist. "Yay. Can't wait to taste your rainbow."

The rest of the ceremony goes off in a bit of a blur, but I do manage to finish my drink, as does Daylen.

We leave the chapel with a few mementos stuffed into my purse and a delicious pizza pie. We're attacking that pizza like we haven't eaten in months when we bump into a large man.

Looking him over, I see he's in head-to-toe leather and covered in tattoos.

He gives us a warm smile. "You two having fun tonight?"

I nod. "The best time ever ever ever. We got married," I screech.

He lets out a laugh. Not sure why getting married is funny. "Congratulations."

"Are you the welcoming committee?" I absurdly ask.

He smirks as he shakes his head. "Nope, I own this tattoo parlor." He points to the sign above our heads that I hadn't noticed before. "Why don't you two come inside and have a look around?"

I examine the green, well-lit sign. Sure enough, it's a tattoo parlor named *Inkognito. What a brilliant name,* I think.

We follow him in and look at all the photos of intricate tattoos on the wall. I've never been a tattoo person, but I'm finding it particularly fascinating tonight.

The man asks me if I want one. I shrug. "I wouldn't know what to get, but my husband had another woman's name tattooed on his abdominium...abdomino...abdicate..." Crap, why can't I think of the word? "Abdomen!" I eventually shout. "Yes, he has another woman's name on there, and I'm jealous. He should get my name too, don't you think?"

The man looks at Daylen, who nods. "She makes a good point. Where should I get her name?" he asks the man.

He motions toward our newly ringed fingers. "Lots of married couples get each other's names on their ring fingers."

Daylen's face lights up. "That's a *great* idea, leather man. Then I can show the world I'm married when I play ball. My wife can show them when she plays ball too." He straightens his shoulders and wraps his arm around me proudly. "She's a stud athlete. The best basketball player in the world. I'm so proud of her. I love watching her play. I wish their uniforms were tighter though, because she's got a bangin' body, doesn't she?"

The man runs his eyes up and down my body while he licks his lips. "She sure does."

Normally that would bother me, but not tonight. Tonight I'm loved up by my new husband's words. Warmth floods my body for him, and while I do want us to get the tattoos, I want to get him naked even more.

I look at the guy. "How long will it take? I have a date to ride my husband's dick." I then grab his dick through his shorts again.

The guy chuckles. "It won't take long at all."

THIRTEEN

KENNEDY

We stumble into the hotel lobby as we polish off the last two slices from the most delicious wedding chapel pizza ever created. Wait, why were we at a wedding chapel? Were we guests at someone's wedding?

He licks the last of the pizza sauce from his fingertips. "*Teehee,* that's the best pizza I've ever had," he screams in delight. "Where did we get it? I need to go back there tomorrow…and every single day for the rest of my life."

I shrug, suddenly forgetting where it came from. The good news is that I think it's helped absorb the booze a little bit. The last hour is spotty—I don't remember how we got back to the hotel—but I'm feeling much less dizzy now that I have some food in my belly. Daylen still has a goofy smile on his face, but he's always goofy. And handsome. Oh man, he's so handsome.

I trace his square jawline with my fingertips. "You're pretty," I tell him as I lean the front of my body onto his. He doesn't budge an inch. He's so big and strong. It's not often I'm around men who are significantly bigger and stronger than me. It's such a turn-on.

He tweaks my nose. "No, *you're* pretty."

His breath still smells like strawberries, and it's the sweetest thing. I want it all over my body.

We unsteadily make our way to the elevator and use my keycard to get us access to the top floor. I look at us in the mirror of the elevator wall, taking in our appearance for the first time in hours. We're a mess. My once-perfect ponytail and makeup look like I ran through a tornado to get here. His hair is sticking up all over the place, though that's normal for him. I don't think he owns a brush or a comb.

I go to move the loose hair out of my face when I realize my left hand is bandaged. What did I do to it? Am I hurt?

My hand is quickly forgotten as soon as Daylen begins kissing my neck. I look at him, the man I've hated for nearly a year, the man who is wearing the most ridiculous outfit in creation. Clarity slowly starts to set in. What am I doing? Am I about to have sex with him?

I can't have sex with Daylen Humblecut, but oh god, the kissing feels good. I can't manage to do anything but tilt my head back and let it continue. I moan at how nice his lips feel as they move down to my cleavage. I have a physical throbbing situation between my legs. Maybe one time with him won't be so bad? It's been a long time for me. Maybe this hate-passion between us will make for explosive sex. I can fuck him out of my system.

Yes! That's a great idea.

No! It's a terrible idea.

I'm still deep in my thoughts when he pins me to the side of the elevator. I can feel his massive erection pushing against my stomach. I want it lower. Why is he so damn tall?

He grabs me by the hips and growls into my ear, "I need to see your tits. I've dreamed about them for months. Fuck, I don't want to want you, but I do."

I feel the exact same way, but I'm still tormented over

whether I should see this through. Even in my hazy state, I'm wondering if this might not be a colossal mistake.

When the elevator doors open, he lifts me like a bride and brushes his lips over mine. "I'm going to make you come so hard, over and over again. You'll be feeling me in your cunt for days."

He does make a persuasive argument.

I grab fistfuls of his hair with both hands and pull them hard. He growls again. "It makes my cock leak when you're rough with me."

I lift my hand back and then bring it forward with force, slapping him across the face. Hard.

He smiles and then tap-slaps me across my face. Not nearly as hard as I slapped him, but it stings a little…and I love it.

Fuck it. This is happening.

We stare at each other as we approach the door of the suite he's sharing with Vance. I narrow my eyes at him. "I hate you, Freddy Krueger."

He narrows his eyes right back at me. "I hate you more, Nurse Ratched."

At that, his lips crash to mine while he pushes open the door to his suite. Our teeth clank and our tongues duel for supremacy. Why do I love the way he tastes so damn much? No real man tastes like strawberries, but I seem to be intoxicated by it.

He places me on my feet and backs me into his bedroom, all without breaking our lip lock. He slams his door shut behind us and grabs for my breasts, but I bite his lip hard enough to draw blood.

He breaks the kiss, though his face lights up as he pushes his erection onto me. I've been dying to get my hands on it all night after feeling how impressive it was earlier in the club. I rub my hand up and down his crotch and call him a freak for how much he clearly got off on me biting his lip.

He wiggles his eyebrows as he pinches my nipple so damn

hard, I wonder if it's still there. "Takes one to know one," he growls in return.

I guess we're both gluttons for punishment because I bark out, "Do it again."

Before I know it, he's shirtless and I'm standing there in my bra and panties. He pretends, through words, that he doesn't like what he sees, but his eyes tell another story. If you can be fucked by eyes, his are doing so as they roam my body unashamedly. I know what a man's lustful look is, and that's all I'm seeing from him right now. That and his dick, which is rock solid, practically poking out like a third leg from his shorts.

I can't take it anymore. I want his dick. I want to see it, touch it, taste it, feel it inside my body.

After I pull his shorts down, he nearly falls over as he attempts to kick them away. I do my best to swallow down my laugh. He's totally trashed.

He takes a brief moment as if to check to see if I'm of the right mind to do this. Only one word flitters through my mind at seeing this thoughtful hesitation written all over his face. Trust. Despite all our shit, I trust Daylen to take care of me. To never take advantage of me. This thought alone pushes me to tell him I'm fine enough to take that next step.

I walk toward him and run my shaky fingertips over the defined muscles of his stomach like I've been wanting to do since the pool today. I both love and hate how sexy this beast is. Goosebumps spread all over his body from my touch.

And then finally, *finally*, I remove his boxer briefs. My mouth is agape at his size. I knew he was big because I saw the tip a few months ago and I've felt him through his clothes, but holy shit. His dick is in exact proportion to how much of a pain in the ass he is. Let me assure you, he's a *big, wide, long, angry* pain in the ass.

My former veil, which returned to its original place as panties, is now flooded. And I mean flooded, as I physically ache for that giant cock to be inside me.

I can't help but rub and then taste the oozing tip with my thumb. It tastes like I'm about to get fucked hard, just how I want and need it from him. Figures that this asshole would have the right tools. Why can't green flag guys be built like this? Instead, I'm faced with the man who encompasses every red flag I've ever dreamed of, draped in the body of a god with the dick of a porn star.

I look down at myself. Where did my bra go? When did he take it off? I see it on the floor, but I don't remember it being taken off. Maybe he's a sex magician and took it off via telepathy.

Fortunately, I remember that I stuffed my purse full of condoms before I left for the evening, hoping I'd muster up the courage to be with a man tonight. I never expected it to be this man, but I'm currently okay with the change in plans. There's something deeply comforting about it being him and not a stranger. I may hate him, but I know and trust him.

Soon after I toss the condoms on the bed, he tosses me on the bed as if I weigh nothing. I'm over six feet and very muscular. I've never once had a lover manhandle me like this. And holy fucking shit does it make my pussy ache with need.

Before I know it, he's on top of me and his thick fingers are pushing deep inside me just like I imagined them doing earlier tonight. Giving into the myriad of sensations, I beg for them deeper, even though I'm not sure fingers can go any deeper than his are. He's so rough with me. I love that he doesn't treat me like a porcelain doll. I hate it when men do that.

His lips and teeth are all over my breasts, devouring them, undoubtedly marking them. He mumbles something about how long he's waited to worship them and how perfect they are.

I can feel his teeth sinking into my lush flesh. Damn, I love this harsh treatment. I get off on it, even though I know I'll have his teeth marks all over my body in the morning.

Fuck that. I'm marking him too. I scrape my nails all over his back, breaking skin and making him moan in pleasure. He loves the roughness as much as I do.

His fingers continue to expertly stroke my insides, knowing how and where to touch me. I can feel my pussy pulsing with deep-seated need as my arousal rockets into space and fluids physically pour from my body.

I'm close to coming already, but I want his dick. The thought of that big dick inside me is consuming me. "Fuck me now, red," I yell out.

He lifts his head and quirks a brow. "Red?"

"Red flag. Fuck me like you're the biggest red flag on the planet."

He pauses briefly, as if in deliberation, so I slap him across the face again just as hard as I did earlier.

His eyes burn with desire as he removes his fingers from my pussy and brings them to my throat, squeezing the sides hard. His cock is now lying heavy on my pussy, with his crown pushing against my swollen, pulsing clit.

He grits out, "All I have to do is squeeze." He tightens his hold a drop more.

I'm confident I've never been more turned on in my life than I am right at this moment. My eyes roll back in my head. Between the choking, the pressure on my clit, and his words, I lose my mind, shaking uncontrollably and screaming into a full-body, all-encompassing orgasm. It feels like my body is levitating off the bed even though a two-hundred-and-sixty-five-pound mountain of a man is on top of me.

I have never—I mean *never*—come from something like that before.

When my eyes regain focus, I see him staring at me in disbelief. "Did you just come from that, weirdo?"

"No," I lie. "It was a…minor tremor. Like the sudden jolting of a speed bump along the road."

"Liar. You came," he accuses with his big hand still holding firm around my neck.

I twist my lips. "Hmm. Must have been beginner's luck for you."

One of the corners of his mouth raises in amusement. "Why can't you admit you're attracted to me?" he asks.

"Back at you, hypocrite."

His eyes move down to my chest. "I'm attracted to your tits...and your legs. You have an amazing body; there's no denying that. If I could just muzzle you, maybe we can get through this without killing each other."

"Do your worst." I open my mouth in invitation for him to muzzle me.

He smirks as he reaches for one of the condoms. He tears it open and rolls it down his length, but before he does anything else, he shoves the condom wrapper into my mouth. "Bite on this. Don't talk."

I happily oblige, clamping my teeth over the rubber-tasting plastic wrapper.

He grabs my hips and flips me over like I'm a well-done pancake. Again, my pussy oozes at his brute strength.

Just as he's lifting me to my knees, we hear a woman screaming Vance's name from across the suite. I turn my head back toward Daylen and mumble with the condom wrapper still in my mouth, "You better fuck me well enough that I'm louder than that random bitch."

He smacks my ass hard before thrusting into me in one fell swoop. The impact of it causes me to fall from my knees to the bed. Thank god I was already wet, or he would have torn me in half. My fall causes me to lose the condom wrapper from my mouth.

"Fucking hell, Daylen," I spit out. "A little warning next time. Ease a girl into that thing."

"I said no talking. You can scream. That's it." He spanks my ass hard again. Hard enough that I know it will be red and bruised in the morning.

It only serves to cause more liquid lust to gush from my pussy.

I feel his lips on my ear. "You like it when I hurt you, don't you?"

I nod.

He pushes my legs together and spreads his own wide in a domineering position as he begins to piston into me. God damn, this is intense. My hands are flailing about trying to grip everything in sight so he doesn't send my body through the wall.

"Grab the headboard," he barks out.

"What?" I breathe, unable to comprehend words during this onslaught.

He spanks me again and grits out, "Grab the fucking headboard so I have some leverage to fuck the bitch out of you."

I can't help but smile. Why do I get off on him treating me like that? What does it say about me?

Releasing my hair tie, he wraps my hair around his fist and yanks it hard.

The man is a fucking beast. In this position, given the magnitude of his size, I can feel the ridges of his cock as it drags through my insides, drawing pleasure from my body like it was made to do so. I might be conscious of my screams as I battle with the nameless woman next door, but they are real—screams of pure ecstasy.

Orgasm after orgasm is wrung from my body as I hold on for dear life. As the hours go on and I sweat the alcohol away, I begin to sober up but don't stop him from the animalistic way he's attacking my body. I don't want to stop him. Drunk or sober, I'm exactly where I want to be.

FOURTEEN

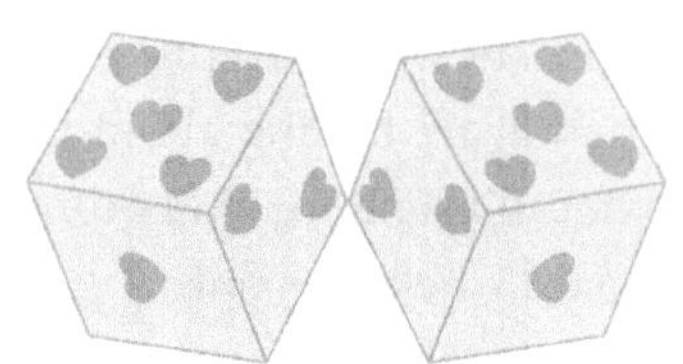

KENNEDY

After the greatest marathon sex of my life, where we explored every position imaginable and I lost count of the orgasms he gave me, though I'm sure it's got to be some kind of world record, I lay in bed next to Daylen. He's passed out cold.

I study his face carefully. He truly is a handsome man. It's too bad he talks…and dresses himself…and shaves himself.

My eyes move down his entire large body, which is completely uncovered right now. He's lying on his back in all his naked glory. His body belongs in one of those firefighter calendars. He must live in the gym.

I gently trace his tattoos of the rose and the matching name with my fingertips. Who is she? I have a strange urge to know. I don't know why I care and why I have a pang of jealousy for her. Who is the woman who was so important to him that he forever marked his body with her name?

As I consider the tattoo, memories begin to flash through my mind. It hits me that we were in a tattoo parlor last night. Panic sets in, and I quickly scan my body, not seeing anything. I jump out of bed to find a mirror. Ouch, I'm sore. My pussy took a pounding. Cheez, walking hurts. I might need a soak in that giant tub of ours today.

I approach the mirror and immediately check my lower back. Phew. No tramp stamp. Nothing on my ass either.

As I lift my left hand and notice a bandage, it hits me hard, like I just stepped out in front of a moving bus. Oh. Fuck. I got a tattoo on my finger. What was it? I can't remember.

Daylen starts to stir in the bed. Shit, I don't want to be here when he wakes up. I don't regret sleeping with him—the sex was incredible—but I won't be able to handle it if he wakes up and I see regret in his eyes. By the time we reached his room and got into things, he was undoubtedly more trashed than I was.

I catch a fleeting glance of my face in the mirror. I guess this is the official raccoon look, complete with smeared makeup and *I just got the shit fucked out of me* hair.

Not having time to fix anything, I slip back into my undergarments and dress, grab my purse and shoes, and then quietly exit his room. As soon as I do, I see Sulley exiting Vance's room with the same *just-fucked* look as me.

We stare at each other in wide-eyed disbelief.

I quickly tell her how trashed I was and lie that I'm disgusted over the fact that I allowed Daylen to touch me. I'm not disgusted like I should have been. I loved every second of it.

She eyes me skeptically, but she's just as embarrassed as me so we agree to never speak of this night again. Ever.

We make our way down the hallway with a slight case of the giggles, given how ridiculous we look. We walk into our suite, where the most shocking thing happens. Palmer is standing in the kitchen, downing a gallon of water, looking the same as us with messed-up hair, smudged makeup, and still in her dress from last night.

Sulley and I burst out laughing, but Palmer is mortified. We make a group pact to act like last night never happened.

I beg for the first shower, and they acquiesce. Turning on the water, I remove my dress and undergarments. I'm able to more closely examine my naked body in the mirror, and I see marks everywhere. *Everywhere.*

I have hickeys and bite marks all over my breasts and the surrounding areas. The same goes for my neck and shoulders. I also have a fully formed necklace of a bruise from all the choking. Tracing it with my fingers, I smile at the memory of how rough he was with me. Turning around, I can see my ass is marked, as are my inner thighs. Man, he worked me over good. I shiver at the memories flooding through my brain.

Exhaling a deep breath, I look up at the ceiling. Why? Why did the best sex of my life have to come from him? The man I love to hate.

My eyes find the bandaged fingers again. I start to remove the gauze. As soon as the final strip is gone, I suck in a breath. Holy shit. I got a tattoo of his fucking name on my ring finger. Why would I do that?

Like a light switch was just turned on, the walk from the club to the hotel starts to come into focus. Indian Elvis singing to us before and after wedding vows.

Wedding vows!

Oh my god. Oh my god. Oh my god.

I frantically dump the contents of my purse on the vanity, with a few smaller, insignificant items falling into the sink with a clank. Ignoring the fact that all ten condoms I had packed are gone, the vanity is quickly littered with my makeup and a bunch of weird novelty-looking items. One is a mug with a photo of Daylen and me smiling at an altar. An actual altar. With shaking hands, I make my way through everything. There's one of those old school keychains that you look through and there's usually a picture at the end of it. I look, and it's an image of Daylen holding me like a bride. We're smiling while happily lifting up our ring-clad fingers at the camera. And that's when I see them sitting at the bottom of the sink, too big to get swallowed up by the drain. Two fake gold wedding bands. I have a vague recollection of taking them off to get the tattoos and then dropping them into my purse.

My heart rate must be two hundred beats a minute. I clutch it. I feel like I'm having a heart attack. Did we really get married? Did I marry Daylen Humblecut? *Holy fuck.*

I lean over, placing my hands on the vanity. I have to take several long, calming breaths in an attempt to rein myself in. I'm completely freaking out. This can't be happening. There's no way it was a legal marriage. We were trashed. They can't let drunk people get married, can they? There's no consent in that.

I need to talk to him. Maybe I'm misremembering. Yes, I must be confused from all the liquor. Like a nightmare you wake up thinking was true.

I'm going to shower and then go talk to Daylen. Maybe his memory will be better than mine.

I scrub my body clean and wash my hair as fast and efficiently as I can. Throwing on a T-shirt and shorts, I realize it doesn't cover all my marks. I slip into a hoodie over my T-shirt and throw my wet hair into a messy bun, not remotely caring what I look like.

Walking back out into the living room, I put on a mask of calmness as I tell them I'm going to run to the lobby for some coffee. They're both too mortified to question why I would do that when we have a coffee machine in the room.

Sprinting down the hallway toward Daylen's room, I pound on the door. It doesn't take long for him to open it in his cock boxer briefs with his hair sticking up all over the place. He looks as shocked as I feel.

He points toward Vance's door and then brings his finger to his lips, indicating I should be quiet. I nod in agreement and follow him into his bedroom, where he closes the door behind me.

I immediately hear an intruding man's voice. "Ah, there's the wife. Mazel Tov," the strange voice rings out before I hear a deep chuckle.

I snap my head around and see Tanner's smiling face on Daylen's laptop. His grin widens when our eyes meet. "Where are you kids going on your honeymoon?" he asks and then starts laughing hysterically.

"Cut it out, Tanner," Daylen snaps. "This isn't fucking funny. It's the least funny thing that's ever happened in the history of the world. It's a catastrophe of epic proportions."

Tanner doesn't bother to hide his amusement at the situation. "Oh relax. This kind of shit happens in Vegas every day. We'll get it taken care of. I'll let you two kids talk. The courts out there will be open in ten minutes. I'll call you back after I've made the necessary calls and set things in motion. Sit tight and figure out how you're going to break it to the kids," he jokes.

He starts laughing again, but Daylen snaps the laptop closed, cutting off the offending noise. He inhales and then exhales a long breath. "He's going to look into how quickly we can get this annulled. He said it shouldn't be a problem. It's slightly discretionary from judge to judge, but, like he said, people get annulments after drunken nights in Vegas all the time."

A shaking hand moves to my mouth as reality sets in. "So it's true? We really got married?" I start pacing as I rub the spot between my eyebrows. "Oh shit, Daylen. How did this happen? Fuck, why is last night so spotty? It's like a puzzle and I can't figure out where all the pieces go, even though I can see them each individually."

He nods. "I know. For me too. I don't remember shit except an Indian Elvis whose real name is Pinky who also gave us pizza for some unknown reason."

Right. Elvis/Pinky. I remember him. "Are you sure we really got married?" I ask hopefully. "Maybe it wasn't legal. Maybe Pinky is a fraud who just wanted our money."

He shakes his head as he hands me a piece of paper. It's a wedding certificate. "Tanner and I already looked into the place. It's legit. We're fucking married."

My eyes fill with tears. "This is nuts." I start hyperventilating as tears begin to stream down my face. I croak out, "I hate you. I don't want you to be my husband."

He runs his fingers through his hair. "That's one thing we can agree on." He approaches me and wipes the tears from my face. "Don't cry. You know I hate it when women cry. Tanner will take care of it. I promise. This will be a distant memory in no time. Only you, me, Tanner…and Pinky will ever know about it."

As if just noticing something, he gently tugs down the neck of my hoodie and sucks in a breath as his face fills with horror. "Did I do this to you?"

I nod, and he stumbles back until he falls into a seated position on the bed. His eyes well with tears as he looks up at me with a genuinely devastated look on his face. "I'm…I'm so sorry. I don't remember. Does…does it hurt? I would never knowingly hurt you."

I shake my head. "No, it doesn't hurt at all." Maybe it's a little sore, a lot sore, but it doesn't hurt, and I don't want him to feel bad about something I wanted.

He visibly gulps as he begins to fidget nervously. "Did I force—"

"No," I immediately interrupt as I shake my head emphatically. He thinks he forced himself on me, or at least did something to me while I was in no condition to consent. As much as I can't stand him at times, and as much of a nightmare as this marriage is, I was with it enough by the time we got to the room to consent. In fact, I was more with it than he was.

Sitting next to him, I take his hand in mine and look into his blue eyes, currently filled with fear and uncertainty. "Daylen, I'm still piecing together everything that happened from the last hour or so at the club to the time we got back to this room, but I remember most of what went on here. I think I was more sober than you at that point. The sex was consensual. I'd be lying if I told you I didn't want it. I did."

With a shaking finger, he points to my neck. "What…what about that?"

"Consensual," I assure him. "I like it…rough. I wanted it rough. I asked you to be rough with me. You gave me what I wanted."

"So what you're saying is you were sober and I was drunk." He cracks a small smile. "*You* took advantage of *me*."

I elbow him hard in the stomach. "Shut up, asshole."

He starts chuckling. "There's my nasty witch. I missed her."

"You came three times," I remind him. "I think you enjoyed yourself."

"How many times did you come?" he asks with a bit of an amused tone to his voice.

"Once or twice," I look down and mumble the lie.

He lifts my chin with his finger until our eyes meet and then raises an eyebrow.

I sigh. "A lot of times, okay?" I admit. "No need to dwell on it. Hate sex suits us both."

He grins widely as he looks me up and down. "I've never seen you all messy like this."

"Screw you, Daylen. Not all of us get off on looking our worst all the time. I'm sorry I didn't primp properly. I was worried about the fact that we fucking got married," I whisper-scream at him.

He rolls his eyes. "If you'd let me continue, I was going to say I like you better this way. You don't need all that makeup and fancy hairdos. You're a beautiful woman. You should go natural more often. You're sexier this way, fresh-faced with your hair all messy."

I'm contemplating whether or not he's fucking with me when his computer rings and "Waterfalls" plays throughout the room.

I shake my head. "Are you serious with that song?"

He lets out a laugh as he walks toward his computer, opens the screen, and accepts the video call. "Tell me you have some good news, Tanner."

Tanner nods. "I do. I was able to get a judge to agree to a video annulment. He'll log on in a few minutes. As I suspected, they have immediately available resources for this kind of stuff in Vegas. Like I said, waking up in need of an annulment is nothing new out there."

We both let out a huge and audible sigh of relief. I feel like I can breathe for the first time in an hour.

"I want half," I joke to both of them with a smile on my face.

Daylen gives me the finger. "Annulment. Not divorce. You're not getting shit, *wifey*."

I shrug with a small giggle. "Can't blame a girl for trying, *hubby*."

"I'm most definitely not equipped to give you the princess treatment you so clearly need."

I cross my arms in annoyance at his words. "My tits bounce when I walk, so yes, I do expect princess treatment."

He stares shamelessly at my chest. "They bounce when you fuck too, sugar tits." He thumps his head. "That's one memory that will never leave me."

As I'm giving him the finger, another video box pops up on the screen, and an old man appears. And I mean old. He looks like he's on his way to his own funeral. He's all wrinkly with very little hair remaining. The sprinkling on the left is completely white. He appears to be in a home office and doesn't realize he's on with us yet as he fiddles with the screen, cursing about technology.

All I can think is this nightmare will be all over in a few minutes. No one ever has to know I was married to Daylen Humblecut for a few hours.

Phew.

DAYLEN

The judge coughs for a solid five minutes before even saying a word. He may not live long enough for the ink to dry on the annulment documents he's about to sign. We'd better get on with this.

The first thing I did when I woke up and found the marriage certificate was to call Tanner. He's not only my agent and close friend, but he's also an attorney. He laughed his ass off for minutes on end. Asshole.

He then assured me this kind of shit happens in Vegas all the time and annulments aren't too hard to come by. We just needed to wait for the courts to open.

Kennedy walked in looking a little less murderous than I would have expected. I freaked out when I saw her neck, but she was nice enough to reassure me. She could have fucked with me, but I'm glad she appreciated the severity of the situation and gave it to me straight. I'm even more glad she was into it. I may not remember everything about last night, but I'm starting to remember just how amazing the sex was. The passion was on a level I've never before experienced. It was like the hate we feel poured perfectly into the sex and made it so damn good.

I have to adjust myself as I look at her. I've never once seen her without an ounce of makeup and without her hair perfectly done. Even when she plays ball, she looks camera ready. I wasn't kidding when I said I prefer her this way. I may hate her personality, but she's gorgeous. There's no arguing that.

The judge skirts death by asphyxiation and finally begins talking, albeit with a giant scowl on his face. "Good morning. I'm Judge Salvetti. I'm a retired judge, but we retired judges volunteer and rotate taking on the requests for annulments that flood the office every morning so as not to disturb the real work needed." He says all this in a very judgmental tone as if scolding us. "Drunk youngsters who don't take the sanctity of marriage seriously are a waste of time for active judges dealing with real-world problems."

Kennedy whispers to me, "Don't hold back. Tell us how you really feel."

"What was that, young lady?" Judge Dog Ears snaps.

She smiles. "I was just telling my husband how generous it is for you to donate your time."

He eyes her skeptically, and I subtly elbow her while mouthing offscreen, "Don't piss him off."

The judge continues, "I remind you that even though we're not wasting court space with this nonsense, you're still under oath."

We both nod that we understand.

He obtains all our information, including names, birthdates, social security numbers, addresses, and the wedding details from last night that we remember. He's clearly judging our actions with snippy replies, but I don't care as long as he signs the damn annulment document.

He asks, "Do you own any joint property?"

"No," I answer.

"Any joint assets at all?"

Kennedy shakes her head. "No. Nothing like that."

"And you didn't consummate the marriage, right?"

Kennedy and I look at each other but otherwise remain silent. The judge stares at us before placing his pen on his desk. "A reminder that you're under oath. Did you or did you not consummate this marriage?"

I lick my lips nervously while Kennedy's shoulders fall. Nodding my head, I admit, "We did, but we were both drunk and barely remember it."

He scowls at my answer and then picks up his pen. He brings it to the papers in front of him several times as if about to write, but never actually does. Eventually, he places his pen back down on the desk and looks back up at the screen. "You know what, I'm not giving you your annulment."

"What?" Kennedy, Tanner, and I all yell in unison.

He nods. "I'm sick of people taking the institution of marriage so lightly. You two aren't irresponsible kids. You're thirty-two and twenty-six with college degrees and real careers."

Kennedy scoffs. "You're punishing us for being responsible adults?"

His eyes blaze with venom. "Yes, young lady, I am. You're both adults who should know there are consequences to your actions," he spits back at her.

Tanner clears his throat. "Respectfully, Judge Salvetti, you have to admit this is highly unusual. You have two adults who admittedly made a mistake in Las Vegas. It happens all the time, just as you said. Annulments are granted on a daily basis in similar situations. There's a lot of precedent to grant this annulment."

The judge leans back in his chair. "But we have discretion. I know you're aware of that, counselor." He crosses his arms as an eerie, smug look takes over his face. "What happens in Vegas doesn't always stay in Vegas." He cracks a small smile as if he's amusing himself. "Here's what we're going to do. I want you two to give this marriage a chance until the end of the calendar year. That's a little over nine months from now. I want—"

"Judge," Tanner interrupts. "This is not how it's done. You can't force them to stay married. They've been married for all of five hours. This isn't equitable in light of the brevity of the term of the marriage."

The judge narrows his eyes. "I can and will do exactly as I please, Mr. Montgomery." His eyes toggle between Kennedy and me. "I want you to go on a minimum of two dates a week. You will date and otherwise attempt to make this marriage work. I want you to give it a real chance. And you must remain true to your vows or the clock starts fresh."

"What?" Kennedy sputters. "I can't have sex for nine months?"

That only seems to enrage the judge more. "You can, young lady. With your *husband*."

"What if we don't want to have sex with each other?" I ask. "You can't force us to have sex. We. Were. Drunk. We're not dating. I don't even like her."

"Of course I'm not forcing you to be intimate," he replies. "I'm just telling you that you can't be intimate with anyone else." He has another smug, satisfied look on his face as he picks up his pen. "Let's do monthly video call check-ins so I can keep an eye on you lovebirds. I remind you that you'll remain under oath when we chat, so don't try to pull a fast one on me. I won't hesitate to put you in jail for perjury. I'll send your attorney all the information. Good day."

He cuts the feed abruptly, and his square on the screen goes black, leaving me with a sense of complete and total hopelessness.

You've never seen three more shocked faces than the three of us. Tanner breathes, "Wow. I've never seen anything like that in my life." He runs his fingers through his beard. "I'll try to appeal his decision, but I wouldn't get your hopes up. These retired judges are respected. No one likes to interfere with them. We got unlucky in getting one with an obvious axe to grind. I'm sorry, you two. You may have to weather this storm through the year."

We're both quiet. Still in complete and total shock.

In light of our silence, he says, "I'm...going to run. We'll talk later, D."

FIFTEEN

KENNEDY

I spent the rest of the Vegas trip in a bit of a fog. I couldn't even look at Daylen, let alone talk to him. He seemed to be feeling the same way as me and didn't glance my way. We didn't fight. It was as though the other didn't exist. I'm sure he was processing the gravity of our situation as much as I was. When Tanner disconnected the feed, I wordlessly walked out of Daylen's suite in shock and never looked back.

I guess we faked our way through the weekend successfully because no one asked me a single question about our demeanor. I can only assume the same went for him. I wouldn't know.

The only communication we've exchanged since Vegas was via text to set up two times to meet up this week. I can't believe it's come to this. I can't believe I'm going to be married to him for nine months, and that I can't have sex with anyone else during that time. I ordered five new vibrators on my way home. They're going to get a lot of use in the coming months. I haven't gone nine months without having sex since I started having sex.

With Booster hot on my heels, happily bouncing around like a moron in his new sneakers, I walk into practice and notice a familiar blonde woman in Beavers' merch shooting baskets with some of the girls on the team. She's super attractive, though tiny compared to the rest of us. She's probably nearing forty but looks to be in great physical shape. Where have I seen her before? What is she doing here? She's obviously not a new player.

Once everyone arrives, Coach Lakshmi blows her whistle for us all to huddle up. We take a knee as she, Coach Carroll, and the familiar blonde stand in front of us. Coach Lakshmi begins, "Ladies, we have a new Beaver staff member. This is Fallon Montgomery. As you know, Noah was fired after last season."

Noah was our team trainer. He was creepy as fuck, uncomfortably and unnecessarily touching all of us. When the season was over, I told Reagan how we all felt, and she fired him immediately without conducting an investigation or inquiring further. She said the fact that we were uncomfortable around him was reason enough for her.

Coach Lakshmi continues, "Fallon has an extensive background as a physical therapist. She's worked at Pennsylvania Hospital for years, rehabilitating those with major injuries. We're fortunate to have her with us now. As luck would have it, she was a highly decorated high school basketball player so she's going to help the coaching staff a bit when she's not busy managing your injuries and ailments. With Coach Carroll likely to be heavily pregnant during the summer, Fallon has kindly offered to handle some of the more physical tasks involved in coaching. Fallon has a daughter, Harper, who's nine years old. Harper will occasionally be around, so keep it clean." She stares right at me when saying that last part.

Sulley giggles. "Yes, Kennedy, keep it clean." She wiggles her eyebrows with amusement before looking back at the group. "I've met Harper. She's an awesome kid with a ridiculous vocabulary. We're excited to have her around, Fallon."

Fallon smiles in gratitude. "Thank you. I appreciate it. She's in school now and spends half her time with her dad, but she'll probably be with us a bit more as the summer approaches."

"Montgomery, as in Tanner Montgomery?" I ask.

She nods. "Yes. That's my ex-husband and Harper's father," she says with zero edge in her tone. "The three of us came to a lot of your home games last summer. Harper is a huge Anacondas fan, being that she loves softball so much, but I've been trying to convert her into being a Beavers fan too. Anyway, I'm excited for this change in my career." She winks at Sulley. "Our friend over there was relentless in pursuing me and helped talk me into it, but I think the change of scenery will be welcome, and the schedule is a bit more favorable for a working single mom like me."

I whisper to Sulley, "How do you know Fallon?"

She whispers back, "She helped to rehabilitate Bailey."

I nod in understanding. Bailey Hart was in a terrible car accident this past fall. Tanner was driving the car. She broke her back and had to relearn to walk. Apparently her recovery was nothing short of a miracle. Sulley and Bailey are friendly, and I know Sulley was in touch with Bailey throughout her recovery process.

Sulley continues, "And Bailey just married Tanner. She's now Harper's stepmom."

The fuck?

"Fallon helped rehabilitate her ex-husband's new wife?" I ask, my tone filled with shock.

She smiles. "And Bailey is pregnant with twins. I heard it was a shock to all, Bailey and Tanner included."

"The fuck?" I verbally express this time.

She giggles. "It's like a soap opera, right?"

"Yes, it is," I agree. "I don't understand how people accidentally get pregnant. Birth control isn't that fucking hard to manage. No glove, no love."

An indecipherable look crosses her face. I point at her. "You and I need to chat about a certain sexy quarterback and the fact that you were screaming from his hotel room all night."

She narrows her eyes at me. "Will this conversation include a certain sexy tight end and the fact that you were screaming from *his* hotel room all night?"

Definitely not. She's got me there. I don't respond.

She smiles in satisfaction as we both return our attention to our coaches. When the huddle breaks, Fallon walks over to me and takes my left hand in her right one. "Kennedy, right?"

I nod. "Yep. Last I checked."

"What happened to your finger, sweetie?"

My left finger is wrapped in white gauze, still very raw from the horrific tattoo. I need it to heal before I'm able to cover it with makeup. And then I need to figure out how the hell to have these things removed. It's supposedly a long, painful laser process that takes several months. I'm going to have to wait until after my season ends before I do anything.

"Oh," I stumble a bit, "I burned it on the stove," I lie. "It's fine. Nothing for you to worry about."

With a pretty face full of genuine concern, she rubs my arm in a maternal, comforting way I'm not used to. "Are you sure? Do you want me to take a quick look at it to make sure it's not infected? Burns are no joking matter. If bacteria invades the wound, an infection could take on a life of its own."

I shake my head. "It's fine. Really. I swear. Nothing more than a flesh wound."

"Okay. I'm here if you need me." She smiles kindly as she squeezes my hand before dropping it. "You're my daughter's favorite player. She wears your jersey to games all the time."

I point to myself in a bit of shock. "Me? Not Sulley? I thought *all* the little girls love Sulley."

She shakes her head. "Nope. It's you. She likes your toughness. She's *obsessed* with softball. Her stepmom is a pro player. Harper thinks you're more like a softball player because your style of play is so rough and tough. She loves watching you push people around. She gets the biggest kick out of it. I honestly think it's the only reason she comes to the games."

A bizarre sense of pride washes over me. I'm not used to any type of adoration from little girls. "Thanks for sharing that with me. I'd be happy to sign her jersey, take photos, or do anything else she needs."

"She'd truly love that. Thank you. Some of the Anacondas players came to her birthday party last year. It was like she died and went to sports heaven."

"That was nice of them. I've only met them in passing, but Sulley says they're a good crew."

She nods. "They're the best."

Once again, there's zero edge in her tone. You'd think one of the players marrying her ex-husband would give her sour grapes, but I sense none.

Hmm. I think I like Fallon Montgomery, certainly a lot more than I liked Creepy Noah.

DAYLEN

I wake in my bed with BJ practically on top of me. When I return from trips, she gets unusually clingy for a few days. I think she's afraid I'm going to leave her again.

I aimlessly stroke her head for a few moments, and she sighs in contentment. I suppose she's the only girl I'm going to have in my bed for a long while.

I look at my ring finger, currently wrapped in a Band-Aid. I guess I'll be wearing Band-Aids for the foreseeable future. Tattoo removal is a long process that will have to wait. My hands are a little too valuable right now.

My phone rings and I see that it's my father. I answer it right away, always happy to hear from him. "Hey, Dad," I say in a cheery tone.

"Hey, stud. How was Vegas?"

Isn't that a loaded question? I can't very well say, *I got drunk, got married to the woman who I hate most in this world, banged her, and now I'm stuck being married to her for nine months. Oh, and we are being forced to spend time together every week, which may or may not end with one of us murdering the other.*

Instead, I happily reply, "It was a blast, as always."

He breathes a sigh of relief. "Phew. Every year you go, I'm afraid you'll come home married to some prostitute like in the movie *The Hangover.*"

Not a prostitute, but does a bitchy basketball player count?

I let out a nervous laugh. "Ha! Not married to a prostitute." Technically, that's true. "I've never been the pay-for-sex type."

"That's because you're a stud muffin like me." He lets out one of his big laughs. The kind that never fails to make me smile.

"Yep. It's genetic. It's my curse for having such a hunk of a dad."

"Sure is," he chuckles. "Any special ladies in your life lately?" he asks in the same hopeful tone he uses each time this topic comes up.

"No one to speak of," I nervously reply.

"What's wrong, son? You don't sound like yourself."

I'm the worst liar ever. Especially to my father. I *never* lie to him. It physically pains me to be anything less than truthful with him. The fact is, he never judges me, but I know the sanctity of marriage means something special to him. He would be wildly disappointed in me for treating it so frivolously.

"Nothing," I answer. "I'm just tired. I might be a bit jet-lagged. I'm still in bed with BJ. She missed me."

"Oh, I hope I didn't wake you."

"No," I reply. "I was just getting up. We have a team workout." And then I have an afternoon date with my wife. I wisely keep that last part to myself.

"Okay. I'll let you go. One of these days, the right woman

will come along, and you'll be a goner. Just like I was with your mother and Ashleigh. I'm a lucky man. You'll hit the jackpot one day too. I have no doubt."

I love that even though he lost his wife so young, he always has a positive outlook on love, relationships, and life in general. That's how I need to handle this situation with Kennedy. I can't change the facts, but I can make the best of them. Moping around about it won't change anything. I don't want to be miserable for nine months. In the often-repeated words of Hank Humblecut, 'When life gives you lemons, make lemonade.'

"Thanks, Dad."

"For what?"

"For always knowing what I need to hear when I need to hear it. I love you, you big hunk of stud muffin sexiness."

"Back at you, you beefcake burrito."

I smile as I hang up, determined to make myself a big pitcher of lemonade.

VANCE ELBOWS ME. "Dude, what's wrong with you? You're so quiet. No jokes for the team?"

"Oh...umm...why did the sperm cross the road?"

"Why?" he asks.

"Because I put the wrong sock on this morning."

The guys all laugh from their various workout locations in our team gym. Even Coach cracks a smile.

My stomach lurches when I see him smiling at me. He's technically my father-in-law right now. How crazy is that? What will happen if he finds out about Vegas? Will he hate me? Cut me from the team? Kill me? All of the above?

"Coach, how was your pickleball tournament this past weekend?" I ask. He mentioned having one before we left.

His face falls. "I came in second place. If Kennedy were around, we would have won. Such a bummer."

Apparently, my wife is a good pickleball player. She's a freak of an athlete, so I suppose that makes sense.

I shrug. "I'm sure you'll win the trophy next time, Coach," I offer in a hopeful expression of support.

He crosses his arms. "Would you believe they tried to give us a second-place trophy? When I grew up, trophies were for first place only. Now they have tenth-place ribbons. What a joke. I *refused* the trophy," he announces with a large dose of pride.

Vance and I both chuckle. Coach is so funny. He doesn't even try to be funny, but he is.

Vance nods at me. "Want to run a few plays this afternoon?"

I shake my head. "I...umm...can't. I've got plans."

"With whom?" he asks.

Beau leans over and says, "I appreciate the correct use of grammar, Vance. Not everyone knows how to use *whom* properly when it functions as the object of a verb or preposition."

I have no idea what he just said, but Vance nods, so I do too.

"You're the master, Beau Fudd," Vance replies.

He winks. "That's what she said."

I let out a loud laugh at Beau's uncharacteristic humor.

He shrugs. "What? I can be dirty too."

I pound my chest. "I feel like I've imparted that wisdom to you. I'm proud of you."

He rolls his eyes, and I laugh before turning back to Vance. "Just an appointment." I don't want to lie to him. An appointment to spend time with my wife.

THREE HOURS LATER, I'm waiting in the park for Kennedy while I shoot hoops. I see her form tentatively approach. She's hard to miss. Exceedingly tall, attractive women don't grow on trees. And I'm noticing for the first time that she has a sway to her hips when she walks. Maybe when it comes to athletic wear, I'm used to seeing her in baggy basketball clothes. Today she's in tight leggings and a small, hooded zip-up sweatshirt that shows a hint of her flat, toned stomach.

I get flashes of her in bed in Vegas. The way her body moved under and over mine. Pieces of that night are slowly coming back to me, especially the sex. I keep replaying it in my mind. It was electric. There's no denying that.

I adjust my half-chub in my sports shorts, knowing she won't appreciate it making an appearance. I pull down my white T-shirt a bit, hoping to cover it.

As she approaches, I notice she looks so sad. I offer her a small smile when she draws closer. "Hey, wife," I joke to try and lighten things.

She stops short and throws her hands on her hips. "Don't call me that."

I shrug. "We've got to practice me calling you wife and you calling me husband. Wife, wife, wife. My wife is here to play ball. See, it's not hard. Now it's your turn to use husband in a sentence."

She thinks for a brief moment before giving me a smile full of attitude and saying, "My husband will be home in five minutes. You'd better crawl out the window to be safe."

I let out a laugh. "Oh shit, that was funny. See, we can have fun."

"Why is your laugh so damn loud?" she asks with a tone of embarrassment as she looks around to see if anyone heard me.

"Pft, you should hear my father. Your father-in-law," I jokingly remind her.

Her face immediately falls. "Stop."

Even though her hair is in a perfect ponytail and she's wearing makeup, I notice bags under her eyes. "You look tired, wife. Is something keeping you awake at night?" I ask.

She gives me a bit of an incredulous look as she exaggeratedly scratches her chin. "Hmm, what could it be?" she asks sarcastically. "Well, nothing big and stressful is going on in my life right now, so it must be something smaller. Oh, I know. I was up all night wondering how a blind person knows when to stop wiping."

If she thought my laugh earlier was loud, it's nothing compared to what comes out of my mouth at that comment.

She shivers. "Fuck, you're so loud. Do you realize every person in this park stopped what they were doing and looked this way when you laughed?"

"Can't help it. My wife is legit funny."

"I swear to god, Daylen. I will kill you in your sleep if you keep calling me that."

And just like that, I'm committed to calling her *wife* as much as possible. It's good to know marriage hasn't changed our dynamic.

"Got it, wife."

She exhales an annoyed breath of frustration. "Why are we here?"

"We're being forced to date," I answer. "Remember?"

"I know that. Why are we in the park where people can see us? And why are you holding a basketball?"

I shrug. "I figured joint meals at restaurants would make it look *more* like dates. Two athletes shooting hoops in the park isn't that big a deal."

"You do know I'm a professional basketball player, right? I just came from basketball practice. I don't need *more* basketball from a non-expert in the field."

I throw my shoulders back. "I'll have you know I was an all-conference basketball player in high school."

She lets out a laugh.

"What's so funny, wife? I was. I have the height for it."

"It's funny because that's a red flag of mine. Men who brag about their high school athletic awards."

I sigh. "Is everything I say and do a red flag of yours?"

"Pretty much," she answers without any hesitation.

"Mean bitches are a red flag for me," I spit in response but immediately regret my words. I don't want to fight with her. She just makes it so easy.

I run my fingers through my hair. "Listen, I'm not thrilled about this situation either, Kennedy. I'm just trying to make the best of it."

"You're making light of it. This is horrible. Gut-wrenching. Catastrophic. A—"

"I get it," I interrupt. "I'm not making light of it. I'm just trying to make the best of the cards we were dealt. We're in this for nine months, whether we like it or not. There's no sense in being miserable. It's a beautiful spring day. I thought it would be nice to be outside. I know a lot of female athletes use male athletes to work against. Is there anything in particular you want to work on? Maybe I can help."

She runs her bottom lip through her teeth before it pops out. "Can you dunk?"

"Of course."

She fidgets nervously. I'm not sure I've ever seen her nervous. It's kind of cute. "I can't. I've been trying for years. I worked on my vertical jump this off-season and am up an inch or two, but I still need at least two more full inches to have a chance at dunking. It feels impossible."

I grin. "You've seen me fly through the air to catch Vance's passes. I have a forty-three-inch vertical. Jumping is my middle name. I can definitely help. Let's work on it," I offer in a genuinely hopeful tone.

After a brief moment of hesitation, she nods. "Okay. Forty-three inches? For real?"

"My cock and my vertical are the same." I wink before I

turn and dribble over to the hoop, leap into the air, and dunk the ball with ease.

After retrieving the ball, I motion for her to come to me, which she does. "I have some drills my trainer does with me, and we'll do those too, but we can also work on your arm and leg interplay. You need both in sync to get extra height. You have strong leg muscles. It's clearly visible." I point to her legs. They're long and extremely well-defined. "You obviously spend time in the gym. You must have your dad's work ethic."

She rolls her eyes. "I have his coloring. Eyes and hair. That's about all I want from him."

"What's the deal with you two?" I ask.

"He was an absentee father. I barely saw him when I was growing up. He was married to football, not his family."

I twist my lips. "I'm surprised to hear that. He's so involved with Pierce."

"How many times have you met my brother?"

I shrug. "I don't know. Hundreds. I feel like I've watched him grow up in our locker room."

She nods. "Exactly. You've played for my father for a decade. How many times did we meet before Layla brought us together?"

My shoulders fall in realization. "Zero."

She nods again. "Right. I was in high school when you started playing for him, yet we never met. Nannies raised us. I'm not sure what happened after I left for college because I rarely come home, but my parents were never around for us when I was growing up. I'm happy that Pierce is having a different experience, but it wasn't mine."

"Both of them? Your mom too?" I ask.

"She's worse than him. *Way* worse. I tolerate him now and then, but I don't speak to her at all. I can't even look at her."

"Why?"

She grabs the ball from my hands and starts dribbling toward the basket while shouting back, "Enough marital therapy for the day. Let's play ball. Time for me to kick your ass, Humblecut." She easily lays the ball into the basket and places her hands on her hips. "Let's see what you've got, Mr. High-School-All-Conference."

She proceeds to kick my ass for the remainder of the afternoon, but it's the most fun we've ever had together. Maybe there's hope for us to get through the next nine months relatively unscathed.

SIXTEEN

KENNEDY

"Ah, that hurts," I whine to Fallon as I lie on one of the padded tables in our training room.

She kneads her fingers through my right quad muscle. "I need to work out these knots. I don't feel like this should be happening to you from your team's practices and workouts. Are you doing any extra-strenuous activities I'm not aware of?" she asks.

"For the past month or so, I've been doing some…extra training with a friend to work on my vertical. I want to be able to dunk. I think I'm getting a little closer," I tell her hopefully.

Daylen and I have channeled our bi-weekly dates into training sessions for me. It's honestly been a lot of fun, and my vertical is clearly improving. He brings a measuring apparatus each time we meet, and I've added another full inch to my vertical leap. I think I'm only one more inch away from making my dream of dunking a basketball a reality.

She shakes her head. "You guys practice twice a day, and you hit the gym most mornings. You're overdoing it, and now your body is revolting." She points to my ankle. "And I see some swelling from when you turned it at practice this morning."

I mumble, "I was trying to hide that."

She raises an unamused eyebrow. "Don't hide things from me. I see everything. Do you have your period right now?"

"Holy shit, you do see everything. Why do you know that?"

"A woman's body is more susceptible to injuries, especially ligament injuries, when she's on her period. It's got something to do with the added hormones in your body. I'm sorry, Kennedy, but I'm shutting you down for the rest of the week."

"What?" I yell out. "No fucking way. The season is about to start. I can't shut down now."

Harper lifts her head and gasps from her seat, coloring at Fallon's desk. "Kennedy. No cursing. You owe me a bag of Skittles. You're very capricious with your word choices."

Harper Montgomery is officially the coolest kid I've ever met in my life. She's like a mini adult. Her vocabulary is insane. Apparently she has word of the day toilet paper and remembers to use the words in her daily conversation. I think *my* vocabulary has increased tenfold since meeting her just a few weeks ago.

Despite having a slightly darker hue to her hair than Fallon, she otherwise looks just like her mother, meaning she's gorgeous. They both have button noses and blue eyes that are nearly turquoise. Harper is a lucky little girl in more ways than one.

Fallon has quickly become my friend. More than a friend. A confidant. I almost told her about the Vegas wedding last week. She's just so easy to talk to and has taken a genuine interest in my life, always asking questions, and always vested in my answers. For the first time in my life, I have an older woman who I look up to. She's not quite fifteen years older than me, but she's a mother and acts like one. A *real* one. Watching her interactions with Harper shows me what motherly love and affection are supposed to look like. I know I'd be less fucked up if Fallon was my mother. I would have done anything to be loved the way Harper is so obviously and outwardly loved.

Fallon also does way more than I'm guessing she's under contract to do for the Beavers. She talks to us about our diets, clearly fascinated by the science of food intake and muscle building. I know Beau believes in that too. I think I'm pretty good about what I eat, but I don't make myself crazy. I'm lucky I don't have to. Yet.

She's also participatory in practices with an endless supply of energy. Coach Carroll's belly is getting bigger by the minute. Fallon steps in all the time to help with the more physical drills. She's like the Energizer Bunny, and every single person on this team loves the breath of fresh air she brings to our group.

I jokingly narrow my eyes at Harper. "Why do you like Skittles so much?"

Her chin drops in shock. "Because it's the greatest candy ever created. Mommy says every woman has a sweet tooth. There's one sweet item that's their weakness, and they can't live without it. It's a rite of passage, and it's okay to indulge from time to time." She whispers, "Mommy indulges every night in her weakness."

"What's her weakness? I need to know how to bribe her to clear me to play."

Fallon covers Harper's mouth, but Harper manages to mumble, "Rum raisin ice cream."

Fallon scrunches her nose. "Traitor."

Harper giggles. "It's true. Mommy eats a pint of it every night I sleep at her house."

"Harper," Fallon jokingly chastises, "enough with the big mouth."

I both love and envy their relationship. Even though I know Fallon shares equal custody with Tanner, she and Harper are just as close as mothers and daughters are supposed to be. I missed out on so much by having a shitty mother.

Harper and I smile at each other. I offer her a high-five. "Thanks for the intel. You just earned yourself two bags of Skittles."

She smacks my hand hard and then pumps her fist. "Yes!"

I look back at Fallon and then point to my thigh. "Can we negotiate this? I don't want to be shut down the whole week. It's an important week."

Our season begins in two weeks. I can't be shut down now when the intensity of practices is reaching its height. Our team is gelling. We could very well make a run for the championship this year.

Fallon toggles her head back and forth in contemplation. "Three days. Give me three days of solid rest, and then I'll reevaluate. If I feel any tightness in the leg or see any swelling in the ankle, I'm extending it. Get as much protein, fruit, and veggies as possible into your diet. Make yourself a good piece of steak or salmon for dinner each night. Lunch too."

Harper hangs on every word her mother says as if it's gospel. She nods in agreement and says, "Daddy is crazy about Bailey's diet with my sisters in her belly. He makes her dinner every night and forces her to make it all gone. I heard him whisper to her the other night that he was going to spank her if she didn't finish her veggies. The weird thing is that Bailey smiled. It was like she wanted to get spanked."

I can't help but let out a laugh. Fallon and I share bemused looks, and she says, "Yep, that sounds like your father."

As if on cue, Bailey walks into the training room and asks, "What sounds like Tanner?"

Fallon and I remain tight-lipped, but Loose Lips Little Harper responds, "That Daddy spanks you if you don't finish your veggies."

Bailey stops short and pinches her lips together, trying to fight a smile. She shakes her head. "Your father is the worst whisperer on the face of the planet."

Fallon lets out a laugh as she walks toward Bailey and pulls her into the warmest embrace. They act like best friends, not like an ex-wife and a current wife.

She rubs Bailey's back, "How do you feel?"

Bailey exhales a long breath. "Tired. I'm always so darn tired."

Fallon nods. "When I was pregnant with Harper, I'd sleep under my desk or in my car during my lunch breaks. I can take her tonight if you need to rest."

Bailey shakes her head. "No, I promised Harper a few rounds in the batting cage tonight. Plus, don't you have a hot date?" Bailey wiggles her eyebrows up and down.

Fallon's eyes widen a bit. She probably doesn't want Harper knowing about her love life. She calmly offers, "I can always cancel my plans if you need me. It's not a big deal."

Bailey squeezes her hand. "Not necessary, but thank you. Harper has a big game tomorrow. We need to hit the cages hard tonight, right, sweet girl?" She smiles at Harper.

Harper nods enthusiastically. "Yes, my championship game is tomorrow." She turns to me. "Bails and Kam coach my team. Do you know Kamryn Hart? She and Bails are twins, but they're nothing alike, even though they look alike. Some people can't tell them apart, but I can. Daddy says Bails is sweet as pie and that Kam is a pain in the A-S-S. But Kam is super funny. And now she lets me call her Aunt Kam. I play second base just like Bails. Sulley came to my championship game last year. Do you want to come to my championship game this year?"

The kid talks a mile a minute. Sometimes it's hard to keep up.

Before I can process all that information, Fallon says, "Sweetie, I think Kennedy is busy tomorrow night. Maybe another time."

"I'm not," I happily announce. "I'd love to come, Harper." It might be fun to see her in action.

Harper's eyes widen. "For realz?"

I nod. "For realz."

"Awesome," she exclaims with a huge level of excitement. "I

can't wait to tell Andie. She's one of my two best friends and my teammate. She's the shortstop. She—"

Bailey clamps her hand over Harper's mouth. "Miss Motor Mouth and I are going to head out." She winks at Fallon with a small smile. "Have fun tonight. Call me in the morning with all the juicy details. Love you."

Fallon sighs. "Love you too. Feel good. I'll see you at your game tomorrow, Harper."

Harper waves before Bailey removes her hand. "Bye, Mommy. Love you millions."

Fallon smiles. "Love you billions."

Harper responds, "Love you trillions," before Bailey physically removes her from the room.

I look at Fallon. "I love your kid. She's a riot."

"Hmm," she responds as she begins wiping down her equipment. "She's something. You don't have to come tomorrow. I'm sorry if you felt cornered."

I shake my head. "Not at all. According to my pain in the ass physical therapist, I can't do anything but sit anyway. I might as well sit and watch your little prodigy play ball."

She giggles. "Fair enough. Thank you. She'll be flipping over you being there. I appreciate it very much."

I look out the door to make sure Bailey and Harper are gone. When it appears as though they are, I ask, "Knowing Bailey is married to your ex-husband doesn't bother you? I can't believe how well you two get along."

She shrugs. "What's the alternative? Should we hate each other because society tells us we're supposed to? I happen to adore Bailey. She's a wonderful person. Tanner and I have been divorced for nearly seven years. Bailey had nothing to do with it. They're good together, and she loves Harper like she's her own. What more could I ask for in a stepmother? At the end of the day, it's about what's best for my daughter. The three of us having a healthy co-parenting relationship is best for her. She's happy and thriving. We're doing something right."

I absorb her words. "You're so…mature."

She lets out a laugh. "Oh, trust me, I have my moments of immaturity too. I'm constantly questioning my life decisions. Switching from my hospital job to this one was among the biggest. I still don't know if I did the right thing, but I can tell you this job is more fun and certainly pays better."

"You *definitely* made the right decision. Everyone on the team loves you. We hated your predecessor. No one would come see him and would instead let their injuries fester."

She scrunches her face. "That's no good." She sighs. "Are you sure about tomorrow? Feel free to change your mind."

"It's fine," I assure her as I pull out my phone. "I just need to cancel my plans."

Daylen and I were supposed to work out, but I'm on Fallon-mandated rest anyway. It can wait. We'll have to find another way to get in our two dates this week.

DAYLEN

"When strippers get money with jizz on it, they have to report it to the IRS. It's reported as gross income," I smirk as I announce that little tidbit at Tanner's poker table.

All the guys start laughing. Tanner, Layton, Trey, and Vance are here. Cheetah texted that he's running late, which is code for banging Kam.

"Speaking of jizz," Vance announces, "D is having a bit of a dry spell. I haven't seen him go home with a woman in weeks." He looks at me with some uncharacteristic mischief in his eyes. "When was the last time you got laid, D?"

He's awfully opinionated for a guy who rarely used to get laid but is now secretly banging Sulley every chance he gets.

His once sour demeanor is downright cheerful right now. It's off-putting.

"Hmm," I twist my lips as if I don't know the exact minute I last got laid. It's my biggest dry spell since I started having sex, and there's nothing I can do about it. "I'm not sure of the date, but let's just say I'm at the point where my bills come more times a month than I do."

The guys all laugh again, but then they all share amused glances. "What am I missing?" I ask as I pop a celery stick into my mouth.

Layton shrugs. "That's what happens right before you find the right one. You start to get fed up with the whole faceless, nameless, emotionless sex scene. The right woman enters your life and, *bam*," he shouts, "she grabs you by the heart and the balls and there's no looking back."

Trey nods. "He speaks the truth. Listen to the man. I suppose the real question is, have you met *the one* and who is she?"

I have zero hesitation when I respond, "Definitely not," but then I feel like I've betrayed Kennedy for some reason. Yes, she's my fake wife, but she's still technically my wife. Maybe the hate isn't as strong as it once was, but it's not like we're friends. Okay, I suppose we've sort of become friends over the past month. Maybe I enjoy our workouts. Maybe I look forward to them a little more than I should. But *the one*? Hell no.

Bang. Bang.

I look at Tanner. "What the fuck is that noise? It's been going on all night."

He smiles. "Bailey and Harper are in the batting cage." Tanner had a professional-grade batting cage installed for Harper so she could practice whenever she wants. "Harper's championship game is tomorrow night. I'm pretty sure she'll be out there all night."

"How's Bailey feeling?" I ask.

"Tired, but otherwise good."

Trey wiggles his eyebrows up and down. "Is she horny all the time? Gemma was on sex crack when she was pregnant."

Layton nods in agreement. "So was Arizona." Arizona just gave birth a few weeks ago. They have a little girl named Ryan. She's so adorable, with light blonde hair like her mom.

Tanner raises one of his dark, thick eyebrows. "I'm not into locker room chitchat. You all know that." Tanner never talks about his sex life. Even before Bailey, he was always tight-lipped. A small smile finds his lips though. "But let's just say I'll be looking to wrap this up early so I can feed the beast."

We all chuckle as Cheetah races down the stairs. "Sorry, I was late. Duty called." He doesn't look sorry at all. Lucky fucker.

Layton turns to him. "You were the last to arrive. What do you have for us? Hit me with some smart shit. At a minimum, you must be getting smarter by banging Kam."

Kam might be the only person I know who's smarter than Beau.

Cheetah nods as if in thought. "You know what? I think I *am* getting smarter. Intelligence by penetration. I'll have to research if that's a real thing."

"Well?" Layton prods, waiting for an answer.

The Cougars play a game of whoever is last to arrive has to give the group a random fun fact. It's kind of interesting, and no one is better than Cheetah and Kam at coming up with those fun facts.

Cheetah thinks for a brief moment before answering, "Men and women are either right or left-nippled. One is always more sensitive than the other. Kam is left-nippled. It drives her a little crazier when I lick around her left cupcake cap."

Like morons, each of us starts tweaking our own nipples, trying to figure out which one is more sensitive.

"What are you preposterous men doing?" Harper's little voice intrudes.

We all turn as she and Bailey stand at the bottom of the steps to the mancave basement, staring at us. Tanner clears his throat as we quickly remove our hands from our own nipples. "Oh, sweetie, Cheetah told us one of his interesting facts. We were just confirming it."

Harper gasps. "I love fun facts. Aunt Kam has a ton of them."

Tanner makes a look of disgust. He may love Bailey Hart, but he barely tolerates Kamryn. "Hmm, no doubt she's full of them. This fact was that the heart is not technically on the left side of your chest, as we're often told. It's in the middle, just slightly left of center. Not all the way over. We were trying to feel our heartbeats to confirm that."

Harper's little eyebrows shoot together as she feels around the top of her chest. "Hmm, I'm not sure I feel it."

Tanner looks almost relieved. "Well, next time you go to the doctor, be sure to ask her and let us know if it's true.

She nods. "I will."

Within ten seconds, she bounces onto my lap, "What's up, Uncle Daylen?" She looks at my cards. "Oh wow, three kings, that's a great hand."

I don't have three kings. The mini genius is a card shark. Bailey and Kam are professional-level poker players, and they taught Harper how to play. The little hustler conned us out of hundreds of dollars just a few weeks ago at Tanner's bachelor party.

Harper and Bailey shared bemused looks. Layton narrows his eyes at Harper. "Does he really have three kings?"

She shrugs. "I'll guess you'll have to throw more money in the pot to find out, Uncle Layton."

Harper looks up at me and winks. Little fucking devil. I love this kid.

After I win the hand, thanks to the ringer in my lap, I feel my phone buzz. Pulling it out, I see that it's Kennedy.

Wifey: Can we reschedule tomorrow?

Why am I hit with a pang of disappointment? I look forward to our twice-weekly practice sessions.

Me: Sure thing. Everything okay, wife?

Wifey: I better not still be listed as wifey in your contacts. You're listed as dickless in mine.

Me: The way you were limping in Vegas suggests otherwise.

Wifey: Can you feel my eyes rolling?

Me: I can! Know that you're just a black flag emoji in my contacts. Black like your soul.

Wifey: You flatter me. You're not really dickless in mine. You're a red flag emoji.

Me: Your husband would like to know why you're canceling our date.

Wifey: I'm going to a nine-year-old's softball game.

I glance down at the little nine-year-old softball player in my lap. She smiles up at me. "Who's wifey?"

"You're a nosy little thing. I'll give you a carton of Skittles if you promise not to tell anyone at this table about the name wifey."

"Make it two cartons," she immediately negotiates.

I narrow my eyes at her. "You're a con artist. One carton, and I'll come to your game tomorrow night."

Her eyes light up. "Really?"

I nod. "Yes."

"Deal."

We do our little, semi-complicated handshake that we've perfected throughout the years.

Me: I happen to have a very cute nine-year-old softball stud helping me win at poker right now. Am I correct to assume it's Harper's game?

Wifey: Yes. Coolest. Kid. Ever.

Me: True. I was thinking of coming to that game too.

Okay, I thought of it ten seconds ago when I found out Kennedy was going.

Wifey: See you there. That can count as one of our forced dates.

Ouch.

Me: What are you up to tonight?

Wifey: Watching a movie and deciding which vibrator to use. I have a variety of them on hand to keep me on my toes...and to help make those toes curl.

Me: Can I watch?

Wifey: No, perv.

Me: ...the movie? Always assuming the worst of me, wifey.

Wifey: I'm usually right. Warning: the movie might be girlie.

Me: I love girlie movies. You know my taste in music. Doesn't it make sense that I would like girlie movies too?

Wifey: Fair point. Fine. See you in a bit.

I lift Harper off my lap and stand. "Gotta go, boys."

"Breaking your dry spell?" Vance asks.

"BJ needs me," I answer.

Harper looks at Vance. "What's a dry spell?"

I smile. "I'll let you handle that. See ya."

With a bizarre and unexpected rush of excitement, I head straight over to Kennedy's apartment. I haven't been here since her drunken New Year's Eve debacle. I wait for her annoyingly slow elevator and eventually arrive at her door, where I excitedly knock on it.

She opens it looking like she did the morning after in Vegas. Messy hair and not an ounce of makeup. She's in tiny shorts and a tank top without a bra. I smile. "I see you got dressed up for me."

She flips me the bird.

"You know it's my favorite look on you, wifey."

She rolls her eyes. "I look dreadful. It's because I couldn't even get myself off with my vibrator. My body is so damn sick of silicone stimulation. It needs dick. Real, soft-skinned, hard-muscled, veiny, angry dick that reaches deep inside me until I can't see straight."

I raise my hand. "I volunteer as tribute."

She makes a look of disgust. "Ew. No. Do you think I'd dress like this if I thought I might have a chance of getting laid?" She exhales a breath. "I can't believe we still have seven months and seventeen days of this."

I chuckle. "Do you have a countdown?"

She nods. "Yes I do. I'm gonna fuck ten guys one minute

after the annulment is finalized. Every hole, orifice, crack, crevice. *Everywhere* on my body will get drilled."

I adjust myself. "Fuck, that's hot. Can I watch?"

She sighs as she turns and walks toward her living room, shouting back, "I opened a bottle of wine. Want a glass?"

"Sure," I answer. I'm not a big wine guy but I don't want to be difficult.

We sit on her sofa, and she pours me a glass. Taking my first sip, I know right away it's the good stuff. I pick up the bottle and read it aloud. "2018 Screaming Eagle?"

It's not a cheap bottle at all. In fact, it's damn expensive.

She shrugs. "It's the closest to screaming that I'll be getting for another seven months and seventeen days." She takes a sip and closes her eyes as if savoring the taste. "Yum, this is the good stuff. This wine's history is more complex than your entire personality."

I smile. "Did you get this expensive little habit from your father?"

Coach Jeffries is obsessed with good wines. I know he maintains a huge collection in his wine cellar and is known to take a lot of time to order it at restaurants. He's probably the only other person I've ever had wine with.

Her shoulders fall. "I suppose. I started stealing wine from his cellar at thirteen. I didn't appreciate how much the bottles were worth at the time. Then when I got older and started drinking shitty wine, I could taste the difference. It's kind of a curse, to be honest. At least with my expensive clothes, I can wear them again and again. With wine, it's gone once you drink it. Another in a long line of problems gifted to me by my parents."

I open my mouth as she holds up her hand. "Don't ask. I'm not talking about it with you. I don't discuss it with friends, let alone frenemies."

"Ooh, we've graduated to frenemies?" I ask with excitement.

She twists her lips. "I suppose you're more tolerable than you used to be."

"Back at you, Cruella. You're more like the redeemable villain instead of the irredeemable villain now."

"How lucky for me," she says with a heavy dose of sarcasm. She grabs for the remote. "There's a documentary on the making of *Cobra Kai*. It's my favorite show. Do you mind if we watch that?"

"What?" I shout. "That's *my* favorite show."

She tries to fight it, but a small smile forms on her face. "About time Johnny got to be the good guy. He was always the good guy, but nobody else saw it."

I gasp. "I have a T-shirt with that written on it."

She giggles. "Stop it. You're making fun of me."

"I'm serious. Dixie Chicks serious."

She lets out a laugh at my *Pitch Perfect* movie line reference. "I'm guessing you love that girlie movie?"

"Of course. It's one of the best movies ever. BJ loves to sing to it."

"Your dog sings?"

"Yes, she has a majestic voice."

"Hmm. I might have to see it one day."

"You can't. She hates women."

"All women?"

"All except my sister. She doesn't like to share me."

She sighs in disbelief as she turns on the documentary. We watch in comfortable silence for about an hour. My hands are clasped together behind my head, causing my T-shirt to lift a drop. I see her eyes staring directly at my tattoo, though she's trying unsuccessfully to hide that fact.

"You can ask me about it if you want," I eventually offer.

"About what?" she asks.

"The tattoo. You're staring. You've mentioned it before. I'm an open book. Ask whatever you want to know."

She chews her lip nervously for about ten seconds. I have

flashbacks to what those lips felt like on my lips, on my chest, on my neck, on my cock. They're so plush and feminine. I love them without lipstick even more. They have a natural pink hue. I bet women pay for lipstick in a shade that she has naturally, yet she always chooses to cover them. I have an urge to storm into her bedroom and throw out all her lipsticks.

She eventually interrupts my thoughts by admitting, "Fine. I want to know. Who is she? Your high school girlfriend? College girlfriend? The love of your life? The one that got away?"

I lift my shirt a bit more, and her eyes move all over my stomach. If I didn't know better, I'd think lust was washing over them. She even goes so far as to lick her pretty pink lips. I don't think she's aware that she did it, but she did.

"Look closer," I instruct.

"Is this just a way to get me to put my head in your lap?"

I chuckle. "No, but I might use that in the future. It's a good tactic. Thanks for the tip."

She rolls her eyes before bending a bit to get a closer look. She gently rubs her fingers over the rose, starting at the flower itself and then working down the stem. I see the moment it hits her. "Are these birth and death years?"

I nod. "My mom. Her name was Rose. My dad and I both got them shortly before he got remarried. It was his way of telling me that while he might be marrying another woman, she wasn't taking the place of my mother for me or for him. That he would always love my mother."

She lifts her head back up. "Was your stepmom pissed?"

I shake my head. "Not that I know of. She's kind of ditzy, but she doesn't have a bad bone in her body. I despised their age difference, but she makes him happy, she's good to him, and she gave me my little sister, who's the most important person to me in the world. If he hadn't married Ashleigh, I wouldn't have Jagger."

Her face softens a bit as she nods in understanding. "I'm

trying to build a better relationship with Pierce. I've been a shitty big sister for most of his life, but I'm doing my best to make up for it now."

"He can't be that mad. I think he came to every home game of yours last season. You can hear him cheering for you all over the stadium."

She smiles. "You're right. It was awesome to have him there. He knows my stats better than I do."

"He's a good kid, Kennedy."

She nods. "I know."

"It's not too late."

Her eyes uncharacteristically fill with tears. "I hope you're right."

She shifts a bit and stretches her back as if it's stiff.

"Do you want me to rub your shoulders like a good hubby is supposed to?" I offer.

Her eyes widen a bit. "What made you ask that?"

"When I carried you home drunk on New Year's Eve, you told me no less than a thousand times that you measured a good marriage by shoulder rubbing. That you never once saw your father rub your mother's shoulders, but your friends' dads did. That it's probably why you love having your shoulders rubbed as much as you do. You then begged me to rub them."

"Did you do it?" she asks softly.

I smile. "I did…over the toilet."

She smacks my arm, and then I tickle her side, but she doesn't laugh. "You're not ticklish?" I ask.

She shakes her head with a mischievous smile. "If a woman doesn't like to be tickled, it means she likes to be choked. And you know firsthand how much I like to be choked."

I gulp as I will my dick to stay down at the thought of wrapping my hands around her neck again.

Not able to help myself, I slowly run my fingertips over the smooth, firm skin of her neck. The bruising is long gone, though I have the sudden need to give it to her again. To mark her as mine again.

I expect her to slap my hand away, but she doesn't. Her eyelids flutter, and she emits a sound that's something between a breath and a moan.

It goes on for a bit, but I eventually move my hand to her shoulder. "Come sit on the floor in front of me. I'll rub your shoulders like a good hubby is supposed to."

She wordlessly nods as she does as she's told, and I think to myself, *good girl.*

SEVENTEEN

DAYLEN

"What's the difference between a mosquito and a hooker?" I ask Beau, Champ, Presley, and a few other guys in the team kitchen at our practice facility.

"What?" Presley asks in reply.

"When I slap a mosquito, it stops sucking."

The guys all laugh while we watch Beau work the blender like a bartender with nearly the entire team lined up to indulge in the fruits of his labor. He's finally making us those Boner Shakes. He insists that if we drink them now, the muscle building we'll have tomorrow will be next level. He said we'll feel stronger than we ever have in our lives, and we'll be able to increase the weights dramatically. I'm excited to try it.

Not having sex for the past two months has forced me to focus on some other areas of my life. I haven't gone out as much because I'm not on the prowl, so drinking has been cut to a bare minimum. I've been waking up earlier and exercising more. I feel stronger than I ever have, and apparently tomorrow I'll be the strongest I've ever been in my life.

Beau has managed to talk nearly the entire team into trying it. Everyone believes in Beau. He's so damn smart and so full of knowledge. I'm always learning new things from the guy.

Vance isn't out of the locker room yet, but I take it upon myself to order him one too. I'm sure he'll want to try it.

Like he always seems to when I tell dirty jokes, Coach walks in and hears the punchline. He glares at me. "I don't want to know the joke. The punchline was enough for me. You're going to have to grow up at some point, Humblecut." He shakes his head. "God help the unlucky woman who's saddled with you one day."

The other guys chuckle, but I have to fake my smile. If he finds out about my marriage to Kennedy, I wholeheartedly believe he'll kill me. Instead, I offer him a Boner Shake. "Beau is making Bon...I mean protein shakes. Would you like one, Coach? He says we'll feel like Superman at our workout tomorrow if we drink it now."

Coach turns to Beau. "That true, Fudd?"

Beau nods curtly. "Yes, sir. It's a proven formula. It will be the best workout of your life. Guaranteed."

"Any potential side effects? I'm not young like you lot."

Beau gives him an uncharacteristically tentative smile. "Well...umm...you'll be stronger in everything you do. *Everything,*" he adds with a heavy dose of suggestiveness and emphasis.

Coach remains clueless. "Fantastic. Maybe my eyes will reap the benefits, and I won't need my reading glasses tomorrow." He smiles as he downs the shake in one large succession of gulps.

Beau and I trade glances. He's nervous. Are the boners from this shake that different from regular boners? I've basically been a walking boner for the past two months. How much worse could it be?

KENNEDY

"Whose house are you sleeping at tonight?" I ask my brother as he, Booster, and I sit at the fancy steakhouse I'm taking them to because I've been on a major protein kick for the past few weeks, and I'm doing my best to spend as much time with Pierce before my summer season begins.

"Mom's," he answers before shifting uncomfortably and scrunching his face. "She's bringing her new boyfriend to your opening night game tomorrow."

He doesn't look happy about it.

"How old is the guy?" I inquire.

Pierce shrugs. "I don't know. I haven't met him yet, but she wants me to meet him tomorrow. I don't want to. All I asked both of them was to either date when I wasn't around or to wait until I leave for college, which is in less than three months. I don't know why she felt compelled to introduce me to someone now."

"Because she's a bitch who only cares about herself. What about Dad and his bevy of bimbos? That doesn't bother you?"

He gives me a look of complete and total confusion. "What bimbos? Dad doesn't date. Or if he does, he never lets on. He's respected my wishes. I've never once seen him with a woman, and he always makes sure to be home on the nights I stay with him."

Now it's my turn to be confused. "Then why does he post all those thirst trap videos of himself working out?"

Pierce lets out a laugh. "Do you honestly think Dad would do that, or even know how to do that? He doesn't have social media. He only just got a real phone last fall."

That's true. I had a similar thought when I saw his new phone.

"Who posts those videos?"

Pierce smirks. "Daylen, obviously. He takes sneaky videos of Dad when he's not looking. I've done it with Daylen a few times. You can even hear us laughing in some of the posts. He's such a funny guy. He created those accounts right after the divorce. I think he thought he was being a good wingman, but then the silver fox thing took on a life of its own. I'm not sure he still does it, but now people just take old videos and splice them into content. It's kind of gross, albeit funny as hell. The best part is that Dad is totally clueless."

I lean back in my chair in a bit of shock. "So he doesn't post those shirtless videos of himself?"

"Fuck no. Dad would never do that. Not in a million years. I doubt he knows the term thirst trap, let alone would participate in one knowingly."

I'm going to kill Daylen. I should have known.

I'm a clusterfuck of emotions over the guy. On one hand, I hate him; on the other, I dream about those hands. They're big and strong, and when they were back on my body massaging me a few weeks ago, I almost combusted. I kept willing him to move them lower from my shoulders, but he didn't. He proceeded to give me the best shoulder rub imaginable. For over an hour, I couldn't pay attention to the show we were watching.

At least when he left, my new vibrators got the workout of a lifetime. I'm sure it's nothing about me suddenly being attracted to him and more about the lack of sex in my life. I crave physical contact. I miss it terribly, and that night was the only kind I've had in two months.

And I felt something strange in my chest when we were at Harper's game together. He and Harper had this whole intricate, choreographed handshake. It was like my ovaries actually swooned at how sweet and gentle he is with her.

Gah. What the fuck is wrong with me? I'm getting soft in my old age.

Pierce continues, "Dad is the nicest guy on the planet. He

offered to get himself another seat tomorrow night so Mom's boyfriend can have his. I think Vance got him an extra ticket."

I think about what Fallon said that day in the training room. About it being better for Harper to keep the peace. I guess that's what my dad is doing. Keeping the peace for Pierce's sake. It's a shame my mother can't do what's right for Pierce. If he asked her to keep her love life on the down low, why would she insist on bringing a boyfriend to a public venue like my game? It's basically shoving it in my father and Pierce's faces. Typical for her.

I decide it's best to switch topics. "Are you two excited about rooming together this fall?"

They're going to a college right here in Philly. Pierce told me that his final decision was weighted heavily by his desire for him and me to be geographically close so we can continue rebuilding our bond.

They both nod enthusiastically. "Queen," Booster says, "I'd like to continue my internship with you if you don't mind."

I shake my head. "No." His face falls until I add, "I think it should be a job. An internship was good while you were in high school, but now it should be more. I'll only let it continue if you let me pay you. It can't be much, I don't have a lot, but I want to pay you for the time you give me."

His face lights up. "Really? I'd do it for free. I love being around you and your friends. You're all so much fun. And it's good for my resume."

"Absolutely. We'll figure out a fair salary and appropriate times with your class schedule. You're going to be a busy college man. I don't want you spending too much time doing my errands. Maybe a few hours a week. Oh, and I got Reagan Daulton to agree to make you the official towel boy. So now you get to be on the bench for all our home games this season. And she's paying you for it."

He gasps with a huge smile. "Ahh," he squeals like a girl. "Thanks, Queen. You're the best."

Pierce mouths, "Thank you," and despite the insanity of my marriage, I'm feeling good for the first time in a long time. It's like removing men from my life has given me more time to reflect on what I want. I have clarity I haven't ever had before.

Repairing my relationship with my brother is priority one for me, and I'm excited we're well on our way. I'm equally excited about the women in my life. I have a solid and supportive female group of friends. Feeling like people have my back is new for me. Fallon and I discussed it the other day while she was working on my leg, which healed nicely. She told me she has a circle of women in her life who have become her lifeline and maintaining those relationships is important.

It's only been a few months, but having a strong, stable, nurturing maternal figure in my life has given me an inner peace that I didn't know was missing. I'm so grateful for Fallon coming into my life.

We had a conversation recently about my father. She strongly encouraged me to rebuild my relationship with him. She encouraged me to rebuild my relationship with my mother too, but she doesn't have all the facts. Fallon is close with her parents and credits them with getting her through the lows of her divorce. Between that and what Pierce told me tonight, it's given me a lot to consider when it comes to my father. It won't be overnight, but I want to try to find a place for him in my life.

Speaking of Fallon, she's now officially an assistant coach. She was anyway, but Coach Carroll is on bed rest. There were some complications with her pregnancy, and she's gone for the season. It was a no-brainer to move Fallon into that role. Every single person on the team is happy about it. Fallon insisted on maintaining her role as our trainer too, so now she has two jobs.

I TOSS and turn throughout most of the night, exactly what I don't need the night before my first game of the season. I think I ate a bad piece of shrimp because I got sick as soon as I got home, but I drank about two gallons of water to make sure I won't be dehydrated for my game, and my stomach is feeling fine now.

I texted Pierce and Booster. They both had the same reaction. That was an expensive steakhouse. It's such bullshit that we got spoiled shrimp, but at least the three of us are feeling better after expelling the bad food.

What I really needed was a few orgasms to help me get a good night's sleep, but the silicone orgasms aren't the same as the touch of a man. Sadly, there's only one man on my mind right now.

I've replayed my time with Daylen over and over again throughout the past two months. The big asshole has managed to worm his way inside. I hate how much I've begun to look forward to our dates; almost sad on the evenings I don't get to see him. His previously annoying jokes are now somehow funny to me. Our hate-banter has become lighter and fun, given that neither of us truly means it anymore. We've sort of become… friends.

When we had our monthly counseling session with the judge the other night, we were practically finishing each other's sentences. We've learned one another inside and out without realizing we were doing it. It was bizarre. I've never had that with a man before. He seemed as shocked as I was by our knowledge of each other's subtle nuances.

Judge Deathbed had a self-satisfied look on his face the whole time. I had to throw in some jabs about Daylen just to wipe the smug smile off his face.

It's early in the morning. The sun hasn't even made its way over the horizon just yet. I'm going to give an orgasm one last shot, hoping it will help to give me another hour or two of sleep before the sun comes up and I have to start my day.

I pull out my biggest vibrator. Truth be told, I ordered this one recently because it sort of resembles Daylen's dick in a weird way. I came across it online, and it was…familiar. Eerily familiar.

I grab some lube and spread it over the tip and then down a few more inches, just enough to give me what I need. I'm about to get to work when my doorbell rings. Who in the fuck is at my door at this hour?

I quickly pull up my sleep shorts and, without realizing that the vibrator is still in my hand, I run for the front door, fearing that something is the matter. Is the building on fire? There's an elderly couple across the hall. Maybe one of them is in medical need.

Without bothering to waste time looking through the peephole, I open the door in a rush and see Daylen standing there with a tormented look on his face. He's in a T-shirt and athletic shorts but is holding a sweatshirt in front of his waist.

"Daylen? What the hell are you doing here at this hour? Are you injured?" He looks like he's in genuine pain.

He lifts the sweatshirt away from his waist, and I see a giant —I mean *giant*—boner tenting his shorts.

I burst out laughing. "Oh my god. What the fuck?"

He's practically hyperventilating as he breathes heavily. "I will write you a million-dollar check if you let me fuck you right now. I swear. I brought my checkbook. Whatever it takes."

Still unable to control my laughter, I ask, "What happened?"

He holds up four fingers, dropping one with each word. "Beau. Fudd. Boner. Shake."

My laughter only grows. Holy shit. He had a Boner Shake and now has the biggest boner in creation. I guess that stuff really works.

He practically weeps, "I've jerked off more times than you can imagine. It won't go down. I need a pussy. I need your pussy. My wife's pussy is the bestest pussy I've ever had. I swear." He drops to his knees. "Please. Name your price. I will take you on a shopping spree that puts *Pretty Woman* to shame.

Richard Gere is my bitch. No, he's *your* bitch. Anything in the world you want. Please help me," he whimpers.

"Get up, you moron. Come inside before you wake my neighbors. The old couple across the way have bat ears." I point to his boner. "You're going to scare them with that thing."

He stands up and walks inside, still with a massive tent in his shorts. I close the door behind him, uncertain what to do.

He nods toward my vibrator, which I forgot was in my hand. "Busy morning for you too?"

I twist my lips. "Hmm. Something like that."

He studies it more carefully. "Is that the JimmyJane 8800 Special Edition?"

I blink a few times in shock. "Why do you know that?"

He smirks. "Because I dated Jimmy and Jane's daughter once. She asked me if I would be the dick model for it." He nods toward it with a satisfied look on his face. "That's my dick. Didn't you recognize it?"

I narrow my eyes at him. "Are you fucking with me right now?"

He grabs the vibrator and pulls down his pants. A massive boner bounces up and down. It's oozing. He wasn't kidding about the effects of the Boner Shake. Good lord, that thing is pulsating and angry. *And mouthwatering.*

Grabbing hold of his cock, he points to a slightly uneven ridge on the lip of the head. With his other hand, he turns the vibrator to show me it has the same ridge.

With a shaking finger, I point at the vibrator. "This is actually your cock?"

He nods emphatically. "Yes, just like I said. I was her dick model for this. Why do you think it's the 8800? It's a subtle nod to my jersey number. And why the hell else would I know the vibrator make and model number? I don't usually see vibrators. In fact, it's the only one I've seen in my life."

I think my chin is on the floor. I'm speechless. The odd thing is that I bought it because I noticed the damn resemblance. I think he might be telling me the truth.

He clears his throat as he strokes his cock a few times, making a dull ache begin to take form between my legs, knowing the itch that beautiful cock could easily scratch for me. I can't take my eyes off it.

"Can we please negotiate?" he pleads as I snap my head up so my eyes meet his again. "Anything, I mean anything you want is yours. Full disclosure, I will need at least three or four rounds to get this under control."

I chew on my lips. Truth be told, I need this too. I want it. I wanted it weeks ago when we were watching television together. If he pushed things, I would have said yes back then.

I'm not giving in so easily though. I wouldn't be me if I didn't fuck with him a little bit. An idea occurs to me. Staring at him, I announce, "I have conditions."

Without hesitating and without an obnoxious reply, he nods. "Name them. Anything." He reaches down to his shorts around his ankles and pulls an actual checkbook out of the pocket. "*Any*thing."

I grab the checkbook and toss it to the ground on top of his sweatshirt. "I'm not a hooker. I don't want money."

"Oookay. What do you want?"

I bite back my smile as I hold up two fingers. "I want two things. First, I want you to wear my jersey to my game tonight."

"Done. Easy. I'll wear it until the end of time. I'll buy a thousand of them and wear them to every game."

I nod. "Good. Condition two. Your first orgasm will be wherever and however I want to give it to you. There may be some spanking and other actions involved, but it's one hundred percent under my control. After that one, you can fuck me however and wherever *you* want."

He narrows his eyes at me. "Can I do the minivan?"

"What's that?" I ask.

"Two in the front and five in the back."

I bark out a laugh. God, this man does make me laugh sometimes. With a smile on my face, I nod in agreement. "Whatever you need to get off, but remember, your first orgasm is entirely under my control. If you don't give it to me, the rest of the activities are off the table. And no visible marks on my body that could be seen in a basketball uniform. I have nationally televised games all week."

He reaches for my flimsy tank top and rips it straight down the middle, all while shouting, "Deal," before bending down and latching his mouth to my nipple.

I slap him across the face. Hard. He jerks his head up in obvious surprise. "What?"

Tossing the vibrator to the ground with the checkbook and the sweatshirt, I press my finger to his chest and poke him several times. "I said *I'm* in charge of your first orgasm. Do not test me, Humblecut. I won't hesitate to leave you hanging." I look down at his cock, which is seemingly defying gravity. "More like I'll leave you standing at attention."

He sighs as he stares shamelessly at my chest. "I think I could come from sucking on your tits right now. I love your tits. I dream of your tits. I jerk off to your tits. I—"

I reach up and clamp my hand over his mouth. "Stop talking. Get naked and place your hands on the wall. I'll be back in a moment. Blink twice if you agree, and we can get started on rectifying this whole situation for you." And for me.

He blinks twice, and I smile in satisfaction before removing my hand and walking out of the room. I hear him yell, "No need for sexy lingerie. I'm already turned on, and I prefer you naked anyway."

Fucking idiot. He has no idea what he's in store for.

As I gather a few items, I yell into my living room, "You better be naked with your hands flat on the wall. Spread your legs and stick out your ass while you're at it."

"I'm ready. I swear. Please come back," he yells out pathetically in return.

I inwardly laugh at his desperation as I remove my shorts and remnants of my tank top and return to the living room in all my naked glory.

His head turns, and his eyes initially drink in my body until he catches sight of what's in my hands. Those once-lust-filled eyes widen in fear. "W…why do you need a spatula and a bottle of lube?"

"I'm in charge," I bark at him with authority. "Face forward and shut your mouth. Come will be pouring out of you in mere minutes. That's all you need to know."

He smiles as he turns his face toward the wall. "Yes, ma'am."

I walk over to him and rub his ass cheeks with my hands. He has a great ass. Some men have that flat, pancake ass where you think their pants might fall down with a minor tug. Not Daylen. His ass is big, muscular, and smooth. It always fills out his pants nicely.

I lift my arm and then bring my hand down, smacking his right cheek with the spatula.

He releases a little yelp but otherwise remains quiet.

I do it again, this time a little harder. I have to admit, seeing red marks take shape on his ass is making me drip with anticipation.

This time, I do it with a lot of force. "Ow. Fuck. That hurt," he complains. "I don't think I can come from this."

I shake in laughter, trying to keep quiet so he doesn't realize I'm laughing.

One more time. I bring my arm back and, *smack*. I come down as hard as I can, and the sound reverberates throughout the room.

"Ahh," he screams.

I bend down and kiss his now reddened ass, taking a few small bites along the way. I even give a little lick up his crack, causing him to jerk forward a bit in surprise.

Standing back upright, I grab for the lube and squirt some onto my index and middle fingers, coating them completely.

He's got panic in his voice when he questions, "Oh god, what are you about to do, you psycho bitch?"

I can't help but release a small giggle as I say, "Just let Dr. Kennedy work her magic." I grab his hip with one hand and then take my two fingers and rub them around his back entrance.

He sucks in a breath. "Oh shit, oh shit, oh shit."

"Have you done any ass play before, Daylen?"

"Not on *my* ass."

"Hmm. Then allow me to rock your world."

"Wait," he exclaims. "A crazy bitch once shoved a remote control up there. Does that count?"

I smile at the New Year's memory before instructing him to relax. I slowly insert my two fingers into him. He jerks forward a drop, but he impressively doesn't otherwise complain.

Knowing he's never been touched here before, I'm gentle at first, moving slowly inside him. "Just give me a second to find your P-spot." I feel around for it. "It's a little bump about four inches in. Sometimes it takes a minute or two to find."

"Four inches?" he screeches as he begins to freak out a bit.

I scoff. "Daylen, your cock is at least nine inches and I took it. Stop being a baby."

"You didn't take it up your ass."

"Yeah, well, I've had more than two fingers and more than four inches in my ass before, so stop whining like a little bitch and focus. You're going to be begging me for more in just a few minutes."

It doesn't take long for me to find the right spot. He gasps when I do, and then I start to massage it with my fingers.

He lets out a slight moan. "Oh wow. I…I…keep doing that." His hips even rock a little to the rhythm of my strokes.

I gradually begin to increase the pressure and make a figure eight pattern with my fingers, knowing what it will do to him. He starts involuntarily circling his hips much more so than before. He's fully getting into it. I knew he would. It feels too good not to.

Once I know he's sufficiently built up and on the brink, I change my finger patterns to more of a come-hither motion.

He begins moaning loudly, before yelling, "Holy crap. Holy crap. Oh god. Don't stop. It's building. I'm almost there. I'm gonna go off like a firehose. Fuck, Kennedy. Fuck."

When I know he's nearly there, I reach my hand that was gripping his hip around to his front and wrap it around his rock-hard cock, giving it three tight, hard pumps in sync with my movements in his back entrance.

He starts banging the wall with his fist, and then practically roars down the building as he loses his load all over my wall. And I mean *all* over my wall. There's a lot of fucking semen. These Boner Shakes cause insane production levels. Wow, I've never seen anything like it.

I continue to pump him voraciously through it. The noises coming out of his mouth are extremely satisfying.

When I'm confident he's done, I slowly remove my hands from his body. As soon as I do, he falls to his knees with his whole body shaking, completely out of breath. With his head bowed, he asks, "What," breath, "the hell," breath, "was that?"

I pat his head like a good dog. "The best orgasm of your life, Humblecut. It's called milking the prostate. You're welcome."

He sits there wordlessly, panting, but nods his head in agreement.

"You'll need a little while to recover," I tell him. "I'm going to wash my hands in the kitchen. Let me know when you can stand again and then we'll work on me."

I leave with a giant smile of satisfaction on my face. He might not be able to walk for thirty minutes. There's no way he'll be able to go again, not for a long while.

I'm at the sink washing my hands when I hear his voice from the living room. "Out of curiosity, why was the spatula necessary for that?"

I let out a laugh. "It wasn't. I just wanted to wallop you and leave marks on your ass. That was for *my* satisfaction, not yours."

Before I know what's happening, his muscular arms wrap around me and lift me effortlessly into the air. I screech in surprise.

"You are mean," he teases playfully, "with a big mouth that would be better served sucking dick."

He places me back down and turns me around, the front of his naked body pressed to mine. My nipples harden as they rub along his chest, immediately ramping up my arousal. God, this feels good. I've been starved for the touch of a man for far too long.

He runs his thumb over my lower lip and breathes, "But I do love these pink lips."

I look up at him, realizing just how much I want him. "I have two pairs of lips for a reason. You can either shut me up or fill me up; the decision is yours."

He leans forward and mumbles into my mouth, "My wife is insane." I can feel him smile against my lips. "In the best way possible."

His lips finally take mine in a hard kiss while he again lifts me and encourages me to wrap my legs around him, which I do.

His tongue pushes into my mouth, and it still tastes like strawberries. Why does this man always taste like strawberries? It's weird, but I sort of like it. I thought it was the drink in Vegas, but it's obviously not that. The man just tastes like damn strawberries.

I can feel him harden against my stomach. How is that possible, given the orgasm he just had? What is in those damn boner shakes? Though I suppose his turnaround time in Vegas was impressive too. Maybe it's just him.

I can feel and hear him reach behind me to shut off the water before turning us and depositing my ass on top of my kitchen table, all without breaking the kiss. I run my fingers through his hair, basking in the intimacy of the moment. His calloused, massive hands move all over my body, leaving no inch untouched. Vegas was full of hard, aggressive hate touches. These are slightly different. Still aggressive and hard, but there's a reverence to them this time. Hate has been replaced with something else. Savoring. Longing. Desire.

He licks and bites his way down my neck, but not in a way that will leave marks. Damn, I wish I wasn't playing on television, or I'd encourage him to be rougher with me.

He spends *a lot* of time worshiping my nipples. He grabs, he licks, he sucks, and he bites. Most importantly, he remembers how sensitive they are. I could probably come from this, especially right now while I'm so on edge.

While certain parts of my body are off limits from marking, my breasts aren't, and he's taking full advantage of that. His teeth graze and clamp down on every inch of my flesh, undoubtedly leaving bite marks again.

Fuck, it's so good.

The wetness between my legs is unmistakably growing with each skillful touch from him. He unashamedly rubs his chest through it, covering himself in my juices. The friction over my sensitive skin threatens to set me off into a blaze of glory.

His mouth. I want that big, obnoxious mouth to pull my orgasm from me.

I grip his hair and yank it hard until I pull him off my chest. "I'm close. I need to come so badly. Stop pussyfooting around and get your mouth between my legs, Gaston," I command with authority.

His lips twitch in amusement at my *term of endearment*. "You got it, Regina George."

I let out a laugh at his *Mean Girls* reference. Of course he's watched that movie.

He sits down on one of my kitchen chairs, bringing him eye to eye with my most intimate region. It's almost weird to be with him like this while completely sober. I've hated him for a year, and now we're naked in my kitchen with his eyes homed in on my bare pussy. I feel so exposed but equally feel turned on by the whole scene. One thing is for sure; I'll never look at my kitchen table the same way again.

Realizing this may be too much, I start to close my legs a bit, but he lifts his head, and our eyes meet while he runs the rough pads of his fingers along my inner thighs and then pushes my knees far apart in one swift movement until they're pinned to the table. He calmly says, "Get out of your head. You're beautiful. Your pussy is mouthwatering. Relax, spread your legs, and let me drain all the chaos from your brain."

He hit the nail on the head. That's exactly what I need. All the chaos drained from my brain.

I lean back on my elbows and relax my legs, allowing them to remain as wide open as they can go.

His satisfied gaze moves back down to my pussy before he licks his lips and then ever so slowly runs the tip of his nose through me while audibly inhaling me. Our moans are mutual and in perfect sync.

My pussy physically flutters. I can feel the moisture building. This isn't going to take long at all.

He slowly circles his nose over my clit a few times as if he's savoring the smell of me. My breath catches at the unexpected yet deeply erotic move. Most men latch on and go from zero to sixty in two seconds. Daylen is giving me the slower seduction with his examination and worship of my body.

It's hot and has me slickening by the second with deep-seated need. I ache for his touch. I want his fingers and his mouth on me. In me. I'm feral for it.

He teases me with the tips of his fingers, running them through me over and over again. I grab the edge of the kitchen table, attempting to get him to push deeper inside. It doesn't work. He remains in control. He's silently communicating that this will very clearly be done his way.

When I stop fighting, he gives me a smile of satisfaction before whispering, "Good girl."

He inserts all his fingers through both sides of my lips, spreading my pussy as far apart as it is capable of going. I'm wide open and bared to him and his penetrating, focused gaze. Again, his eyes scan my intimate region as if he's studying it. He blows air on the sensitive flesh, and I jerk in response.

He breathes, "So beautiful," before his tongue runs up and down my slit and then probes my entrance, shallow at first, but then deeper and deeper while stretching me beyond my limits. It equally burns and feels good.

My legs are already shaking. My nipples are tight and achy. I have to fall back and grab them for some relief.

With his tongue now deep inside my channel, his thumb moves to my throbbing bud, and I jerk at the cacophony of sensations running rampant through my body.

Again, he doesn't rush things, merely teasing my clit with what's to come, building me up until I feel like I'll die if he doesn't move things along.

Take note, gentlemen. This is how a man is supposed to eat a woman.

For the first time in as long as I can remember, my brain shuts off to the outside world. The only thing going through it right now is the pleasure Daylen is expertly coaxing from my body with his slow, methodical seduction.

I want to grip the table to ride out what is seconds away, but my breasts need me more. I have to pinch my own nipples as hard as I can, causing another shot of need to dart straight to my pussy.

My back arches involuntarily as the orgasm rises to the surface. My throat begins to hurt. At first, I can't figure out why, but then I realize it's because of my screams. I can't control what's coming out of my mouth. He's the master of my body right now. I'm powerless, and it feels so damn good.

My hips start to thrust, searching for that one final move to push me over the cliff. And then it's there, his synchronic, perfect movements have me falling over that cliff.

I plunge into the deepest abyss of pleasure. My vision is dark at first before it's quickly covered with a rainbow of the most radiant, vivid colors I've ever seen.

For one brief moment, I forget all that plagues me. All that weighs heavily on me doesn't exist. My parental issues. My career reputation issues. The fact that this man is my forced husband. The fact that I sort of hate him. They're all gone, if only for a few minutes in time.

Right now, I'm in the present, and he's doing exactly what he said he'd do. He's draining all the chaos from my brain. It feels like a blank slate, and it's glorious.

My vision hasn't returned yet when I feel his mouth on mine and his tip teasing my entrance. The tangy essence of me immediately envelops my taste buds as his tongue deliciously spreads it all over my mouth.

His body is big and warm on top of mine. He's all-encompassing. It feels so good. So right.

My vision hasn't returned yet, but I wrap my arms and legs around him before scraping my nails along his back in a way I know will leave marks, if not break skin.

He lets out a guttural moan before driving deep into me with one long, hard thrust. He feels massive and so damn hard. Every pulsating vein rubs my insides. It's a sensation I've never encountered before. He's by far the biggest I've ever had inside me, and I feel the delicious burn of his unprecedented possession over my body.

He lets out a loud grunt into my mouth. "Oh fuck. You feel amazing wrapped around my cock. I'm in pussy heaven."

It's the word *wrapped* that's got me snapped back to reality. Did he have time to put on a condom? Was I too lost in my post-orgasm fog to remember him doing it?

I try to talk, but I can't because his tongue is plundering my mouth as he begins to move inside me. Even inside me, I can feel his skin on mine. I can feel the ridges and the contours of the head of his penis as they scrape along my sensitive insides, drawing a pleasure I've never known.

He's not wearing a condom. I know it. For a few moments, I don't care because it feels too good and I don't want it to stop.

Our hips work together as if we've practiced it a million times before. He showers me with words and sounds of praise, as lost in the pleasure as I am.

I can hear the scraping of the kitchen table across the floor until it eventually crashes into the wall. The noise breaks me from my dick trance.

"Daylen," I breathe.

He pinches my nipples hard, and I lose another ten seconds of sanity before finally shoving his chest as hard as I can. He doesn't budge, he's too strong for that, but it snaps him out of it enough to lift his head and give me a concerned look of question.

"Condom," I pant. "We forgot a condom."

He sucks in a breath as he immediately stands and withdraws from me. I hate losing the sensation of both his body and his cock, immediately feeling empty and cold without him.

He stands in front of me, pulling his hair, with worry written all over his handsome face. "I'm so fucking sorry. I've…I've never once done that. I've never been inside a woman without a condom. Holy shit. What's wrong with me? I got so carried away by you. Wanting you. I'm so sorry." He keeps apologizing over and over.

I sit up and tenderly rub his arm. "Relax. Take a breath."

His shoulders do drop a bit as he inhales and exhales a few deep breaths, clearly conflicted over what just happened, but eventually settling down.

I nod in approval of his calmer state. "Better. Don't get crazy. I'm clean and I'm on the pill."

He nods. "I'm clean too. I swear. I'm…I'm so sorry. It's my responsibility, and I failed you."

I shake my head. "It's *our* responsibility. *We* failed. And it was only a minute or two. It's not like you came."

We both instinctively glance at his dick, currently extremely tall and hard, glistening with my juices. I've never seen a bare dick glisten with my juices before. It's fucking hot.

He seems as mesmerized by it as I am.

I can't help but lean over and grab him by the base before running my tongue up and down his shaft, tasting my own essence.

The defined muscles of his stomach contract. "Fuck, don't do that. I'm trying to…oh fuck. Oh fuck. Keep doing that. God damn, your tongue is magical."

I lift my head and lick my lips in an exaggerated fashion. "Yum. I taste good."

A small smile forms on his lips at my attempt to lighten this heavy situation.

"It's delicious pussy pie, isn't it?" he asks.

I smile briefly before my face turns more serious. "I have condoms in my bedroom. If you're up for it, we can go finish what we started." I wink at him. "Beau Fudd Boner Shakes pair well with Kennedy's Pussy Pie."

He barks out a laugh before easily lifting me and throwing me over his shoulder, smacking my ass hard, and then marching us straight into my bedroom.

In less than a minute, the condom is on, we're lying on my bed, and he's back inside me, moving in and out. He feels great, but I'd be lying if I said I didn't prefer it without the condom. Experiencing every vein and ridge of him was an indescribable sensation.

He's on top of me and is moving so damn slowly and carefully. His mouth alternates between my neck, breasts, and lips, like he's worshiping them. It feels perfect, but I sense emotions bubbling to the surface, and I don't like it.

I thrust my hips up and breathe, "I need more. I need it violent."

While the force of his thrusts intensifies, he's still too tender. I don't want tender. I can't do it.

I try to increase the rhythm myself, and then I try to flip us so I can control this, but the mountain of a man is too big and heavy. I can't manipulate anything from the bottom. We're doing this his way.

It's like he's…making love. I prefer it when he hate-fucks me.

The sounds of my ringtone momentarily break my slight mental breakdown.

Do I normally answer my phone during sex? No. Am I going to right now? Yes.

I reach over, grab my phone, and answer the call. "Hello?"

He stops his movements and lifts his head, staring at me in bewilderment.

I plaster a big smile on my face as I pleasantly answer the lady on the phone's question. "No, I'm not looking to change my cable provider."

I discreetly end the call, but he doesn't know that. I continue talking into the phone, pretending the saleswoman is still on the other end. "No, I'm not doing anything important. I've got some random guy inside me, but he won't fuck me like I need, so I'd rather talk to you. Tell me about your various cable plans in extreme detail. I have oodles of time and nothing better to do."

I try to bite back my smile, but he grabs the phone and looks at it, quickly realizing I already ended the call. He narrows his eyes at me. "You're a nasty woman."

I nod. "Yes, I am. So fuck me like I'm nasty. Fuck me like you want to hurt me. Punish me," I command.

He withdraws and violently spanks my pussy hard enough that I think it might leave a mark.

Now we're talking.

He then reaches down and taps his dick on my pussy a few times and says, "I'd like to restore to factory settings."

I giggle, but it's short-lived when he climbs up on me, straddles my chest, and grabs me by the throat with both hands. "Is this what you want?" he growls.

"Yes," I cough out, barely able to speak with his massive body on my chest and the brute strength of his hands limiting my ability to do so.

With one hand still on my throat, he pulls off the condom and tilts his hips forward until his tip reaches my mouth. "You want something to choke on? I'll give you something to choke on. Open wide, sugar tits."

I happily oblige.

He drives his hips forward so damn hard that I think his tip enters directly into my windpipe. He begins fucking my mouth, shouting things like, "Take that, you masochistic bitch."

Yes, this is what I want and need.

With both hands on my throat and his cock down my throat, he does his best to choke me into submission…and I love every minute of it, lapping him with my tongue and sucking as hard as I can.

He thinks he's pushing my boundaries, but he's only ramping up my arousal.

He begins to lose control a bit before pulling out. "Fuck, I don't want to come in your mouth. I want to come in your pussy after you have another orgasm."

"Then fuck me to the brink of unconsciousness and I'll have one."

He quickly rolls another condom on and slides down my body again. He continues choking me while only running his dick through me, never into me, until I feel like I'll die if he doesn't get inside me again. He's driving me crazy.

"Fuck me now," I yell out.

He shakes his head. "You don't deserve the D yet. Earn it. Beg for it."

He removes one hand from my throat and squeezes my nipple so damn hard that I think it might pop off. My eyes roll back in my head, and I let out a moan.

"You're one deranged bitch."

"You flatter me," I croak out.

He narrows his eyes at me. "Are you ready to beg for it?"

I smile as I shake my head. I like this game.

He slaps my nipple harder than I've ever felt, and my pussy leaks in happiness.

"Say, *please fuck me*."

I shake my head even though my pussy is weeping for him now.

He brings his arms under my knees before returning his hands to my neck. I'm beyond open and exposed to him in this position. I'm not sure I've done this with choking before. His long, muscular arms afford a few extra benefits.

I think he's finally going to reenter me, but he continues running his cock through me as though he has all the time in the world. Bending his head, he bites my nipple with bruising force, and I swear I nearly come from everything he's doing to my body.

I can't take it anymore. I give in. "P…please. Fuck me."

He immediately impales me with his monster cock and then proceeds to give me the pounding of a lifetime all morning until it's time for me to get ready for my game.

EIGHTEEN

KENNEDY

I've been in my shower for more than thirty minutes with the temperature turned up as high as I can stand it. I'm sore. *Really* fucking sore. It's making me a little nervous about my game today. I hope I can move like I need to.

I look down at my body. He marked me all over but did a nice job of limiting it to areas that will remain hidden by my basketball uniform. My breasts and ass took the brunt of it. I can't help but smile, remembering what was undoubtedly the best sex of my life.

He was so overtly domineering in bed…once I poked the bear a little bit. It's in complete contrast to his silly, laid-back demeanor. My fingers run over my red, raw nipples as I replay the morning inside my head.

Once again, he pulled countless orgasms from my body, over and over. He's got talent. I'll give him that.

He didn't want to leave, but I kicked him out, knowing my body couldn't possibly take any more sex, and I needed to get myself prepared to play today.

As he left, he thanked me for taking care of him in his time of need. I'm guessing that means this was a one-time thing, which is probably for the best. I hate that I'm sad at the notion of not having him again.

I blow-dry my hair and then style it into one of my perfect runway-ready ponytails. I then apply my makeup. I don't overdo it for games, but a little foundation, mascara, and light lip gloss while on national television can't hurt. I don't want to look like Casper the Ghost.

They're starting to photograph us when we walk into the stadium, so I'm doing my best to get creative with my gameday walk-in outfits. In fact, Daylen lost a bet to me before we left for Vegas, and I get to dress him for his opening day walk-in outfit. I shudder to think what he would have chosen for me to wear today if he had won. I'd probably be dressed in a 1950s dad lawn-mowing outfit. That or my gold bikini, which he mentioned countless times when we were drunk in Vegas.

I shimmy into expensive, high-end skinny jeans, which show off my figure nicely. I can't help but smile as I grab the shirt I purchased to wear today. It's a retro, fashionable, flattering one-of-a-kind version of Sulley's college jersey. It has her school, number, and name on it. She has no idea about it. I can't wait for her to see me wearing it.

Slipping into my stiletto heels, I leave my apartment and head to the stadium. As I enter, I'm accosted by photographers, all shouting questions at me about my outfit choice. I will no doubt be all over social media within the hour.

"Kennedy, why Sulley O'Shea's jersey?" one of them stupidly asks.

I smile as I stand in front of our team's step and repeat banner backdrop and pose for the flashes going off in my face. "Because she's a superstar and my friend. I'm sick of the women in this league bashing her when they should be thanking her for bringing so much attention to the sport."

It's true. No one used to give a shit what we wore when we

walked into the stadiums. We never got this type of media attention before Sulley came into the picture.

I continue, "She should know her teammates have her back, even if the rest of the women in this league feel threatened by her. We love and support her wholeheartedly."

I blow them a kiss as I ignore the remaining questions, pose for another minute, and then head into the locker room.

Sulley's eyes tear up when she sees me, offering me a huge hug and whispering into my ear, "I love you, Kennedy Jeffries. You're the best friend I've ever had in my life."

I crack a few jokes to mask the emotions swimming inside me over what she just said to me. I suppose I've never had a best friend, but I do now. It feels good to admit that I'm happy. For the first time in a very long time, I'm truly happy.

Shortly after we break apart, Fallon walks into the locker room in a white pantsuit. I let out a whistle. "Wow, you're looking every bit the sexy coach. I've never seen you dressed this nicely. You look amazing." She's absolutely stunning.

She winks at me and whispers, "It's a Prada suit. I knew you'd appreciate it more than anyone else."

"You look hot," I offer. "All the men in this stadium won't be watching the game. They'll be looking at you."

She twists her lips. "Not really my goal for the day, but I appreciate the compliment."

"Do you date?" I ask, realizing we've never once spoken about her love life. I know Bailey mentioned a hot date that one day, but I've never heard anything from Fallon about her love life.

She shrugs nervously. "A bit. Dating when you're older has its…challenges. I'm a single mom. All the men in my age bracket are either single dads or career playboys. There are things going on that weren't when I was young and single, without all the responsibilities and emotional baggage I have now." Her eyes move down to my chest, and a small smile forms on her lips. "I certainly can't get away with marks like those anymore. Harper would see them in a second and ask a million questions."

I look down and realize my shirt has slipped a bit. Bite marks are clearly visible on my breasts, even though they won't be once I'm in my sports bra and jersey.

She lets out a laugh. "I guess you had a good night."

I offer a cheeky smile as I turn toward my locker. "It was a good morning."

A *really* good morning. *The best ever.*

WE'RE on the court in our warmup layup lines when I notice my mother walk down the aisle toward her seat with a guy who must be at least ten years her junior following closely behind while holding her hand. She smiles and waves at me with her other.

The fuck? We don't communicate. She's lucky there are kids here, or I'd give her the finger.

Pierce is trailing behind them, looking miserable. He and I make eye contact, and he throws his hands in the air, conveying his frustration to me. Why is my mother parading her boy toy in front of him? She has no shame.

I refocus on my warmups but have to tug on my shorts a bit. I'm so damn sore. I think I'll need an icepack between my legs after the game. Sulley notices and asks about it. I lie that some random guy I met on Tinder gave me a pounding.

I assume Daylen's on Tinder. It could be true. I hate lying to her, but I have no choice. I don't want anyone ever knowing about Daylen and me.

On the other side of the floor, I see Vance sitting and chatting with the Cougars guys and Anacondas women. They're all super tight.

Just then, Daylen comes strolling down the aisle in my jersey.

I can't believe he really wore it, and I truly can't help the huge smile it brings to my face to see him wearing it.

He smirks at me before grabbing his junk and mouthing, "I'm sore."

I point to my crotch and mouth back, "Me too."

His grin widens with obvious pride. Deviant.

My father then walks in wearing my jersey. He narrows his eyes at Daylen as he takes in the fact that he's wearing the matching jersey. Daylen looks nervous. Oh man, it's fun to watch him squirm as I see him try to explain it away. I wish I could hear what they were saying.

My attention is pulled when my mother yells my name. She knows well enough to never do that. It's not like I'll respond. She's showing off for this guy. I can feel my rage rising to the surface.

As if I'm not angry enough, an opposing player, Diane Garma, who's the biggest Sulley-hater on the planet, walks by Palmer and mumbles, "What do you do, eat potato chips and french fries all day?"

Palmer's eyes immediately fill with tears.

I see red and march right over to stand protectively in front of Palmer. I cross my arms and puff out my chest. "Fuck off, Diane," I spit at her. "Stay on your side. Don't you even look at her, let alone talk to her ever again."

She snarls. "What? I'm just speaking the truth. Unlike Palmer, I care what goes into my body."

I narrow my eyes at her. "I've seen your ex-boyfriends on Instagram. Let me assure you, you don't care what goes into your body."

I hear Palmer snort in laughter behind me. I'm happy to hear her laughing and not crying over Diane's cruel and unnecessary treatment.

Diane grits her teeth and shoves me. "Fuck you, Kennedy. We're not all whores like you."

I bring my lips to her ear and whisper, "I've seen the guy

you're currently dating. I've also seen photos of him with other women. How pathetic that you're satisfied being second best. Do you see the giant, blond, hot pro football player sitting over there in my jersey?" I motion my head toward Daylen.

She turns her head and looks at him.

I continue to whisper, "Yes, that one. He fucked my brains out all morning. For hours. I might be a whore, but I'm a whore who had a dozen orgasms from that big-dicked stud before I came to the stadium today. And he liked it so much that he's wearing my jersey. He's not out with another woman. In fact, I can guarantee you that you won't see him with anyone else for the foreseeable future because unlike you, I know how to keep my man satisfied."

As if sensing what's going on, Daylen brings his index and middle fingers to his mouth in a V shape and then flicks his tongue through them suggestively.

I smile at him, and he winks back at me.

"Enjoy your shitty lays, Diane. It shows in the way you play."

I wave at her innocently just as Coach Lakshmi calls us into our pregame huddle. If looks could kill, Diane would kill me right now. It seems I've struck a chord. My hours of stalking her on social media are paying off today.

Palmer bumps my hip with hers. "Thank you. What did you whisper to her?"

I shrug. "Just a little friendly chatter among competitors."

She giggles. "I doubt it was very friendly."

Nope, it wasn't friendly at all. Fuck Diane. She's been a thorn in my side for years. She used to play for another team, but now she plays for my old team out of New York. They traded for her when they released me. Yes, I dislike her because of that, but no one mistreats Sulley more than her. She's had a tongue-lashing coming for a long time, and I did my homework to prepare for it.

The first half of the game is a little shaky. Sulley, Palmer, and I are all a bit off. I know why I can't move properly. I wonder what their excuses are. It doesn't help that my fake-as-fuck mother is acting like a schoolgirl, touching and laughing with her boyfriend while my brother is obviously suffering.

And then I saw some random girl flirting with Daylen. I don't know why it bothered me, but it did. It's not like he paid her much attention.

By the second half, we get it together and start working well as a team. Diane can't handle it and starts pushing Sulley around and getting in her ear about how overrated she is. She's giving Sulley hard elbows every damn time she touches the ball. It's driving me nuts.

The refs are useless, failing to call any fouls on her. They're supposed to protect us from this kind of thing, not turn a blind eye.

At some point, Layla is dribbling down the court. Diane strips her of the ball and starts moving toward their basket. As is often the case when an opposing player is about to go in for an easy basket, Sulley hustles and wraps her arms around Diane before she can score, taking her to the ground for a hard foul.

Diane goes absolutely berserk, popping up and putting her nose right in Sulley's face while screaming obscenities at her.

Per normal for Sulley, she doesn't engage, turns around, and starts walking away. Diane's eyes widen in rage at the sight of Sulley ignoring her. There's something to be said about the way Sulley handles herself. If their words and actions are getting to her, she certainly never lets on. She's always cool as a cucumber. I think that pisses off our opponents even more.

Once Sulley has walked about ten feet from Diane, I see the moment Diane snaps and she begins to charge at Sulley.

Fuck that. I try to put my body between Diane's and Sulley's, but Diane doesn't stop. I'm not exactly sure what comes over me except a feeling of complete and total protectiveness over my best friend. When Diane doesn't alter course, I pull my fist back and pop her right in the nose.

I swear I didn't mean for it to be as hard as it was. I didn't mean to knock her out cold and very obviously break her nose.

But I do. And mayhem ensues. Both benches clear as players start to tangle. Every referee is blowing his or her whistle. Players and fans are all screaming. People are throwing things onto the court. It's madness.

I'm the intended target for most of their players as they thrash at me, grabbing my hair and my jersey. I'm taking elbows left and right. Before I realize it, both my father and Daylen are pulling people away from me.

The next ten minutes are a blur. I get ejected from the game, and I know a big suspension is coming my way. Maybe even worse. Reagan warned me about my behavior. I completely lost control out there today.

Tears are streaming down my face. Fallon wraps her arm around me protectively and escorts me off the court to the locker room. Once the locker room door closes and the buzz of the mayhem is more distant, I fall to my knees and begin sobbing.

Fallon gets down on the ground with me and pulls me into an embrace. "Hey, hey. Don't cry. You were protecting your teammate."

I sob out, "Reagan is going to kill me. She told me this was my last chance, and I blew it. She might release me. I may never play ball again." I suddenly feel like my world is falling apart.

I cry on her shoulder while she caresses my hair. "Don't worry. We'll take care of it. We're not losing you. Everyone loves you. You're important to this team on and off the court."

I pull my head up and look at her. "Why are you so nice to me?"

Confusion crosses her face. "Why wouldn't I be?"

"People aren't normally nice to me," I raise my voice. "In case you haven't noticed, I'm not easy to get along with. I have resting bitch face, and I'm kind of cunty to people."

She releases a small laugh. "Well, I get along with you. You're not cunty to me." She grabs me by the shoulders and looks into my eyes. "You're going to get through this. I promise. Everyone on this team will have your back, just like you always have theirs. That's how real friendships work."

I nod as my tears begin to slow down. I look at the state of her stained top from my crying. It's covered in blood and makeup. "I'm sorry I ruined your nice suit," I cry.

She holds me closer, clearly not caring what it's doing to her outfit. "It's okay. It was last season's design anyway."

It's not. It's new. I know fashion, but I appreciate that she's trying to make me feel better about it.

I've only known this woman for a few months, but somehow, she's giving me comfort that I've never received before. And it feels nice.

I WAKE in the morning to my doorbell ringing. I left the locker room shortly after my embarrassing meltdown in Fallon's arms, not wanting to talk to anyone or face the proverbial music. My phone started blowing up immediately, but I ignored that too, powering it down before I even got home. I crawled into bed and cried myself into a restless sleep.

I groggily make my way to the front door and look through the peephole. It's Reagan. Reality sets in. She's going to release me. No other team will want me. My career is over. At least she has the decency to tell me to my face.

I take a deep breath, trying to build the courage to deal with what I know is coming my way. I open the door, expecting her to look venomous, as I'm sure she was one of the many people calling me last night, but I can't read her impassive expression.

"Can I come in?" she asks calmly. I nod, and she walks into my apartment with me closing the door behind her.

As always, she's dressed impeccably with perfect hair and makeup. I find myself wondering if she doesn't have stylists living at her house. I guess she's rich enough to have them on payroll. Why not?

She turns around and places her hand on my shoulder with nothing but concern written on her face. "Are you okay?"

I chew my lip nervously. "I suppose it depends on what you're about to say. Am…am I off the team?" I ask as I unsuccessfully attempt to swallow down my emotions.

She jerks her head back as if surprised by the question. "Off the team? Are you crazy? You're the heart and soul of this team."

"I am?"

She lets out a laugh. "Yes, Kennedy, you are. I don't condone you knocking out another player in the league, but you were defending Sulley. I've watched the tape a million times. She was about to hurt Sulley—there's no denying that. Kennedy," she looks into my eyes, "you've been everything I've hoped you would be and more. You've done exactly what I asked of you. We're not bailing on you just yet, sweetie."

I exhale a long breath in relief. "Thank you so much. How… how long is my suspension?"

Her face tightens a bit. "Well, the league called me this morning and told me you're being suspended for a month and being fined five-thousand dollars."

My eyes widen. "Holy shit, I've never had one that bad."

"Have you ever knocked another player out cold and broken her nose?"

I lower my head and shamefully admit, "No."

"Right. Sulley insisted on covering your fine."

"She doesn't have to do that. I'll take accountability for my actions."

Reagan shakes her head. "She did have to do that. You saved her from certain injury, and she can more than afford it with everything she's got going on. Let her pay. You've been a good teammate to her, and now she's returning the favor the best way she can. As for your suspension, I was able to negotiate it down to two weeks."

I perk up at that bit of news. "Oh. That's not so bad. I'll only miss four games."

Her face twitches a bit. "There's a condition."

"What condition?" I ask with both fear and suspicion.

She briefly pinches her lips together. "They want you to go to rehab. It's technically for anger management. We're going to officially call it *a wellness retreat,* but it's a certified rehab facility."

"What?" I turn and walk toward my living room with anger bubbling inside me. "No fucking way. I'm not doing that weird, talk about your feelings shit."

She follows me into my apartment. "You are," she announces with authority. "Like you said, with a two-week suspension, we only lose you for four games. With a month suspension, we lose you for nine. That's twenty percent of our season. You're too important to this team to lose you for so long. Think of it as a little rest and recovery time. I found you a nice facility in Maine. It's beautiful up there in the summer. Unplug. Take some time to chill out and recharge."

I'm quiet. I don't want to do this, but I feel like I have no other choice but to acquiesce.

She cracks a small smile. "You're going to like what I have to say next."

"I doubt it," I mumble, pouting like a spoiled child with my arms crossed.

Her smile widens. "Have you been on social media this morning?"

I shake my head. "No, I turned off my phone last night. It was blowing up, and I didn't feel like talking to anyone."

She holds up her phone. "You should check your phone. You're being hailed a hero. The real-life Black Widow is what they're calling you. My phone is ringing off the hook with endorsement offers for you." She points her finger at me. "Let me tell you what's going to happen. You're going to head to Maine for two weeks and decompress. They'll have you talk to therapists, which you will do without *any* problem." Her tone sharpens for that bit. "They'll have you connect with animals, nature, and some other Kumbaya shit like that, but you'll do so with a smile because they'll be sending a report to the league when your time there comes to an end to confirm your utmost cooperation. After that, you're going to come back home and find yourself a bigger agent to represent you. Trust me, you're going to need it. I advise striking while the iron is hot."

I'm processing all the information she has given me. This morning is going exactly the opposite of how I expected it to. When I cried myself to sleep last night, it was to images of me being forced to clean out my locker today, not this. I even let my mind drift to having to ask my father for money, which I've refused to do since I left for college.

She's right. I need to pay the piper for my actions and then pick myself up like I always have. If there are new opportunities, I need to seize them. What other choice do I have? This woman hasn't led me astray yet.

I swallow. "Okay. I'll do whatever you tell me to." My eyes meet hers. "Thanks for having my back, Reagan. Thank you for everything."

She smiles again. "My pleasure. By the way, I had six calls this morning from other teams in the league wanting to trade for you. Do you still want out of Philly?"

My brother's face pops right into my mind, followed shortly thereafter by my amazing group of friends. Even Daylen's face unexpectedly makes a brief appearance. I'm realizing that in just a year, I feel more at home here than I ever have anywhere else.

I shake my head. "No. I want to stay."

She nods. "Good, because I already told them no. We're not letting you leave us. Be at the small airstrip in two hours. I'll have my private jet take you up to Maine so the press doesn't bother you just yet."

"Okay. I'll be there."

"Good." She walks toward my door, and I follow her. "This is going to work out. Stop worrying and stay the course. And let's retire the brass knuckles for a bit. At least for the rest of this season."

I playfully salute her. "Yes, Captain."

She grins as she opens the door. "You're much more amiable than you used to be. I sort of miss your snarkiness. It was more of a challenge for me."

I let out a laugh. "I promise to be a bigger bitch moving forward."

"Perfect."

As she steps out into the hallway, Daylen is exiting the elevator, walking toward my apartment. His worried eyes meet mine.

Reagan looks at him and then back at me before walking toward the elevator and mumbling, "I swear to god, every athlete in this town is fucking other athletes in this town. There must be something in the water."

She steps onto the elevator as Daylen stops in front of my door. "What are you doing here?" I ask with a heavy amount of edge in my tone.

His brows crease. "I was worried about you. I called and texted a million times."

I turn and walk into my apartment with him hot on my heels. "I can't talk right now. I need to pack."

"Where are you going?"

"Rehab. My suspension will only be two weeks if I agree to go to rehab."

"Rehab? For what?" he asks in a shocked tone.

"For my anger issues, what else?"

I walk into my bedroom and remove a suitcase from the top shelf in my closet, opening it on my bed.

"Where's the rehab?"

"Maine."

"Maine!" he exclaims loudly. "That's so far. I'll…I'll drive you there."

I turn and look at him. "It's a ten-hour drive, Daylen. That would be twenty for you round trip."

He shrugs. "It's fine. I don't have other plans for today."

I shake my head. "I don't need to be driven. Reagan is flying me there," I say as I begin to toss my clothes into the suitcase.

He runs his fingers through his hair. "I'll drive you to the airport."

"Not necessary," I answer as I continue packing. "I'll get an Uber."

He grabs me by the arm so I'm forced to look at him. "I'm driving you."

"I said no," I grit out.

"You're my wife. You've had a rough twenty-four hours. You're hurting. I will be driving you, and I will stay with you until I'm convinced you're okay, which you're very clearly not. Even if it means getting on that damn plane with you."

"Stop it," I violently pull my arm away from his hold on it. "I'm not your wife. I'm not yours to worry about. You don't really know me. Don't pretend like you do. You spend time with me because you're legally obligated to do so."

And then it hits me. "Oh, you're just worried about our court-mandated dates."

He tightens his face in anger. "Are you for fucking real right now? I don't give a shit about Judge Dies-A-Lot. I'm worried about my wife."

I close my eyes. "Stop calling me that."

"No, I will not stop. It's exactly what you are. You're. My. Wife."

"I don't have time for this bullshit. Please just leave."

He ignores my request and paces in my bedroom while I pack, refusing to talk to him. I don't understand why he's here.

Once I'm done, I reach for my phone and turn it on. It pings with notification after notification. Thousands of them. Countless texts from Daylen, Sulley, my father, Pierce, my mother, everyone on the team, Alyssa, Coach Lakshmi, Fallon, Booster, and a few other Camels guys.

I breathe, "What the fuck?" I stand there dumbfounded before I realize Daylen is looking at it from over my shoulder.

"People care about you, Kennedy. A lot of people. Me included." He wraps his arms around my chest from behind and kisses my head before whispering into my hair, "Please let me drive you to the airport. I'm much cheaper than an Uber. I'll only charge you twenty bucks," he jokes.

I roll my eyes. "Fine. What do you want to do about Judge Dinosaur?"

"Don't worry about it. I'll have Tanner handle him. Is there anything I can do for you when you're gone?"

I turn around and try not to be overwhelmed by the sincerity written all over his face. "Reagan said a bunch of new endorsement offers have come in and I might need a new agent. Someone a little bigger than the one I have. Do you know anyone?"

He smiles. "That makes sense. You're fucking exploding on social media right now. You should wear a Black Widow costume to your first game back. It will feed into all the dialogue."

I scrunch my nose. "Ugh. No. I've always hated that nickname."

"I'd embrace it. And you'll look hot as fuck in that tight bodysuit." He wiggles his eyebrows up and down.

I punch him in the stomach. "Aww," he chuckles. "You're so violent. Maybe I should protect my nose." He covers it with a smile. "I'll talk to Tanner about representing you."

My eyes widen. "What? No. He handles multi-million-dollar deals. I'm not big enough for him. I need a mid-level person."

He shakes his head. "He'll take you on." He straightens his shoulders with visible pride. "Consider your new agent taken care of. When I pick you up at the airport in two weeks, it will be done. I promise."

NINETEEN

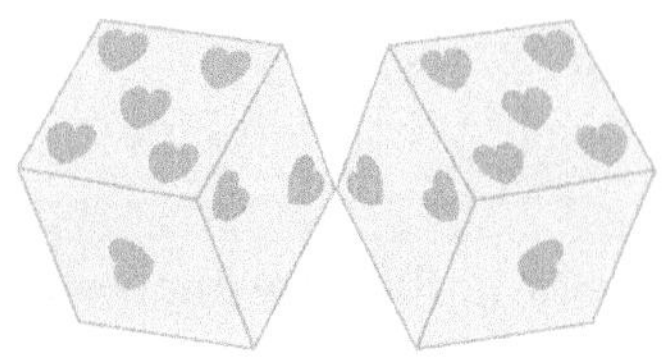

DAYLEN

After dropping Kennedy at the airport, I head straight to Tanner's office. It's in a big downtown office building. He's been here ever since he moved his company from New York City to Philadelphia. While I was sad for him that he was getting divorced, I was extremely happy when he relocated. I love having my agent and friend so close by now.

When I walk off the elevator, I smile warmly at his longtime, middle-aged secretary, Shannon, "Good morning, beautiful lady."

She looks up from her computer and blushes shyly at the compliment. "Good morning, Mr. Humblecut."

"Shannon," I scold.

"Good morning, Daylen."

"That's much better, pretty woman. Is he in?" I ask.

She nods. "He's in with Mrs. Montgomery right now, Mr.... Daylen. Let me tell him you're here."

I wave my hand dismissively. "No need. He loves my visits." And I'd like to see Fallon and congratulate her on the new job. I know how much the ladies on the team love having her around.

Shannon begs me not to go into his office and scrambles to pick up her phone, but I ignore her and open Tanner's office door, completely forgetting there's a new Mrs. Montgomery.

I'm reminded. Quickly.

Bailey is sitting on his desk facing him with her legs spread. She's giggling while his head is buried under her dress. Her back is to me. I can't see anything I shouldn't be seeing, but I know what he's doing to her.

"Oops. Sorry," I mumble.

His head quickly pops up, and Bailey pulls the bottom of her dress down to cover her thighs. Shannon appears behind me. "I'm so sorry, Mr. Montgomery. He wouldn't wait until I called you." She throws a death stare my way.

Sitting up straight in his three-piece navy-blue suit, Tanner practically growls at me in annoyance. "There's a reason Shannon is out there. There's also a reason for closed doors."

"So you can get office action?" I ask innocently while batting my eyelashes.

Bailey smiles, but Tanner scowls. She hops down from the desk and pecks him on the lips. "I'll leave you two alone. See you at home tonight."

"No," he barks out. "This will be quick. *Very* quick. Stay. I'm not done with you yet." He grabs her by the waist and pulls her to sit across his lap, refusing to let go despite her soft protests.

He nods his head toward Shannon. "That will be all," he barks at her. "In the future, when my *wife* is in here, *no one* is to disturb us," he commands with authority as he glares at her, and she practically shrivels while closing the door.

I'm glad he's on my side. He can be a scary dude sometimes.

Though as soon as he looks at Bailey, his face immediately

softens. He practically has hearts in his eyes when gazing at her and her baby bump lovingly.

It's weird to see him this way. It's not at all how he was with Fallon when they were married. They were more formal around each other. Always appropriate, but there was no spark. They lacked the playfulness my parents had and that I hope to have one day. In fact, in all the years they were married, I don't remember him ever touching Fallon the way he's always touching Bailey. He can't keep his eyes or hands off her when she's around.

I have an uncharacteristically brief moment of jealousy for what they share. They're lucky to have it.

His face hardens as he turns his attention to me. "What *else* is it that I can do for the man who I recently helped become the highest-paid tight end in all of football?"

I grin at him. "That's why I'm here. Because you're the best in the business. The only one I'd ever trust. Kennedy needs new representation, and you're the only man for the job."

Bailey's eyes widen. "I bet offers are pouring in after last night's excitement. That was the craziest thing I've ever seen in women's sports. We don't have much of that in softball. It was so intense."

I nod as I sit in a chair in front of his desk. "Yes, she's gotten a lot of offers. She needs a better agent. She needs you, Tanner."

His eyes toggle between me and Bailey. Appropriately, he hasn't told her about Vegas, and now he's cornered himself by keeping her in the room with us.

I decide to let him off the hook. "As long as she can be trusted to stay quiet, you can tell her everything."

He nods and then proceeds to tell Bailey about our Vegas wedding and the judge's mandate about us staying married through the year and all the other conditions that came with it.

"Holy shit," she breathes. "That's the wackiest story I've ever heard."

I nod. "Sure is. Anyhoo, my wife needs your help, Tanner. Please draw up the contract right away. I want her to have it when she gets home."

His shoulders fall. "I'm at my capacity. I'm beyond it. I can't take on more clients, D, especially with the babies coming. I just don't have the time or bandwidth to give her what she needs."

My jaw tightens, and I increase the grip on the armrest of the chair until I think it might break. I don't take up much of his time. I don't ask for much, so I'm asking for this. "Make fucking time for my wife."

His eyes widen in obvious shock. I rarely get heated, but I care about this. A lot.

He licks his lips as he studies my unusually aggressive demeanor. "Is something going on between you two?"

"We're married. Duh."

"You know what I mean, Daylen."

I exhale a long breath. "She's my wife and my friend. I care enough to want to make sure she's in good hands, as I do with all my wives and friends. There are no better hands than yours. You're the only person I trust to manage her career properly."

Bailey runs her fingertips over his beard. "Come on, baby. It obviously means a lot to him. She's a Philly athlete. She should be with you. Help her out."

He stares lovingly at her compassionate, soft face. His shoulders fall as he says, "Fine," as though he's in a trance. I'm pretty sure she could ask him anything and he'd agree to it.

I gasp in mock shock. "All I had to do was massage your beard, sit on your lap, and call you baby? It's good to know for the future."

He narrows his eyes at me. "I have a condition."

I twist my lips. "Hmm. Is it that you want me to join you and Bailey in bed? Fine. No problem, but I like to be cuddled afterward for a solid twenty minutes. And I like to be the little spoon."

Bailey giggles, but Tanner doesn't. "No, asshole," he growls at me. "You know I've been searching for the right woman to lead my women's division, right?"

I nod. I do know that. He's been interviewing for the position for over a year, never finding the right person for the job.

He continues, "This will stay between us for now, but Kam is going to run that division."

"Kam?" I ask. "As in Kamryn Hart, Bailey's sister?"

He nods. "Yes, she's been taking law school classes at night for years. She's almost done with her legal degree. She's going to run that division as soon as she graduates, if not before. We're in the process of getting her set up because I'm in negotiations for her to represent the star of the new women's football league, Jordie McNamara. I planned on her being Kam's first client, but Kennedy might beat her to the punch."

"Cool. Yeah, Kam would be perfect. I think she and Kennedy would get along great." I smile. "I can totally see Kam being a barracuda at this. That's awesome for her."

Bailey grins widely. "I know. I'm so proud of my sister." She turns to Tanner. "And of you for being nice to her and giving her this opportunity."

I know Tanner and Kam don't get along all that well, but I love this idea.

Tanner also agrees to help deal with Judge Eternal Sleep. He said he'll probably just want to tack on extra dates when she returns, which is fine by me. It's becoming more and more appealing to spend time with Kennedy. In fact, I've begun to look forward to it.

The sex we had yesterday was out of this world. It's so damn hot between us. Who knew that once hating each other would produce this level of passion? I've never come as long or as hard as I did yesterday. My brain was such mush that I momentarily forgot a condom. But, hell, it felt so good being inside her like that. She handled my miscue much better than I would have anticipated. She was calm and took equal responsibility even though it was all my fault.

I can't wait for her to get back so we can have a repeat performance. She let me kiss her long and hard at the airport before she left. It will have to tide us over until she gets back in two weeks.

I leave Tanner's office feeling hopeful for Kennedy. I'm excited to tell her about Kam. She's going to flip out.

On my way home, I decide to call my sister. We're due for a catch-up session.

"Hey, D," she answers right away.

"Hello, lovely sister of mine. What's the latest on Cherry Tree Lane?"

She giggles at my *Mary Poppins* reference. That was her favorite movie growing up. "Good one. Everything is fine." She snorts in obvious annoyance. "You should see what my mom wore to my softball game the other day. It was ridiculous. She wore a tight Versace dress, Jimmy Choo shoes, and held a Gucci purse while sitting on a dirty metal bleacher next to the bearded lady who's doing her best to keep K-Mart in business."

I burst out laughing. "Holy shit, that's so damn funny. You painted an excellent picture. I can imagine it perfectly. She used to do the same thing at my high school football games. And she was only, like, twenty-five then. Everyone assumed she was my sister."

"Yeah, I bet that sucked big time. You probably hated her back then."

I don't really like to Ashleigh-bash in front of Jagger. No matter what, she's still Jagger's mom. If my sister wants to complain, I'm happy to give her an ear, but I usually steer clear of fueling the flames.

"Nah. It wasn't so bad," I lie. "She made Dad the town hero. It could have been worse. He could have married that K-

Mart-loving bearded lady. Then my sister wouldn't be as stunning as she is."

"You flatter me, D. Speaking of stunning women, I saw on TV that you were at the crazy basketball game last night. You ran on the court to pull people off Kennedy Jeffries, and you were wearing her jersey. Do you know her?"

"I do. She's a...friend. I was sitting with Coach Jeffries. She's his daughter."

"Hmm," she says skeptically. "A gorgeous female friend whose jersey you were wearing. Who you ran out to defend on the court. Sounds like more than a friend to me, D."

I suddenly wish she had gotten her mother's brains instead of our father's. I try to play it off. "She's a cool chick. We hang out sometimes. Our friends are all friends."

"Pft. What a load of crap. Anyhoo, did Dad talk to you about us coming up for a visit in a few weeks?"

I smile at that bit of news. "No. When?"

"When I get out of school next month. I want to tour some of the colleges in Philly."

"Hell yes. Stay as long as you want. I'd love to have you. BJ could use some female companionship, and you're the only female she likes. The only one she doesn't try to kill."

She giggles. "Still? What happens when you bring women home?"

"I don't bring any home. She attacked an Amazon deliverywoman a few months ago." Though that was worth it because after I cleaned her injuries, she gave me an amazing blowjob on my back deck. I choose not to share that with my sister.

"Oh man. Poor woman."

Poor woman? I gave her three orgasms after the blowie. I'm sure she, too, agrees a few scrapes from BJ were worth it.

"Yep. Poor woman."

"Okay, I'll talk to Dad, and we'll figure out a few days for him to take off work. I'll text you the dates."

"Can't wait."

TWENTY

KENNEDY

"Sometimes I feel like Bruce Banner becoming The Incredible Hulk, and I'm powerless to stop the transformation once it starts. Does that make sense?" I ask the therapist who was assigned to me for the past two weeks.

We're sitting on perpendicular hunter-green velvet sofas in what can best be described as a cozy library, complete with shelves of books and an always roaring fireplace. I initially questioned her about the necessity of a fire in the summer, but she said it creates a relaxing atmosphere. Maybe she's right, because I got comfortable talking to her much more quickly than I would have anticipated. It's like staring into the crackling fire opened the floodgates, and it all came pouring out of me.

She smiles. "It does make sense, and while it's not ideal, it's good that you recognize it. Tell me the things that enrage you."

"Nouns enrage me."

"Nouns?" she questions with confusion written all over her face.

I can't help but crack a smile. "People, places, and things."

"Kennedy…" she warns. She's gotten used to my sass.

I sigh. "Fine. Assholes enrage me. Obviously."

Dr. Ludwig twists her lips. "Hmm. Can we be more specific?"

I sigh. "My mother, those who are mean to people I care about, and it used to be Daylen, but...well...you know."

She nods. "I do. As we've discussed, he's morphed throughout the past year from a thorn in your side to a bit of a protector, and you've never felt protected before."

She thinks that's why I have this hard exterior. Because I've always felt the need to protect myself, not feeling like anyone else was doing it.

On the same note, she thinks I've done a lot of personal growth throughout the past year, well before I got here, but, as she's said many times, *Rome wasn't built in a day.*

She's not wrong about Daylen. I probably feel safer around him than I've ever felt with a man. We can yell and scream and poke at each other until we're blue in the face, but I can't deny the fact that he's proven to be someone I can trust. I know he would never let anything bad happen to me, and I can't say I've ever felt that way about a man before.

I nod, having no interest in discussing him further.

"And Fallon," she continues. "She's the first true maternal figure you've ever had, at least in a very long time."

Dr. Ludwig knows everything that's gone on with my mom and understands why I have no interest in rebuilding that relationship. She tried to prod me further on that, but I shut her down. Not happening. I know I'm fucked up and have some relationships in need of improvement, but that one is beyond fixing.

I exhale a long breath. "Yes, but I haven't known her that long. It's only been a few months."

"You can't help how you feel, Kennedy. You feel drawn to her. You feel safe with her. Safety is a big thing for you. Again, she's filling this void you've had for a very long time and have clearly been craving. It's okay to admit that. Sometimes a girl just needs her mom. You haven't ever had that, and now this nurturing, maternal figure has entered your life and given you things it's very normal to want."

I nod again and reply, "I didn't know I needed it until someone gave it to me."

She smiles. "Good. And your father?"

I swallow. "While he wasn't father of the year when I was growing up, I acknowledge I may have misunderstood a few things about him and am more open to mending fences with him at some point. My brother is my priority, but I'll be more communicative with my father moving forward. I promise."

She nods, obviously pleased with my response. "Wonderful. I hope these two weeks have been helpful. Sometimes we need an outsider's perspective to open our eyes to things. Two weeks of working on yourself doesn't cure all, but I hope you feel as though this therapy has been enlightening."

I pinch my lips together, wanting to be honest with her because she's been honest with me. "I think parts of this have been helpful, but the thing about therapy is that people who go are there because of other people who actually need therapy but don't get it. It's kind of chicken-egg."

"I understand what you're saying. You can't control how other people act; you can only control your own reactions to them. We can always work on ourselves even if others choose not to. Every single one of us is a work in progress. I think you've progressed quite a bit in your two weeks here. Maybe you'll consider opening up to people in your life now that you have quite a few who you trust. Sometimes just talking about things helps, whether with a professional or not. I'm not telling you that you need therapy. I'm telling you that you don't have to feel alone. You don't have to carry all your burdens alone. You have people in your life with whom you can share them. Let them carry that weight with you. I promise it will weigh less heavily if you do."

A year ago, I would have laughed in her face for that comment. Now I think she's right.

A year ago, I hated Sulley O'Shea with a passion. Now she's the reason I have a relationship with my brother, always pushing and encouraging me on that front.

A year ago, I didn't have a circle of girlfriends who I felt I could depend on. Now I do.

A year ago, I had no interest in a relationship with my parents. Now I'm considering spending more time with my father.

And then a quieter voice inside my head reminds me that a year ago, I knew that no man on this planet gave a shit about me. Now I have one who does. And he's my damn husband. For now.

I've spent a lot of time thinking about Daylen over the past two weeks. While I'm starting to feel close to him, what will happen at the end of the year when we get the marriage annulled? Will he want nothing to do with me? Will we go back to hating each other like we always have? The way he kissed me at the airport had my head spinning and only served to confuse me more.

I don't want to be enemies, but I equally don't want to get hurt. I feel like I'm on a one-way train to heartbreak. There's only one solution to this. I need to derail the train before it reaches its inevitable destination.

DAYLEN

I'm sitting at the dining table by my pool, eating juicy steaks I cooked. Vance, Beau, and Champ are sitting out here with me. Kennedy returned yesterday. She didn't contact me. In fact, she was radio silent for the full two weeks she was gone. I assumed they didn't let her have her phone, but she could have contacted me on her way back or when she got back.

The fact is, I've missed her. Terribly. I've gotten used to having her around all the time, and then she was gone. Nothing. It was...lonely.

I'm trying to figure out why she didn't reach out when she returned. I kissed her at the airport when I said goodbye, and she let me. It was an amazing kiss. I know she felt it too. I had to steady her on her feet afterward.

So why didn't she call? Why do I sound like a girl?

Sulley is taking the Beavers' team out to a nice dinner tonight to celebrate Kennedy's return. It's her way of thanking Kennedy for her sacrifice. Then we're all meeting at a club to celebrate. I don't know why I'm so nervous, but I am. I'm not sure how to act around her anymore.

Sulley's family was in town this week so Vance didn't see much of her. He's just as much on edge for tonight as I am, so much so he doesn't realize I, too, am freaking out.

I'm aimlessly rubbing BJ's belly because she swallowed her steak whole and is now suffering the effects, when Beau interrupts my thoughts. "What's wrong with you, D? You're a million miles away."

I look down at BJ, willing her to help me come up with an adequate deflection. "Oh...umm...I was just thinking about what a dog and a near-sighted gynecologist have in common."

He narrows his eyes at me. "What?"

I plaster the biggest, fakest smile I can muster. "A wet nose."

The guys all burst into laughter and don't bother me about my weird mood anymore. Crisis averted.

We talk and laugh throughout dinner. Vance keeps checking his phone to see when the girls are done with their dinner, anxious to get to Sulley. I wish my girl was texting me when they're done.

My girl. Fuck, why do I think of her that way? Is she my girl?

Champ tells us about a new guy he's been dating. We tell

him to invite the man to join us tonight, but Champ maintains that he doesn't want to be the poster child for gay professional football players.

I shake my head. "That's bullshit. Fuck what anyone thinks. You should be free to be you, however and wherever you want. We've got your back, brother."

He gives me a small smile. "I know. But for every one of you, there's someone else who's ignorant. You've seen the bigotry I've dealt with, and that's just on our team. Imagine how bad it is in the world."

I nod in understanding. We have a player on our team, Reece Sanders, who treats Champ like a leper because of his sexuality. It drives us all nuts. A new rookie is threatening his job. We're hoping Reece gets cut before the season. If he doesn't, Vance, Beau, and I have discussed talking to management about Reece's unacceptable behavior. Coach hates him too. We know he'll have our back on this issue.

"They're ready," Vance excitedly announces as he stands, holding up his phone.

I chuckle. For a guy in a secret relationship, he's not doing a very good job of hiding it. Beau and Champ aren't supposed to know about him and Sulley.

Beau raises an eyebrow at me in question. I shrug, pretending I have no idea why Vance is wriggling around like a virgin on prom night.

I stand too. "Can you guys clean the dishes? I'm going to change my clothes. I'll be right back."

"Why?" Beau asks. "You never give a shit about what you look like. It's weird enough that you have a real haircut and an evenly shaved beard. Clean clothes too? What's this world coming to?"

I want to look nice for Kennedy tonight, but I can't say that, so I just give him the finger and say, "I smell like the smoke from the grill. I slaved away making nice steaks for you fuckers. You can give me ten minutes to jump in the shower and change my clothes."

Forty minutes later, we walk into the club. I'm in khaki slacks and a clean, fitted, black T-shirt that shows off my muscles. The guys were relentless with me over how nicely I'm dressed. Do I really always look like shit? I suppose I know the answer to that. I've never cared about how I look for anyone. *Until now.*

The bouncer allows us to butt to the front of the line and tells us the girls and Presley are already at our usual table in the VIP area.

Vance takes the steps two at a time. It's good that he's taking all the attention because my own excitement would otherwise be hard to hide. I'm right behind him, barely able to contain the quickening beating of my heart.

My eyes immediately find my girl. She takes my breath away. She's so beautiful. Her ponytail and makeup are perfect, as they always are when we go out...and pretty much all the time. I don't know what she did with her eye makeup tonight, but her green eyes sparkle particularly brightly.

She's wearing tight, black leather shorts that show off her mile-long legs with some sort of tiny white silky top that leaves little to the imagination. And I don't have to imagine anymore because I've seen the sultry perfection that lies underneath those clothes.

I have to adjust myself just thinking about her naked body. I'm hoping for a repeat performance tonight. How much longer do we have to stay here before she and I can leave together?

The table erupts in laughter just as we approach. "What's so funny?" I ask with a smile.

Kennedy's eyes meet mine, but I can't get a read on her. She's looking at me like she used to. With annoyance. I must be misreading it.

She gives me a less-than-warm glare. "I was just telling

them that I can sit on TikTok for hours, watching videos of cement being power washed, thinking it's absolutely brilliant. Then I'll watch some award-winning documentary on Netflix and think it's total crap."

I chuckle. "That's very true. I watched two straight hours the other day of someone popping pimples on TikTok. I couldn't stop. It's intoxicating."

She doesn't smile. She narrows her eyes at me. "You know what else pops up on my feed? Topless videos of my father working out. I've recently learned he doesn't post them himself. Someone else does it."

I grimace, but the guys burst out laughing. Champ elbows me. "Oh man, you're so busted." He looks at Kennedy. "Does Coach know? He'll tear Daylen a new one if he finds out."

She shrugs. "I don't know. Maybe I should find out," she threatens.

I gulp down the giant knot in my throat. I forgot about those videos. I haven't done one in a while, but they never seem to leave TikTok. People respond to them, comment on them, share them, and duet them all the time. I swear I created the account to help Coach after his divorce. How was I supposed to know the whole #SilverFoxTok thing would go viral? There are an awful lot of Daddy videos of Coach Jeffries out there. He would be pissed if he found out.

I don't respond as we slide into the booth and order drinks, hoping they quickly move on to a new topic of conversation.

They do, and for two solid hours, everyone has a good time. Everyone except me. Kennedy doesn't even glance my way. It's as if the day before she left didn't happen. It's as if we're not married. It's as if we're not getting closer.

At some point, my hurt morphs into anger. How dare she treat me like this.

Presley and Layla are doing their usual bantering thing. At some point, he announces, "Let me explain marriage in a nutshell. Your wife can spend four hours getting ready while you sit there waiting, but if your shoes aren't on when she's ready to go, you're the problem."

I shrug while my eyes meet Kennedy. "Maybe marriage isn't for everyone. Why buy the cow when you can get the milk for free?"

The girls all moan in annoyance, but Kennedy fires right back, "Why buy the whole pig when you can get the itty-bitty sausage for free?"

She holds her thumb and index finger less than an inch apart to emphasize her point, and the ladies all laugh with her.

Itty-bitty sausage? She knows that's not true.

I've had enough of this ice queen treatment. I pull out my phone and text her.

Me: Can we talk?

I see her react when her phone pings. She reads it and then just shakes her head and places the phone back in her purse.

She's ignoring me. Why?

I've spent most of the evening managing Vance and his raging hard-on for Sulley. God, he's obvious. He needs to tone it down. She's barely paying attention to him, but he's practically burning a hole through her.

After a while, I stop listening to him, unable to take my eyes off Kennedy. Why is she acting like this? What did I do wrong?

Vance and Sulley eventually disappear at the exact same time. Like that's not suspicious. They're probably off fucking in the stairwell. Lucky him.

I look at Kennedy and loudly announce, "I got you a new agent, like you asked me to do."

Her eyes widen.

Palmer appears confused. "Why would you ask Daylen for help with a new agent?"

Kennedy's face turns murderous at me. "Oh…umm…I was

talking about it with my father, and Daylen overheard us. He offered to do some legwork while I was gone because he has a few connections." Her mouth tightens. "Why don't we go somewhere and chat about this privately, Daylen? Somewhere quieter."

Finally.

I nod. "Yes, let's go have a private chat."

We both stand and excuse ourselves. She's walking briskly like she's on a mission. I almost have trouble keeping up. I may have poked the bear a little too hard, but I need to be alone with her. I itch to touch her.

We keep going until we find ourselves in a private bathroom stall. When we walk inside, she locks the door behind me in a manner that suggests I'm in big fucking trouble.

"Why would you say that in front of them?" she immediately spits in anger.

"What?" I ask innocently, even though it was anything but. "You asked me to find you an agent."

Her hands ball into fists at her side. "There's no good reason for me to have asked you. It was private. You did it to get a rise out of me. Grow up."

My shoulders fall. "I'm sorry. You're right. You were ignoring me, and I wanted to get your attention." I run my fingers through my nicely styled hair. "I...I missed you. And you haven't called since you got back. I wanted to pick you up from the airport. I wanted to know how your two weeks went. I don't understand why you're ghosting me. What did I do wrong?"

Her face softens a bit. "I'm sorry, Daylen. You've done nothing wrong. The past two weeks gave me some time to consider things. I think us sleeping together again was a mistake."

I grab her hips and pull her body flush to mine. "It can't be a mistake when it feels so right. I wasn't alone in there. I know you felt it too. We're good together."

Her eyes fill with tears, and she briefly relaxes into my body, placing her hands on my shoulders. I've missed her touch so damn much. For a few seconds, I can sense that she missed me too.

Eventually, she gently places her hands on my chest, pushing to give us a little more distance. "It *was* amazing, but we both know it can't last. We should stop now before one of us gets hurt." She briefly looks down before she looks back up at me. "This arrangement has an expiration date. Our friends are close. It's taken me a long time to find a circle of women who I can depend on. I won't do anything to mess that up. I think we should do what we're asked to do by Judge Jurassic and then try to part at the end of the year as the frenemies we've always been."

I open and close my mouth a few times. I'm in shock. "That's what you really want?" I ask.

She looks away and nods, croaking out, "I think it's for the best."

I'm not begging. Daylen Humblecut doesn't beg for women. It's the other way around.

I step away from her, puff out my chest, and steel my expression. "Fine, Cruella. If that's what you want. Back to frenemies it is. Meet me at the park tomorrow afternoon, and we'll pick up where we left off, per court orders. Judge Geriatric said to add an extra day each week until we catch up from your time away. I guess you'll have to suffer through seeing me three times a week for the next month. After that, it's back to status quo."

She wordlessly nods, but I can't drop it quite yet. "Why are you like this? Why do you enjoy misery?"

Her lower lip wobbles a bit, but she otherwise doesn't emote. "It's all I know. Why are you always so overly happy?"

I stare at her in disbelief. "Why wouldn't you want to be happy? It's like you go out of your way to be unhappy. Who chooses to live their life like that?"

An errant tear drops from her eye, but she says nothing.

I unlock the door and open it. Before walking through it, I announce, "By the way, you're now represented by Montgomery Sports Management, the top agency in the country. Kamryn Hart will be your agent."

Her face jerks in surprise.

"Yes, *that* Kamryn Hart. She can be the one to explain it all to you since we're nothing but frenemies. She's expecting your call. You're welcome."

I walk out the bathroom door and straight out the door of the club, no longer interested in being around anyone but my dog.

TWENTY-ONE

KENNEDY

It's been the worst few weeks. Daylen's words have cemented themselves into my head. I can't escape them. Am I choosing misery over happiness? I'm certainly miserable now.

He's been cold as ice to me. We meet as scheduled at the park to work on my vertical skills, but it's all very robotic and formal. There's no playful banter. No intimate touches. At a minimum, he used to find creative ways to touch my boobs which he thought were slick, but I always knew and let it happen. He's not even attempting that anymore.

I think I may have made a mistake in pushing him away. I miss him, and I miss the way we were with each other. The look of devastation on his face when we were in the club bathroom hasn't left me. Why has the big doofus gotten under my skin so much? Why am I so damn emotional lately? I cry every night in bed while downing a pint of ice cream, too tired to go out.

Per his idea, I wore a tight, leather Black Widow costume as my gameday walk-in outfit for my first game back. It. Was. Genius. The internet flipped.

After that, every designer on the planet reached out about

dressing me for my gameday outfits. I basically have my choice of anything I want to wear, and it's sent to me immediately for free. Some even pay me to wear their clothes.

I texted him about it to thank him, and he responded with a thumbs-up emoji, which is basically more of an FU emoji than the middle finger one. I suppose I can't blame him, given the way I treated him, but it still hurt. I wanted to share it with him. To celebrate with him.

I've done my best to put my head down and focus on basketball. I'm having a career season. I've never played better. Our team chemistry is off the charts, and we're on a collision course to make a run for the championship this year.

Kam is a fucking animal. She's gotten me endorsement deal after endorsement deal. I've never had this much money in my life. I'm thinking about buying a house. Initially I thought I'd buy something near Sulley, but she barely lives in her house anymore. She's had some issues with crazy fans, so she sleeps at Vance's almost every night. Even though she insists it will never happen, I know it's only a matter of time before she moves in with him.

I'll wait until my off-season, but I'm ready to buy, and I couldn't possibly be more proud or excited that I'm finally in a position to do so.

I'm stopping by Kam's office on my way to practice this morning. She said she may have a huge makeup endorsement opportunity for me and wants me to meet the head of marketing for the company. I have no idea which one it is. She said she had to sign an NDA, and I would meet them in person after I signed one too. But to say I'm excited about working with a makeup company would be the understatement of the century. This is my lifelong dream. I've been fantasizing about the possibilities since she mentioned it.

I make my way up to reception, where a woman named Shannon greets me warmly. "Good morning, Ms. Jeffries. Ms. Hart is in her office in a meeting." She slides over what appears to be a two-page contract. "She asked that you review this, sign it, and then join the meeting."

I don't know what the fuck I'm looking for. Shannon must sense my trepidation because she offers me a small smile. "Ms. Hart has reviewed it on your behalf. She said you should feel comfortable signing but should always review anything you sign as a matter of practice."

I nod. "Thanks."

I take a seat and pretend to read it for a few minutes. My head is too jumbled to comprehend anything. If Kam says it's fine, that's good enough for me. I sign it and hand it back to Shannon.

"Wonderful. You can head right in. They're expecting you."

I offer a quick knock before opening the door. When I do, I notice two other people sitting in her office. One is Jordie McNamara. I recognize her right away. She's the star of the new women's football league. She's beautiful, with a wavy blonde ponytail and eyes that remind me of Fallon and Harper's in their unique blue shade. She looks like she's a little younger than me, which makes sense because I think she recently graduated from college.

The man is remarkably attractive. He's probably around Daylen's age, but not nearly as big as my man.

Nope, Daylen's not *my* man. My husband, yes. My man, no.

The stranger has stylishly messy dark-brown hair, blue eyes, and the cutest dimples you've ever seen that frame the huge smile he has on his face as he stands to greet me. Holding out his hand, he warmly says, "Kennedy Jeffries. I'm so excited to finally meet you. I have a little girl who watches your games. My name is Phoenix Hale. Please call me Phoenix. I'm the director of marketing at Hale Cosmetics."

Taking his hand in mine, I do everything I can not to scream with excitement like a lunatic. Hale Cosmetics is the top cosmetic company in the world. This is the gold medal of endorsements. If I could pick one endorsement, this would be it.

I look at Kam, and she grins widely. "I'm good at my job, aren't I?"

"The best. Whatever they're offering, I accept," I immediately reply.

Kam's face falls as she shakes her head and mumbles something about me being a terrible negotiator.

Phoenix barks out a loud laugh. "I think we're going to get along just perfectly. Kennedy, do you know Jordie McNamara?" He points to her.

Jordie stands, and I realize she's just as tall as I am. "No, it's nice to meet you, Jordie. I'm excited to watch you play."

Her face lights up. "Oh man, I love watching you. Are you sure you're not better suited to play football? I've seen you take down quite a few players. You could be a linebacker."

I shrug. "My father always said I'd make a great football player."

She nods. "I think you would. I'm a huge fan of your dad's too. I used to watch him as a little girl. It must have been cool growing up going to his games."

Not as cool as you'd think, Jordie. Of course I don't say that out loud. I pretend that having a superstar of a father was as fun as everyone assumes it would be.

Phoenix's gaze toggles between me and Jordie. "You were right, Kam. Both their eyes are uniquely gorgeous in totally different ways. And both have such full lips," he admires, but not in a creepy way. "I have a million ideas churning through my head right now. This campaign is going to be special. Two talented superstar female athletes with model good looks? The possibilities are endless."

Jordie cowers under the praise. I look at her in bewilderment. Phoenix notices and sighs. "She doesn't love the cameras or wearing makeup, but we let her help create and find makeup that makes her comfortable. We even let her name it."

I gasp. "Do I get to name it too?"

He chuckles. "I suppose I walked into that one. Absolutely. Why not?"

I'm internally doing cartwheels while trying to maintain a cool demeanor.

We sit and chat for about an hour about a few concepts. I've probably never been more excited about anything in my life. My melancholy mood of late is immediately lifted.

After they leave, Kam and I talk for a few more minutes. "Don't fucking cockblock me in my negotiations," she jokes. "Play it a little cooler moving forward."

I giggle. "Crap, sorry. My bad. You should have told me who it was beforehand so I had time to calm down. I was flipping my shit when he introduced himself."

She nods. "I understand. It's a big deal. Fortunately, you and Jordie will get the same deal, which is very good." She shows me the number, and I nearly faint. In fact, I actually get lightheaded, and she forces me to sit while Shannon fetches me a glass of water and a protein bar.

For the first time in weeks, I'm genuinely happy as I walk into practice. Sulley looks at me skeptically. "Why are you so happy? It's weird."

"Me? I'm always cheery."

She raises an eyebrow. "Hmm. Seriously, you're awfully smiley. Oh, you must have been with one of your Tinder guys. I've been calling you for, like, an hour. Now I know why you didn't answer."

"Calling me? I hate when people call my phone. I don't use it for that. Text like a normal person."

She giggles. "I'll keep that in mind."

"Why were you calling?"

She shrugs. "Just checking in on you. You've been kind of distant. I know I've been spending a lot of time with Vance, but I…umm…don't want to lose our friendship. I'm just a little afraid to be in public right now with all the stalker crap going on."

I throw my arm around her. "I know. We're good. Honestly? I haven't gone out at all lately. I'm trying to stay focused on our season and staying out of trouble."

And I'm always exhausted and a little heartsick.

She wiggles her eyebrows. "Lots of Tinder guys coming by?"

Did I really used to spend so much time with Tinder men? I suppose I know the answer to that.

I shake my head. "Nah. No men and no liquor. I'm off all of it." I thump my head. "I'm going for clear-headedness this year. Men and liquor fog the brain."

Shay overhears us. "What? No men and no liquor for Kennedy? Has hell frozen over? You've been like a zombie lately. Are you sure you're okay, sausage jockey?" she jokes.

I cross my arms. "Sausage jockey? Hmm. I kind of like that name." Knowing they need me to be more like my normal self, I ask, "Speaking of liquor, how does a lesbian control her liquor?"

Shay bites back a smile. "How?"

"By her ears."

The two of them laugh, and all is normal again. I appreciate that they've noticed my off demeanor of late and were checking in on me, but I'm keeping things bottled up for now. My therapist in Maine would disapprove, but that's what I need to do for my own self-preservation. It's the only way I know how to handle things.

After practice, I'm in the training room with Fallon. She's kneading and stretching my lower back. It's been bothering me for a few days.

"Does anything else hurt?" she asks.

I move around a bit, testing my body. "Not right now. When my back flares up, I occasionally feel something between a shooting pain and numbness down my legs. It's like pins and needles at times."

"Oh," she says knowingly, "it's probably sciatica. It's a nerve inflammation in the lower back that can impact the nerves down your legs. Lie down and put your legs straight out. I'm going to raise them one at a time. Tell me when the pain gets bad."

After doing a few physical tests on me, she's confident it's sciatica. "We'll start with ice and then move to heat. I'll give you a few exercises which should help. We don't want to lose you for the playoffs. I'd prefer you sit for a week or two sooner rather than later. If it gets worse or moves to another part of your body, please tell me right away."

"I will. What causes it?" I ask.

"It could be a bunch of things. It's not a lack of core strength for you, but it is for some. Same with obesity, which is obviously also not the cause for you. It could be overuse. Are you still doing those extra workouts?"

I nod. "Yes."

"It's probably that. I used to get it all the time when I was pregnant with Harper. Pregnancy is a known cause, but I assume it's not that," she says in a jovial tone.

And that's the moment it hits me like a lightning bolt. I haven't gotten my period in a while. In fact, we're over six weeks into the season, and I haven't had it at all. Never since I got my first period at age thirteen have I been anything but perfectly on schedule. Did I fuck up my birth control pills?

I practically leap off the table and grab my bag. Rummaging through for my cosmetic case, I pull out my pills and open them. No, everything is in order. Did I miss one? No, I didn't. I never do.

Did I get drunk and throw up my pill? No, I haven't been wasted since Vegas.

And then I remember the night with my brother and Booster. We all got a small bout of food poisoning. I was sick that night, and the next day was the day I had sex with Daylen. We didn't use a condom for a few minutes.

Fallon walks over to me and notices the birth control pills in my hands. "Kennedy, could you be pregnant?"

I think I'm in shock. It takes me a while to respond, but when I do, I say, "I…I…I think I might be."

She sucks in a breath. "Oh shit. Who's the father?"

I'm completely speechless, at a loss for words as my brain starts to spin. My breathing becomes labored.

She places her hand on my back. "Relax, sweetie. Deep breaths. It's going to be okay. Sit down. You look like you might faint."

She helps me to sit, and I exhale a breath I didn't realize I was holding. "I…umm…wow. I can't believe this."

"Keep breathing," she instructs while continuing to rub my back.

Once the room stops spinning, I blurt out, "I need to go."

"Tell me what I can do to help," she offers.

I shake my head. "I don't know. I really have to go." I stand and look at her. "Please don't tell anyone."

"Of course not." She squeezes my arm one last time. "Don't hesitate to reach out. I'm here for you. You don't have to do this alone. You have plenty of people who care about you."

I nod robotically, still in shock. "Thank you."

I practically sprint to my car. Do I buy a pregnancy test first, or do I tell Daylen first? I don't need a pregnancy test to tell me I'm pregnant. I know in my core that I am. Besides being uncharacteristically late for my period, I've had obvious symptoms recently. I've been tired, my breasts are tender and bigger, I've had some lightheadedness, and the sciatica. Not to mention I've been horny as hell. I had assumed that was because of the dry spell, but it's very clearly the potential pregnancy. How could I have been so blind?

TWENTY-TWO

DAYLEN

I jump high into the air and catch the ball at practice before my feet fall back down for the completion. I'm immediately tackled hard to the ground by a giant linebacker falling on top of me. Fuck, that hurt.

I writhe around a bit, and some of the guys chuckle at my dramatics. Okay, maybe I'm exaggerating a little. I tend to do that at times.

In actual pain, I'm a tad slow to get up, and Coach shouts, "You good, Humblecut?"

Isn't that a loaded question. Physically, I'm fine. Mentally, I'm a mess. I miss her. I'm with her three times a week and still miss her. Because when we're together, it's as if we're not. She's so distant. I think I preferred it when we hated each other because the fire was there. I have no read on her. She's stoic, so I try to be the same way. I honestly don't know if I can make it through the rest of the year like this.

As I've reflected on our time together, I realized I was starting to fall for her. I'm not sure how or when it happened, but it did. And this iciness between us is messing with my head and hurting my heart.

I pretend that all is good in my world and nod. "I'm good, Coach," I wheeze as I spit a little blood.

"At least your teammates laughed," he says. "You know you're getting old if you go down hard in front of people and they panic instead of laughing. If I went down like that, they'd call the paramedics before bothering to check on me."

I chuckle. "Valid point, Coach."

I return to the huddle, and Vance looks at me. "All good?"

"As good as strippers when a bunch of drunk, wealthy frat boys walk into a club after having visited an ATM."

He cracks a small smile. "Nice catch."

I lick my fingertips and then circle them in the air. "A tongue and finger combo isn't just for flipping the pages of a book."

His smile widens while he simultaneously rolls his eyes and calls the next play.

As practice draws to a close, the team of trainers ask to examine my ribs. I remove my shirt, and they immediately wince. "D, you're all bruised. We should get them X-rayed."

I wave my hand dismissively. "Nah, I'm fine. It's tackle football. Bruises happen. They're not broken. Trust me, I would know." I've broken my ribs countless times. It's extremely painful—a hell of a lot more pain than I'm feeling now.

They instruct me to come get ice from them after I shower, which I assure them I will.

Before I head to the showers, I open my locker and pull out my phone to see if I missed any calls or texts while at practice. I see a notification of a text from Kennedy.

> Wifey: Need to talk. Rang your doorbell, but I guess you're not home. That, or you're ignoring me. Heading through your gate to the backyard. I'll wait for you by the pool. It's important.

The pool? Shit. BJ has access to that area. She's going to eat Kennedy.

I quickly call Kennedy's cell to warn her, but there's no answer. Oh my god, what if BJ already hurt her? Images flash through my mind of Kennedy lying on the ground in my backyard, bloody and injured, with BJ's mouth around her throat.

Without bothering to shower, and still in my uniform pants, I grab my keys and run out the door toward my car. I'm racing home, fearing the worst. I keep calling her cell, but there's no answer. Why isn't she answering? What does that mean?

Twenty-five long minutes later, I pull into my driveway and jump out of my Jeep. I sprint toward the gate to the backyard at full speed.

I'm fearful of what I might find back here, but nothing prepares me for what I see when I walk through. Kennedy is fast asleep on one of my chaise lounge chairs. She's on her back. BJ is peacefully sleeping, cuddled up next to her, with her head and paw on Kennedy's stomach almost protectively. Kennedy's hand is resting on BJ's neck. They look like best friends. What the hell? That dog hates women.

I quietly walk toward them so as not to disturb their sleep. They're both out cold.

Looking down, I notice Kennedy is wearing spandex shorts and a white tank top, leaving very little to the imagination. My wife truly is a stunning woman. Physically, she's perfect. Too bad she has to open her mouth.

Okay, I miss that mouth because lately she's been saying nothing to me at all. I'd rather snark than the silent treatment.

Her eyelids start to blink open. I can see her green eyes

take me in. There's something different about her right now. I can't place it. It's like she's softer. Impossible. This woman is as hard as nails. She's managed to spend three days a week with me all month without barely looking at me.

I think she's about to say something sweet, but I should have known better. She croaks out, "Why are you topless and in football pants? Do you ride around town like that? You're such a tool."

And...there's the bitch I know and love to hate. Pathetically, I perk up at her comment. It's the most she's given me in a long while.

"BJ hates all women," I tell her as I run my fingers through my messy practice hair. "I saw your text and was a little freaked out that she may have hurt you. Sorry I didn't stop to shower and change while worried about my *precious* wife."

She raises an eyebrow as she scratches behind BJ's ear. "Hurt me?" She looks down at BJ, and in a baby voice that mimics the one I use with my dog, she says, "This angel showed me nothing but love. She's a cupcake, right, baby girl?"

BJ coos and nuzzles her nose into Kennedy's belly like they're best friends. She doesn't even acknowledge me. Her father. The man who loves and feeds her every day.

Only one word comes to mind. *Traitor.*

Her eyes home in on the bruising on my chest, and her brow creases. "What happened?"

I wiggle my eyebrows. "My wife likes it rough."

She cracks a small smile before her face falls serious as she looks back up at me. "We need to talk."

I sigh. "Sure. Can you give me ten minutes? I really need to jump in the shower. I can smell myself."

She nods as she stretches her arms and yawns, revealing a sliver of her silky stomach that I miss licking. My dick stirs, and she notices. "I can't believe you guys wear those tight pants to play ball." Her eyes, shaded with obvious lust, stare unashamedly at my cock. "They leave *very* little to the imagination."

I roll my eyes and start walking to the house. "Stop ogling me, Ursula. I'll be back in a few minutes." I admit that I walk extra slowly toward the house so she can admire my ass.

I can't help the smirk that finds my lips. That felt like the old us. I can't believe how much I missed our banter this past month.

I'm in my oversized shower, just about to finish, when the thick, seamless glass door opens and Kennedy walks in naked. I swallow down the large gulp in my throat. "W...what are you doing?"

She exhales, as if in resignation. "I'm so fucking horny. I helped you a few weeks ago. Now it's your turn to pony up." She nods at my rapidly growing erection. "You appear to be on board with the plan. Don't pretend otherwise."

My lips curl in amusement. "This is what we needed to talk about? You chomping at the bit for some Humblecock?"

Her face scrunches, and she makes a look of disgust. "Ugh. Humblecock? I'm adding men who incorporate cock into their last names to my red flag list."

I chuckle. "You can't get enough of my Humblecock. Just admit it."

"It has nothing to do with you. I just need some cock, and *Humblecock* is the only one on the menu. Can you just shut your pretty mouth and give me a few orgasms? I need it."

We both smile in amusement. This is how we used to be, and I don't think I'm the only one who's missed it.

I scratch my fingers through my beard, pretending to contemplate this even though my dick is giving my excitement away. "Hmm. I suppose I can take one for the team. What are you gonna give me?"

"What do you mean?" she asks.

"When I needed to fuck, you had conditions. First, you sodomized me, and then you made me wear your uniform to your game, where I had to deal with a whole thing with your father over it. What do I get if I give you what you need?"

She calls my bluff and spins on her heels before placing her hand on the door handle. "Forget I asked."

She's about to push it open when I grab her by the throat and pull her back flush to my front. With my other hand I cup her pussy, and her breath catches. "Fuck yes," she moans.

I whisper into her ear, "Is this where you want me?" I tighten my grip on her neck and slowly run my middle finger through her. She's swollen and dripping wet. "Where you need me?"

Her breathing deepens as she relaxes back into me. "Yes. Please. God, I need to be touched. Touch me, Daylen. Touch me everywhere with your big, rough hands."

She places her hand over my lower one and pushes my finger into her tight, slick warmth while tilting her hips to deepen it. "I need to come so badly. You have no idea."

My hand slides down from her throat and grabs her breast, twisting her nipple until it's nice and hard. I add another finger inside her pussy, and together they push easily in and out of her slick channel while my thumb finds her clit. My lips latch onto her neck, tasting her unique sweetness.

My cock is painfully hard and leaking. I rub it through her ass cheeks in hopes of gaining some relief. I'm annoyed with how my body reacts to hers. I want to hate doing this with her, but I can't. It's not just that she's hot and I haven't had sex in several weeks. I think there's something about the push and pull of our relationship that stirs something in me. I've always had it easy with women. I thought I liked the easy, compliant type, but it turns out that this infuriating, mean bitch turns me on like no one else ever has. There was a level of passion when we were together that I've never achieved with a woman before. I assumed it was the after-effects of the boner shake, but my attraction is just as strong right now as it was then. Maybe even stronger, considering how terrible the past few weeks have been between us and how much I've truly missed her.

I get into a rhythm, stroking her inner walls while working her clit and hardened peaks. Her hips gyrate to my movements while the sounds leaving her mouth are feral. I guess she really did need this.

Her tits feel slightly fuller than I remember. Heavier. Regardless, they're undoubtedly the most perfect pair ever created. I've never been around a woman with more sex appeal. She oozes it in every movement she makes.

In what feels like mere seconds, she's exploding all over my hand as wave after wave crashes over her trembling body. Hearing her scream my name has moved to the top of the charts as my favorite music.

When she's done, she turns around so our eyes meet. Water trickles over her long, dark eyelashes that frame her green eyes so perfectly. They're a slightly deeper shade of green right now, but I can see them very clearly oozing with the same torment I'm feeling. She wants to hate this as much as I want to, but she can't help but feel the passion and chemistry we so obviously share.

We breathe the same air for several long beats with our lips nearly touching but never meeting.

She whispers, "I want to hate you."

I whisper back, "I want to hate you too."

She takes several long breaths. Oh, how I've missed the scent and taste of her sweet breath. We kissed for hours that night in her apartment. It was probably the only tender thing we did. I love the way she kisses. It's aggressive and passionate.

I can feel her swallow as she looks up at me with pleading eyes. "I need you to fuck me like you hate me, Daylen, because you're going to hate me again soon."

I tilt my head to the side in confusion. Why would she say that? Why would I hate her again? Is she assuming I'll hate her again once our marriage is over? Is that what the ice queen treatment has been all about? Self-preservation?

I rub her lower lip with my thumb, and her whole body shivers. Goosebumps spread all over her tan, soft skin.

Needing to reassure her, I breathe, "I don't think I could ever hate you again, Kennedy, no matter what."

Pain crosses her face. What's going through that enigmatic head of hers? I have no read on her right now. She tells me she wants nothing to do with me, that having sex was a mistake, and now she's naked in my shower begging me to fuck her like I hate her because I'm going to hate her when it's over. Is she going to blow me off again when we're done? I can't handle that. Maybe we should talk before this happens. I need clarity on our situation.

She reaches for my cock, but I grab her wrist. "Don't."

She jerks back in surprise. "You don't want me?" There's no edge to her tone. She thinks I don't want her.

"You know I do, but you're messing with my head. You hurt me when you slammed the door in my face," I admit. "I'd be crazy to let you do it to me again."

Tears well in her eyes. "You are the last person on this earth that I want to hurt." She cups my face so damn tenderly. "My feelings for you were beginning to run a little deeper than I'm accustomed to. It took me by surprise."

"Then why did you end things before they truly got started?"

"We had an expiration date."

"Had?" Her referring in the past tense is bizarre.

She throws her arms around my neck and presses our bodies close together. Her nipples rub against my chest. I love having her soft body on my hard one. "I have missed you so much, Daylen. The past few weeks have been horrible for me. Please, I need you. When we're done, we'll have an honest conversation. I promise. I need to feel you inside me again."

I'm conflicted, but I'm powerless to her when her naked body is close to mine.

This time when her hand reaches for my cock, I don't stop her. She begins to stroke me, and her touch feels so good I nearly weep like a baby.

I run my hands down her back. "Let's get out before things get too heated. I don't have a condom in here."

She shakes her head. "We don't need one. I want you here and now."

I assume that's because she's on the pill and we haven't had sex with other people since before Vegas.

It felt so good being inside her without one, even though it was for a short time. I ache to feel that again, so I let all rational thoughts leave my brain.

I move her hair out of her face and look into her eyes. "I can't fuck you like I hate you because I don't. Not one little bit."

She peppers my chest with kisses and breathes, "I don't hate you either, but fuck me like you do. Please. I need it rough. It makes me feel alive."

She takes my hand and places it on her neck. I squeeze it a little but then release it and smack her pussy hard with that same hand. She gasps, but her eyelids flutter in response.

I aggressively walk into her until she's forced back and pressed flush to the tile wall. Looking down at her, I grit my teeth and growl, "You're not in charge, I am. I'll choke you when I want to choke you. I'll slap you and bite you as I please. Hell, I'll spank your naughty ass if I want to do that. Do you understand me?"

She nods enthusiastically as her face lights up. She loves when I'm bossy, and she equally loves being manhandled. She's nuts in the best way possible.

I grab her by the throat and pin her to the wall much harder than I normally would. I'm careful to apply pressure to the sides, not the windpipe. I don't actually want to constrict her airway.

I wonder how far I can push this. I lift her slightly off the ground by only the neck. Her tippy toes are still supporting some of her body weight, but not all.

Her reaction? Her nipples harden, and her cheeks flush. This chick is *off the reservation* crazy.

"You want more?"

She can't nod because I'm supporting her weight by her neck, so she whispers, "Yes. More. Harder. Rougher."

I lift her a drop more until her feet are off the ground. I've never once done this to a woman. Choking? Yes. Holding her entire body up by her neck? No.

Her only response is to start stroking my cock again, which couldn't possibly be any harder. "Do you feel me, baby? Do you feel what you do to me?"

She moans.

I lick across the seam of her mouth before covering it with my own. She gives it right back to me in spades, with her tongue immediately invading my mouth like she's dying for a taste. We brutalize each other's lips with punishing kisses that will undoubtedly mark us both.

God, she's so hot.

I pull her leg until both are wrapped around me. Most of her weight sits on my waist now, but I still have a strong hold on her neck and squeeze it a bit harder, seeing just how far she'll let me go. She moans into my mouth as the pressure increases. The woman loves to be choked, there's no doubt about that. Not just a light image of choking. Squeezing hard until I think she could pass out type of choking.

I kiss her hard and long, as my other fingers flick and torment her nipples until I'm sure they're tender and aching. I can see them getting red and raw, yet she doesn't even flinch. In fact, she claws at me like I'm bringing her the greatest pleasure she's ever known. Even with the rain shower pounding down on us, I can feel her juices gushing all over me.

When I slap her breasts a few times, she thrusts that wet pussy over my cock and scratches her long nails down my chest in response.

Damn, I think I get off on the pain too, because she broke skin, and my cock is leaking in excitement.

I have no idea if this is hate or lust or something in between, but holy hell, it's hot, and I just want inside her body. The way she's gyrating her hips tells me she's ready.

Without bothering to prepare her, knowing she's soaked, I move my hips and slam straight into her in one powerful thrust. Her mouth breaks from mine as she tilts her head back and screams out at the unexpected intrusion.

I take the opportunity to suck and bite her collarbone and breasts, as I finally remove my hand from her throat. Noticing the dark red ring around her neck spurs me on to move in and out of her at a barbaric, merciless pace.

She leans her head forward and sinks her teeth into my shoulder. "Ahh," I scream as she undoubtedly breaks my flesh. More liquid lust fills her pussy as I glide in and out of her like I'm trying to kill her with my dick.

I can feel her pussy wrap around me like it's trying to suffocate me before she screams her way into an orgasm that has her whole body convulsing in my arms. It's honestly a thing of beauty. I take a moment to admire how sexy she looks when orgasming. Lust practically spills from her pores. I've never seen anything more perfect in my life.

Her head eventually falls on my shoulder as her body heaves from exhaustion.

"How do you feel?" I ask.

She pants, "Like my organs have been rearranged. I think I need to ice my vagina."

I bite back my smile. "Lock that shit down and suck it up, buttercup. We're not done."

Her head immediately pops up. "You didn't come?"

"Not yet. You wanted it hard. It's about to get harder. Feel free to say mercy," I challenge in a more playful tone.

Her lips curl in amusement. "Bring it, big boy. I can take it."

I turn off the water because it's getting cold and annoying. Walking us out of the shower and not caring about the water on the floor, I set her down and then violently spin her and bend her over my vanity.

I grip a healthy fistful of her hair and snap her head back until our eyes meet in the mirror. When they do, I mouth, "Say mercy."

She mouths back, "Never."

At that, I thrust right back into her as she yells out and squeezes her eyes shut. Quickly grabbing her throat with my other hand, I grit out, "Open your eyes when I'm fucking you, sugar tits."

They pop open right away and again meet mine in the mirror. I'm being so damn harsh and demanding with her, but she's not scared at all. She's loving this. I've never been this rough with a woman, but this woman is lapping up every second of it. The crazy thing is that I am too.

I've now got one hand pulling her hair and the other squeezing her throat, while I savagely move in and out of her body. I don't know that I'd want this every time I have sex, but she's awakening something in me I didn't know I needed. She's significantly taller and stronger than anyone I've ever been with. I love that she can take everything I'm giving and still want more. I'm so big and always afraid of hurting women, but with her, I can unleash my beast without any worries.

There's nothing gentle about what we're doing. It's brutal, hard fucking at its finest.

Her hips slam onto the vanity over and over again. It will undoubtedly leave bruises and other marks on her body, but she never breaks the pace. She never asks for the mercy I imagine most would.

She reaches her hand under her body and grabs my balls so fucking hard. I think I black out for a second. The unexpected pleasure is indescribable. It takes everything I have not to let go right on the spot and spill my seed inside her.

I get it together enough to give her what she needs again. Looking down at her apple of an ass, I have a sudden need to own it. I release her throat before smacking her ass as hard as I can. It immediately reddens. I look in the mirror for some reaction from her, but I see a damn smile on her face.

With our eyes still meeting, I take two of my fingers and stick them in my mouth before shoving them right up her ass without any preparation. Her eyes roll back in her head.

It doesn't take long for her to reach another release. This time I go over the edge with her as I come inside a woman for the first time in my life.

TWENTY-THREE

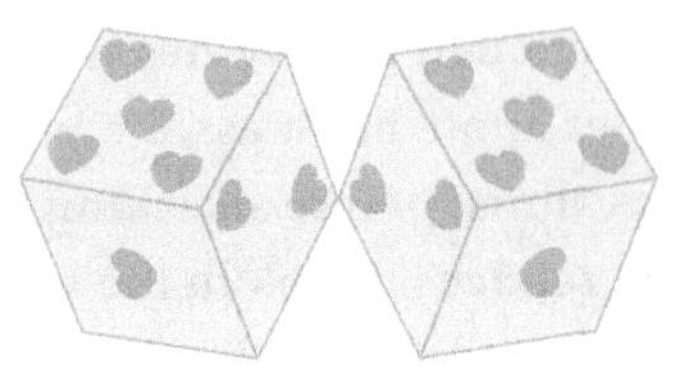

KENNEDY

"How many guys have you slept with?" he surprises me by asking as we lie in his bed during our post-coital bliss.

I couldn't move if I wanted to. The man fucked me into a near coma. After the bathroom smackdown, we got into bed and did it all over again.

Every inch of me is sore. My throat, shoulders, and breasts are all marked up from his mouth. I'm going to be applying cover-up to my body for weeks when I play ball. That's if I can walk. But I wouldn't change it for anything in the world. That sex was everything I needed and then some. The mind-blowing chemistry we share is undeniable.

I condescendingly pat his chest. "Just you," I answer. "The rest didn't let me sleep."

He chuckles. "Really. Tell me. I won't judge."

"Umm, you will most definitely judge, because it's a lot, but I don't know the precise answer. Do you know your body count?" I challenge, knowing there's no way he has the answer.

He shakes his head. "I have no idea."

"Right. We're both whores. Let's leave it at that."

He turns his head on his pillow and looks at me. "I prefer to think of us as experts in the field. It sounds better."

I nod. "Well said. I think you might get smarter after you come."

"It's called post-nut clarity," he informs me. "All men are smarter after they come."

I twist my lips at his fun pillow talk. "I can see that. Unfortunately for me, my mind is most active right when I want to fall asleep. It's extremely inconvenient."

He smiles. "I love when you tell me what keeps you up at night. It's always amusing. What's keeping you up lately?"

I think for a moment, wanting to keep it playful, not quite ready to get into the heavy. "Last night I was thinking about *The Cosby Show*."

"The eighties television show?" he asks in obvious surprise.

I nod. "Yes. I used to watch it on Nick at Nite all the time when I was a kid."

"I did too," he admits. "Why were you thinking about it?"

"The mom's name was Clair Huxtable," I state, "the dad's name was Cliff Huxtable, and the show followed them and their Huxtable children."

"And?"

"Why was it called *The Cosby Sh*ow? Yes, it was the main actor's real name, but no one on the show was named Cosby. Why wasn't it called *The Huxtable Show*?"

His loud, booming laugh threatens to shake the house off its foundation. I used to hate that laugh. Now I miss it when I don't hear it for a while. I've missed it terribly this past month.

"Holy shit. You're right. I never thought of it."

I smile. "This is the random crap that goes through my mind at night and keeps me awake."

I start to crawl over him to his other side. "Switch sides with me," I instruct.

He shoves me back down. "No way. This is my side. All my stuff is on the night table."

"I don't want to lie in the wet spot. It's your fault you made me do that. You lie in it."

He chuckles. "I'll do my best not to make you come so hard next time." He pulls my body until we're both snuggled closely on his side of the bed. "Better?"

"I suppose."

He's now lying on his side, facing me in all his naked glory while leaning on his elbow. I turn to him as well, with our faces only inches apart. He runs his fingertips back and forth over my bare hip. "This is my favorite part of a woman's body. It's so uniquely feminine."

"Not my tits?" I half joke. He's obsessed with my tits. He's always staring at them and, when we have sex, his mouth or hands are always on them.

"That's my favorite part of *your* body," he answers, "because they're complete and total perfection. In fact, they felt fuller today. Is that part of a woman's cycle?"

If it's the cycle of being pregnant, then yes, I think to myself.

I swallow hard. It's time. This is my opening.

I take his hand in mine, threading my fingers through his. "I did come here for something…other than the orgasms. Thanks for those, by the way."

He wiggles his eyebrows up and down. "Back at you."

I exhale a long breath. "I got sidetracked by the sex, but I do want to talk."

He nods. "Me too. I've hated the past month. I don't want it to be like that betw—"

"I'm pregnant," I blurt out because there's just no easy way to drop this kind of bomb.

He blinks in rapid succession over and over but otherwise remains wordless.

"I'm sorry to just say it like that," I continue. "I had a whole speech planned, but I forgot it. Anyway, I'm pregnant. I only just realized it today. I know you didn't come inside me before tonight, but I guess they're right in health class about precum possibly causing pregnancy. Whoda thunk it?"

Oh Christ. Discussing precum and health class were not in my planned speech.

"I…I…I." I keep stuttering like an imbecile. Shit, Kennedy, get it together. "I don't expect anything, but I feel strongly that you have every right to know. I hate when women keep it a secret as if it's not also the man's child just because he isn't carrying it."

Silence. More blinking by him. Maybe he's having a stroke. Should I call an ambulance?

"Do you have any questions? I'm not sure I'll have answers, but I'll try my best."

He continues blinking but doesn't otherwise move.

"Please say something. I was flipping my shit the whole way over here. If you hate me and want me to leave, I will, but I need you to emote in some way."

In light of him not moving, I start to get up, planning to get dressed to leave, but before I can do so, he grabs my arm and says, "Beau. Fucking. Fudd."

I shake my head. "No, it's not Beau's. It's yours. I know that for sure. I haven't been with anyone else since last year. I was a little trigger-shy about being intimate with anyone after New Year's Eve."

He shakes his head. "Boner Shake. We're having a child conceived via Boner Shake."

I bite back my smile. "I suppose that's accurate. Perfect, let's blame Beau."

He looks at my stomach as if it shows anything, which it doesn't, and then his eyes widen in what appears to be…delight. "Our kid is going to be the greatest athlete of all time," he proudly and loudly announces.

I stare at him, dumbfounded. "That's the first thing to come to your mind when I tell you, my forced husband, that I'm pregnant? That the kid will be a great athlete?"

"Not a great athlete," he corrects. "*The greatest* athlete of all time. Think about her genes. Yours and mine together. She'll be a prodigy. She'll have the height, the coordination, everything."

"It could be a boy," I remind him.

This conversation is not going how I thought it would go. Not at all.

He shakes his head. "No way. It's a girl. I'm already a #GirlDad. I have a #GirlDad hat that BJ gave me for Christmas last year."

"BJ gave you a hat?"

He nods. "Yes."

"Did she order it herself?"

He nods again. "Yes. She's very smart." His eyes widen again. "Holy crap, our kid will be smart too. You're super smart."

Maybe he really is having a stroke.

"Can we take a step back here?" I suggest. "I'm not sure you're processing this information properly. Maybe you're in shock."

He shakes his head, and then BJ lets out a bark before climbing onto the bed, collapsing next to me, and resting her head on my stomach.

He gasps. "BJ knew. That's why she didn't attack you. That's why her paw was lying protectively over your stomach. She knew her little sister was in there. It all makes perfect sense now."

Yep, the guy has officially lost the plot.

I study his face carefully. "Do you have any questions?"

"When are you due?"

I shrug. "I don't know. My best guess would be nine months from Boner Shake day?"

"What did the doctor say?"

"I haven't seen a doctor yet," I inform him. "I realized I was pregnant two hours ago."

"And then you took a pregnancy test?" he asks.

I shake my head. "I came straight here when I realized it. I… I…" Tears well in my eyes. "I didn't want to deprive you of anything…if you want to be a part of it."

His face falls, and he pulls me close to him. "Why are you crying?"

I wipe the tears. "I'm not."

"You are. You're not happy about this?" he asks with worry written all over his face.

"I don't know how I feel," I answer honestly. "I haven't had time to consider it. Frankly, I was more worried about you. I realized I was pregnant and came straight here. I didn't think you'd be so damn happy. I thought you were going to hate me, and I wanted to rip off the Band-Aid."

His brows crease together. "Why would I hate you?"

I point to my stomach. "Duh?"

"It's not like you did it on purpose. You're the one who stopped things that day. I was the irresponsible one, not you. You should hate me." He gasps. "Wait, do you hate me?"

What in the fuck is happening here? This is the weirdest conversation to ever take place.

I stare at him and shake my head. "No, Daylen, I don't hate you for getting me pregnant. We both did this…and Beau Fudd."

His shoulders relax. "Phew." He sits up suddenly and gasps again. "We need to get you a pregnancy test. I don't want to get all excited only to have my heart broken."

"Excited? You're excited about this?"

"Hell yes. I can't wait to be a dad. I had the best dad ever. Oh my god, he's gonna flip his lid about being a grandpa. I need to call him right away."

I grab his arm. "Daylen, I don't want anyone to know yet."

He shakes his head. "I can't keep secrets from him or Vance. I won't last. He and Vance are my best friends." A dreamy look takes form on his face. "I hope I'm as good a dad as mine is."

I plop my head back down on the pillow. "I had the worst mom. All I hope is that I'll be nothing like her." Realization finally starts to settle in, and I begin to freak out. "Oh god, I can't do this. I don't know how to be a mother. I'm not like you and your dad. I had no one to show me how to act."

He wipes the tears beginning to form under my eyes. "You're going to be a great mom," he confidently assures me.

I shake my head, no longer able to control the tears from spilling from my eyes. "I can't do this," I sob.

He takes my hand in his and kisses it. "You can. I know you can."

I look up at him and croak out, "What makes you so sure?"

He runs his knuckles over my cheek and looks at me with all the sincerity in the world. "Moms are nature's ultimate protectors. No one protects the people she cares about better than you. There are literally a million memes out there about you being a superhero protector. We're going to make mistakes, all parents do, but we're going to do a lot of things right too, because we're going to love this baby. That's all you have to do as a parent. Love the shit out of your kid. I know we can both do that. I don't have any doubts."

I'm silent. It's like this guy has a handbook on how to handle this kind of situation perfectly, and he's hitting every single mark. The man is a walking, talking green flag.

He sits back up and takes my hand in his. "Here's what we're going to do. First, I'm going to make food for my three best girls. I need to keep you all well fed."

"Three?" Oh crap, are they twins? Triplets?

"You, baby prodigy, and BJ."

I nod in understanding while simultaneously breathing a sigh of relief.

"Then we're going to buy a test to confirm the pregnancy. If it's as you think, we'll make a doctor's appointment to make sure baby prodigy is growing as she should be."

"You're so…level-headed. It's freaking me out."

He barks out a laugh. "Would you rather I freaked out? Did you think I'd freak out?"

"Honestly? Yes."

He stands and starts to put on his clothes. "No way. I'm already thinking of which room will be the nursery. We can talk to Layla and Presley about things babies need. You should move in right away so we can start planning everything."

He says it nonchalantly, like it's not a big deal that I'd be moving in.

I can't get a single word in as he seemingly plans the rest of our life before exiting the room to make us lunch.

What the fuck just happened?

I TAKE my time getting dressed because I don't think I'm processing everything that has gone on today. When I woke up this morning, insta-family was *not* on my bingo card.

It's like he decided the rest of our lives without consulting me. I have no idea what I want, but Daylen has unilaterally decided what it will be.

I think we need to confirm the pregnancy, and then we'll have a conversation about things. I'm not ready for all this. *We're* not ready.

Mary Poppins is out there whistling while making lunch as if he doesn't have a care in the world. If I'm not mistaken, I think I hear BJ whistling with him. That can't be.

The doorbell rings, and he shouts, "Can you grab that? I'm at the stove, and BJ and I are just finding our groove."

"Sure," I respond with my mind still spinning on its axis.

I open the door and see a blonde-haired, blue-eyed, unusually attractive Amazon delivery woman holding a small box. Her pretty face drops when she notices me. "Oh, is Daylen home?"

I cross my arms as a jealousy I've never before experienced runs through my body. "Are you on a first-name basis with all your customers?" I ask with a heavy dose of edge to my tone.

"Oh…umm…I…" She holds up a small box. "I have a delivery for him."

I go to reach for it, but she pulls it back. "It has to be…signed for," she lies. No one has to sign for Amazon deliveries. In fact, most of them don't even ring the bell anymore. They just drop it, take a picture, and then leave.

I offer her my biggest fake smile. "Oh, well, I'm his *wife*, so I can sign for it."

Her face drops about twenty stories. Oh man, this is fun.

"He's m…married?" she scream-asks. It's more of a high-pitched squeal.

I nod. "Yep." I rub my non-existent belly. "And we're expecting our first baby. My crazy husband is convinced it's a girl, but I don't know. What do you think?"

If I thought her face was painted in horror before, I was wrong. She practically throws the box at me and leaves a trail of smoke as she runs back toward her truck and takes off.

I inwardly laugh as I close the door and walk back into the kitchen. Tossing the small box at Daylen, I nonchalantly say, "I can't believe you banged your Amazon delivery woman. Is it the blue polyester uniform that does it for you?"

He turns his head from the stove and raises his eyebrow at me. "Don't judge. She's hot."

"She is. Judge Century Club will not be happy," I joke.

"It was before Vegas," he immediately responds. "I've kept my word. Do you doubt me?"

In reality, I don't doubt him. We're not even together and yet I know he would never cheat on me. That realization is also a bit mind-blowing.

I shake my head. "No, I don't doubt you at all."

"Good. Honestly, I forgot about her. I guess a new Amazon delivery person is in my future. I hope the new one has the same gag reflex. Do you think that's an Amazon hiring prerequisite?"

I cross my arms. "No way her gag reflex is better than mine."

His smile widens. "Why don't you get on your knees so I can

reevaluate? Suck a Dick Sunday is coming up. It's my favorite weekly holiday, but I'm willing to let you celebrate it a few days early."

"Is that what I'm having for lunch? Humblecock cream?"

He lets out a huge laugh. "Oh man, you make me laugh. Our daughter will be funny with us as her parents. This kid is going to be the whole package."

I sigh. He really has adjusted to the notion of fatherhood quite quickly.

An hour later, we're both in hats and sunglasses at the drugstore. I suggested hats and sunglasses in case we're recognized while buying a pregnancy test. I don't need this leaked to the media.

Daylen has placed every pregnancy test in the store in our basket. I stare at him. "I don't think we need thirty of them."

"We want to be sure."

"I don't think I could possibly pee enough to manage all these tests."

"I can pee on some of them," he offers. "We're a team, right?"

I pinch the bridge of my nose. "I hope this kid has my personality, not yours."

He chuckles, but I stare at the overflowing basket with my hands on my hips and disapproval written all over my face.

He scrunches his nose. "Fine. We don't need all of these." He then places one of them back on the shelf. One.

We head to the cashier, and he hands her the basket. She smiles at him. "Will this be all, sir?"

He shakes his head and deadpans, "No, I just wanted to show you what I've got so far."

Her face falls in confusion.

I interrupt, "Ignore him. He thinks he's a comedian. This will be all, thank you."

We get in his car to drive back toward his house, which happens to be unexpectedly nice. I was shocked when I went there today.

"Why do you have such a big house?" I ask while he's driving. "You're a single man."

"I'm not single, I'm a married man, but yes, I bought it while single. I had a place in the city, but then I got BJ. She was antsy being cooped up in an apartment all day. She needs space. The house has a doggie door and a huge backyard. Now she can come and go as she pleases and run around out back when I'm not home. She's got a lot of energy, like her daddy."

"What do you do with her when you go on road trips?"

"I told you before. I have Chef Benny. He takes care of the house and the dog. He also does a lot of grocery shopping and meal prep for me. I should call him. He needs to start meal prepping for you to ensure you're eating a healthy diet. If you give me a list of things you do and don't like, I'll give it to him."

"You have a butler?"

He turns to me. "You have an intern."

"True, but I don't even pay him yet. Though I'm giving him a few bucks starting soon."

"Benny isn't a butler. He's more of a…household manager."

I roll my eyes. "That's modern-day nomenclature for butler."

He smiles.

"What's so amusing?"

"That was a big word. I told you our kid will be smart."

I lean my head back on my headrest and admit, "I learned that word from Harper last week. She's smarter than me and she's nine years old."

He chuckles. "I love that kid. I hope we get one just like her. We should use the same word of the day toilet paper she has. It works." He then rattles off about a million other things he wants us to do for this child. He's making my head hurt, planning our future. I don't even know what I'm having for dinner tonight, let alone what school system my kid will be in, which apparently Daylen has now mapped out.

"Daylen," I plead, "please slow down."

He looks at the speedometer. "Oh shit, you're right. Precious cargo on board. See, I told you that you'd be a good protector."

I wasn't referring to the speed of the car. Tears form in my eyes. I have to turn to the window to hide them from him. Things are moving at warp speed. I can't handle it.

Though apparently he was actually speeding because we're hit with the sounds of a police siren about five seconds later and are pulled over.

We're parked on the side of the road when the police officer walks up to the driver's side and knocks on the glass. Daylen rolls down the window. "Sorry, man, my girl needs to pee on twenty-nine sticks. I was rushing home."

The middle-aged male police officer removes his aviator sunglasses and stares at Daylen. "Sir, have you been drinking?"

Like an idiot, Daylen nods. "I have. Do you really think I'd take this woman home sober?"

I swear to god, he has a propensity to choose the worst times to make jokes.

The officer's eyes toggle between me and Daylen before busting out into a huge grin. "Holy Toledo. It's you. I'm a huge fan."

Daylen removes his hat and gives him a big grin. "Always happy to meet a fan."

The police officer scrunches his eyebrows in confusion. "I don't know who you are, but your friend is Kennedy Jeffries, the famous basketball player. My three daughters are huge fans. They never miss a game on television."

I can't help but let out a laugh, my bad mood temporarily forgotten. Removing my hat, I offer a million-dollar smile of my own. "That's nice of you to say. Thank you. I apologize for my slow friend. He was dropped on his head a lot as a baby. I assure you, he hasn't been drinking. In fact, he's rushing me to the stadium for our practice. That's why he was speeding."

The police officer appears conflicted.

"Listen," I continue, "how about you let my butler get me to the stadium on time? As an expression of my gratitude, I'll leave you and your daughters four tickets right on the floor for our next game. I'll even stop by myself with signed jerseys for your girls. It will be a night they never forget. You'll be their hero."

His face immediately brightens. "Oh wow. That would be incredible. Thank you, Ms. Jeffries."

"Mrs. Humblecut," Daylen mumbles grumpily.

I snap my head to him and give him a look of warning. He has seriously lost his marbles. Every single one of them.

The police officer lets us go, and we pull back onto the street, making our way to Daylen's house in silence because I'm still processing his insane behavior since I told him about the baby. At least I do have the wherewithal to text Booster to have him take care of the police officer's tickets and jerseys for me.

We're now waiting for the first two pregnancy tests to marinate properly. I appropriately had enough pee for two tests, rendering the other twenty-seven completely useless. Frankly, they're all useless. I know the answer.

I'm fiddling with my phone to waste time, but the reception is terrible. I go to the Wi-Fi settings to try to find Daylen's network, but none of them make sense. Nothing with his name or address. "What's your Wi-Fi network?" I ask.

"Police Surveillance Van #2," he answers without hesitation.

Sure enough, that's on the list of networks in range.

"I know I'll regret asking this, but why?"

"Because I like fucking with my neighbors. Duh. Can you imagine the looks on their faces when they went to log onto their networks and they saw a police van network on the street?" He laughs as he amuses himself.

The father of my child, ladies and gentlemen.

I look through his belongings on his vanity. I notice a tube of Crest Kids' strawberry-flavored toothpaste that I must have missed earlier when he was pounding into me and choking me in this very spot. I pick it up and look at it. Holy shit. Now it all makes sense. "This is why you always taste like strawberries? You use kids' toothpaste."

He smiles. "I use real toothpaste too, but then I use this at the end. Doesn't it taste good? Every man can taste like mint, but very few can taste like strawberries. Don't deny that you like it. Who doesn't like the taste of strawberries?"

I'm marveling at his thought process when his alarm pings that it's time. He's physically bouncing up and down with excitement. What's wrong with him?

He hands me one and keeps one for himself. I glance down at mine and see that it's got two lines, meaning I'm pregnant. He makes a whole show of doing a countdown, so I pretend like I don't already know the results. "Three, two, one..."

He looks at his and then he does one of his touchdown dances. The Cabbage Patch, as he often does at his games when celebrating a big play.

The guy does have shockingly good rhythm for a big man, but I truly can't get over how happy he is about this. He then lifts me in the air and twirls me around before bringing his lips to mine for the sweetest kiss as he happily breathes into my mouth, "We're going to be parents. You and me. Forever."

Forever? All I'm thinking about right now is the math. Math to make sure I'm okay to play this entire season and will be back in time for next season. Given that it's easy to calculate the exact date when the baby was conceived, I should be due in March. The real question is how quickly I'll be showing. It's July now. If we progress into the playoffs like we hope to, my season won't be over until mid-October. It will be close. I've never wished more that I had a real relationship with my mother. I could ask her when she started showing, though our bodies are nothing alike so it would probably be meaningless anyway.

There's only one person who I want right now. Fallon. The therapist told me to lean on those who give me comfort and support. She gives that to me. My friends do too, but she's a mother, and she already knows about the possibility of me being pregnant.

I tap Daylen's arm. "Put me down."

He does.

I wave awkwardly. "I'm heading out. I'll catch you later."

His face falls. "What? We need to celebrate. I'll get the champ…oh crap, no liquor. I'll get rid of all of it. Don't worry."

For some reason, that's the straw that breaks the camel's back for me. "I'm not worried about fucking liquor, Daylen. I have about a thousand things I'm worried about, but the temptation of alcohol isn't one of them." I try to shuck out of his embrace but can't budge an inch. "Let me go." Why is he so damn strong?

He doesn't. He strengthens his hold around me and asks, "What can I do to help?"

"You can stop suffocating me," I yell. He finally releases me, and I quickly step back away from him, practically gasping for theoretical air. "I appreciate that you're excited, and I truly appreciate how amazing you've been, but I'm still figuring out how *I* feel about this. Being a twenty-six-year-old single mom during the height of my career wasn't exactly in the plan."

"Single mom?" he questions in complete and total shock. "You're *not* going to be a single mom. We're married. You're going to move in, and we'll raise her together as husband and wife. We're going to be a family."

I ball my fists, ready to explode on him. "Move in?" I scream. "Husband and wife? Family?" I shout. "Do you even hear yourself? Daylen, we hated each other a few months ago. *Hated*. Like I couldn't stand the sight of you, and I know you felt the same way about me. Then we got drunk in Vegas and got married. It should have been annulled hours later but Judge Decrepit decided to fuck with us for his own morbid amusement. We're getting the marriage annulled at the end of the year. We won't be husband and wife when this child is born. I'm absolutely not moving in here. We're not together and never will be. Get all that through your thick skull."

His face falls like he's going to cry. It's as if none of this occurred to him. I don't understand why he would think we're going to be one big happy family.

It pains me to see him so upset. Shit, that was harsh. I didn't want to hurt him, but he wasn't living in reality.

He trembles a bit. His hands are shaking while his brow creases in a way I've never seen from him before. He's genuinely shocked and saddened by my words.

"Where's the happy ending in all that?" he asks, looking like a lost puppy. "Where's *our* happy ending?"

I touch his arm, needing to comfort him. "Not all stories have happy endings, Daylen. If they did, they'd just be called endings."

As if sensing his need, BJ nuzzles into Daylen's side, and he instinctively rubs behind her ear, much to her obvious delight. I don't think he realizes he's doing it. It's second nature for him to take care of her.

"Daylen," I continue with a more even tone, "I have zero doubt that you're going to be an amazing father. You had an amazing father. You're already an amazing father to BJ. You're such a good man and a natural caregiver. Our child is so fucking lucky to have you as a father." I tap two fingers on my chest. "I'm the one who's fucked up. I'm the one who might not be a good mother."

I lick my lips nervously as I prepare to say something out loud that I've only said once before, and that was to the therapist in Maine. "When I was in high school, I was dating a college guy. We were together for several months. I thought I was in love with him. I came home one day and found him fucking my mother on my family's kitchen table."

"What?" he breathes in disbelief.

Tears fill my eyes. "Yes. My mother slept with my boyfriend. That's the woman who raised me. That's who set an example of motherhood for me. I'm not sure I'm equipped for this."

He stands there completely dumbfounded. An absolutely

normal response to what I've just told him. Because no, it's not fucking normal for a mother to have sex with her daughter's boyfriend.

Tears now spill from my eyes. I see his internal battle, but because he's such a good human being, kindness wins out, and he pulls me into his arms. I fight it at first, but he doesn't let me go. He holds me, rubbing my back and kissing my head while whispering, "Let it out. You need this."

And then I sob in a way I haven't in the ten years since it happened. I sob and sob and sob until his T-shirt is soaked all the way through.

Damn her. I swore I'd never cry over her again.

When there are no tears left and my shaking has subsided, he finally releases me. "Let me get you some water."

I follow him to the kitchen, where he secures me a bottle. I take it from him. "Thank you."

He nods with a somber look on his face. "Are you okay?"

I let out a nervous laugh. "Honestly? I don't know. I'm sorry if I was harsh. I'm still processing this. But, Daylen, I'm not going to be someone who stays married for the sake of the children. I'm confident my parents did that, and it didn't turn out so well for them. They were both miserable for years. I care about you, I truly do, but you have to admit this situation is nuts. We're not in love. Don't you want to be in love with your wife?"

He runs his fingers through his hair. "I care about you. A lot. I could love you one day, I know I could," he admits with complete and total sincerity.

"But you don't love me now, and I feel the exact same way about you." I hold up my hands almost in surrender. "I need us to slow down. I need to wrap my mind around this unexpected news. I need to figure out how it impacts my life and my career. Right now, the only thing on my mind is making sure I can finish this season. I have no idea when I'll pop or how I'll be feeling. I've been so damn tired for the past few weeks. Is it going to get worse? Will I have enough energy to play ball? Will my body changes end my season early?"

His eyes widen in realization as he sucks in a breath. "The way you play, Kennedy. It's so rough. There are always elbows flying and hard falls to the ground. It might be dangerous for the baby."

A bit of anger bubbles inside me, but I do my best to remain calm as I state, "To be perfectly clear, while I value your thoughts on our child tremendously, I'm not asking for your permission on this issue. My style of play will not change. You're about to become a father. Will your style of play change?" I challenge.

He's quiet. It's not a battle he should fight, and he realizes it.

TWENTY-FOUR

KENNEDY

I left Daylen's house with us on shaky ground. I needed to get away from him. At least he promised to keep things under wraps until we have a more concise plan. That guy would happily walk into his next practice wearing a #GirlDad shirt, and we don't even know if we're having a girl.

My mind is a clusterfuck, and I need a level-headed person to talk to. I texted Fallon asking if I could come by her house. She said Harper was home but I was welcome.

I pull into her driveway. She lives in a McMansion not too far from Daylen. I guess she did well in her divorce settlement. I'm confident a physical therapist's salary can't quite make a house like this happen. It's very in keeping with the area, with a stone façade and black window frames. The white vertical siding on one section of the house looks new and is a nice touch. There are two large bay windows, and I smile as I see Harper's face pressed to one of them. I guess Fallon told her I was coming by.

I walk to the door, but before my finger reaches the doorbell, the door swings open with a grinning Harper standing there. I hope my kid is as happy as she is. I certainly wasn't when I was her age, being raised by nannies because my parents couldn't be bothered.

Holding my hand in the air for a high-five, I say, "What's up, little genius? Any fun words for me today?"

She jumps in the air to smack my hand. "Yep. Petard."

"Umm, what's that?" I ask, having never heard the word before.

"A small bomb," she answers. "I'm not exactly sure how I'm going to incorporate that into my daily life, but I'm going to try."

I think a petard was just detonated in my life. Look at me. I used it in a sentence.

"I'm sure you'll think of something," I offer. "Can you say, *I'm the petard*?" I make a bomb-exploding motion with my hands.

She giggles. "No, silly."

I shrug. "I tried. Is your mom around?"

She nods. "Yep. She just got out of the shower. She said for me to bring you to the kitchen if you arrived before she was done and offer you some water because you should always offer guests a drink when they arrive."

I suddenly feel the need to write all these parenting tips down. That's a smart one. Teaching your kid how to be a good host.

We walk through the house, which is nicely decorated with elegant yet warm and homey touches. "Your house is awesome, Harper."

She nods. "My grandma helped Mommy decorate it when we moved here. I was a little girl. I barely remember."

"Does your dad live nearby?"

"Yep. He and Bails are super close. I felt the babies kick in her belly yesterday. It was freaky," she exclaims with excitement.

I look down at my stomach. That will be me soon. Hopefully not too soon.

As I sit on a stool in the kitchen and Harper excitedly fetches me a glass of water, I hear Fallon yell from upstairs. "Harper, is Kennedy here yet?"

Harper yells back, "Yes, Mommy. She's eating all your rum raisin ice cream." She smiles with mischief.

"Don't lie to me, Harper Montgomery," Fallon scolds.

Harper places her little hands on her hips. "Santa, The Tooth Fairy, and The Easter Bunny. 'Nuff said, Mommy."

A laugh bubbles from my throat. This kid is a riot.

Fallon walks into the kitchen with wet hair, small shorts, and an equally small T-shirt. I don't think I've ever seen her wearing so little. She's got a great body. She must get hit on all the time.

She glares disapprovingly at Harper. "Stop spending time with Aunt Kam. Her attitude is rubbing off on you."

Harper smiles. "She taught me a new phrase yesterday. Beef Walk."

I start laughing, knowing what it means, but Fallon obviously doesn't. "What's that?" she asks.

Harper giggles. "Going away from people to fart so they don't hear or smell it. She said if she has milk chocolate, she has to Beef Walk every time."

Fallon sighs. "God help me, Aunt Kam is going to be the death of me. Harper, why don't you go do your homework so Kennedy and I can talk?"

"Already done," she proudly announces.

"Then please go and read for a bit."

"Okay, Mommy." She turns to me. "Don't leave without saying goodbye."

"I won't," I assure her.

Harper exits the kitchen. It sounds like she walks upstairs. I look at Fallon. "It's cool that she's willing to read. I would never have agreed to that at her age. I would have gone right to the television."

Fallon nods. "Me too. She's only allowed a certain amount of time in front of the television on a school day. She'd rather use it up later for *The Real Housewives of Beverly Hills* tonight. It's our embarrassing guilty pleasure."

I let out a laugh. "I get it. Those bitches are nuts, but I can't look away either. Their crazy drama is like crack."

"Agreed."

I notice her pickleball racquet on the counter and motion toward it. "Do you play?"

She shrugs. "I recently started. I'm not very good just yet. It's hard at my age to find ways to be competitive. I'm liking it a lot though. I think I'm already addicted."

"We should play sometime," I offer. "I'm pretty good. I play with my dad now and then. In fact, I'm playing with him and my brother tomorrow."

She grins widely. "That's wonderful. Happy to hear it."

I'm honestly not sure why she cares so much. Weird.

She stares at me. "I'm guessing this is a big conversation." I nod. "Would you like some hot chocolate? I have lots of marshmallows," she excitedly offers.

"Sure. That would be nice." I narrow my eyes. "How did you know that I like extra marshmallows in my hot chocolate?"

As she begins making it, she shrugs as she says, "Doesn't everyone?"

"I suppose."

It was one of the few positive young childhood memories I have of my dad. He'd always sneak extra marshmallows into my hot chocolate when my mom wasn't looking. It kind of became a running joke between us until I was slightly older and stopped drinking it as often.

Minutes later, she's handing me a warm mug with a few too many marshmallows. I take my first sip as we sit at her kitchen table. It's soothing. It's like she knows just what I need. It's that maternal instinct I fear I'll never have.

My eyes meet hers. "I confirmed it. I'm pregnant."

She nods in understanding. "How do you feel about it?"

"I'm not sure," I answer honestly. "The father is over the moon. He's so fucking happy. I can't get over how damn excited he is about it."

She smiles. "That's good news, isn't it? Anyone I know?"

"Obviously it stays between you and me for now, but it's Daylen Humblecut."

Her eyebrows practically shoot into her hairline. "The football player?"

I nod. "Yes."

"I didn't know you two were dating. You're kind of an unlikely pair. He's so…goofy. At least on TV and in the handful of times I met him when I was married to Tanner. We lived in New York City when we were married, so we didn't see Tanner's Philly clients as much as he does now. I can't believe you've been able to keep your relationship with Daylen out of the press. You're both so popular in this town."

"We're not really dating. It's…complicated." I then go on to tell her everything. *Everything*. It feels so good to finally unload it all on someone. A small amount of the weight I've been carrying on my shoulders is lifted. The therapist in Maine was right about that.

Fallon sits there with shock written all over her pretty face. "Holy shit," she breathes. "That's intense. And crazy. You're *married* to him?"

"I am."

"Does anyone else know?"

I shake my head. "Just Tanner. He tried to help us get the quickie annulment, which sort of backfired on us."

"Right. Makes sense. How do you feel about Daylen?"

I exhale a long breath. "He's a great guy. I hated him at first, but I don't feel that way now. Not at all. He's different from any other man I've spent time with. It's hard to articulate." I take another sip of my hot chocolate. "He makes me feel…safe. I trust him, and no matter what happens with us, I know he'll be a loving, attentive father."

She gives me a small smile. "Well, that's important, sweetie. More important than you could possibly imagine."

I nod. "I know it is, but we're not in love. We're not even together. I can admit the physical chemistry is strong, *very* strong. But we were thrust into this situation. We've never even gone on a real date."

"You spend two or three days a week with him playing ball. You don't have to go out for a meal for it to be considered a real date. I'm sure you know a lot about him at this point, more than plenty of others who get married, trust me. Some of my friends married men they barely knew."

I twist my lips. "Fair point." I take another sip. "He had it in his head that we would be moving in together and living the happily ever after life. I had to put the brakes on things. I won't just be with him because of the baby. The baby should have nothing to do with us as a couple."

"I understand that, but don't close the door on things working out between you two. They could. It's obvious you have real feelings for him." She shakes her head and lets out a small laugh. "Man, this is the most chronologically fucked up relationship ever. First comes hate, then comes marriage, then comes sex, then comes dating, then comes friendship, then comes baby. Maybe the next thing will be love?" she adds hopefully.

I can't hide my smile. "Yep, fucked up. That's me and my life in a nutshell."

"You're not fucked up, Kennedy. You have some demons, as does everyone. You don't think I was fucked up after my marriage ended? Let me promise you, I was. I am. It's been seven years, and I still don't have my shit together most days."

"You? You're perfect."

She lets out a laugh. "Ha. Perfect. Right." She turns toward the staircase; I assume to ensure Harper isn't within earshot. She then leans toward me and lowers her voice. "My husband was ignoring me, so I went out and fucked his best friend in the alley of a bar while that husband was at home with our two-year-old daughter. Does that sound perfect to you?"

I think my chin physically drops to the floor. I'm rendered speechless. In a million years, I never would have guessed that about her. In my mind, I assumed the divorce was Tanner's fault. How could it ever be hers?

"Yep," she reacts to what must be shock written all over my face. "It's the worst thing I've ever done in my life, and not a day goes by that I don't regret it, even all these years later. I ran home and tearfully confessed to Tanner right away. We were legally separated by the next day." She leans back in her chair and nods her head in satisfaction. "No one is perfect. We all have demons. We've all made mistakes. And none of us has a time machine to allow us to rewrite the past. I wish more than most that we did, but we don't. All you can do is learn from those mistakes and move forward. Try each day to be better than you were the day before. Try to raise a good kid who isn't an asshole."

Harper gasps as she descends the stairs. "You said a bad word, Mommy."

Fallon raises an eyebrow as if to remind me just how imperfect she is.

I WENT HOME after Fallon's and spent the evening doing a lot of thinking. Yes, we've done everything in a messed-up order, but I can't control the past. As crazy as it sounds, I think the best thing is for Daylen and me to date. I'm pregnant with his child, but we'll have to put that out of our minds if we want to get to know each other properly. I do like him and can't deny that I'm attracted to him, but there are certain things that can't be rushed. It's got to be this way or no way at all. I won't just be with him because of this baby. It's not fair to either the baby or us. I know what it's like to grow up in a house with parents who don't belong together.

It's morning and I'm on my way to my father's pickleball club. My brother and I are playing with my father and Double Dees. Pierce and I are going out for lunch afterward. He leaves for college next week. I'm so happy he'll be close by. I want him in my life. I want him in his niece or nephew's life too.

I see the three of them already sitting on a bench when I arrive at the club. Double Dees is yapping away, and I overhear him asking them, "What's the useless skin at the end of a penis called?"

"A man," I answer before any of them can, as I approach the group.

My father and Pierce chuckle while Double Dees smiles. "You're ruining my joke, Triple Dees. The next part was supposed to be: What do you call a man with too much foreskin?"

I shrug. "I don't know." I do, but I don't want to ruin it for him.

"Fiveskin," he cackles.

I let out a laugh. "Good one, old man."

He gasps in mock shock. "Old man? I'll have you know, young lady, that I have a lot going for me." He pauses for dramatic effect. "My eyes are going, my knees are going, my back is going, and my patience is definitely gone."

My father clears his throat. "You're not the only one getting old, Dave. Last night, I was in bed for twenty minutes when I heard the pizza guy cough. Then I remembered I originally came to my bedroom for my wallet."

Pierce barks out a laugh. "Ha! You got jokes, Dad."

He nods. "Those dipshits on my team are rubbing off on me. Humblecut keeps everyone laughing through every damn workout with his dirty jokes. The whole team hangs on every word that guy says."

I can't help but smile. I suppose I've learned to love Daylen's sense of humor. While occasionally ill-timed, like in front of police officers and cashiers, his jokes are clever and funny. He's such a happy person and takes genuine joy in making the people around him happy. I hope our child gets that from him more than anything else.

"Are you listening?" Pierce asks.

"Sorry, I was daydreaming. What did you say?"

"Do you want to be partners?"

"It's a little uneven putting the young people on one side, but sure. We'll kick their asses, baby bro."

The truth is, my father and I are by far the best two players. It's better for us to split. Pierce and Doubles Dees are about the same. Pierce has youth on his side, but Double Dees plays more often. It's a fairly even match this way.

My father and I exchange glances, letting me know he's thinking the same thing as I am.

The game gets underway and, as expected, it's a back-and-forth affair. Pierce is cool as a cucumber, seemingly unaffected by the ebbs and flows of the game. My father was right. He doesn't have the competitive fire you need to play sports at the next level. I'm happy that my father recognized it and encouraged Pierce to pursue medicine over a football scholarship. It's best for him. You need that killer instinct to succeed at a high level in athletics.

I've gradually come to the realization that my father isn't a bad guy after all. It's clear he and Pierce are close. I'm happy for my brother that he has a good relationship with my dad. I know how much Daylen treasures his relationship with his father.

At some point, I slam a ball a little too hard. It would have gone out, but Double Dees couldn't get out of the way in time and it hit him in the stomach, meaning it's our point.

"Damn it," he curses, "if I weren't so fat, it would have been our point."

Pierce and I share a bemused look. Dave is a funny, self-deprecating guy. I enjoy playing with him.

We go on to win five of the nine games played. It's been a fun morning. When I return to the bench to place my racquet in my bag, I pick up my phone and see a text from Daylen.

> Red Flag: My family is visiting. We're about to have lunch by my pool. Any chance you can stop by and join us? When the time comes that you let me tell them about the baby, I'd like for them to have met the mother of my child at least once.

Sometimes he's so damn sweet. I can give him this.

> Me: Of course. I have Pierce with me. Is it okay if he comes too?

> Red Flag: Absolutely. He can talk to my sister about colleges in the area. She's here looking. Thanks, I appreciate this.

DAYLEN

I was up all night tossing and turning. I've never been more excited about anything than when Kennedy told me that she's pregnant. I was so consumed by my happiness that I didn't stop to consider how she was feeling. How it would impact her body and her career.

I came on strong, and she was overwhelmed. I've just never considered raising a child without two parents in the same household. I had it for six years, and I cherish those memories. I want that for my kid. Having my child half the time isn't appealing to me, but she's right, we're not ready for more. Yet.

And then she told me about her mom. Now I understand

why she refuses to talk to her. I'll never look at Ginny Jeffries the same way again. I wonder if Coach knows. It was on the tip of my tongue to ask Kennedy that question, but then she started sobbing in a way I'm not sure I knew she was capable of. It was like she needed to purge herself. It's clear to me that she doesn't talk about it with other people. I'm happy she felt comfortable enough with me to tell me. That must mean something.

God, we could be good together. I believe that. I just want a chance to prove it. I'm determined to win her over.

And the sex? It's phenomenal. There's something magical between us. It's explosive every damn time.

I have to adjust myself, getting hard just thinking about the way we were yesterday. The way her body reacts to mine. The way I feel when she touches me. How rough I'm finding I like things with her. She's opening my eyes to a part of myself I didn't know existed.

But it's not just great sex. There's a connection I've never shared with another woman before her. She's different, and I'm starting to think that's a good thing.

Vance clears his throat from the leg press machine. "Dude, you're really going to town over there. Is everything okay? Did one of your bimbos give you more than you bargained for?" he asks while nodding toward my junk, which I've got my hand on.

I shake my head. "Nah, my underwear is a little tight today."

"Maybe you should wear your own," he deadpans.

I can't help but smile. "Vance McCaffrey, did you just make a funny joke?"

His face remains stoic. "I'm an underrated funny guy."

"Ooh. Not sure about that."

I really want to tell my best friend what's going on, but I promised Kennedy I wouldn't tell anyone yet, and the last thing I want to do is piss her off. It's killing me though. I'm about to be a father, and I can't even share the good news with the people I love.

Hmm, I wonder if I can tell one or two people. She'd never know.

I look at Presley as he works hard on the quad extension machine. "Elvis, do you ever lie to Layla?"

He stops what he's doing and stares intently at me. "Absolutely not. I'd never get away with it." He points at me. "Never lie to a woman because she's going to find out anyway. Most women investigate better than the FBI. I told her I didn't cut my toenails in bed last month because it drives her nuts when I do it. Last night, four weeks later, she found a tiny nail clipping under the bed and was able to do her own little forensic analysis to determine that it was from the time I told her I didn't do it. FBI, like I said. It should be all women. Every crime would be solved within a matter of hours if they ran the whole show. Guaranteed."

I chuckle. "You're sexy when you're scared of your wife."

He nods. "My wife still thinks I'm sexy. Every time I walk by her, she says, *What an ass.*"

I burst out laughing. Even Vance smiles. Sometimes your friends give you what you need without even knowing you need it.

After a fun, distracting morning workout with my teammates, I'm driving home. Coach wasn't at the workout. One of the assistant coaches said he was playing pickleball with his kids today.

Of course, in my manic Google searches last night, I learned that a pregnant woman shouldn't let her body temperature get too high. Now I'm worried she was too hot when playing pickleball. I can't imagine how I'm going to feel during her basketball games. Kennedy practically plays tackle basketball.

I'm preoccupied as I walk through the front door to BJ

leaping into my arms. "Hey, baby girl. Daddy missed you all morning. Did Chef Benny give you lunch?"

Bark.

"I'll take that as a yes."

I walk into the kitchen and see Benny chopping and prepping. "Hey, man." I notice several steaks and other accompanying foods. "Why so much food? Am I having a party?"

He nods toward my backyard pool area. "Did you forget that your family is staying with you for a few days while Jagger looks at schools?"

My eyes widen. "Oh fuck. It's been a crazy day. I totally spaced."

He laughs. "I figured. I told them you had a morning workout and told me to let them in. They put their bags in the guestrooms and are out back by the pool now. I made them margaritas and set out a few appetizers."

I slap his back. "Thanks, Benny. You're the best, man."

He winks. "You bet. I was...cleaning up a few things upstairs. Did you have a woman here last night?"

I nod. "I did. Yesterday afternoon."

"How was BJ?" he asks with obvious concern, given BJ's behavior around women. He knows I never bring women here.

"She loves this particular woman. In fact, I might have you grab a few things for her. She's going to be around for a long while." *Forever.*

He stops cutting and turns to me. "In all my years working here, this has never happened."

I smile. "I'm getting old. Maybe it's time. I'm gonna go see my family. Thanks for your help."

He returns to cutting, and I start to walk toward the back glass doors, but before I open them, he says, "And congrats. I saw the tests when I was emptying the trash. You're gonna be an awesome father, man."

It hits me straight in the heart. I'm going to be a father.

How the hell am I going to get through this visit from my family without spilling the beans?

I offer a small smile in gratitude. "I hope so."

I take out my phone to text Kennedy about Benny getting some of the foods she likes when I look out to see my family laughing. I want them to meet her. When the day comes that I tell them about the baby, I want them to know who I'm talking about. I want them to know who the mother of my child is.

I decide to text her asking if she'll come by.

TWENTY-FIVE

DAYLEN

"If she doesn't rip a fart, she doesn't have your heart," my father happily announces.

My sister and I burst out laughing, while Ashleigh covers her face in mortification. I have to hold my stomach. "That's the funniest story I've ever heard."

Apparently, Ashleigh came to watch my dad in court this week, and during a particularly tense moment, she accidentally farted. Of course my dad is trying to make her feel better about it, telling her that farting in front of your significant other is a sign of being comfortable and in love.

She shakes her head. "In front of *you*, maybe. All those people? Horrific. They all knew who it came from."

My sister is hyperventilating, she's laughing so hard.

I hear BJ release her protective bark and then go running toward the gate. My father sucks in a breath. "Oh shit. D, do something."

I turn in time to see Kennedy and Pierce walking through to my backyard. BJ stops right in front of Kennedy and then gently lifts her snout for a kiss, which Kennedy happily obliges along with a sweet rub behind her ear.

It's like BJ knows to be careful around Kennedy. It's unbelievable.

And Kennedy looks fucking hot. I knew she was playing pickleball, but perhaps it's time for me to take up this sport. She's in a tiny little white skirt and a sleeveless matching top that is only slightly more material than a sports bra. There's about an inch or two of her sexy stomach showing. I can't help but stare at it, knowing my baby is growing inside her. My heart swells with affection for both of my girls. Three, if you count BJ.

Yes, I'm convinced it's a girl. I was born to be a girl dad. I keep imagining holding her little body in my hands and loving her, the same way I did with Jagger.

Pierce is wearing athletic shorts and a T-shirt. His eyes immediately zero in on my sister in her bikini. Little fucker.

I turn to my family. "I invited some friends. They're Coach Jeffries' kids." I look at my sister. "Pierce is going to be a freshman this year at a college nearby. I thought you two could chat about it. He might have some insights for you."

She stares at him and licks her lips. "Thanks, bro. You're the best."

What the fuck is happening?

I stand and make my way over to them, first shaking Pierce's hand and then kissing Kennedy's cheek. I whisper into her ear, "Thanks for coming. You look edible. I'm going to fuck you in this skirt sometime."

She takes a sharp inhale. I lift my head in time to see her face flush and her lips part. She likes that idea. All hope isn't lost.

"How was pickleball?" I cheerily ask both of them as if I didn't just tell her I was going to defile her.

Pierce answers, "Kennedy carried us. She ate and left no crumbs."

"She's a professional athlete," *and the mother of my child*, "of course she was awesome. She's good at everything. Come," I wave in invitation, "meet my family."

I introduce everyone. My father takes one look at Kennedy and then wiggles his eyebrows up and down at me. Yeah, no shit she's hot. She looks like Wonder Woman with all those curves and her height. Ooh, I bet she'd look amazing in a Wonder Woman costume. New fantasy unlocked.

I offer Pierce a bathing suit of mine. It will be big on him, but he can tie it tight. He disappears inside to get it. I told him to ask Benny where to find it. In no time at all, he and Jagger are yapping away in the pool like long-lost friends.

Dad looks at them. "I think we have a love connection."

I lean back. "Normally I would intimidate the crap out of any potential suitor, but I happen to like Pierce."

Kennedy smiles with amusement as she watches them interact. She's probably never seen her brother this way before.

My dad and Kennedy talk for a while. I sit back and let nature take its course. I'm just happy they seem to be getting along so well.

Eventually, I stand. "I'm going to visit Uncle Charley."

Kennedy rolls her eyes. "Stop announcing it, freak."

Dad chuckles. "He loves doing that. Always has. Why don't you pee in the pool like everyone else in the world?"

"In my own pool?" I ask with genuine disgust. "Pass."

He shrugs. "I pissed in the deep end at our neighborhood pool last week." He smiles. "The lifeguard blew the whistle so hard I almost fell in."

Kennedy starts laughing, as does my father. "Oh my god," she says, "you two have the exact same laugh. It's scary."

Ashleigh, who I'm confident didn't get my dad's joke, nods. "Oh yes, since baby boy was little. Always the same laugh."

Ashleigh didn't know me until I was a teen, but whatever. I don't correct her. I never do.

I return a few minutes later, and Chef Benny is serving the steaks. "Thanks, Benny. These look awesome. Did you make one for BJ too?"

He nods. "Of course. All dogs should eat expensive steaks because they know the difference," he says sarcastically.

"Exactly," I happily agree.

He motions his head toward Kennedy and mouths, "Is it her?"

I nod.

He mouths back, "She's hot."

I mouth, "I know, right?"

The lovebirds emerge from the pool to eat. Pierce smiles at me. "Thanks, man. These steaks are lit."

Dad agrees. "Maybe I should have Chef Benny cook for Ashleigh's birthday next week instead of..."

He purposefully stops speaking and then pretends to zip his lips.

Ashleigh smacks his arm. "Darn it. I thought you were going to spill the beans. Ugh. Where are you taking me?"

Dad kisses her cheek and answers, "Hopefully from behind."

Jagger squeals, "Dad! Stop it. You're so embarrassing."

He lets out his loud, booming laugh, and Ashleigh giggles before not so quietly whispering, "You got it, *Daddy*." Yes, she calls him *Daddy* all the time.

Kennedy's body shakes in laughter at the whole interaction.

Dad gives Jagger a bemused look. "Don't worry, sweetie, I've got the perfect spot all picked out for *yo mama*." His eyes then move to mine as they sparkle in amusement. He loves busting out the *yo mama* jokes in front of new friends. Embarrassing Jagger in front of her new crush is just an added bonus.

Jagger sighs. "I beg you not to do this right now, Dad. Please."

Dad wipes his mouth with his napkin and then places it on the table. It's his sign of what's to come.

Jagger knows it. She then explains to Kennedy and Pierce what's about to happen. She also apologizes in advance.

Dad steals his face. "Yo mama's so stupid, she went to the dentist to get a Bluetooth."

Everyone snickers but me. I take a breath as I think of my next line. "Yo mama's so fat, when she sat on an iPhone, it turned into an iPad."

Everyone else bursts out laughing. Dad actually has to bite his lip to keep his own laughter away. That's progress for me.

He eventually wards it off and asks me, "Do you know the difference between a washing machine and yo mama?"

I smirk as I shake my head that I don't.

"When I dumped a dirty load inside the machine, it didn't follow me around for two weeks."

I can't help but laugh loudly, right along with the rest of the table. "Oh my god. Classic. You're the master, Dad. I can't beat you." *And I never want to.*

Dad winks. "Your time will come, son."

About an hour later, Kennedy is exiting the bathroom, but I push her back in and close the door. I pull her hips to mine and brush my lips over her mouth. "You look so sexy in this outfit. I've been hard since you got here."

She smiles into my mouth as she wraps her arms around my neck. "I *love* your family." She shakes her head in disbelief. "Is this how meals always are with them?"

I nod. "Yes. *Exactly* like this. Every single time. Never a dull moment."

She gently and lovingly runs her fingertips through my scruff. "I hope you realize how fortunate you are."

"I do." I lick my lips nervously. "It could be like this for us one day. If you want."

She looks down. "Daylen—"

"I know I went a little crazy yesterday," I quickly interrupt before she can shoot me down. "I was excited. I saw the future I wanted and pressed the fast-forward button. It was wrong of me to make assumptions like I did, but I won't give up on the possibility of us. There's something here." I toggle my finger between the two of us. "Maybe we're not at the marriage or baby-making phase of our relationship, but there's a spark I've never shared with anyone else, and I personally want to see where it goes."

She looks up at me and nods. "I do too."

I can't help but smile widely at her unexpected response. "You do?"

"Yes. We've done this in the weirdest order ever, but I feel it too." She runs her hands up and down my arms. "You make me feel so safe, Daylen. I've *never* felt safe with anyone in my life before. It's a big deal for me."

My chest swells with pride. "I know it is. Thank you for trusting me. I promise I won't let you or our daughter down. Ever."

She rolls her eyes. "I hope it's a boy just to spite you."

I chuckle. "Of course you do. Not a chance. BJ said she wants a sister."

"Did she say that? In those precise words?"

"Yes," I joke.

"I bet."

I pull her as close as possible again, and she happily obliges me. "Can we maybe go on a real date?" I beg. "One that doesn't involve basketball. We can still practice all the time. I'm committed to you dunking one day, but can we go to dinner? Anywhere you want. I know you don't want to be seen in public. We can go off the beaten track. I don't care. I just want to give things a real go. I want to spend time with you talking and doing normal dating things."

She smiles softly as she nods again. "I'd like that."

I can't help but kiss her, and she lets me. In fact, she also allows my hand to move under that sexy skirt. I've been dying to do that since she got here.

An orgasm later, when we're walking back to the pool, she asks, "Why does Ashleigh use WTF inappropriately? Does she not know what it means?"

I chuckle. "It's a funny story."

KENNEDY AND PIERCE stay through most of the afternoon until Pierce has to physically tear himself away from Jagger. They exchange telephone numbers under the guise of him answering any questions she may have about college, but I'm not an idiot. They were both smitten.

I appreciate how much time Kennedy spent with my family. She could have stayed an hour or two, but she stayed for several hours until Pierce had to leave for a prior commitment. If I didn't know better, I'd say she was disappointed to have to leave. She and my father got along better than I could have possibly hoped.

It's later at night now, and everyone has gone to bed. I'm out back throwing a ball to BJ while brainstorming ideas for my first real date with Kennedy. I want it to be special. I already told Benny to find me some fashionable clothing to wear. I want to look good for her.

I hear my backyard glass door slide open, and my father walks out in his matching pajamas. I look him up and down. "Did those PJs come with one of those sleep caps?" I jokingly ask.

He gives me the finger. "It came with a hot chick twenty-five years my junior handing them to me, so I wear whatever the hell she tells me to wear to bed just thankful she still wants to be in the same bed as me."

I chuckle. "Fair enough."

He pulls out his cigar case and a lighter. I lift an eyebrow. "I'm pretty sure said hot chick doesn't like you smoking those."

He smirks. "Said hot chick had one too many margaritas from Benny and is now out cold. And if I want to sit and have a cigar with my son every once in a while when I know he needs to talk, I can and I will."

He motions toward the chairs at the table. "Have a seat, son."

I throw BJ's ball as far as I can and then sit down. He hands me a cigar and lights it for me. I take a few puffs and smile. "This reminds me of my eleventh birthday."

He nods. "Ah, your first cigar. You coughed for two straight days after that. I think your school nurse wanted to report me to child services for giving you a cigar at that age."

"I remember. She kept asking me if you gave me any other *drugs*." I air quote the word *drugs*, as if a cigar is a drug.

"Hmm. That's right." He blows out a long plume of smoke. "It was the same time as the fifth anniversary of your mother's death. You were having a particularly tough time. I thought it would help to do something special together. You didn't articulate anything specific that was bothering you, but sometimes a father just knows when his son is in need. Like right now. Something is going on with you. Talk to me."

I let out a laugh. I don't know how he does it, but he always knows. "I love you, Dad. I don't know if I say it enough, but you're the best father. I never felt like I missed out by not having my mom around because you're twice the dad of all others. I hope I'm half the father you are one day."

He nods. "Thanks. Now start talking. Does it have to do with the pretty lady here today?"

I nod and exhale a long breath. "I'm not sure where to start." So I start at the beginning and tell him every little detail, from our hate-filled beginnings, to Vegas, to the pregnancy, to my developing feelings for her. All of it. He listens without interruption, even though I know he's dying to interrupt.

When I'm finished, he shakes his head. "Wow, that's quite a story." He reaches across the table, grabs the top of my hand, and smiles widely. "I'm going to be a grandfather."

"Yes, you are. The best in the business, no doubt."

He squeezes my hand in gratitude before releasing me and leaning back in his chair again. "Did you know your mother and I were law school adversaries competing for the top spot in the class?"

I shake my head. "No."

"We were. I hated her, and she hated me." His blue eyes turn glassy. "She had this fire in her belly. I both despised and respected it."

"I get that. How did it turn from hate to love?" I ask with genuine curiosity.

"I accepted that she was smarter than me and learned to be content with my number two spot."

I let out a laugh.

He continues, "And then when I stopped hating her, I fell head over heels in love with her. I just knew. She was different from anyone else I had dated. She challenged me in ways no woman ever had. I always had it easy with the ladies, but not her. She rejected me at first, but she was the one, and I was persistent. I wooed her. I learned her likes and dislikes and then planned accordingly. She eventually softened on me, and things progressed rapidly from there. The hate turned into passion, which turned into...storybook love." He says the last bit with a whimsical look on his face as if he's remembering something special about her.

"I think Kennedy has softened on me, but sometimes I'm not sure. She was pretty mad at me yesterday. She stormed out of here after putting me in my place. Rightfully so, but it still happened."

"Sometimes men like us need that. You don't spend five

hours with a man's family if you still hate him," he says. "You don't spend five hours asking his father to tell you stories of his childhood if you don't care. She cares. I can see it."

"I'm not sure how to woo her. She's different from every girl I've ever been with."

"Isn't that what makes her special?"

I nod. "I suppose. She has a lot of baggage though."

He waves his hand dismissively. "Everyone has baggage. Think of the baggage Ashleigh had to take on when marrying me. I was a heartbroken widower with a slightly out-of-control teenage son who consumed ten thousand calories a day."

"Why Ashleigh?" I ask. "She's so different from Mom."

"That's why. I didn't want a cheap carbon copy. I didn't want someone I'd compare to her. There will never be anyone like your mother. I needed someone totally different. I know Ashleigh is a little loopy at times, but she takes good care of me and keeps me young. And I desperately wanted another child."

I twist my lips. "Your first one was no good?"

The corners of his mouth raise slightly. "Nope. He's defective."

I chuckle. "Kennedy would probably agree with that."

"Tell me what you like about her."

I think for a moment. "I like her strength, her mind, her drive, her sense of humor, her character, her convictions, her fierce independence, the way she protects those she cares about—"

"Her rack," he interrupts.

I smile. "I was trying to keep it clean, but obviously her body is a dream. Physical attraction is most definitely not the problem."

"And the physical connection?" he prods.

I blow out a breath. "The best of my life. Off the charts. She fries my brain and my balls."

He lets out a laugh. "Well, that's promising." He wraps his

lips around his cigar and takes a few puffs. "All you can do right now is listen to her, respect her, and be there for her in her times of need. Nature will otherwise have to take its course. If love is in the cards, it will happen over time. You can't force it. But I have a feeling about you two."

"Me too, Dad. Me too."

TWENTY-SIX

KENNEDY

We've had the best time tonight. There are vineyards I never knew existed only forty-five minutes away from the city. While I couldn't imbibe in the product given my current state, the owner gave us a private tour and taught us about the process of making wines. We picked and ate a few of the wine grapes, tasting the different varieties. She showed us the difference in leaves from the vines of various types of wine.

It was fascinating. We even got to participate in some of the planting for the next harvest, and she promised to send us a case when the wine from those grapes is ready, which should be after the baby comes. She's even going to create a private collection for us from it, which she's allowing us to name.

We got to stomp on grapes with our bare feet and participate in every step of the process. Given how much he knows I enjoy good wine, it was a really thoughtful date. The fact that *we* couldn't drink didn't spoil the fun at all. Yes, he refuses to drink if I can't.

We then went to a nearby restaurant with farm-to-table dining. It's a one-table restaurant that seats sixteen people, but he paid for all the spots so there would be no one else around to see us.

We've talked and laughed throughout the best meal I've had in ages. We learned so much more about each other. I got to hear about how those *yo mama* jokes started between him and his father, which makes it all the sweeter. I learned the reasoning behind why he hired Chef Benny. When I first heard he had a house manager, I judged him for it. Now I realize how generous and sweet it is of him to take care of a former teammate that way. There's so much more to Daylen Humblecut than meets the eye.

He even dressed nicely for me in designer duds. I guarantee he didn't own those a week ago.

I'm in a simple, black dress that sits mid-thigh. There's a sheer element to it where it's a bit revealing in the right light. I knew every time I hit that light today because Daylen's eyes were on my body, practically undressing me. He's not remotely hiding his attraction, and I can admit that he's been driving me crazy with need all day with his loving demeanor and sweet touches. I initially wasn't sure if I should go home with him tonight, but now it's inevitable. I want him badly.

We're just finishing the best blueberry pie I've ever had in my life when he takes my hand and kisses it. "Sometimes I can't get a read on you. What are you looking for? What do you want in a partner?"

I smile at his thoughtful question. "I just want someone to care for me as much as Netflix cares if someone has logged onto my account from another device at another location."

He lets out his loud laugh. I think the whole staff looks at us from the sheer volume. That laugh used to annoy me so damn much. Now I live for it. It automatically makes me smile.

He squeezes my hand. "Seriously. Tell me."

I think for a moment, wanting to give him an honest response. "I can't say I've put a lot of thought into it. I'm still young. I haven't spent my time looking for *the one* like a lot of women my age. *Mr. Right Now* has been all I've ever been interested in. I know I'm a little messed up about relationships, so I've never let myself go there." I pause to take a sip of my water before continuing. "If I dig deep, which I did a bit during my time in Maine, I suppose I want to truly matter to my partner. I want to be prioritized. It doesn't take a degree to figure out why. I've never felt that way. My father didn't prioritize me. My mother most definitely didn't prioritize me. Hell, my basketball team in New York didn't prioritize me. When is it my turn to matter?"

I'm taken aback by that revelation. I'm not sure I've ever admitted it to myself, let alone spoken those words out loud to another person.

His normal jovial face turns serious. I think maybe tears briefly pool in his eyes. He brings my hand to his lips and kisses it again. "You matter to me, Kennedy." He reaches over and rubs my belly tenderly. "You matter to our daughter. You'll be the most important person in the world to her. To both of us."

I fight back the threatening tears caused by his sweetness. "Don't make me cry, Daylen Humblecut. I was looking to get laid tonight," I joke to keep things light. "Carrying your baby is making me hornier than a two-dicked billy goat."

And this time when he laughs, every single head undoubtedly turns. I think the huge wooden table and all sixteen chairs shake too.

His glassy eyes turn mischievous as he takes out a coin from his pocket. Holding it up, he says, "Tails, I give you head. Heads, I get your tail."

I smile widely. I like this game. Wiggling my eyebrows, I say, "Why choose? Who says we can't have both?"

"For real?" he asks excitedly.

"As long as you make me come over and over, you can do with me as you want."

He holds his hand up in the air. "Check, please."

WE CRASH through his front door with our lips locked, not too different from Vegas, but this time, there are so many more emotions involved. We're also stone-cold sober, so there's no sloppiness. It's passionate, purposeful touches. Lots of them. I'm not sure I've ever been more ravenous for a man than I am for him right now.

Because I've never cared about one until now.

I fell just a little harder for Daylen Humblecut tonight, and now I want to jump his bones. I normally have a healthy sexual appetite, but pregnancy has me going crazy all the time. It's a constant need, and I plan to get my fill tonight.

He lifts my dress over my head and tosses it on the floor before lifting me so my legs wrap around him. Just as our lips are about to meet again, I feel a giant paw on my bare ass. Just one, though, because the other is wrapped around Daylen. She wants to join us.

I giggle. "This isn't the kind of threesome I'm into."

"Does that mean there are threesomes you *are* into?" he asks with sudden curiosity.

"What woman doesn't want to get railed by two guys?" I joke. *Sort of.*

He scrunches his face. "Men? Forget it. I'm not sharing my wife with any other man." He kisses down my neck. "She's all mine. For better or worse."

For the first time ever, I don't hate it when he calls me his wife. In fact, it gives me chills.

"BJ, bed!" he commands. And I swear I nearly come from his authoritative tone and the way she immediately obeys.

"That turned you on," he accuses with amusement. "Your nipples are practically poking through your bra."

I nod. "Fuck, it was hot. Now get all bossy with me and fuck me hard."

He looks down my body until his eyes find my stomach. "Maybe I should take it easy on you tonight. I was super rough with you last time. I didn't know you were pregnant."

I grab fistfuls of his hair and pull it hard. "I swear to god, if you take it easy on me, I'm milking your prostate every damn day throughout this pregnancy."

He shrugs. "I'd be good with that. It felt weird, but the orgasm was killer. It literally brought me to my knees."

I narrow my eyes at him, and he smiles. "Fine, I'll choke you to near unconsciousness if that's what you want."

I nod emphatically. "Yes, that's what I want. Get to work."

"Okay, okay, Ms. Bossy." He pauses briefly, almost as if he's nervous. "Can I show you something first?"

"Your dick? I've seen it. I know it's big. I'm mentally prepared."

He chuckles. "Not my Humblecock. Something else."

"Is it a red room of pain? Oh god, please let it be that."

He shakes his head in amusement. "You have a one-track mind, Jeffries."

"Your child is causing increased blood flow to my downtown, and since you put said child in there, I need you to take care of business for me."

He places me back on my feet. "Five extra minutes, then orgasms galore. I'm gonna be like Oprah." He points to my mouth and yells out, "You get an orgasm." Then he points to my pussy. "You get an orgasm." Finally, he points to my ass. "And you get an orgasm."

I smile at his ridiculousness. "Fine, I'll wait an extra five minutes for all those *alleged* orgasms," I say with a heavy dose of sarcasm.

Removing his sports coat and throwing it over the kitchen chair, he takes my hand and leads me to the stairs. We ascend the first flight, which is where all the bedrooms are. But then we walk down the hall to a smaller second flight I hadn't noticed before.

As we climb the second set of much narrower stairs, I look around at the unfamiliar space. "I didn't know there was a third floor."

"There's not. It only leads to one thing." He stops in the middle of the stairs and looks at me. "Just so you know, I've never brought another person up here before. Chef Benny knows this space is off limits. Even BJ hasn't been here."

Where the hell are we going?

We continue to climb until we reach the top of the stairs, where French doors sit. They have thin, white, silky curtains. While they're not opaque, I still can't see where they lead. I'm half hoping for a red room of pain.

He opens them, and I can't help but smile. It's a small balcony facing the back of the house. It provides a great view of the stars in the late-night sky, which appear to go on as far as the eye can see. There's a huge circular hybrid of a sofa and a lounge chair. It's got a back to it with a small overhang and is filled with pillows and blankets. It kind of looks like a soft, cushiony cloud.

"What is this?" I ask.

He intertwines his fingers with mine. "I don't have a ton of memories of my mother. You know I was so young when she passed, but I do vividly remember the small second-floor balcony at our old house. I wasn't allowed out there. My parents called it their adult space, but I used to spy on them late at night when they would spend time out there. They would sit for hours and talk, laugh, dance, kiss, and I'm sure they did *other* things too, though fortunately I never saw that. It was their special space. No television, no phones, no crazy son, and no other responsibilities except spending quality time together. For some reason, it always stuck with me. I didn't build this house, but I did build this balcony in hopes of one day having someone special to share it with."

I absorb his words and how much this space must mean to him. "Why did you bring me out here?" I ask with genuine curiosity.

He tilts his head to the side and looks at me as if the answer is the most obvious thing in the world. "Because you matter to me. Because you're my wife. Because you're the person I want to share this space with."

This man is really getting to me emotionally tonight. I'm not sure I can handle it.

His thumb runs across my cheek, wiping away a tear I didn't realize had escaped. He brings that thumb to his mouth and tastes it.

I can feel my heart pounding in my chest. Even though I'm in my black bra and thong, and we're outside, I've never felt so much warmth in my life.

He holds out his hand. "Do you want to dance with me?"

Even though there's no music, I wordlessly nod as I take his hand. He pulls my body to his and wraps his big arms around me, with his comforting hands resting on my back. It's like a cocoon of safety. Nothing and no one can get to me right now.

I place my hands on the nape of his neck and run my fingers through his hair, which is a little long right now. It's normally messy, but he styled it nicely tonight. I know he did that for me.

He commands, "Alexa, play wifey."

I look up at him. "If 'Waterfalls' starts playing, I'm leaving."

I can feel him shaking with laughter. "No, I have something else in mind."

"You have a playlist named *wifey*?"

He smiles. "I made it today, hoping we'd spend time up here together. I wanted to, but I wasn't going to tell you about it unless I was truly feeling it. This space means a lot to me."

Oh boy, this man might break me.

"Ordinary" by Alex Warren starts playing on the speakers I hadn't noticed before.

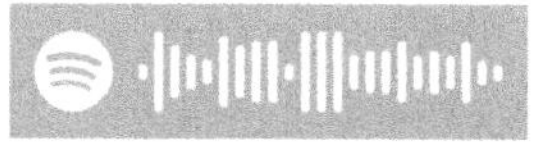

He smiles. "I couldn't possibly think of a more perfect song for you."

"Ordinary?" I question with a heavy dose of skepticism.

"Have you ever listened to the lyrics?" he asks.

I shake my head.

"He wrote it for his wife. It's about finding an *extra*ordinary partner. Listen to it closely one day."

I sense none of the usual joking in his tone. He means it. I desperately want to read the lyrics as soon as I can.

"I will," I promise.

We comfortably sway to the sweet song. I try to listen carefully, but I'm too absorbed in all things Daylen. It must be the pregnancy hormones because I'm so overcome with emotion for this man right now. I've never felt closer to another person in my whole life.

His hands move all over my body as if he's memorizing and cherishing every inch. It's driving me wild. I can feel his erection growing in his pants just as my own need begins to intensify. With slightly trembling fingers, I begin unbuttoning his shirt until it's completely open. I need his skin on mine with a desperation I don't recognize.

Running my hands all over his chest and abs, I breathe, "You're a beautiful man. Your body is incredible. If the football thing doesn't work out, you could totally be a stripper."

He chuckles. "I'll keep that in mind. The same goes for you, except most strippers have fake tits. Yours are real and perfect."

"You're obsessed with them."

"Guilty as charged," he happily announces as he flicks my nipple. "I can't wait to taste milk from them."

I smack his chest. "No way, freak. I'm not breastfeeding you."

He smiles while wiggling his eyebrows. "We'll see about that." He pulls one of my bra cups down, runs his thumb over my nipple, and breathes, "So sexy." It hardens immediately. "And responsive to my touch."

He bends and makes an exaggerated show of slurping it into

his mouth, causing a burst of liquid desire to shoot directly to my pussy. He continues sucking while circling his tongue over the painfully tightening bud.

He's now pulled down the other bra cup and is tweaking and rolling that nipple with his other skillful hand. I can feel the callouses of his thick fingers rubbing against my sensitive flesh. I'm loving how rough he's being. His touches aren't gentle. They're exactly what I want and need. It always feels like he reads my body like a book. His favorite book.

My clit is swollen, and it's pulsing with the need to be touched. I don't think it will take much to push me over the edge.

My chest is heaving with the cacophony of sensations running through my body right now. I grab onto his hair, encouraging his actions, moaning, "I'm close. Don't stop."

He switches his lips to the other nipple, sucking that one into the wet warmth of his mouth and swirling his tongue around and over it with expert precision. He tugs the other nipple so hard that the first tremor of a small orgasm bubbles through the surface.

"Oh god," I yell. I think I also thrust my hips a bit, searching for relief, but I'm too lost in the pleasure to know exactly what I'm doing. My body is in his hands as I begin to lose control.

He shoves his thick thigh between my legs and pushes hard to my most sensitive region, all while increasing the pressure of his sucking and tugging. It's my official undoing. I bite my lip hard as my entire body shakes through the unexpected orgasm.

I can't believe I just came on his leg. I'm still in my thong. He barely touched me. It doesn't seem to bother him at all, as he doesn't stop until he's milked every last drop from me, ensuring that I'm satisfied.

I didn't do anything, but I'm breathless. He practically has to hold me up, I'm so depleted of energy.

He eventually lifts his head from my chest with a huge grin on his face. "That was hella hot. Let's give you another orgasm."

I'm too drained to respond with words, so I nod.

While he unclasps my bra, I regain enough consciousness to do the same to his belt. In mere seconds, we're both stripped of our clothing, and my energy has returned, eager for more of what this sexy man has to offer.

He lies down on the round lounge sofa and waves me over. "Come sit on my face, but I want your ass north and your pussy south. Watch the stars as I eat *your* blueberry pie."

"My ass will be right on your nose. It's hardly whipped cream."

He smiles. "It's whipped cream to me. I need to get that ready too." He flicks his tongue suggestively. "Get that sweet ass on my face, sea witch."

My lips curl in amusement. "You're such a caveman."

"I am, but I know you dig it."

Yes, I do. I can't believe it, but I do.

I climb up and position myself over his face just as he asked. His tongue immediately runs through my back entrance several times without an ounce of trepidation. Is there anything better than an uninhibited man who will go to town on your ass?

In fact, he grabs my hips and pulls my ass even closer, and then shoves his face between my cheeks, leaving no inch untouched. His tongue pushes into my back entrance. I can feel my stomach muscles tighten at the sensation

Grabbing my ass, he removes his tongue and slowly slides his thumb into my puckered hole, while his tongue then moves to my other entrance and plunges inside.

My hips begin rocking of their own volition as he fucks me with that magical tongue and thick, long thumb at the same time.

Before I know it, he adds fingers circling my clit. It's a trifecta of heavenly sensations, and I'm the lucky one drifting into a sea of pleasure.

It's a struggle to keep my eyes open, but I look down at his cock. It's so hard and masculine. It's twitching with need of its own as precum oozes from the crown. I'm suddenly dying to taste it. To give him some amount of the pleasure he's giving me.

I bend forward and lick what has already pooled on his stomach before taking him into my mouth and letting the saltiness invade my tongue while inhaling his deeply masculine scent. Now it's his turn to let out a loud moan along with a few other undecipherable sounds of ecstasy.

Wrapping my hand around his length, I pump him with long, hard, fast strokes. It only serves to spur him on as his thumb and tongue push deeper inside me. His fingers are increasing in speed over my sensitive bundle. It all feels so perfect. I know my body is about to lift into orbit.

I've now got two hands and my mouth working him over, twisting those hands with every movement. We're both making loud noises as we let the pleasure overtake us. The stars may sit light-years above us, but we're both floating in them right now.

My orgasm is cresting. It's within reach. I have to lift my head to yell out as the multiple sensations become too much to bear, and I let myself explode all over his face. I open my mouth to scream just as long, salty ropes of his come squirt onto my mouth, chin, and his stomach.

I can't believe we came at the same time. That's no small feat in this position. I'm confident it's never happened to me before. I'm equally confident that no one has ever done to me what he just did to me. There was a lot going on back there.

I can feel him licking through me to clean me, so I do the same for him, licking every ounce of his semen from his stomach until it's all gone.

He easily manipulates my body until I'm lying half on his body and half on the sofa with my head resting comfortably on his chest.

"You're a dirty woman," he happily and proudly announces.

"You're a dirty man," I spit back in a playful tone.

I can feel him shrug. "I guess that's why we work so well together. I could feel the back of your throat on my tip, but I couldn't see your face. Were you gagging? Were your eyes watering?" He asks as though he's hoping for those things.

"Your dick was in my mouth. Why can't that be enough? You need me choking with tears streaming down my face? Don't be so selfish," I joke. In reality, he's the least selfish lover I've ever had.

He releases that belly-shaking laugh of his.

I can't help but bow my head down and suck his crown back into my mouth, running my tongue through his tip. But this time, I do it in a way that he can see my face.

"W…what are you doing?" he stutters as his cock twitches with sensitivity.

I let him fall out of my mouth with an audible plop onto his stomach. "That coin also landed on heads. That means it's time for some real tail action."

And that's all it takes for him to harden again. What is it with women's asses that makes men lose their minds?

"Do you need me to get lube or will a healthy dose of saliva do?" he asks.

"Saliva is fine," I answer. "Just make sure it's a lot and get me ready. You're a whole lot of man to take back there."

"Yes, ma'am. Let's get you another orgasm first."

He moves me so I'm seated on top of him, facing away from him. I sit up on my knees while he positions his cock at my entrance before gloriously sinking down onto him. We both let out moans. I can feel every long inch of him. He feels so perfect inside my body.

We're both still, acclimating to the sensation, when he sits up so that I can feel his broad chest cover my back with his comforting body heat. His fingertips trace the skin of my neck, and his lips run along my ear. "Why do you like to be choked so much?" he asks. "Why only rough sex?"

"I'm not sure. It's just something I enjoy. I guess I get off on the danger of it."

"Hmm. Can I tell you why I think you enjoy it?"

"Sure, Dr. Humblecock."

He tightens his hold on my neck a bit while keeping his lips close to my ear. "I think you're always in control of every little thing in your life, but sex is the one time you let yourself give up a little of that control. The roughness allows you to do so without opening yourself up to any real emotions or intimacy because you don't trust anyone."

I consider his words for a moment. He might be right.

He whispers into my ear, "You can trust me, Kennedy. Not just in bed. Everywhere. I'll never hurt you." He places his other hand on my stomach, and chills run up and down my body. "No matter what happens, I'll always be here for you both."

Tears well in my eyes as I think I experience every emotion possible. I can feel my heart beating wildly in my chest. I can equally feel his calm and steady heartbeat on my back. He's truly the yin to my yang, and I think it's just what I need. *He's* what I need. What *we* need, the baby and me.

I've been wronged so many times, and I know I've wronged others, but I did something right to bring this man into my life. To have him as the father of my child.

I relax my body into his, subtly letting him know that I'm giving up some control to him. I'm trusting him. He kisses under my ear and again whispers, "I've got you."

Eventually I begin my movements on top of him. While some of the rough aspects I like are still present, there's something a little different about the way we move together tonight. It's not about pain. It's not an animalistic battle. It's something more. Two people totally in sync with each other, relishing in every movement and every touch.

It's a new and unfamiliar sensation for me. All of my concerns are momentarily put on hold while I completely lose myself in all things Daylen Humblecut.

He makes good on his promise to take care of me, giving me two more orgasms in the front and then another in the back as I ride him reverse cowgirl and sing my pleasure into the starlit evening sky.

He manipulates my body perfectly, with his big, rough hands worshiping my breasts, clit, and throat. It's a true mix of rough and soft. My way and his way somehow blended into a perfect balance.

By the time we're done, we're both completely spent. I don't even remember falling asleep, but I know we do so under the stars on his special balcony while we're tangled together, neither of us willing to let go of the other.

I WAKE in the morning to both my and Daylen's phones ringing at the same time. Peeling my eyes open, I realize we're in Daylen's bed. I have no idea how I got here.

I'm under the sheets, but Daylen is out cold, spread out naked on top of the bed. He's on his back with his hand wrapped protectively around his massive erection.

I grab my phone and answer without checking to see who it is. I bring it to my ear and croak out, "Hello."

"Ms. Jeffries, hold the phone out so I can see you."

Oh, it's a FaceTime call. Because I'm not fully awake, I do as instructed. Judge Darth Vader's ugly mug appears on the screen. Oh shit. I forgot that we have our monthly video call today.

Daylen moans, rolls to his side, and throws his arm over me. His hand grabs for my breast over the sheet, and he squeezes it in his sleep.

The judge snarls, "That better be your husband's hand on you. If it's not, we're going to have a big problem. Let me see right now, young lady."

Daylen's eyes pop wide open. I'm sure mine match his.

Because I feel like I have no other choice, I tilt the phone so the camera can pick up Daylen, but only from his chest up. The judge would definitely meet his maker if he saw all of Daylen and his astonishing manhood.

Daylen grins widely and, in a cheery voice, practically sings, "Morning, Judge. Just catching me in bed with the wife. We must have slept in. Can we possibly chat another time?" he asks nonchalantly as if we're both not naked and his hand isn't *still* on my breast.

The judge gives a smile that's something between evil and self-satisfied...and then coughs up a lung. Daylen and I both jerk at the intrusive noise and share a look of disgust at how bad the judge sounds.

Because it's not enough for Judge Necrosis to see us this way, Daylen's bedroom door swings open, and Vance walks in. He stops short when he sees me and yells, "Holy fuck."

"Who's that?" the judge barks.

"Just my friend, Judge," Daylen answers. "Again, can we reschedule?"

The judge narrows his eyes. "Fine. In light of the good news of seeing you being…together like this, I'll allow for one reschedule, but you must take these meetings seriously. Have Mr. Montgomery contact my office. Good day," he wheezes before hanging up the phone.

Vance's eyes toggle between me and Daylen. "I'm literally in shock. Don't you two hate each other?"

Daylen releases my breast and rolls onto his back again in all his naked glory. I motion my head toward his dick. "Don't you care that Vance can see you?"

He shrugs. "Vance has seen me naked thousands of times. We've shared a locker room for ten years. He has a big dick too. We have a club for guys like us. There are very few members. It's exclusive. We're thinking of taking in large-breasted women too. Are you interested in joining?"

"I'll pass, but thanks for the offer." My eyes move to his still erect penis. "Does he normally see you hard?"

"Sometimes. We share hotel rooms on the road. I wake up hard every morning."

"*Every* morning?"

He nods. "Yes. Morning wood is a sign of health for men. If you don't have it, it's like a check engine light telling you something is wrong." He looks at Vance. "Right?"

Vance also nods. "True."

Daylen continues, "Beau told us to go to the doctor if we ever wake up without it. And then he gave us a long lecture about testosterone levels and diets. Morning boners are super important. That's all I remember from the speech."

Vance sighs. "As interesting as this morning wood conversation is, what in the actual fuck? Again, don't you two hate each other?"

"Don't you and Sulley have family bad blood?" I challenge back, knowing they're fucking like rabbits right now.

He twists his lips. "Hmm, fair point. I'll let you two get dressed. I'll be downstairs trying to avoid your slobbering beast."

I scowl at him. "Be nice to that dog or you'll be on my shitlist, McCaffrey."

Vance stares at Daylen with disbelief written all over his face, and Daylen smiles. "She loves BJ, and BJ loves her."

He scratches his head and exits the room, closing the door behind him.

Daylen looks at me. "He's going to have questions. What should I tell him?"

I sigh in resignation. "Tell him whatever you want. I know he's your best friend, and I'm sure we can trust him to keep our secret. I was thinking about talking to Sulley about everything anyway. It's so hard keeping all of this from my best friend."

He nods. "Thanks. It will be such a relief to tell him. I've never kept anything from him before."

I turn in his bizarrely soft bed. "How did I get here? Didn't we fall asleep on the balcony?"

He nods. "Yes. It started drizzling in the middle of the night. You slept through it, so I carried you inside and tucked you into bed."

I snuggle in. "Why is your bed so comfortable? I don't remember it being like this the last time. I don't want to move. I could stay here all day."

He twists his lips. "The bedding is new. I know you like high-thread-count sheets. I remember them from your bed. I just bought this set. Do you like it?"

"I do, but that was…presumptuous." I smile. "What made you think I was a sure thing last night?"

He purses his lips. "Hmm, just a guess. I knew you were horny and wouldn't be able to resist my Humblecock."

I roll my eyes at his arrogance as I sit up. "My dress is on the floor downstairs. Can you get it for me? I'll have to walk of shame out of here."

He scrunches his nose. "Don't be mad…but I got you a few things."

"What things?"

"That sexy red robe you were wearing at your apartment? I got you one just like it to keep here. I also got some of your toiletries, like girlie shampoo and stuff. They're in the bathroom. And the second closet has a few items as well. They're not fancy, just some Camels sweatshirts and sweatpants in your size so you don't have to walk of shame out of here."

I stare at him in shock. "You're bizarrely thoughtful, albeit slightly creepy."

"Are you mad? I was afraid you would be."

I shake my head as I rub my fingers through his scruff and peck his lips. "No, I'm not mad. Thank you for thinking of me."

You're the first person who ever has.

TWENTY-SEVEN

DAYLEN

It's been a great few weeks for Kennedy and me. We've found our groove. We rarely spend a night apart, except when I have team obligations like mini-camp. She even stayed with BJ the few nights I was gone because she didn't want BJ to be lonely. I think she loves that dog nearly as much as I do. I know the feeling is mutual, and it warms my heart to see how protective BJ is of Kennedy. She follows Kennedy everywhere in the house, and if a delivery person approaches the door, she always places herself between Kennedy and the visitor, usually scaring them away. Kennedy is amused by it, but it hits me right in the heart seeing my two girls interact like that.

More and more of her belongings have slowly trickled into my house. Without speaking of it, I've cleared plenty of space for her. I have two giant walk-in closets in my bedroom. I moved my stuff to the smaller one. I'm pretty sure closet space is the way to her heart, so I happily gave up mine for her.

We've continued her training. She's so darn close. Millimeters away from making a dunk happen. It might not be this season, but hopefully next. I even installed a basketball net for her so she can practice anytime she wants.

I haven't broached the future at all with her. I'm trying to live in the moment while slowly and subtly making space for her in my life and house. I think I've fallen in love with her, but I'm not telling her. She'll feel pressured. She needs to get there in her own time.

What I don't love is what she's selected for me to wear to walk into our first game. I lost a bet to her months ago, well before Vegas, and she has done her best to do me dirty.

I wouldn't want it any other way. I would have done the same to her if I had won the bet.

I'm in our stadium parking lot, sitting in my car and bracing for the chaos that will surely follow from what I'm about to wear into the stadium. I slowly step out of my car in my green fleece robe and take a deep breath as I think about the huge amount of humiliation I'm about to face. A bet is a bet, and I lost it. Time to pay up.

I slip the swim cap on my head and place the swim goggles over my eyes before grabbing my bag and tossing the robe into the car.

I open my Spotify app and press play for the song "Stayin' Alive" by the Bee Gees, blasting it on the speaker as loud as my phone will allow. In only the tiny pink Speedo that leaves nothing to the imagination, I strut into the stadium like I own the place. Did I mention that the speedo has a beaver over the crotch? I'm not sure where she found this thing, but she was mighty excited when it arrived last week.

Teammates begin to notice me and laugh hysterically. The press goes berserk, as I knew they would. Flashes are going off at a pace that's hard to imagine. Yep, this will be all over the internet in mere seconds. I hope that spiteful bitch, who I think I love, is enjoying herself right now. I have no doubt she's following online with a mischievous glint in her gorgeous green eyes.

I might as well own it. It could be worse. At least I look good. *Damn* good.

I pose like a swimsuit model for all the cameras, sucking in my cheeks and placing my hands on my hips. I even shake my ass a bit for a little something extra. They're eating it up. I knew they would.

Vance walks over and holds his cowboy hat over my family jewels to cover them but then laughs and removes it. I'm not sure I've ever seen him smile as much as he is right now.

Coach then walks by. He stops short, and his face drops when he takes in my wardrobe. "You know, Humblecut, I used to judge your generation for being so adamant about supervised playdates. My generation certainly never had any, and we managed to survive. But right now, I'm thinking you could have used a little *more* supervision."

Vance laughs. "Blame your daughter for this horrific scene."

He turns to look at Vance. "Why would I do that?"

"He lost a bet to her months ago. The terms stated she got to pick his outfit for today. This is what she chose."

I nod. "I'm a man of my word, but your daughter is batshit crazy." *And I dig the fuck out of her for it.*

He shrugs. "Tell me something I don't know, Humblecut. What was the bet?" he asks.

Vance smirks. "Whether she could knock him down with one karate chop to the side of the neck?"

Coach raises an unamused eyebrow. "She's a blackbelt in karate, Humblecut. You never stood a chance."

My face falls. "What?" I yell out. "She never mentioned that. That cunning bitch had hidden skills. Holy crap. It was fixed."

Coach grins like I've never seen before, and Vance nearly pees his pants in laughter.

KENNEDY

My long-awaited Google alert pings just before we're about to leave the locker room for warm-ups. We have a game early this afternoon. The Camels have a late afternoon game that we'll go to when ours ends. I was hoping Daylen would make his grand entrance before my game started so I could see his outfit. Sure enough, it's happening.

Sulley, Layla, Palmer, and Shay stand behind me, looking over my shoulder. We've all been waiting for this. They have no idea what outfit I selected. They just know today is the day.

I pull up the picture and hear gasps and giggles behind me. Sulley says, "Holy cow. That's incredible. I don't know how you think of this stuff."

Palmer mumbles, "Now *that's* a sausage I would happily eat."

I burst out laughing and turn around to her. "Palmer, do you incorporate food into your sex life?"

She turns a bright shade of red and chews her lips nervously. "As you've said many times before, we all have our kinks."

I hold up my hand for a high five, and she smacks it. I'm proud of my girl. She's really come out of her shell.

Layla mumbles, "Ay, dios mío. He's packing un salchichón grande."

Yes, ladies, that is one large sausage. There are going to be a million memes of his beaver-covered package all week. It could be worse. I could have exposed a small sausage.

"He should be thanking me," I proudly announce. "He'll have half the women in this country begging for a date." And I owed him this for having Booster post the small dick pic last year.

Sulley scoffs. "Pft. Are the other half blind? His body is amazing."

I know. I traced it with my tongue last night. And again this morning, after he woke me up with his head between my legs.

He said he'd now like to eat me for breakfast before all his games, calling it his breakfast of champions. I'm happy to oblige that request.

Our budding relationship is getting harder and harder to hide, but he's been amazing at respecting my wishes. We've had the best month of doing normal dating. A lot of it has been hanging out at his house because we'll be recognized in a public restaurant, but he sometimes finds creative ways for us to go out. Honestly, I don't mind staying in with him because he's so much fun. Plus, being in his house isn't exactly a chore. His backyard pool situation is fun, I enjoy the serenity of his roof balcony, and I'm obsessed with his dog. BJ can sing in tune. It's the craziest thing I've ever seen. She gets on her hind legs and dances with Daylen while they sing together. Seeing him as the father of my child gets easier by the day. He'll be everything my father wasn't. He'll be present and involved and will make our kid feel so damn loved. I have no doubt.

He's working so hard on us. Without mentioning it, he moved his stuff into the smaller closet and my stuff into the bigger closet, even though I only keep a few things there, though it seems to grow by the day. That closet is my dream come true. It's massive, with rows and rows of hanging space, shelves, and a whole seating area in the middle. Though I did find a bunch of my lipsticks in the back of one of his drawers. They had gradually been disappearing from my apartment and my purses, and I thought I was going crazy. I can't manage to be upset with him, knowing he did it because he prefers me au naturale.

He makes sure Chef Benny has all my favorite foods on hand. There's nothing that man doesn't think of to make me feel loved and happy. How did I misjudge him so badly when we met? He's perfect.

I hear Palmer giggle as she stares at her phone. "Oh my god. #HumbleCock is already trending."

I roll my eyes. Oh, cheez, he's going to have a field day with that one. He's probably already had T-shirts and hats made with the hashtag.

Sulley lets out a laugh as she looks at her phone. "Ha! This post has a picture of him from today and reads: *I thought it was a game of inches, not feet*. So funny. And this post says the Camels should change their name to the Tripods."

Shay smiles as she looks at her phone. "This one reads: *There's the Super Bowl and there's the Super Bulge. One already down for Humblecut. Will he get the other?*"

I can't help but smile. "I'm kind of a genius, aren't I? I should go into marketing when I retire."

Palmer sighs. "I could use marketing help."

My good mood immediately sours. Palmer has been the subject of a hate campaign this summer. I don't know why, but she's getting crucified for her body on social media. We haven't been out much as a big group lately, with the guys in training and our playoffs about to begin, but Beau body slammed a guy at a club last week who was hassling Palmer. I know it's weighing on her. We've been trying to find other fun things to do as a group that are a little less public. It works for me because I can't drink. It's easier to stay away from the club scene.

I hate seeing my friend this upset. It's carried over to the court, with some of the mean girls in the league mumbling comments to her. I'm trying not to get into fights since my suspension, but some of the girls make it hard for me not to retaliate.

Fallon walks over and looks at my phone. She sucks in a breath. "Holy crap. I hope no children can see that thing. It will give them nightmares for weeks."

She squeezes my shoulder and whispers into my ear, "And congratulations."

I can't help but giggle. Yep, I'm a lucky bitch. Hands off, ladies. He's all mine.

I'M RIDING over to the football game with Sulley and her bodyguard, Keith. He's been with her for a few months. I'm glad I'm only in the famous-*ish* category. Famous enough to get endorsement deals and occasionally recognized, but not famous enough to have stalkers like Sulley. She's had a few scares of late, and Keith gives her peace of mind. He's big, bald, and doesn't say a word. I love having him around. He drives us everywhere, doesn't bother us, and keeps people appropriately at bay. I'm grateful for the opportunities my newfound celebrity has given me, but sometimes fans can get a little too close for comfort. There's a time and place for that.

Reagan purchased a suite for all the Camels' home games and gives us uninhibited use. Is there any better owner in professional sports than Reagan Daulton? I'm pretty sure there's not.

We're the only team in the league with a private jet. She said she doesn't want us to have to be delayed on the whims of the commercial airlines. We're also the only team in the league that plays to sell-out crowds every single game. Thank you, Sulley, for that. Coming to this team from New York has been the best thing to ever happen to me.

We clinched the three seed in the playoffs tonight. If things go as I hope, we could be on a collision course to play New York in the finals. We have to get there, and so do they, but nothing would make me happier than beating my old team for my first championship. The way our team is gelling right now makes me think it's within the realm of reason.

Sulley and I chat about our secret relationships. Me with Daylen and her with Vance. She had already told me about her relationship, but I finally opened up to her about Daylen and me a few weeks ago. I think we both needed the ability to talk to someone without judgment, and that's what we give each other. It's nice to have her to talk to, and I think she feels the same way about me. I'm the only one on our team who knows about the two of them, though I think others suspect it. Vance practically undresses her with his eyes anytime they're around each other.

I also finally opened up to some of my teammates about the drugging incident on New Year's Eve. I'm not sure I realized how much it impacted me until I finally confided in my friends about it. They all cried for an hour. Sulley felt so bad for not being in town, and the rest for not noticing. Obviously it wasn't their fault. It was an unfortunate, eye-opening situation, and I will be forever grateful to Daylen for doing what he did for me. In discussing it further with Sulley, we determined it was the moment things took a turn in my relationship with Daylen. How could I ever again hate a man who did that for me?

The Camels' game is underway when we arrive. Because I'm with Sulley, we enter through a private, secured entrance and are escorted to a private elevator that leads directly into the suite. Yep, there are perks to being Sulley O'Shea's best friend.

It's a back-and-forth, tight game, with both teams not having any trouble moving the ball up the field. I can see Beau fired up on the bench, yelling at the other defensive players. I wouldn't want to be on Beau Fudd's shit list. It looks scary.

The Camels have the ball now on their own twenty-yard line. The ball is snapped, and the entire defensive line is running uninhibited toward Vance. I can't imagine having five three-hundred-pound men running at me wanting to crush me into tiny pieces. Poor Vance.

It's a screen pass to Daylen just a few yards down the field. He breaks one tackle and then another. One of their cornerbacks grabs onto his waist, but Daylen drags him as if he's not there until the guy falls off him. Daylen manages to zigzag and stiff-arm defenders until he runs all the way to the other end zone and then unnecessarily leaps headfirst into the endzone, capping it off with a somersault.

He stands and does a little freestyle swimming routine with

his arms, followed by doing the official swim dance move by holding his nose and shimmying down.

He then looks up to our suite with a big smile and makes a heart with his fingers before lifting his jersey to reveal a Beavers T-shirt underneath.

I can't help but laugh, as does everyone in our suite and the rest of the stadium. I know people assume the heart is for the Beavers, but I'm pretty sure it was for me.

After a winning game, the guys like to celebrate at a nearby bar with the fans. I send Sulley over without me. I want to wait for Daylen at his car. I'm like a lovesick puppy. I can't get enough of him, and I can't publicly embrace him like I want to. I'll do so by his car before we head over to the bar.

While I'm standing by his Jeep, I get a text from Pierce. He was at my game today with my mother and her boy toy. She kept trying to get my attention, but I ignored her. I always do. I don't know why she keeps trying.

Pierce: Awesome game today. Can you stop by my dorm room? Need to talk.

That's very unlike him. I respond right away.

Me: Of course. Are you okay?

Pierce: Yes. How long?

Me: About thirty minutes.

Pierce: See you then.

I'm worried. I saw his room when he moved in, but he's never asked me to come by. It must be important.

It's now dark outside, and the parking lot is nearly empty. All the fans are gone. It's just players' cars, and some of them have already started leaving. Daylen should be out any minute now.

I hear Daylen before I see him. His laugh is hard to miss. I can't help but smile when I hear it.

When he finally notices me waiting by his Jeep, his entire face lights up. He's so freakin' happy to see me. It feels good.

"Nice game," I say.

He wordlessly approaches, drops his bag, and immediately pins me to his Jeep with his body as his soft, plump lips caress my mouth. The familiar taste of strawberries delights my taste buds. I should be worried that someone could see us, but I have zero fucks to give right now.

He grabs my face and deepens this kiss like he hasn't kissed me in weeks, when in reality it was just this morning. It's seductive. It's intoxicating. It's perfect. I'm falling deeper and deeper for him every day that passes.

An intruding noise eventually causes us to breathlessly break apart, though our faces remain close together. I breathe, "Wow, I should wait for you more often."

He traces my lipstick-smeared, swollen lips with his thumb. "I like you waiting for me."

"I like your dance moves. Nice touchdown celebration."

A big grin breaks out on his face. "That was for you."

I nod. "I know. I loved it. I wanted to thank you before we got to the bar, but my brother just texted that he needs me. I'm going to Uber over there. I'll come by later tonight."

He shakes his head. "I don't want you alone in an Uber. I'll drive you."

I roll my eyes. "I'll be fine. I've been Ubering alone for a decade. You should go and celebrate with your teammates. It was a big win."

He scowls. "Not happening. I'd rather celebrate alone with you anyway. Get in the damn car. We'll stop by Pierce's and then go to my house, where I will feed you and then fuck you."

His protective, take-charge demeanor should bother me, but it turns me on, and he knows it. "You're a Neanderthal, you know that?"

"You love it, Cruella." He points to the passenger side of his Jeep. "Car. Now."

Fuck, he's so hot.

While we're driving, he squeezes my thigh. "Do you know what I learned today?"

"That Speedos are extremely revealing and women love a good bulge?" I cheekily reply.

"No, wise ass. I learned that you're a black belt in karate. I never stood a chance, did I?"

I giggle. "You could have asked. You assumed I couldn't knock your sexy ass down. Don't ever underestimate me. I only make bets I'm confident I can win."

He bites back his smile and breathes, "Unreal. I was set up."

"I owed you one for setting me up with the Champ bet."

He smirks. "I suppose, but I'm pretty sure you got me back with the fake dick pic. I was five seconds away from sending you a real dick pic to prove you wrong.

I laugh. "Newsflash, women don't like dick pics. We like come-shot videos with the sound turned on." I shiver at the thought. "Getting one of those from you would be a huge turn-on."

He raises an eyebrow. "That can be arranged. How about a new bet?"

"I'm listening," I respond.

"The going home from the hospital outfit for our baby. If it's a girl, I choose. If it's a boy, you choose. Either way, I'll send you that video."

I'm not confident I'm winning this one, but I'll take the video. And I've come to love his playful demeanor. He's so fun.

Holding out my hand, I offer, "Deal."

He happily shakes my hand in return. "Deal."

I can't help my smile. "If it's a boy, will we name him Richard Dickgrabber? We can call him little Dickie."

His head snaps to me. "You remember that?"

I nod and sigh. "I suppose I remember a lot of what you've

said since I met you. Like when you told me I was the kind of person who didn't have real friends." I didn't mean for it to come off with as much edge as it did.

His face falls, and he reaches for my hand. "I'm sorry about that. It was a cruel thing to say."

I shrug. "It's okay. It made me think. At the time, you weren't wrong, but I don't think that's the case anymore."

"It's not," he immediately offers. "You're beloved by everyone close to you."

He stares at me for an extra beat. I think he's trying to tell me he loves me but isn't saying the words out loud. I'm glad he doesn't. I'm not sure I'm ready to hear them.

I squeeze his hand in silent acknowledgment. "I like that you call me out on my shit. Truthbombs are good for me. I need that in my life." I barely whisper, "I've never had anyone care enough to do so."

A small smile finds his lips. "Well, okay then. How about a few more? Your personality falls somewhere between Mother Theresa and Mother Fucker."

I spit in laughter, appreciating both the joke and him lightening the conversation. This man somehow makes me laugh and fills my soul at the same time.

Twenty-five minutes later, we're walking into Pierce's dorm building and up to his room. I knock on his door, and he opens it with his head down and a solemn face. "What's wrong?" I ask with concern.

He looks behind him and then at the floor in front of me, like he's unable to make eye contact. "I'm so sorry. Don't be mad at me. She made me do it."

He opens the door further, and I see my mother sitting there. Her collagen-injected lips tighten as much as they can for someone who probably has no feeling in them. "Time for us to talk, daughter. Pierce, wait outside," she demands like he's a child.

I wordlessly cross my arms in the doorway while Pierce hangs his head further and walks out.

"Come inside, Kennedy," she commands.

I suppose this was inevitable. I've been back in Philly for over a year and have successfully avoided a real conversation with her.

Daylen, who she likely couldn't see behind me in the hallway, walks in with me. Her facelifted face attempts to show surprise, but it doesn't move much. "Daylen? What are you doing here?"

He scowls at her. "I was giving Kennedy a ride home when Pierce texted."

She nods in understanding. "Honey, can you give Kennedy and me a few minutes alone? We need to talk about family business."

He shakes his head. "I'll leave if Kennedy wants me to."

"I don't," I immediately respond. "Please stay." I look at her. "He knows everything."

She looks uncomfortable, but I don't give a shit. It's not my job to appease her in any way, shape, or form. "Say what you have to say, Ginny. I have plans. I only came here because of Pierce. How dare you use him to get to me. Don't put him in the middle. It's not fair to him."

She throws her hands in the air in obvious frustration. "You left me no choice. I've been patient, but you won't return my calls or texts. And now I can't even get through. My texts bounce back. What else was I supposed to do?"

"I blocked you. You were annoying me. When someone doesn't return calls or texts, it means they don't want to talk to you. Take the social cue, Ginny."

Daylen subtly places his hand on the small of my back in solidarity. Knowing he has my back, both literally and figuratively, means everything to me right now. It's giving me the strength I need to have this conversation with words and not fists.

Tears well in her eyes. "What can I do to repair our relationship? I'll do anything. I love you. You're my daughter."

My anger bubbles over. "Daughter?" I shout. "Funny how you care most when my star is on the rise. I haven't been your daughter in ten years," I yell at her. "Frankly, I was barely your daughter before that. We both know that."

"How long are you going to punish me for it?" she asks with hardly a shred of remorse. "I made a mistake. People make mistakes."

"A *mistake* is forgetting to pick me up from school. A *mistake* is mixing up my game times and missing a game. A *mistake* is forgetting to pack my lunch. Bending over so my boyfriend can stick his dick inside you is not a *mistake*. It's diabolical. It's not something any real mother would ever do. Mothers are supposed to support and protect. You never did either. Mothers shouldn't get off on stealing their teenage daughter's boyfriends."

"You don't know what I was going through at that time with your father. I was a mess. You don't have a husband or a child. You can't possibly understand. Maybe you will one day in the future, and then you'll have some compassion for me."

I can feel heat emanating from Daylen's body. He grits out, "She'll be a million times the wife and mother you were when the time comes. She will *never* treat her daughter like you treated her. Mothers are supposed to be the only women who hope their daughters are better than they are. Were you happy about Kennedy's successes?"

My mother stiffens. He hit the nail on the head. "Of course I was happy," she lies.

"No, Ginny, you weren't," I snap. "You were jealous. You were jealous that I got what little attention Dad gave our family, you were jealous that I was prettier than you, and you were jealous that I was a superstar. I should have been your pride and joy. Instead you saw me as your competition. While the day you fucked Nick was the day our relationship officially died, in reality, it was never there to begin with because you were too insecure and selfish to ever be a real mother. You weighed social status over your kids every single day of your life. We all have choices. You made yours, and now I'm making mine. I have nothing else to say to you." The tears are starting to form, but I won't give her the satisfaction. As if sensing my need, Daylen wraps his arm around my shoulders and kisses my head. I lean into him before giving her one more parting statement. "To be crystal clear, you will *never* be welcome to be around my family when I have one. Stay away from me. Stay away from the people I love. Stay out of my life. You're toxic, and it's time to take out the trash. Goodbye, Ginny."

I turn and walk away from my mother with Daylen standing right by my side.

I hold it together until we get to the parking lot, when I start sobbing. Daylen takes me into his arms. "I'm so fucking proud of you. You were amazing."

I mumble into his chest. "I want to go home."

I can feel him deflate. "If that's what you want, but I wish you'd let me take care of you. I was hoping you'd stay with me tonight."

I look up at his eyes and know for a fact in this moment that I'm in love with him. He's my home.

I nod. "That's what I meant by home."

TWENTY-EIGHT

KENNEDY

We're now into the playoffs, and we won our first round of games. The Camels have won their first few games of the season. Things are good professionally. Personally, things are even better. Daylen and I rarely spend a free moment without each other. We've achieved another new level of intimacy, especially since that night with my mother. His unwavering support unlocked something in me. I've almost completely thrown caution to the wind.

The only thing I've held back is telling him that I love him. I'm still scared. Those words have never left my mouth in my life, but I know the feelings are there. I know I can no longer imagine my life without him in it. I need to build up the courage to say those three little words out loud.

Alyssa and Shay are hosting a girls' night. I wasn't going to go because hiding the fact that I'm not drinking is hard in such a small group, but Sulley said she'd abstain with me under the guise that we're focused on the playoffs. Having a best friend is pretty awesome.

It's not like anyone will be getting rip-roaring drunk anyway. We're all locked in.

I knock on the door, and Alyssa opens it. I notice she got a haircut. It's a cute bob. "Your hair looks great. You didn't go full lesbian cut, but I like it."

She smiles. "Do you know why so many lesbians have such short hair?"

I shake my head. "I don't."

She wiggles her eyebrows up and down. "Because we get really excited about scissors."

I let out a laugh. She cracks me up, but I came with an arsenal of my own. "What do you call fifty lesbians and fifty politicians in the same room?"

"Hmm, I'm not sure. What?" she asks with an amused expression on her pretty face.

"A hundred people who don't do dick."

She giggles. "Nice. And very true." She waves her hand. "Come in. Sulley and Palmer are here. Layla is running late. She said she's having monster-in-law issues."

I give her a knowing nod. Layla's mother-in-law stays with them for the roughly two months of overlap in our season and the Camels'. It's the only way they can manage childcare for their toddler because there are nights when they're both out of town. It comes with a price though, and that's Layla's sanity. Her mother-in-law drives her nuts, constantly judging her parenting style. It's only getting worse with each passing week.

When I walk into the living room, I notice Palmer and Shay each have a glass of wine in hand. Shay offers me some, but I decline. She doesn't even ask why. I think it's assumed we're taking it easy with a big game later this week. I worried for nothing.

Palmer starts talking about her parents and how close she is to them. She's super excited that they're coming into town for all our remaining playoff games. Their relationship is sweet. I know she talks to her mom every single day. I can't imagine.

Eventually Layla arrives. She plops down on the couch, grabs the bottle of wine on the coffee table, and drinks directly from it before shouting out what I'm pretty sure are a series of Spanish expletives.

We're all staring at her until she eventually sighs. "My mother-in-law just told me I'm a drug addict because I use birth control. She wants us to have another baby and said Presley should take me to rehab because I'm *addicted* to birth control pills."

We shake our heads in disbelief. "That's insane," I offer.

She nods. "It is. It's almost as crazy as last year, when I was breastfeeding, feeling like my nipples were being cut by razor blades, the monster-in-law told me I was *selfish* for breastfeeding for so long because she wanted to be able to feed the baby more often. The bitch is officially off her rocker. I think it's only getting worse with age. I can't take it much longer. I'm not doing this again next season. I just can't have her living with us for two months again."

She exhales a long breath. "Maybe it will end soon. Her birthday is next week. She's suddenly super into taking baths and asked us to get her something bath-appropriate for her birthday." She gives a sly smile. "So I got her a toaster oven. Take that in the bath with you, you pinche puta."

We all burst into hysterics.

She begins sharing a few more mother-in-law and grand-parent stories when it occurs to me that my baby won't have a grandmother. I suppose Ashleigh sort of counts, but Daylen's mother is gone, and I won't let my mother around my child. While I adore Hank and know he'll be an amazing grandfather, I don't want him to be the only grandparent in my kid's life. I'm feeling like it's time to have a real talk with my father.

Probably due to my crazy hormones, I'm suddenly unwilling to wait a second longer, so I stand. "I'm really sorry to bail, but I need to run. I forgot about something I need to do."

Sulley gives me a look as if to ask if everything is okay. I nod that it is.

Everyone expresses their disappointment, but don't push, sensing something is going on with me. When the season is over, I'll tell them everything.

As I drive over to my father's, I'm filled with anxiety. I have so much to say. We need to talk about our relationship, and I need to tell him about Daylen and the baby.

I know Daylen wanted to be here for this conversation, but I need to do it alone. I'm not sure how my father will react, and I don't want things to escalate with him and Daylen. I'm going to absorb the blow for him. Whether Daylen agrees or not, I'm trying to protect him and his job. He's been my protector. Now it's my turn to return the favor.

I ring the doorbell a few times, but there's no answer. I had texted Pierce as to my father's whereabouts, and he replied that Dad was home tonight. I know they speak on the phone or text nearly every day. Maybe Dad's out by the pool. It's a warm evening, and I remember him mentioning that he likes it back there.

He once told me that his code is my birthday, and he encouraged me to use it anytime. I decide to unlock his door myself for the first time ever.

Walking inside, I'm immediately hit with the sounds of music coming from the backyard area. I guess that's why he didn't hear the doorbell.

Wiping my clammy hands on my shirt, I slowly make my way toward the back of the house filled with nerves. As I approach, I see him in only his bathing suit with his back to me. He's dancing to some slow song that's likely from the eighties, knowing my dad. I've never heard it before.

A woman's hands are wrapped around him, caressing his back lovingly. I can't see much of her, he very obviously towers over her, but I can see her bare legs and enough of her body to know she's in a bathing suit too.

I know my parents are divorced, but it's slightly weird seeing my father with another woman, especially since they're half-naked. I've never once seen him with anyone but my mother. I wish I could say the same for her.

A small smile finds my lips. I'm happy for him. If what Daylen and Pierce have said is true, he's waited a long time to find someone. He deserves to be happy, especially after being married to that miserable shrew for so many years.

I've never seen him dance before. He and my mother barely looked at each other, let alone danced. I never once saw them be affectionate or loving. Seeing how Daylen is with me makes my heart ache a little for my father. No wonder he never wanted to be home.

The woman's hair sways into my sightline, and I see that it's blonde. He certainly has a type. Petite blondes.

I'm about to interrupt when he bends his head and kisses her. Her fingers run through his hair. Their in-sync movements are familiar in a way that I know they've done it many times before. She's not new.

Suddenly he lets out a moan, and his hands move down her body. Okay, this is getting creepy. I'm leaving. I'll come back another time when he's not five seconds away from having sex.

I turn to leave when the sounds of a woman's laughter hit my eardrums. Wait, I know that laugh. It's very familiar. Where have I heard it before?

I turn back toward them, and that's when the biggest gut punch of my life hits me. That's saying a lot because I also walked in on the sounds of my kitchen table banging the wall as my then-boyfriend was nailing my mother.

The woman my father is now dipping as they smile and laugh into each other's mouths is Fallon. *My* Fallon. The only maternal figure I've ever had in my life.

Reality hits me like a ton of bricks. It was all bullshit. She never cared about me. She was using me to get to my father, just like every single person in my childhood.

Tears spill from my eyes as I watch them together, acting so damn familiar. How long has this been going on? A long while is the obvious answer by the way they're interacting.

His hands roam her body, and they start kissing again, but this time it's getting even more heated. He lifts her, and she wraps her legs around him.

Fuck this. I'm out of here.

With tears spilling from my eyes like a damn waterfall, I run out the front door to my car. Peeling out of the driveway, I begin to replay every conversation I've had with Fallon in the past six months.

She definitely asked about my parents a lot. She was always encouraging me to mend fences with my dad and spend time with him. Did he send her to manipulate me into reconciling with him? I'm so confused and so damn hurt by her betrayal. Another mother stabbing me right in the back. What have I done to deserve this? Am I that horrible of a person?

My car practically steers itself. There's only one place I want to go right now. My safe space. The only true safe space I've ever known.

I pull into Daylen's driveway. His Jeep is out front, so I know he's home. Using his code, I walk inside and am immediately warmly greeted by BJ. She's so gentle with me. It's such a contrast to how she practically tackles Daylen when he walks into the house. It's like she knows about the baby. Maybe she really is as smart as Daylen thinks she is.

I rub her ear as she nuzzles into my stomach lovingly. "Where's Daddy?" I ask.

Oh god, now I'm talking to her like she understands me, just like Daylen does.

She motions her nose toward the stairs. Yep, she understands me. Genius dog.

I walk up the stairs and hear music. Naturally, it's "Waterfalls," and it makes me smile. Why does he love that song so much?

I know the answer, and it's a sweet one.

Following the sounds, I make my way down the long hallway to one of the guestrooms. I can smell it's freshly painted before I arrive at the doorway and see the new pretty pastel pink color on the walls. Painting supplies are piled in the corner over a plastic sheet.

There are a variety of pastel-colored basketballs and footballs stenciled on the wall with all types of animals. There are new built-in bookshelves filled with children's books and other decorative knick-knacks. I can't help but smile as I notice a mobile on the ground that has both tiny basketballs and tiny footballs hanging from it. He obviously had it custom made.

Looking to the other side of the room, I see a big ivory toy chest with a pink Beaver on the front, overflowing with toys. Dozens of stuffed animals fill the huge lavender and ivory striped rocking chair next to it.

And then I see him. My husband.

He's on the ground with a screwdriver, assembling a crib. He's mindlessly shaking his body and quietly singing the words to his favorite song as he reviews the instructions with determined focus.

The tears run afresh from my eyes as I watch him build our baby's crib. He's one of the highest paid players in the league. He can more than afford to have someone else do all this, but he wants to be the one to do everything.

My heart has never felt fuller in my life.

Only three words cross my mind right now. "I love you," I state without a shred of doubt or regret.

His head snaps to me. "Oh shit. You said you had plans with your friends tonight. I didn't want you to see this room until it was done. I wanted to surprise you." He holds his hands up in surrender. "Don't be mad. I know it's early, but things get crazy once my season kicks into high gear, and I wanted to do it all myself."

"I love you," I again announce with a fresh wave of tears dripping down my cheeks.

As if hearing it for the first time, he smiles so damn big that I can't help but let out a laugh through my tears. "You love me?" he asks. "Love-love or love that I'm assembling a crib?"

"All of it," I answer without hesitation. "Every single thing about you."

He places the screwdriver, instructions, and screws on the ground before standing and walking to me. His arms are open, about to embrace me, but his face falls drastically as he approaches. "What's wrong, baby? Why are you crying?"

I take his hand. "Can we go to the roof balcony and talk?"

He nods. "Of course. Is everything okay?"

I lean into him and bury my nose in his neck, taking in his familiar, comforting scent that wraps around me like a warm blanket. "It is now," I breathe.

We silently walk up to the balcony and lie on the big circular lounger-sofa. I rest my head on his chest, needing to feel his arms around me like I've never needed anything else in my life.

Without hesitation, he indulges me and pulls me close to him. "What's wrong?"

"I think you're my person, and it fucking terrifies me."

"I love hearing that, baby, but what's wrong? Why are you crying?"

"*That's* what's wrong. You called me baby…and I like it." I start sobbing again.

He lets out a laugh. "Because it's always been a red flag, right?"

I nod through my tears while he continues to laugh and hold me. He whispers into my hair, "Do you want me to put on sandals too? I can take a selfie in front of my car if you want… with my Android…while wearing a chain necklace and white jeans…with my fruity drink in my other hand."

I can't help but laugh through my tears. "The fact that you listen to my red flags is kind of a green flag."

"Yeah, well the fact that your tits keep getting bigger is a huge green flag for me. We're a match made in heaven."

I smack his arm. "They are not."

"Um, yes, they are. Trust me. They're my favorite things on this planet. I know when they're changing. I know every inch of your body, and I love all of it almost as much as I love you." He tilts my chin until my eyes meet his. "I love you too. I have for a while, but I knew you wouldn't want me to say it first."

And then the waterworks begin all over again because once again, he knew what I needed and gave it to me. Why am I so damn emotional?

Oh, right. Duh.

He studies me carefully. "Did something happen tonight? I know my girl, and this isn't just lovey-dovey emotions. You're upset about something specific."

Yep, he's my person.

"I walked in on my dad and a woman," I admit.

He smiles. "Good for Coach. He deserves to get laid."

I stare at him. "That's my father, asshole."

He chuckles. "Right. He deserves to make love. Better?"

"No, dipshit."

He chuckles. "Why were you there? I thought you were going to Shay and Alyssa's tonight?"

"I was at their place for a bit." I bite my lip. He's not going to be happy about this. "I decided it was time to have a real talk with my dad. I wanted to lay it all on the table and confess everything to him."

He stiffens. "What?" he says in a raised tone. "I wanted to be there for that conversation. I owe it to him to have that conversation man to man. I would have done it months ago, but I'm respecting your wishes. You should also respect mine. That's how relationships work."

Now I feel like shit. "You're right. I'm sorry," I whisper. "I wanted to protect you from his wrath like you protect me. It doesn't matter anyway. I didn't tell him."

"Then why are you so upset?"

I exhale a long breath. "He didn't answer the door, so I just walked in. He was by his pool dancing with a woman. At first I thought it was sweet, but then I saw her face. It was Fallon."

His eyebrows pinch in confusion. "Fallon who?"

"How many fucking Fallons do you know?"

"Fallon Montgomery? That Fallon? Tanner's ex-wife, Fallon? Harper's mom, Fallon? Your coach, Fallon?"

"Oh my god," I whine. "Stop saying her name. Yes, that Fallon. The one who has weaseled her way into my life over the past few months. I thought she cared about me, but it was about my father, like everything and everyone in my life growing up."

His lips twist a bit. "Nah, that doesn't sound like Fallon. I've known her for ten years. She's a good person. She doesn't have a deceitful bone in her body."

"Did you know that when they were married, she fucked Tanner's best friend? That's what precipitated their divorce."

His eyeballs nearly pop out of his head. "No way. She wouldn't do that."

"She told me directly that she did. In fact, she pretty much used those exact words. How do you feel about those non-existent deceitful bones now?"

His head falls back, and he breathes, "Holy shit. Tanner has never said a word about it. Maybe he doesn't know."

"He knows. She told him right away. They got separated immediately after it happened."

He nods his head as if things are coming back to him and falling into place. "So that's why Fallon was hell bent on getting out of New York City. She wanted to come home to her family. Now I know why. That's fucking nuts. Poor Tanner."

"What about me?"

He's silent for a few beats. "I admit maybe she's not exactly who I thought she was, but I still don't see her as calculated. Trust me, I've been around a lot of calculated women in my life. Fallon isn't one of them. What did she say when they saw you?"

"They didn't see me. I was emotional and ran out of there before they could catch me. I came straight here."

"Because I'm your person?" he says in a lighthearted manner.

I narrow my eyes at him. "Don't push it. I have other candidates for the position," I deadpan.

He silently laughs. "Nah, it's me. You love me. Will you change my name in your phone to *My Person*?" He gasps. "Even better, I want to be your emergency contact."

I roll my eyes. "I'll think about it. It might be too much of a commitment. Honestly, I don't need an emergency contact. I need a person I can trust to clear my browser history, lie to my lawyer, and clean the crime scene."

He smiles. "One day it will all be me." He sighs. "Why don't you just go back over there and have an adult conversation with them?"

I lift my head in shock. "What? They were two seconds away from having sex. I'm not walking back into the lion's den of debauchery."

He shakes his head. "I feel like there's probably a reasonable explanation for everything. Instead of crying about it and making up stories in your head, let's just go find out what it is. Your father loves you and would *never* purposefully do anything to hurt you. Fallon may have a few more imperfections than I thought, but she's just not like that."

He stands and lifts me like a bride as if I weigh nothing. "Let's go. I'll go with you."

"What? No way. He doesn't know about us or the baby."

"Then let's just tell him. I'm sick of secrets. I'm sick of hiding. You told me you love me. I love you. We're married. We're having a baby. He's your father. He's my coach. Let's all just have a little chat and clear the air."

I scrunch my face in disgust. "Ugh. How the hell did you become the mature one?"

He smiles with pride. "Holy crap. You're right." Walking us

back inside, his face turns more serious. "I want to do this. It's time."

I grab his face and look into his blue eyes. "I hear you. Please just let me get through my season, and then we'll do this together. I promise."

His shoulders fall. Disappointment is written all over his handsome face.

"I'll go over there and talk to them by myself," I offer. "I won't mention you or the baby. It will just be about their relationship and my relationship with both of them. You're right. I should confront this head on instead of letting it fester and making up stories in my head."

He places my feet on the ground and mumbles, "Fine," before walking away from me.

I know he's disappointed, but I only have the mental energy for one issue at a time. Daylen is an inherently honest person, but I know my dad. He's not going to take the news of Daylen and me very well. I don't want any more drama than I already have in my life right now.

I find him a few minutes later back in the nursery, working on the crib. Poking my head in the doorway, I say, "I love it, by the way. It's beautiful. And perfect. And I still hope it's a boy so you have to redo everything."

He basically just grunts. He's still pissed at me.

"I'm going to head over to Dad's," I continue, but he's still giving me the silent treatment.

I wrack my brain for a way to get a response from him. I don't want to leave with him pissed at me. "I want to wait ten more minutes to make sure they finish whatever they were about to do. It's Sunday. I know your favorite weekly holiday falls on this day. How about I suck your big dick while I wait?"

His head pops up immediately. "Tell me more about this plan."

AFTER GIVING Daylen the blowjob of his life, I'm driving back over to my dad's house. This is so unlike me. I'd rather be pissed and stew in my anger than confront anything head on, but Daylen's right. I need to hear them out. My intent this evening was to move in a healthy direction with my father, and I still want that to happen. I want him in my baby's life, but the first step is fixing our relationship.

I need to make sure they're done doing whatever it is they were about to do when I left. While I'm more than okay with embarrassing them in their post-coital bliss, I don't want to catch them in the act. I'll be scarred for life.

I quietly tiptoe around back from the side instead of going through the house again. As I'm doing so, it occurs to me that Fallon may have told him about Daylen and the baby. Holy crap. What the hell am I doing here? What am I walking into?

I start to turn back around, but then I hear Daylen's voice in my head telling me to be an adult. Damnit. Adulting sucks.

Resigned to the fact that I'm about to have one of the most uncomfortable, awkward conversations of my life, I continue walking toward the backyard until I reach the final corner, which has some shrubbery hiding me from view.

I listen before I look. I don't hear moans. In fact, I hear more laughter. Most people don't laugh during sex, though sometimes Daylen makes me.

Deciding there's no way my dad makes her laugh during sex, I poke my head out enough to see them lying next to each other on an oversized double lounge chair. They're clearly naked, but at least there's a blanket on top of them.

They're both laughing at something. My dad isn't a big laugher…or much of a smiler. Maybe she brings it out in him.

They're trading sweet, familiar touches, smiles, and kisses. They're actually kind of cute together. I guess physically they make a lot of sense, both being attractive. He's a little older than her, but it's probably around the same age difference as Daylen and me so I won't judge that aspect of their relationship.

As I consider it more and more, I realize I want to know the details. Time to make my presence known.

I pop out from behind a big bush and yell, "Sex police. You're busted."

They both jerk up in surprise into a seated position. Fallon quickly covers her briefly exposed chest with the blanket before she brings her other hand to her mouth and cries, "Oh my god," before tears flood her blue eyes. "Kennedy, I'm so sorry. I wanted to tell you. I…I—"

"It's my fault," my father interrupts as he hangs his head in shame. "Don't be upset with Fallon. She loves you and the relationship you've formed. You can blame me. You already hate me."

The blanket is pooled at his waist, but Fallon is clutching her side up for dear life. They look like teens who were busted in the act. If I wasn't so confused and pissed, I'd probably laugh at this situation.

It's almost comical how they're both afraid of me right now and resorted directly to explanations without any other words spoken. I guess I'm kind of scary.

I silently grab a small chair and place it in front of their double lounge chair before taking a seat. I wish I had a flashlight to shine in their eyes like a police interrogation.

My father studies me carefully. "Why don't you look surprised?"

"Oh, I'm surprised. But that surprise occurred an hour ago, when I was last here and watched you dancing and feeling her up. I left in tears when I realized the one mother figure in my life didn't actually care for me at all. She was using me to get to you."

They simultaneously shout, "That's not true."

My pointer finger toggles between them. "How long has this been going on?"

They look at each other and then back at me before my father answers, "I became interested in Fallon about a year ago. We didn't start seeing each other until about seven months ago."

I look at Fallon. "Made him work for it?"

She's silent for a moment before admitting, "It's complicated."

"What's not complicated," I spit in response, "is that I met you six months ago. Probably not a coincidence."

My dad starts to open his mouth, but Fallon grabs his arm. "I can speak for myself, love."

He nods and wraps his arm around her as a show of support. They're quite obviously more than fuck buddies.

She begins, "Your father and I were already talking when Sulley approached me about the job. She pursued me, not the other way around. You can ask her. That's exactly what happened."

I kind of remember Sulley referencing the same around that time, so I don't question it.

She continues, "I was on the fence because of you. I wanted the job, it affords me a better homelife than my last, but things were complicated enough between you and your dad. I wasn't sure if it was the right thing to do. After talking to your dad about it, we agreed I would take the job. Did I seek you out to try to get to know you? Honestly? Yes. Did I plan on us becoming as close as we've become? No. That happened naturally. And so you know, I would *never* betray any of your confidences to your father."

She widens her eyes at the last part, letting me know that she hasn't told him about Daylen or the baby.

I nod in understanding. The admission softens things a bit for me. At least I don't feel like she was some sort of spy or anything.

My father nods in agreement. "I don't know what you two

talk about, but I do know you are in desperate need of a mother figure in your life. It's something you missed out on, and I was happy to hear you found it in Fallon. I've never met a better mother than her, certainly leaps and bounds above the hand you were dealt. I love that you have her in your life. You've been lost for so long, but there have been so many positive changes in you since you moved back into town. I have no doubt having Fallon in your life has played at least some part in that."

Interesting. It's the first time he's ever ragged on my mother, indirectly or not.

He continues, "Fallon wanted to tell you—she's been wanting to tell you for a long while—but I was afraid you'd clam up like you have for the past ten years."

"Can you blame me?" I yell in frustration. Why is he always so nonchalant about my mother's behavior? We've never discussed it. Not once.

He visibly swallows. "I'm sure it was traumatic walking in on your mother having an affair, but you turned your back on all of us after that day."

"An affair?" I ask with incredulity. "It was way more than that, don't you think?"

Confusion crosses both their faces as they look at each other with creased brows and then at me. Holy shit. They have no idea what I'm talking about.

"Do you know who she had an affair with, Dad?"

He shakes his head. "She never said. I assumed some stranger she met. She never let on that it was anyone we knew." His eyes widen. "Did you know the man?"

I bark out a laugh. Of course my mother lied to me about telling him everything. Why would I ever think otherwise?

"Does the name Nick Castillo ring a bell, Dad?"

I can see on his face that he's running through names and faces in his head, unable to find the answer. He sucks in a breath the moment it hits him. "Your boyfriend? That older college guy you were dating who I wanted to choke to death every time he walked into the house with a smug smile like it was normal for a twenty-year-old to date a sixteen-year-old?"

I nod once. "Ding, ding, ding. You've won a prize," I announce like a game show host. "I didn't walk into *my* house, *my* safe haven, *my* home, and see *my* mother having sex with a stranger. I walked in and found her getting railed from behind by *my* boyfriend. On *my* kitchen table. The same place I used to do *my* homework. The same guy I lost *my* virginity to a few weeks earlier."

Teardrops fall in rapid succession from Fallon's eyes. She breathes my name while my father sits silently, looking like a deer in headlights. He's not faking this. He genuinely didn't know.

Reality eventually hits him too, and tears trickle from his eyes, nearly matching hers.

Personally, I'm fresh out of tears. I'm so damn sick of crying over these people. All I really want to do is to go home to my husband, crawl into bed with him, and then let him help me forget this day.

My dad looks at me with a face full of emotion. Glassy green eyes I recognize from every time I look in the mirror. "I know I wasn't a great father to you. I know I let my own demons take over and wasn't around like I should have been. I'm so sorry for that. You'll never know just how much I regret the way I acted. I've tried my best to be there for Pierce in all the ways I failed you. I've tried to make it up to you as best as I can. But I swear to you, Kennedy, I didn't realize just how horrific it was for you. Your mother told me you caught her in bed with another man, but that I shouldn't bring it up to you because it would be like reliving the trauma all over again. I wanted to kick her out right away, but she said you'd blame yourself for our divorce and that we should stick it out until you left for college. It made sense, so I agreed to it. I had no idea how bad it was." He starts to get choked up. Covering his mouth with his hand, he croaks out, "My poor little girl. You've lost so much. Even more than I ever knew."

I believe him. He's visibly suffering right now. Even though she's grappling with her own emotions over what happened, Fallon moves to comfort him.

I sigh, knowing what I need to say. "Frankly, it makes perfect sense. I never understood why you didn't react like you are right now. Now I get it. You didn't know. She lied to me about having told you because I threatened that I would if she didn't. I'll never forgive her for any of it, and I'll never have a relationship with her, but I don't feel that way about you, Dad. I want you in my life. I need you in my life. I want to move past the painful memories and look toward a more positive future, one I hope you'll be a part of."

I really want to tell him that I want him to be a grandfather to my child, but I made a promise to Daylen, and I intend to see it through. It obviously means a lot to him, and I realized tonight that I need to better respect his wishes. He's more than earned it.

Dad starts to stand but then thinks better of it while holding the blanket in place. One corner of his mouth turns up slightly. "If I wasn't naked, I'd hug you."

I let out a laugh. "Good thinking. Please stay exactly where you are. We can hug another time."

Fallon, meanwhile, is a sobbing, slobbering mess.

I exhale a long breath. "Dad, your girlfriend is a crybaby. Get her under control."

His small smile widens a bit as he pulls Fallon into his arms to console her. Their interactions are so familiar and loving. It's obvious there are real feelings involved.

I suppose she cares about me too or she wouldn't be this upset over everything.

The devil on one shoulder wants to let her stew in misery for lying to me, but now I've got goddamn Sulley *and* Daylen on the other shoulder telling me to console the woman who has come to mean so much to me this year.

The stupid angels win out in the end. I walk over to Fallon and bend over, offering her a hug. She immediately pulls away from my father and wraps her arms around me so damn hard, like she's never going to let me go.

We stay in an embrace for a long while. By the time she calms down and we break apart, my father is standing and dressed.

He kisses my cheek and then hers. "I want to continue this conversation, but I have something else I need to do. I'll be back in a little bit."

"Where are you going?" Fallon asks before I can do the same.

His lip twitches and his nostrils flair. "It's time for me to have a little chat with Ginny." He looks at me. "What happened to you is *not* okay. It will *never* be okay. I know I can't go back in time, but I'm going to do my best to make this right. Your mother won't get away with this. I love you. I've always loved you, and I always will. I didn't protect you then, but I will now."

I should tell him the past is the past, but I don't. It's time for her to face the music.

Without waiting for a response, he storms off, looking angrier than I've ever seen him. I hope he fucking burns her house down, kitchen table included.

Not having any interest in sitting where they just had sex, I slide down and sit on the ground right by Fallon. She wraps the blanket securely around herself and moves down to sit next to me, shoulder to shoulder. Both of us lean back on the lip of the lounge chair with our knees bent.

"Is hanging out in my dad's backyard completely naked normal for you?" I ask playfully.

She smiles. "Sort of. Sometimes it's *my* backyard," she giggles as she says.

My face turns a bit more serious as I look at her. "I hope he tears her a new one and then removes her from his life. I'm sure he's still giving her money. He should cut her off."

Fallon sighs. "That's not what's best for Pierce. He's just a sweet kid who wants his divorced parents to get along."

"He's not a kid, Fallon. He's not nine, like Harper, he's eighteen," I remind her. "He needs to learn how to handle a little adversity. It's time for him to grow a pair. He's too much of a pushover."

She gives me a small smile. "You and your father are so much alike." She reaches toward me and tucks my hair behind my ear. "I've wanted to say that to you at least a million times in the past six months."

"I wouldn't know how alike we are or aren't," I sadly admit.

"He'd love nothing more than for that to change. He's desperate to repair your relationship. It sounds like you're starting to feel the same way," she says hopefully.

"I want him to have a relationship with my child."

She nods. "I know he'll want that too when he finds out."

I rest my head on her shoulder and admit, "I told Daylen I love him."

"Really?" she practically squeals in obvious delight while kicking her feet in excitement. "What did he say?"

"That he loves me too. That he has for a while but knew I needed to be the one to say it first. He's right about that. I would have freaked if he said it first."

She blows out a breath in relief. "Good, can we tell your father now? Please? Keeping this secret from him has been killing me. I've had his secret I couldn't tell you, and then your secret I couldn't tell him. I've been going nuts."

I lift my head and nod. "When my season is over. I can't deal with any more drama until then. I'm teetering on the edge as it is."

She moans in annoyance. "Crap. I'm not sure I can take a few more weeks of this. It's so hard. Deceitfulness is an obvious trigger for him."

"I saw the way you two interact. Do you love him?" I ask, even though it's not really my business.

She turns her head so our eyes meet. "I do. Very much. We

still have some hurdles to overcome, but he's the one for me. The one I feel I've waited a lifetime for."

"What hurdles?"

She pulls herself up into a standing position and offers me a hand to help me do the same. She looks up at me warmly. "Want some hot chocolate with extra marshmallows?" she asks. "We can talk about all the hurdles, and I'll answer any other questions I imagine you have."

I nod. "I'd like that."

TWENTY-NINE

DAYLEN

We're all up in New York City for game six of the WNBA league championship. And by all, I mean my closest Camels teammates, my Cougars friends, and our Anacondas friends sans Kam and Cheetah, who are running late, per always.

The Beavers are playing against Kennedy's old team. She's been emotional over it. She feels they slighted her by releasing her, but she's also happy it happened.

She's been playing incredibly well. Her rebounding and defensive skills are the reason they're up three to two in the series, leaving them only one win away from taking the championship. The girls all want it so badly.

I'm filled with nerves. I want them to win it all tonight, because if they lose, they'll have a decisive game seven on Sunday at home when we're playing across the country. Win or lose, I would hate to miss it. Everything would be perfect if they could just win tonight. We can celebrate with them and then get on a plane for California tomorrow morning without any stress.

Coach and Pierce are here. Ginny is nowhere to be found and hasn't been seen at a single game since that night when Kennedy spoke with Coach and Fallon. From what Kennedy told me, Coach didn't know what Ginny did to her. I had suspected as much.

She came home from her father's that night emotionally exhausted. She crawled into bed naked and then showered me with more love and affection than I would have thought possible for her. It was like she couldn't get enough of me. I loved it and tried to give her everything she needed.

I see Coach glaring at me in my Jeffries number eight jersey. I hope he asks me about it again. I won't lie to his face. There's nothing I want more than to tell him the truth about us. To tell everyone. To be able to love her wherever and whenever I want. She's so damn stubborn about it.

We've gotten into a few fights lately over when we'll tell everyone. I don't understand why she won't come clean. It's basically the only strain on our relationship right now. Everything else has become seamless. I desperately want to jump over this one last hurdle.

Kam and Cheetah make their way to our seats, and Layton glares at them. "Last to arrive. Per always. Let's hear the latest crazy fun fact from you two."

They exchange knowing glances before Kam looks at us with the usual mischief written all over her face, and says, "If a female octopus isn't in the mood, she'll strangle the male octopus and then eat him."

I think every male within earshot winces. I shake my head. "That feels like an extreme response. Can't she just roll away from him like every other woman?"

Kam smiles as she shrugs. "Maybe he's into being choked."

My girl certainly is.

"And eaten?" I ask.

She lets out a laugh. "To each their own."

I suppose.

I see her staring at Kennedy so I ask, "How's it going with your number one client?"

"Great. She just shot her commercial for a big cosmetics company. I can't tell you which one yet, but it's huge. She was amazing. I think you're going to *really* like it." She shoots me a suggestive look.

Not only is the look a little weird, but it's equally odd that she'd tell me that. Does she know about us?

I stare at her skeptically, but she simply winks before taking her seat.

The game begins, and it's a back-and-forth affair, keeping us all on the edge of our seats. It's two great teams battling basket for basket. Kennedy is working her ass off on the boards, as she has for the entire series. Rebound after rebound, she helps her team to either keep possession or gain possession. She's one of the shortest girls out there, but it doesn't matter because she's so strong and tough. She can also jump a mile high. I'd like to think I played some part in her increased vertical leap. Regardless, I love the gritty way she plays. I can't take my eyes off her, even when she doesn't have the ball.

I catch a glimpse of the Band-Aid around her left ring finger. Normally, she wears makeup to cover it, but not during games. She fears the makeup rubbing off so she resorts to a bandage, which I have to do all the time.

For some reason, seeing that Band-Aid is bothering me more now than ever. It should be a diamond, not that piece of shit she's wearing now.

I want to do this right. Even though we're married already, I want to propose and have a real wedding. Not one we barely remember officiated by Elvis/Pinky.

The first thing I need to do is to buy a ring. One that better fits my queen. Second thing, talk to Coach about everything and then ask for his blessing. Third, it's time to get down on one knee.

KENNEDY

We lost on a buzzer-beater the other night in New York. It was heartbreaking. The good news is we're playing in Philly tonight for a winner-take-all game seven. The bad news is that Daylen is on the other side of the country playing his own game today. He said my father made arrangements for them to watch at least the second half of our game on the airplane ride back.

I'm not sure which one of them was more disappointed that we lost, meaning they wouldn't be at the winner-take-all game. I appreciate how much they both care.

Sulley and her bodyguard are picking me up in about an hour. I'm in my bathroom getting ready when my text tone pings.

> Dad: Good luck today. I'm sorry I can't be there. I asked management for a leave of absence, but they said no. I'm so sorry. We'll be watching on the plane. Number seventeen is defending you tightly. If you draw her in, you'll be able to spin away and get open for an easy basket.

I smile. I don't remember the last time I got basketball advice from him. I was probably fifteen or sixteen.

The past few weeks have been good for us. I've spent some time with him and Fallon. They may actually be the cutest couple in existence. They asked for my help in breaking the news of their relationship to Pierce. I'm not sure why everyone treats him with kid gloves—he's an adult and should be able to handle his father being with a woman—but I agreed. We're going to do it next week. The same week that Daylen and I are supposed to talk to him.

When I suggested to Daylen that we delay talking to him

another month or so, he lost his shit. We got into a huge fight, and he boarded the plane yesterday with us not on speaking terms.

I respond to my father.

Me: Good thought. Thanks. Good luck to you too. We'll celebrate both victories this week.

Dad: It would be my pleasure.

I decide to text Daylen. They're probably about to leave the hotel for the stadium.

As if reading my mind, as he often does, my FaceTime rings and I see it's him. I accept the call right away. "Hey," I answer in a solemn voice, unsure of where we stand, though I did go to his house and play with BJ today, so that should please him.

He gives me a small smile. "I needed to see your face. I miss it."

I hear Vance yell in the background, "You're so pussy-whipped."

Daylen scowls in his direction. "If you had that pussy in your bed, you'd be whipped too."

"He *is* whipped," I remind Daylen.

Daylen nods away from the camera. "Right. You're just as bad, *Vile Vance*."

I smile at the nickname Sulley calls Vance.

He turns back to the camera. "What are you wearing to the stadium for the big game?" he asks in his *I want sexy time* voice. This is his way of telling me he doesn't want to fight anymore. He hates fighting. Considering the nature of our relationship for the first year we knew each other, it's kind of ironic that he doesn't have the stomach for any strife in our relationship. It's equally cute that he's trying to smooth things over.

"I'm wearing the gold bikini from Vegas," I answer. I'm not, but I know how much he loves that bikini.

He sucks in a breath. "Oh shit. So hot. Do you know why bikinis were invented?"

"Why?"

He smirks, and I know something ridiculous is about to come out of his mouth. "To separate the meat and dairy."

I let out a laugh. "Good one, but I'm not wearing that. I'm planning to wear a little cowgirl outfit. I'll wear it for you sometime in private. I have a feeling you'll like it even more than the bikini. I could do a little cowgirl action on top of you. I'd be happy to ride that horse between your legs."

Though I have to wear a different shirt than I planned. My belly popped a bit overnight. It wasn't like this yesterday. It's crazy how that happened. I usually hate how unflattering my baggy basketball uniform is, but today I'm thankful for it.

I don't want to tell him about it over the phone. He's going to be excited. I want him to see it in person for the first time, not on his small screen.

Daylen winces. "Shit. Now I'm hard."

I hear Vance groan in annoyance and Daylen gives him some crude gesture.

Our eyes eventually meet again. "Thanks for calling," I say. "I hated how we left things."

He nods. "Me too. The worst thing happened this morning. I went to the refrigerator to get a snack, and you weren't there."

I see a pillow thrown at his head while Vance yells at him again. "Oh my god, you're pathetic."

I can't help but giggle. I think it's sweet how he unashamedly loves me, even in front of Vance.

His face turns a bit softer. "I just want to be able to love you out in the open. Is that so wrong?"

"No, it's not." I exhale a breath. "Daylen, for the first time in my life, I'm happy. I'm content. Everything is working *for* me not *against* me. You're a huge part of that—the biggest part—but I'm afraid to mess it up. If it ain't broke, why fix it?"

"I get that, I really do, but I want…more."

He looks so sweet and sad that I almost feel bad for lying to him. Almost.

I BOX the defender out and grab the defensive rebound, immediately passing it up the lane to Sulley. She dribbles to the basket and overshoots what should have been an easy layup. She's so off tonight. It's very unlike her.

Palmer and I are keeping the team afloat with our rebounds, while Layla and I account for most of our points, but if Sulley doesn't get hot, we have no chance. We need her perimeter shooting. She's the best in the league at popping threes.

We head into the locker room at halftime down by nine points. It's not insurmountable, but we've got a lot of work to do.

Reagan walks into the locker room while we're all toweling off and drinking water. We usually do that for a few minutes until it's time for a speech from Coach Lakshmi.

She's not in a pantsuit tonight. She's in a designer, fancier version of our jersey that has been made into a cute little dress. It's kind of weird to see her like this. I nod at it. "Do we get to wear those jerseys next year?"

"You can wear whatever you want if you win," she answers without missing a beat. "Ladies, I stopped by to tell you I'm proud of you. You've worked hard as a team and have come such a long way in the past two years. Last year, you were equally talented, but you played as separate individuals. This year, you're a true team. The love and unwavering support you have for each other shines through." Her eyes meet mine. "In some ways, don't you feel as if you've already won?"

I nod. That's exactly how I feel.

She continues. "Don't go back out there feeling pressure." I know that's directed at Sulley. She's right. Sulley has the weight of this franchise on her shoulders. It's not fair to her. "Go out there and play because you love the game and you love playing with your best friends. They're your found family."

Everyone is silent, letting her words sink in. Found family. I like that term. She's right. That's exactly what we are.

She eventually leaves, and we all huddle together, vowing to play our hearts out.

We return to the floor as a completely different team. Sulley is on fire as she drops three after three. Unfortunately, Diane the Dick is matching her hot streak, as she, too, drops three after three.

We're now down by two, and there's a stop in play. Diane bumps my shoulder with hers. "Where's your fire, Kennedy?"

My fire? I've just set a championship series rebounds record. What's this crazy bitch smoking? She's just trying to get under my skin.

"Fuck off, loser," I snap.

She lets out a whistle. "Wow. Someone needs to get laid."

I narrow my eyes at her. "I did last night. Just ask your brother."

She pinches her eyebrows in confusion. "I don't have a brother, asshat."

I wink. "You will in about nine months." I blow her a kiss. "Say hi to your dad for me. Or as I like to call him, *Daddy*."

She snarls and shoves me. I do a bit of an acting job and flop to the ground. She's immediately whistled by the referees for a flagrant foul.

I smile at her as I happily sink two technical shots, tying the game. I turn to her and rock the baby. Her teammates have to hold her back while mine laugh at the entire altercation.

We continue to trade baskets throughout the fourth quarter. We're down by one and they have the ball with about fifteen seconds left in the game. There are only five seconds remaining on the shot clock, so we don't foul them.

Diane starts to move for the lane, but Palmer strips the ball from her and quickly calls a timeout. I look up at the clock. There are seven seconds left.

We all jump on Palmer for the big play as we head to the bench to huddle with our coaches. Coach Lakshmi pulls out the clipboard. I'm sure we're going to run a play designed to get Sulley open for the game-winning shot. My job will likely be to pick for her. I'm more than good with that. In the biggest moments, you want the ball in the hand of your star, and my best friend is the biggest star of all.

I smack her shoulder. "You've got this, superstar. I believe in you."

She takes a deep breath and nods.

Coach Lakshmi and Fallon share an amused look as she draws her Xs and Os on the clipboard. "We've got a few plays in mind. Shay, you'll inbound the ball to Sulley at halfcourt and then quickly head to the basket for a possible tip-in if the shot is missed."

Shay nods, understanding her role in this.

Coach continues, "Palmer and Layla, draw your defenders away from the lane, but crash the boards once the shot goes up. Kennedy, I want you to fake like you're about to set a pick for Sulley but then lose your defender and roll toward the basket. Sulley, bounce pass her the ball for the game-winning layup."

I stand there dumbfounded while Fallon tries to hide her smile. I know this was her idea.

"Shouldn't Sulley take the shot?" I ask.

Coach shakes her head. "They're expecting that. They'll likely be double-teaming her. You'll have man-to-man coverage. It will be easier for you to get an open shot."

Sulley smacks my shoulder with a huge grin on her face as she echoes my words from a minute ago. "You've got this, superstar. I believe in you, Air Kennedy." She gives me a look where I know exactly what she's thinking. She's going to alter the play slightly, and I know exactly how because we're at the point where we can read each other's minds.

Layla shouts, "Fuck yeah, let's go win this."

We bring our hands in for a cheer before we break apart and take our positions on the court.

Shay inbounds the ball to Sulley. As Coach expected, two players immediately suffocate her.

I take one sharp step like I'm going to set the pick, drawing Diane close to my body. As soon as I feel her touch me, I do what my dad told me to do and spin away from her, heading straight for the basket.

She bit on my fake. I've got a full step on her now. Instead of the bounce pass Coach instructed Sulley to give me, Sulley tosses the ball into the air for an alley-oop.

I bend my legs low and then leap into the air as high as I can, grab the ball, and dunk it just before the clock expires.

Game over. We win.

I hang on the rim for an extra second or two, enjoying the biggest moment of my life. It feels like a billion flashes go off in my face before I finally drop to the ground, only to be dog-piled by my entire team.

THIRTY

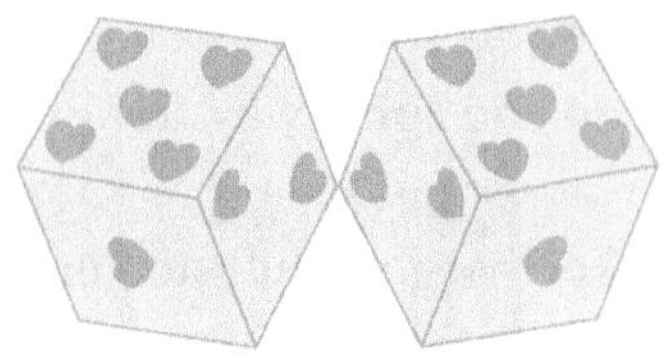

DAYLEN

Holy. Fucking. Shit.

She did it! She dunked. She didn't just dunk, she dunked in the biggest moment to win the league championship as time expired. That play will live on in infamy as the greatest in league history.

My girl. *My wife*. The hero.

Our team was going crazy on the plane as we all watched with nervous excitement. I had to look away when Coach and Vance were embracing, jumping up and down while celebrating Kennedy's big moment. I desperately wanted to join them, but more importantly, I wished I was there to celebrate with her. I can't wait for this damn plane to land in a few hours. I need her like I need oxygen. I would parachute to get to her right now if I thought it was faster.

Vance plops down next to me and lightly punches my arm and whispers, "She was awesome, man."

I nod. "She was. They all were."

His eyes briefly move to Coach a few rows up before returning to mine. "When are you going to tell him?"

I shrug. "I'd tell him now, but Kennedy keeps delaying. I'm frustrated, but she's pregnant. I don't like to upset her."

"Trust me, I get it." He's having similar issues with Sulley. He runs his fingers through his hair. "At least Kennedy will be showing soon. Then she'll have no choice. Sulley is dragging this on forever."

I feel bad for my friend's situation, but he's right about mine. We're on a timeline. She'll be showing any day now. I'm suddenly feeling hopeful that this will be over sooner rather than later.

As soon as we deplane, I sprint to my Jeep and head straight for Kennedy's apartment. I'm dying to hold her in my arms and congratulate her. I'm going to kiss every inch of my superstar's beautiful body.

It's the middle of the night, but she said she'd wait up for me, so I'm going. I know her team was out celebrating. She was with them, but obviously not drinking. I'm sure she's back now. I have her code if she's fallen asleep.

I speed like a madman to her place, impatiently pressing the elevator button a thousand times as if it will make the world's slowest elevator arrive that much faster.

I contemplate taking the stairs, but the elevator doors open just before I'm about to abandon it. When it arrives on her floor with a ping, I see her already standing in her doorway waiting for me. She's fresh-faced with just-out-of-the-shower hair, wearing my jersey. There's nothing but her long legs poking out.

I can't help but stare. She takes my breath away. She's never looked more beautiful to me.

I didn't know she owned one of my jerseys. It must be new, but my heart pumps wildly seeing it on her. My dick thumps too. It's fucking hot seeing her like this.

As soon as she sees me, a huge smile takes form on her face. At the same time, we run toward each other, and she leaps into my waiting arms, wrapping both her arms and legs around me. "I did it," she squeals in delight. "Did you see my dunk?"

My smile matches hers. "I saw. It was amazing. You worked hard for that. I'm so fucking proud of you, baby."

"*We* worked hard. You and me. Together," she humbly corrects.

I nod as I walk us back toward her doorway. "We're a good team." I mean that in about a million different ways.

Sensing my thoughts, she holds my face with both hands and brings her lips to mine for a sweet, soft kiss, before breaking away and whispering, "We are. Thank you for helping me. It wouldn't have happened without you. Everything is better with you in my life."

I kiss her lips and mumble into them, "I missed you so damn much."

"What exactly did you miss?" she asks in her usual mischievous tone.

"Mostly your tits but also being inside you." I wiggle my eyebrows up and down. "How about I get reacquainted with both? We can celebrate your basketball victory with me dribbling all over your nipples."

She smiles. "Ooh, I think I'd like that. Should I grab the spatula so I can have some fun too?"

Before I can respond in the negative, she gasps. "Omigod. You need to see this first. I was dying to tell you this morning, but I wanted you to see it in person." She lifts the shirt a drop. "I popped while you were gone. It just suddenly happened when I woke up this morning. It was hard to hide in the locker room. Good thing our season is over. I'm not sure I'd be able to fit into my uniform by next week."

I look at her little belly in awe. Placing her down on her feet just outside her doorway, I drop down to my knees and rub my hands all over her bare stomach as I look on in wonderment. As if realization is just hitting for the first time, I ask, "Our baby is in there?"

Tears fill her eyes as she releases a small laugh and nods. "Yep. A little bit of me and a little bit of you."

Overcome with emotion, I can't help but kiss her belly before I talk into it, "You're going to be a freak of an athlete, precious baby girl. You might get division one offers before you're even born. We should get Tanner on it right away."

She releases a laugh. "You're a fool. It's definitely a boy."

I shake my head. "Nope. I'm a #GirlDad. Do you think I should start singing her 'Waterfalls' so she knows the words right away?"

She smiles while rolling her eyes at me. "Umm…no. Please spare *him* that pain."

My face turns more serious as I look up at her. "We're not going to be able to hide this much longer. We need to tell people. Our families. Our friends." I cradle her little belly and look up at her hopefully. "I want the world to know my baby is in here."

She exhales a long breath. "I know. Fallon said the same thing. Let me get through this week with mollycoddling Pierce, and then I promise we'll do it after your next two games. Your bye week is after that." That means we have an entire week off. "It will give my dad time to come to terms with everything I've been hiding from him."

We hear a noise at the end of the hallway, but when we turn our heads, no one is there.

I blow out a breath in frustration, but I don't want to dwell on it and ruin her big night. "Two more weeks. I guess I can live with that."

She begins to lift her shirt a little further, revealing the underside of her breasts to me. "Good," she breathes, "because tonight, I need to feel you moving inside me. I want to celebrate with my sexy baby daddy."

I twist my lips. "Am I called a baby daddy if we were married when the baby was conceived? I feel like that's a term for out-of-wedlock conceptions."

She lifts the shirt a little higher, revealing her luscious, bare, perfect tits to me, immediately causing my boxer briefs to tighten. I think they got even bigger in the two days I was gone.

"Do you really care about semantics right now, or would you rather fuck these tits?"

I kiss her belly one more time and say into it, "I love you." I look up at her. "And I love you."

She smiles softly. "I love you too."

I shake my head. "I wasn't talking to you." I stand and grab her left tit, kissing it directly on the nipple. "You. I love you."

She giggles.

I then grab her right tit. "And you. I love you most of all, scarecrow, because your master is right-nippled and she can come when I suck on you and only you."

She narrows her eyes at me. "What do you mean I'm right-nippled?"

"Cheetah once told me we're all right or left-nippled. One side is always more sensitive than the other."

"Is that true?" she asks with a tone of disbelief.

"I wasn't sure at first, but you come when I suck on that nipple not the other."

"Holy shit," she breathes.

I drop to my knees again, sink my face into her panty-covered pussy and inhale her delicious scent. "Hmm, I didn't forget about you, princess." I lick her through her panties. "You're the most delicious of them all."

She looks around the hallway. "Let's go inside before we give the old couple across the hallway a heart attack."

I shake my head. "Nope," I say, running my nose through her. "I'm going to lick your creamy cunt until you come out here, and then I'm going to carry my gorgeous bride inside and make love to her all night."

My eyes move up and give her a look to suggest we're doing it my way tonight. We've begun to toggle between the hard fucking and more tender lovemaking. I'm a little scared of the hard stuff with the baby, but sometimes Kennedy needs the lunatic fucked out of her, and I'm the man for the job. Rough sex is her form of escapism.

She nods. "Okay." I know she now enjoys the tender moments as much as she enjoys the rougher ones. Our emotional connection grows by the day.

I continue to lick her over her panties while lifting one of her legs over my shoulder. She leans back on the wall next to her door, succumbing to the sensations.

Pulling her panties to the side, I blow on her most sensitive flesh, and her hips jolt. "Daylen," she whines, "please touch me."

I run one finger through her weeping flesh. I love how wet she gets for me. Always.

Sucking that finger into my mouth, I close my eyes in reverence. "Hmm, the flavor of champions. I love the way my superstar wife tastes. Non-superstars don't taste nearly as good. Neither do non-wives."

She smiles down at me while running her fingers through my hair. I stare into her eyes as my fingers slowly enter her. I can feel her body contract around me while her pupils dilate and her grip on my hair increases.

I slowly lick through her over and over again. She loves the slow build-up. She shatters so damn explosively when I don't rush things. I'm just as happy to savor it. Being intimate with her is my favorite thing in the world. I've never loved anyone I've had sex with until her. It enhances every feeling and every touch.

With my lips now sucking on her sensitive bundle, I look up at her. Her face is flushed, her hair is messy, my jersey sits high on her chest, resting on top of her full tits, and there's a little bump with our baby inside. All I can think of is *mine. My wife. My baby. My everything.*

It takes mere minutes before she comes apart on my fingers

and mouth. She was a little loud, and the old couple across the hall briefly opened their door, gasped, and then closed it. Kennedy was too absorbed in the pleasure to notice. It's all part of my plan to get her evicted so she has to move in with me. I mentioned it once, and she said it was too soon, but I want her in my house before that baby comes. The sooner the better.

I pull her panties back into place and pat her pussy over them. Staring straight at it, I whisper, "Good girl. Now Daddy is going to tear you up."

She places her one lifted leg, now wobbly, back on the ground before grabbing my shirt and aggressively pulling me into her apartment.

As soon as the door closes, she crashes her mouth to mine. Our lips and tongues explode in a lust-driven marriage, as our hands equally explore one another at a feverish pace. It's like we can't get close enough.

My hands ride up the silky-soft skin of her body and cup her breasts hard, but not as hard as normal. I want passionate lovemaking, not a rough and tough fuck fest. As soon as my fingers find her nipples, they harden, and she moans into my mouth. Her tits are deliciously sensitive.

She rocks her hips, running her now-dampened panties over my hardness. I can feel her heat even through my sweatpants. She's always on fire.

My dick throbs with the need to be surrounded by her warmth. She frantically pulls at my sweatpants until they're around my ankles, mumbling into my mouth, "Get inside me. I need you so badly."

She purposefully falls back onto the floor next to her door, pulling me with her until I'm situated between her legs. She reaches down, slides her panties to the side again, and places my tip at her entrance.

"Now, Daylen. Now," she pleads.

In one fast, powerful drive, I'm home. Deep inside my wife, where everything is perfect. ***For now.***

THIRTY-ONE

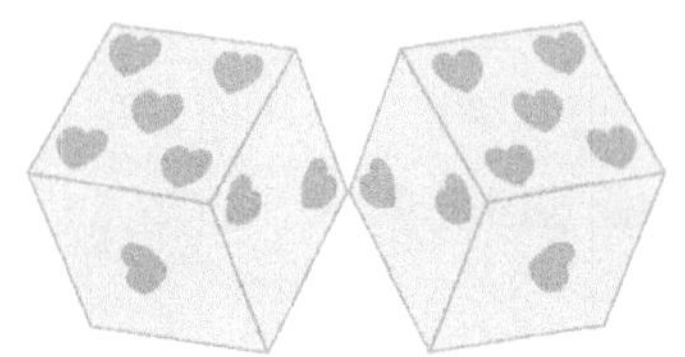

DAYLEN

It's early morning, and I left Kennedy peacefully sleeping in her bed with a note that I needed to get home to BJ. Chef Benny had a family obligation last night and couldn't stay over. I didn't want to miss out on being with Kennedy, but I need to get home to my other girl.

I'm sure Kennedy has a million team obligations today anyway. She's going to be all over the place with her magical championship-winning dunk and the franchise bringing home the trophy. I'm excited about all the attention they're about to receive. It's well-deserved. Those girls work their asses off.

I'm smiling, thinking of all the love she and her teammates are going to get from this often-fickle city, so I don't see anyone hiding as I approach my front door.

My fingers are moving to my keypad when something flies by my head and hits my door hard before the sound of glass shattering reverberates in my ears and my neck is hit with the shrapnel. Ow, fuck, that hurt.

I turn around just in time to see a fist flying at my face

before it lands on the corner of my eye. I go down like a sack of potatoes on my front stoop.

I blink a few times as the pain rattles around in my head and my vision runs blurry.

As things begin to refocus, I see Coach standing over me with glassy eyes, reeking of alcohol, still in the same clothes he was wearing when we flew home last night. His fists are in the air, primed for a fight.

"Get the fuck up, Humblecut," he barks out. "I'm going to beat you senseless."

I hold up my hand in surrender as I try to stand, but then he punches me in the stomach, which sends me back down to my ass. God damn, the fucker is strong.

Holding up my hand again, I wheeze, "Stop, Coach. Please."

He remains in a fighting stance while his jaw tics. "I loved you like a son. How could you do this to me?" His voice cracks while he says that last bit as though he's on the verge of crying.

"What? What did I do?" I ask, completely out of breath with blood trickling down my face and my eye starting to swell a bit, but my cheekbone took the brunt of the punch.

"Kennedy," he grits out. "How dare you touch my daughter! Have you no honor? And...and..." his voice cracks again, "she's pregnant?"

He drops his hands and begins sobbing. His pained eyes meet mine. "Why? Why would you treat her like one of your whores?" He punches his own chest. "*My* daughter. Why? Tell me. I need to know."

My eyebrows crease. That's what he thinks? That she's just some random woman to me?

I stumble to my feet, maintaining a safe distance from him. Shaking my head, I quietly say, "You've got it wrong, Coach. It's not like that at all. I lov—"

As the words are about to trickle out of my mouth, we both

turn to the intruding sounds of a car screeching into my driveway. It's Kennedy.

The car comes to an abrupt halt, and she runs out of it, staring wide-eyed at the situation. She takes in my bloody face and immediately moves to stand in front of me, yelling at her father, "What did you do to him?"

His finger trembles as he points at us. "He touched you. M…my daughter."

"So what?" she screams. "That makes it okay to hit him? I'm an adult who can make her own decisions. Your solution is to attack him? Are you crazy?"

He looks down at her stomach and practically weeps, "You're pregnant with *his* child?"

She nods as she leans her back against my front, reaches for my hand, and places it around her waist and over her stomach. "I am, and I love him."

His face contorts in disgust. "Love him? This guy? The guy who has no respect for women? How could you be so stupid?"

My chest puffs at his word choice, and I spit out, "Don't you dare call my wife stupid."

His eyes widen, and he sucks in a breath. "Wife?"

Whoops. Guess he didn't know that part.

Kennedy nods. "Yes, Dad. I'm his wife. We're married. I love him, and he loves me. We're having a baby, and I'm about five minutes away from moving in here with him."

I perk up at that bit of information, the heaviness of this situation momentarily forgotten. "You are?" I ask excitedly.

She nods.

"Who invited you?" I joke. "I didn't invite you to move into this house."

She turns her head, and I see a small smile form on her lips. "BJ invited me."

"In those exact words?" I inquire cheekily.

Her smile grows. "Yes," she answers without hesitation, "in those exact words."

"Hmm, I suppose that makes sense. She *does* love you."

Coach's face scrunches in confusion. "Who's BJ?"

"My dog," I answer.

Now he appears even more confused. I look at him. "Coach, I've been wanting to talk to you about this for a long while. Months."

"I asked him not to, Dad," Kennedy interrupts. "He wanted to. I wasn't ready to tell you about us. Be mad at me, not him. He hasn't done anything wrong."

I shake my head. "It doesn't matter now. No one needs to be mad at anyone. This is a happy situation." I look him directly in the eyes, trying to convey my sincerity. "I love her. I'm madly in love with her. She and our baby girl are everything to me. They're my family."

His shoulders fall in defeat. "W…when did you get married?" He looks at Kennedy with sadness written all over his face. "Who…who walked you down the aisle?"

"Pinky Punnathanathukunnele," she deadpans.

"Pinky Parpanopolous? Who's that?" he asks.

I bark out a laugh. "He didn't technically walk you down the aisle."

She nods. "True. I walked myself down…I think."

Her stomach grumbles, and I run my hands up and down her arms. "You're hungry, baby. Why don't we go inside, and I'll make you and BJ breakfast. We can fill your dad in on everything. Finally." I whisper in her ear, "And I think your dad needs some food in his belly."

She nods. "Okay. And we need to take care of your face."

I squeeze her and then move my eyes to Coach's. "Coach?" I look at him in question. "Will you come inside so we can talk about this with words not fists?"

He nods silently, clearly still in a bit of shock. He's also not completely sober, stumbling a bit.

I open the door, and BJ comes flying toward me at warp speed, but ten feet before she gets to me, she stops short and then slowly makes her way to Kennedy, nuzzling her stomach.

I mumble, "Traitor," and Kennedy giggles as she bends to kiss BJ's head.

In a baby voice, she says, "It's okay to love me most, baby girl."

BJ coos under the adoration for a few seconds before she turns her head to Coach and growls viciously.

"BJ, bed!" I command.

She immediately turns and runs to her bed while Kennedy mouths, "So hot."

I chuckle as the three of us make our way into my kitchen. I grab various ingredients and food from the refrigerator to start cooking as Kennedy finds a plastic bag and fills it with ice. While I'm at the stove cracking eggs, she places it over my eye while wiping the small amount of blood from my face with a damp washcloth.

I pull my head away. "I'm fine, babe."

"You're not fine. Your eye is swelling by the second. And it's bleeding." She returns the ice and cloth to my eye again, carefully tending to it.

I place my hand on her hip and peck her on the lips. "Thanks for taking care of me."

She nods, solely focused on my eye, and mindlessly replies, "Always," much to my delight.

I work on the eggs and bacon while she stands there and continues to carefully tend to my eye. I motion my head toward the fruit. "Eat some fruit, baby. You have to get your daily dose of blueberries. It's the only naturally occurring blue food. It has vitamins you and Baby Girl Humblecut need that you can't get anywhere else."

"Okay," she replies compliantly.

Still holding the ice on my eye with one hand, she reaches over for the blueberries with her other hand, throwing a few in her mouth and then a few into mine. "You need them too. You have a big game this week."

I take them into my mouth and then playfully nibble on her finger.

She gently moves some of my wild hair from my face. I scrunch my face a bit. "Sorry it's so long and messy. I know you prefer it neat. I'll get it cut today."

She shakes he head. "It looks cute like this, but if you want it cut, I'll do it for you."

"Really?"

She nods, still focused on my eye. "Of course."

Coach clears his throat as he stares at us. "What the fuck is happening here? You two are so…domestic. It's unsettling."

We both smile at each other. We *are* domestic, and I love it.

Kennedy turns to him. "Let me take care of his eye, and then we'll talk. You don't want it to swell so much that he can't see the ball this weekend. He's the best player on your team. You can't afford to lose him."

"You think I'm the best player?" I ask proudly.

She winks. "You know it, stud."

Coach groans in annoyance at our banter. "Ugh, stop talking to each other like that." He plops down on a chair at my kitchen table and tugs on his hair. "He's a buffoon, Kennedy. He doesn't take anything or anyone seriously. He treats women like objects."

Kennedy's lips tighten, and she aggressively points her finger at him. "Don't talk like that about my husband. I'll make you coffee to sober you up, but if you're mean to my husband, I'm kicking you out of our house."

He cowers under her scary gaze, but I'm just trying to play it cool, inwardly combusting over the fact that she called me her husband twice and referred to the house as *ours*.

I have zero chill and am unable to contain my smile. She glares at me. "Don't look so damn happy. We don't have a prenup. Half this shit is mine. And I'll sue for custody of BJ."

Now it's Coach's turn to smile. I think I might even catch a little laugh.

Ten minutes later, the four of us are sitting at the table eating breakfast. Coach motions his head toward BJ. "Your dog sits at the table with you?"

Kennedy rolls her eyes. "Why are people so shocked by this? Where else would she sit?"

I nod. "Right? What's she supposed to do, eat off the floor like an animal?"

Kennedy looks appalled. "That would be uncivilized."

I grin at her word choice. God, I love her so damn much.

Coach exhales an audible breath. "Can someone please start talking before my head explodes?"

We then tell him the whole, crazy story sans the sex stuff. He can read between the lines on that, given the whole pregnancy thing.

He bites into his bacon with a perplexed look on his face. "You two got married when you hated each other?"

Kennedy nods. "We did."

"Are you staying married at the end of the year?"

I nod, but she says, "We'll see. One life decision at a time. It's been a crazy year. A year ago, the thought of being in the same room as him made me sick to my stomach."

Coach mumbles, "I've known him for ten years, and being in the same room still makes me sick to my stomach."

I chuckle. "I love how we bicker like a family. Should I start calling you Dad?"

He stares at me like he's going to kill me. "Why would I ever be okay with this?" he asks me. "You've never taken anything or anyone seriously. Why should I believe you'll take my daughter seriously? For a decade, *a decade*, I've heard you in the locker room talking about women like they're objects. Like they're nothing but punchlines to your immature, ridiculous jokes."

I'm about to defend myself, but Kennedy speaks first.

"Daylen uses humor because he loves to make people happy and hates confrontation. It doesn't mean he doesn't take things seriously. The Daylen you see isn't the same as the one I see." Tears well in her eyes. "He's probably the kindest, most generous and thoughtful man I've ever met in my life. He considers me and our child in every single decision he makes. I'd trust him with my life and not give it a second thought. I have never, and I mean *never,* felt more loved, protected, and seen than I have with this man. If anything, I'm the emotionally immature one, not him. I'm the work in progress, not him. I hope I give him half of what he gives me."

I take her hand, squeeze it, and whisper, "You just did."

She gives me a small smile before looking back at her father. "Haven't you seen changes in me this year?"

"I have," Coach admits.

"I'm working so damn hard on being a better version of me, and Daylen is a big part of that. You can't imagine how many times I've questioned my ability to be a good mother since I found out about the baby. I didn't have one. I'm fucking terrified." She taps her finger on my chest a few times. "This guy, this guy right here, he gives me validation every minute of every day. He sees the good in me on the days I can't find it in myself. He tells me what a great mother he thinks I'll be when I can't see it in myself. There is no one, *no one,* I would want to do this with other than him. I think he's going to be the most amazing father because he's such a natural caregiver. No one has ever taken better care of me. No one loves harder than him. Our child and I are so damn lucky to have him."

I get choked up with emotion at her words, but she's not done.

Her glassy eyes drift to mine before they meet her father's again. "For the first time in my life, someone quiets the chaos always churning through my brain. I'm not saying this to hurt you, Dad, but I've always felt so damn alone. I've never had anyone to lean on. I've always had to take care of myself because no one else was there to do it for me. Daylen is the man who says to me *I know you can do it by yourself, but you don't have to anymore*. He makes my doctor's appointments, he makes sure I'm eating well, he cooks for me, he supports me, he makes me feel seen, and," she looks at me, "he makes me feel like I matter. Daylen Humblecut is the biggest green flag to ever exist, and I was a fool to ever think otherwise."

I'm feeling about a million feet tall right now, knowing how she feels. She's never outwardly expressed any of this to me before. She's more of a *show by actions not words* kind of woman.

I gently swipe the errant tear on her cheek with my thumb as we stare at each other. I love her so much.

I want to drop to my knee and ask her to marry me all over again, but I still want my solo conversation with Coach. Instead, I take her hand, kiss it, and say, "I was planning to wear white jeans and sandals with socks today. Is that okay?"

She giggles through her tears, and it's music to my ears.

I turn to Coach. "In summary, I'm kind of awesome."

He rolls his eyes and mumbles, "I should have killed you out front."

And then it occurs to me that Kennedy arrived here only a few minutes after me. I look at her. "What made you come here this morning?"

"I startled awake when you closed the door," she answers. "When I rolled over to check my phone, I had a million missed voicemails and texts from Fallon that Dad knew and was fit to be tied. She was afraid he'd confront you." She looks at Coach. "You should call her. She's worried sick about you."

He scowls. "Fallon and I aren't seeing each other anymore."

"What?" Kennedy screeches. "Why?"

He stands abruptly with the chair falling over and him stumbling a bit. "I don't owe you an explanation of my love life, Kennedy. Considering you got married and pregnant without so much as a mention of it all to me, I don't need to share *anything* with you." He runs his fingers through his hair in frustration and barks out, "I need to get out of here. I can't handle this."

She stands and yells, "You're not sober. You can't drive. It was irresponsible of you to drive here."

"Don't tell me what to do like I'm a child," he screams back.

"You're acting like a fucking child, so I *will* tell you what to do. I'll lie down in front of your car before letting you drive right now. You're not going anywhere. When you sober up, you can go and apologize for whatever you did to Fallon. Don't fuck things up with her. She's the best thing to ever happen to you."

They're in a stare-down. It's stubborn versus stubborn. I've never once got into an antagonistic screaming match like this with my father. I'm at a bit of a loss, but I know I don't want Kennedy getting upset. It's not good for her or the baby.

I stand and rub her back. "Calm down. It's not good for you or the baby. I'll drive him home in his car and Uber back." I point toward the kitchen table. "Can you take care of this?"

She nods. "Sure. I'll follow behind in my car and bring you home."

I shake my head. "No, I want you to relax. Take a bath when you're done. I bought a big box of some of the salts you like. They're in the linen closet."

She nods as she begins to clear the table before pausing briefly. "When you sober up, Dad, you'll realize that while all this may have started in a fucked-up way, and we've done things in a crazy order, it's a blessing. I consider Daylen and this entire situation to be the best thing that has ever happened to me."

Unable to stop myself anymore, I grab her face and give her a hard kiss on the lips. "Thank you. You and our baby are the best things to happen to me too. Now I can tell everyone," I say excitedly.

She gives me a small smile. "I still want to get through the madness of the next few weeks, and then we can tell everyone. I promise. We have so many team interviews. I don't want them to be about me and my pregnancy. They should be about the team and our achievement."

A pang of disappointment hits me because I'm sick of the secrecy and want to be there to celebrate with her this week, but it's been an emotional morning for her. I don't want to make things harder.

Coach and I begin the short drive to his house in silence before I finally speak. "I'm sorry you found out from Fallon and not us. It's not how I wanted this to go down. I wanted to have a real conversation with you, man to man. I owed you that."

He shakes his head as he aimlessly stares out of the passenger window. "That's not how I found out. I went to her apartment last night to leave her a congratulatory gift, and I saw you two together in her hallway."

My eyes widen knowing what we did in that hallway, but he says nothing further, and neither do I.

His pained eyes eventually meet mine. "I don't want her to suffer the same fate as me. It's like a damn family curse," he mumbles.

"What does that mean?" I ask, not understanding what he's referencing.

He visibly swallows. "This stays between us."

I nod.

"Ginny and I fudged the dates and the story of how we met for our kids' sake." He pinches the bridge of his nose. "She was one of the faceless many when I was in college. You know how it is when you're the big man on campus."

I nod again. "I do." When you're a football star on the rise, with the certainty of millions of dollars waiting for you when you're done with college, every woman wants to hitch themselves to you. They practically throw themselves at you. It's overwhelming at times.

"I barely remembered sleeping with her, let alone her name, when she told me she was pregnant with my child. We waited until paternity was confirmed, and then we got married. I didn't love her. I thought I would grow to over time because she was the mother of my child, but it never happened for me. The same damn thing happened with my parents, but they didn't even make it through me being in diapers before they got divorced. I was determined to give my daughter a different life, but when you don't marry for love, it gets ugly. I was miserable for so many years." His voice cracks, "And now the same thing is happening to my baby girl."

At least now I understand his rage a bit more. "Coach, I know this isn't how you imagined things going for her, but I do love her. I can be honest enough to tell you I didn't when we got married, but I love her now. Very much."

He shakes his head. "You think you do because of the baby. You love the baby, not her. Trust me, I would know."

"No. It's her. Even if there were no baby right now, I'd still want her. I'd still love her. Even with the bizarre circumstances of our union, I haven't broken our vows and never will."

He nods in understanding. I don't need to spell out that part of things further for him.

I need to convey just how serious I am. "Coach, I know I'm the team goofball, but I take your daughter very seriously. I've never been with anyone like her. Honestly, if you asked me a year ago, I would never have imagined I'd want someone like her. She's different. A complete pain in the ass sometimes. She challenges me in a way no other woman ever has, but I think that's what makes her so special. It's one of the reasons I love her. I also love her independence, her strength, and the way she takes care of everyone around her. She's such a loyal friend and teammate. I love her honesty. It's brutal at times, but you always know where you stand with her because she's incapable of being anything other than authentically her. I love that she's shared things with me and has allowed herself to be vulnerable with me. I love her personality. She's the funniest person I know. I love that she takes care of me without realizing it because it's become second nature for her to do so." I risk a quick glance at him when I turn on my blinker. "She told you I take care of her, which I do at times, but she equally takes care of me. I love that she's the first person I want to see in the morning. I love that I miss her like crazy when we're on the road. I love that one hug from her can make a bad day turn good." I shrug. "And if I'm being honest, she's also pretty easy on the eyes."

"Watch it, Humblecut," he growls.

I chuckle. "She's the most beautiful woman I've ever seen in my life, but that's not why I'm proud to call her my wife. It's all the other things I mentioned. I bought a real ring for her and wanted to do this the right way. I planned to talk to you first to get your blessing."

"Blessing for what? You're already married," he spits back.

"I want us to have a real wedding. We barely remember the first, and it doesn't reflect where we are now. I want to tell her I love her and want to spend my life with her in front of all our family and friends. She's been hesitant about us going public, preferring to wait until her season was over. Now she wants to wait even longer."

"What about you?" he asks. "What do you want?"

"I want to tell the world. I have for months, but you know Kennedy. It's her way or the highway, and while I don't let her get away with everything—she likes being called out on her shit sometimes—I've given her this because it's her body carrying that baby and her career is the one that will be affected. She loves playing basketball, and the impact of having a baby weighs heavily on her. I don't want to do anything to upset her. My job is to support her."

He narrows his eyes at me. "Who are you right now?"

A small smile finds my lips. "I'm the man who loves your daughter. I'm the man who's going to take care of her for the rest of her life. Honestly, I regret nothing about the past year other than not being forthcoming."

He's silent for a few beats. "Don't let her walk all over you. She needs a man who will challenge her."

My smile grows. "I know, Coach. Challenging her is one of my favorite pastimes." It's kind of our foreplay, but he doesn't need that detail. "But the timing of telling people about the baby impacts her career, not mine. This decision is hers, even if I don't like it."

We pull into his driveway. When I stop the car, I hold out my hand for him to shake.

He stares at it for a long while before eventually taking it and squeezing it hard. "If you hurt her, I'll kill you. That's not an empty threat. I will literally murder you and not think twice about it."

I nod. "Deal. I'd like to give her the ring and do this the right way. I want you to walk her down the aisle to me. Do I have your blessing?"

His lip twitches. "One of my best friends owns a cement company. I know where to put you so that you'll never be found. Don't fuck with my baby girl, Humblecut. She's the most important thing in the world to me."

"To me too, Coach. I'll take that as a yes."

THIRTY-TWO

DAYLEN

The past two weeks have been crazy. Vance had a family emergency and disappeared to Montana for a few days. Kennedy has been giving interview after interview. I've secretly hoped she'd talk about us, but she hasn't.

Their victory parade was the other day. While the Camels all celebrated with them as a group of supportive friends, I didn't get to celebrate with my girl the way I would have wanted.

It hurt. A lot. I've tried to pretend otherwise, but I'm not very good at lying. I'm sure she senses it.

We have a nationally televised home game tonight. It's also the big reveal for her makeup commercial that she filmed several weeks ago. They decided to debut it during a second-half timeout of our game to try to piggyback on both the Beavers' championship and the introduction of the new women's football league. They're hoping our fans will gravitate to that league too.

I'm having a terrible game. My head isn't in it. I don't want to upset Kennedy, but don't my feelings matter too? Can't she see that the continued secrecy is hurting me? Yes, I know the decision is hers, but I'm struggling.

I spoke to my father about it earlier today. He seemed bizarrely confident that things would work out and that I should be patient a little longer.

He was so damn sure of it. He's never let me down before, so I'm rolling with things. Just a little longer, and we can tell the world. *I hope.* Something tells me she'll delay it again. I'm afraid of how I'll react if she does.

It's finally time for the commercial. It's not only playing for the people at home on their televisions, but they're showing it on the big screen here at the stadium because of Kennedy's local stardom.

The commercial begins, and it's hot as fuck. Holy shit. Jordie McNamara and Kennedy are both in significantly sexier versions of their respective jerseys. They're both beautiful in totally different ways, and the hair and makeup people did a great job accentuating that. While they both have makeup on their faces—it's a cosmetics commercial—it's not overdone or tacky. There's a whole theme about it being okay to look the way they do while playing as hard and tough as they do. It's a female empowering message, and I'm proud of my girl. Good for Hale Cosmetics for highlighting what real beauty is.

The message is so strong and deep that it garners a standing ovation from the huge crowd when it's over. Vance smacks my back. "She looked amazing."

I nod. "Yes, she did." She's smokin' hot.

The screen then switches to an interview with Jordie. She talks a bit about her journey of having played with the boys in high school and having to hide her more feminine side, and how happy she is to now be able to embrace it all. She then explains the reason behind why she named her lipstick and eyeshadow what she did.

When they move on to Kennedy's interview, I can't help but inhale a sharp breath as she appears on the screen. She's wearing my jersey. I blink a few times to make sure I'm seeing things correctly. Yes, it's a number eighty-eight Camels jersey. This is her subtle way of telling the world that we're together. I can't help the big smile that overtakes my face, but the joy I feel is nothing compared to what she does next.

First, she talks about how much she enjoys traditional girlie things like clothes and makeup and how it doesn't impact who she is as a player or how she plays the game. The off-camera interviewer then asks her what she's chosen as the name of her lipstick.

She answers, "*Humble Rose*."

"Why that name?" the interviewer inquires.

"It's named after my mother-in-law, who I unfortunately never had the chance to meet," she states as if everyone knows she's married. "I told my father-in-law my plans to name it after her, and he and I came up with the name together. She was a special woman, and I'm excited to honor her memory this way."

Monkeys could fly across this stadium right now, and I'd be less surprised.

"You're married?" the interviewer asks, failing to mask her clear surprise.

Kennedy grins widely as she nods. "I am. Very happily."

"To whom?"

Kennedy tugs on her jersey. "To the greatest football player on the planet, of course. Daylen Humblecut." She rubs her belly. "And we're expecting a baby this spring." She blows a kiss into the camera. "Good luck in your game tonight, baby. I love you."

All hundred or so teammates and staff on my sideline turn and look at me. There's no masking the shocked expressions on their faces. Hell, I think all sixty thousand fans look at me too while there's collective gasp in the stadium.

My best friend has a huge grin on his face. He's so happy for me.

The interviewer then asks, "What did you name your signature eyeshadow?"

Kennedy bites back her smile. "I named it *Waterfalls.* That song is my husband's happy place, and he's mine." They play the song as the interview ends.

I look up to try to find Kennedy in the Beavers' suite. I see her standing front and center, wearing my jersey in public for the first time. She holds up her left hand and wiggles her ring finger, which I see isn't covered by a Band-Aid or makeup anymore. She then blows me a kiss. I realize she did all this for me. All the waiting was a ruse. She wanted to give me the huge—and I mean *huge*—public display of our love. I didn't think I could love her any more than I already did, but I was wrong.

I wish I could climb this stadium right now just to kiss her.

After I excitedly remove the Band-Aid from my ring finger, I give her the heart sign with my hands. At least people now know why I always do that after every touchdown. All for my wife.

SIX WEEKS LATER

KENNEDY

I stand in the bathroom crying, and Daylen comes flying in. "What's wrong?" he asks with worry written all over his face.

"I can't see my vagina anymore," I sob in response. My stomach has grown like bamboo in the past few weeks. I went from not showing at all to a beached whale in the blink of an eye.

He bursts out laughing. "Holy crap, that's hysterical. I

happen to know your vagina inside and out. Probably better than you. Anything I can help with?"

I hold up my razor. "I wanted to shave for our wedding."

We're having a small ceremony tonight with close friends and family. When I agreed to it after the day I outed us to the world, I didn't expect to be this big yet. I've had to buy six different dresses while trying to play catch-up with my constantly expanding waistline.

Outing us like that was in the works for a while. I knew how upset he was that I kept us a secret, but he's so amazing to me that I wanted to give him the grandest of gestures on the grandest stage possible. I knew a large public display of affection would mean a lot to him.

Hank gave me the idea when I went to him about the lipstick name. I knew I wanted to name it after Rose, but I wanted to make sure it was okay with him. I always suspected Daylen had told him about us. I figured there was no way he was able to keep us a secret from his father, and I was right.

Hank and I talked a lot about Rose and how excited she'd be to see Daylen this happy. We also spoke about how much Daylen was hurting from keeping us a secret. I'm not sure I fully realized it until Hank articulated it. We then devised the plan to reveal it in the biggest of ways. It was my way of showing Daylen just how much I love and appreciate him.

Daylen was floating on cloud nine over it. As soon as we got home after his game, he sprinted inside and returned the gesture by dropping to his knee and offering me the biggest diamond ring I've ever seen in my life. Apparently he had purchased it and was waiting for the right time to give it to me. I'm slightly obsessed with it. He did a great job picking it out. It makes me wonder if he had help, but I've never asked.

He takes the razor from my hand. "I'll do it for you."

I scrunch my face in disgust. "I feel like that's bizarrely intimate."

He raises an eyebrow. "Your hand has been up my ass and

mine yours. I'm pretty sure things don't get much more intimate than that."

I giggle. "True." I rub my pubic hair. "Are you sure? Don't mess up. I like it smooth."

He nods. "I'm the one whose face will be buried in there tonight. I don't want anything to go wrong. I promise. I have a vested interest in the safety of your vagina."

I lay a towel on the tile floor of the bathroom and sit naked before spreading my legs while leaning back on my elbows. He fills two cups, one with hot water and the other with cold for rinsing. He gets down on his knees and then gently runs shaving cream over my center.

"Hmm, I think I like your pussy covered by me in white cream."

I smile as I roll my eyes. "Stay focused."

His eyes don't move from my pussy. "Oh, I'm *very* focused."

I look at his boxer-brief-covered crotch, which has grown a lot in the past minute. "I can't believe you're hard from this."

He shrugs. "It's kind of hot. And your legs are spread wide with your pink pussy on display. Of course I'm hard."

I can't help but lick my lips at the sight of his imposing manhood. Even doing something gentle like this, he's still so big and masculine.

He notices and shakes his head. "Don't even think about it. I'm not that kind of girl. I'm saving myself for marriage. It's a good thing I'm getting married tonight because this sexy image will be playing on repeat for me all day."

"Remarried," I remind him.

He nods. "Remarried. I'll miss Pinky Punnathanathukunnele this time."

I giggle. "Me too. How often does an officiant run the ceremony and sing Elvis tunes at the same time?" I start singing one of those tunes.

"Shh. I'm focusing."

He's so careful as he runs the razor blade across my most

sensitive region. It's quite a sight seeing a giant of a man, nearly naked, being so tender with me.

He pauses to rinse the blade. "It's going well. Perhaps this could be a career for me after football."

"Makes perfect sense. You do love vaginas."

"Vagina," he corrects. "I'm a one-vagina kind of man now. It's a good thing it's my favorite vagina in the world."

I smile. "You have the sweetest pillow talk."

"Your vagina is a philosophical one," he announces with a straight face. "That's why it's my favorite."

"What makes her philosophical?"

He smirks. "It's deep."

I can't help but laugh. "Oh my god. Where do you come up with this stuff?"

He wiggles his eyebrows as he continues to carefully run the razor over me. Time and time again, he strokes me with it, never hurting me.

"Got any more vagina jokes for me while you're down there?"

He twists his lips, all while remaining focused. "Hmm. Why don't witches wear panties?"

"Why?"

"So they can grip the broomstick better."

I spit in laughter. "I love that one. I'm using it."

He places the razor blade in the cup and gives me a satisfied look. "All done. I did a perfect job, if I must say so myself."

I run my fingers between my legs and check on his work for myself. "It does feel rather smooth. Nicely done, Dr. Humblecock."

He gasps. "Oh my god, I need a lab coat that has Dr. Humblecock written on it."

I make a note to order him one for Christmas.

He continues. "My post-football-pussy-shaving business will be called Humblecock Coochies."

I nod. "It has a nice ring to it."

He chuckles. "I think so."

His telephone on the counter rings, and he picks it up before his eyes widen and he looks at me. "It's Judge Demise."

"Crap," I exclaim, "I forgot we have our final meeting with him this morning. Let's fuck with him." I stand and quickly grab my robe.

He wiggles his eyebrows. "Yes, excellent idea, wife. Go answer and pretend like we're not together. I'm sure he's calling your phone too."

I grab my ringing phone from the bedroom and run into the other room. Once I'm there, I answer the video call and smile into the camera. "Hi, Judge."

He scowls. "This is the second time I tried calling. Where were you?"

"Sorry, I was on TikTok watching someone restock their fridge and put things in clear containers for two hours. My bad."

I can hear Daylen laughing from the other room. God damn, he's so loud. He's going to out us to the judge.

He then joins the call. "Sorry I was late. I was walking the snake."

The judge pinches his eyebrows in confusion. "What does that mean? You can take snakes for walks? Do they have snake collars? Do they have necks?"

I can't help but giggle. "No, Judge, that was a euphemism for going to the bathroom. My dear husband amuses himself by finding random ways to tell people he's going to the bathroom."

The judge sighs. "God help me, you two will be the death of me." He then mumbles, "It wasn't worth it."

"Worth what?" Daylen asks.

The judge's trademark scowl turns into something I don't recognize on his face. I think it might be a smile. What the hell?

"Winning the competition," he almost cheerily announces. "Every year," he explains, "each retired judge picks one couple who we refuse an annulment, asking them to wait an unreasonably longer period of time. If we can get them to remain married after that period, we win the pool."

I stand there in shock, but Daylen asks, "How big is the pool?"

He lifts his eyes upward, and his lips move as he appears to count. "Well, there are around thirty-three retired judges in the program, but four are boring and don't like a little fun competition. We each contribute one dollar to the pot, so that's twenty-nine dollars I've got coming my way."

My jaw drops. "You fucked with our lives for twenty-nine dollars?"

His small smile becomes much larger. "I suppose that's one way to look at it. The other is that perhaps I know what I'm doing. I've been married for sixty-eight years. I've been a family court judge for nearly all that time. I've seen what works and doesn't work. I saw a fire in you two that I knew would light with the right kindling. I merely provided that kindling. It was you two who lit that fire and set it ablaze. I saw your speech on the television, Ms. Jeffries…or should I call you Mrs. Humblecut?" He turns his attention to Daylen. "And you, Mr. Humblecut, I could hear your laugh two counties over, let alone a room or two over. I may be getting old, but it's not easy to pull one over on me."

Daylen and I are shocked into silence, and the judge chuckles. I didn't even know he had teeth. "I see I've stunned you." He straightens his collar. "It's good to know I still have it."

Again, we remain silent. Neither of us has any words for this insanity.

He sighs. "Well, I suppose my work here is done. I understand congratulations are in order. Shall I assume it's okay to tear up these annulment papers? I'll sign them today if you'd like."

Daylen walks into the room I'm standing in and throws his arm around me before kissing my cheek. "No annulment needed."

"Ms. Jeffries?"

I shake my head. "No annulment."

He grins. "Excellent. I'll tell the wife she can have dinner at the fancy steakhouse tonight. Twenty-nine dollars goes a long way in Vegas."

I think that was a joke. Did he just try to make a joke?

He laughs as he continues, "I'll give you one parting bit of advice about matrimony. Maturing in a marriage is understanding that if you hit your wife's butt as you walk by, she'll roll her eyes, but if you don't, she'll wonder why you don't love her anymore. Don't ever stop smacking her ass."

He waves, and practically sings, "Best of luck, you two," before he cuts the feed.

A FEW HOURS LATER, Daylen and I are standing in front of each other reciting our vows, staring lovingly into each other's eyes. Yes, our friends and family are here, but we only have eyes for each other.

We're dressed in high-end but not too formal clothing. Daylen happily let me dress him in slacks, a button-down shirt, and a sports coat. It's my favorite look on him. I'm in a silky, long white dress that shows enough cleavage to keep him happy but not be inappropriate. We rented a rooftop restaurant in a downtown Philly skyscraper. It's winter, so we couldn't be outside, but the restaurant has glass walls with three-hundred-and-sixty-degree views of the city, so it's beautiful.

"Do you take this man to be your husband?" the officiant, whose name isn't Pinky or Elvis, asks.

"I do." I smile at Daylen as we hold each other's hands. I decide to add my own vows. "I promise that the only waterfalls I'll chase are the real ones with you by my side. I promise to never judge you, even if you wear cargo pants, white jeans, or sandals with socks. If you want a photo of yourself in front of your car, I'll take it for you. If you want to wear a chain necklace, I'll help you put it on. If you want a fruity drink, I'll make it for you." My eyes well with tears. "I'll never ask you to be anything other than authentically you because I love the real you. With a spatula in hand, I'll love you until the day I die. And if I go first, I'll haunt you for eternity just to ensure you make good fashion decisions."

He smirks as he bends forward and softly kisses my lips.

The officiant turns to Daylen. "Do you take this woman to be your wife?"

"I do," he answers with a mischievous sparkle in his eyes. "I'll never again judge a bra by its cover. I'll put my hands inside and discover."

I smile while everyone laughs.

He continues, "You, Kennedy, are the person who matters most to me in the world." I fight my tears. He knows what that statement means to me. "I want us to grow old together. Old enough so we can complain about how things used to be better, like your dad does. I promise I'll care more about you than how much Netflix cares if you're logging on from a different location with a different device. I promise to dance with you on our balcony. I promise to carry you inside if you fall asleep in the rain. I promise to always make you laugh. And when I die," his face turns serious, "I want my ashes placed in your salsa so I can tear your ass up one last time."

The whole place erupts in laughter except my dad. He barks, "Humblecut!"

Daylen snaps his head toward my father. "Sorry, Coach."

Harper, who's our flower girl, asks Tanner, "What does that mean, Daddy?"

Tanner pinches the bridge of his nose. "Oh Christ. Ask your mother."

I grin widely, point at Daylen, and lightheartedly announce, "My emergency contact, ladies and gentlemen."

Daylen pumps his fist. "Yes! I finally made it as your emergency contact."

A few hours later, we're all sitting around an oversized table. I'm overwhelmed by everyone here to support us. Two years ago, no one at this table would have been here to celebrate me, and now I can't imagine my life without any of them. It's my family, his family, and our found family.

Tears fill my eyes at how much fuller my life has become since my trade to Philly. That day, I thought it was the worst thing to ever happen to me. It turns out it was the best.

This damn pregnancy is making me so hormonal.

Daylen leans over and whispers, "Are you okay?"

I nod as I squeeze his hand. "I'm perfect."

"Damn straight, baby." He pulls a phone out of his pocket. One I don't recognize. "Look, I got an iPhone. No more Android. No more messing up group texts. Green flag for me."

I giggle as Hank holds up his champagne glass. "To the happy couple," he shouts before wiping away his own errant tears and turning his attention to Daylen. "I love you, son. I'm so happy you found a woman who matches your energy. *Yo mama* would have been so proud."

Daylen raises an amused eyebrow. "Yo mama?"

Hank nods. "Yep."

Jagger whines, "Are you two for real? Not now."

Hank nods again. "Yes, now."

Daylen puffs out his chest. "Yo mama is so dumb, she tried to make an appointment with Dr. Pepper."

Everyone except Hank laughs. He stares at Daylen and says, "Yo mama has been sleeping around so long, that she's gotten with the Father, the Son, *and* the Holy Ghost."

Again, more laughter, but Daylen keeps it together.

I raise my hand. "Can I try one?"

Hank and Daylen share a bemused look as Hank winks at me and motions his hand in invitation for me to give it a go. In fairness, Hank had given me the heads up and encouraged me to join their bit tonight.

I first look at Harper and instruct, "Earmuffs." Fallon covers Harper's ears and gives me the all-clear signal. I lick my lips. "Yo mama is as dumb as a bowling ball. She gets picked up, fingered, thrown in the gutter, and yet she still comes back for more."

And they both laugh. I'm the big winner tonight in every way possible.

THIRTY-THREE

SUPER BOWL SUNDAY

KENNEDY

I wake in the early morning to the feeling of Daylen's tongue between my legs. Without opening my eyes, I smile and run my fingers through his hair. "Whoever you are, you need to be quick. My husband is staying in a room nearby and could be here any minute."

The team rules don't permit us to stay together at the hotel. In fact, he's not even allowed in here, but that hasn't stopped him at all. He sneaks into my room at some point every single day.

We've been out in LA all week for the Super Bowl festivities. It's been a blast, and I'm excited for the guys that they get to experience this. What's not so great is being eight months pregnant during a weeklong party. I may have popped late, but Baby Girl Humbelcut has more than made up for it. Yes, it's a girl, but Daylen doesn't know yet. I asked the doctor when Daylen went to the bathroom during one of my visits. I guess I lost the bet. Daylen carries the baby's first outfit everywhere he goes, *just in case*. I don't know what it looks like, and I'm afraid to find out.

He bites my inner thigh hard. "Ah," I shriek. "That's going to leave a mark."

"Good," he mumbles before diving back in and bringing me to orgasm in no time.

As soon as he's milked every last drop from me, he turns me on my side and moves behind me. At this point in the pregnancy, it's the only position I can manage.

He lifts my leg and nudges his tip through me a few times. I flinch, still sensitive from my orgasm seconds ago.

He continues to tease me until it becomes unbearable. "D, get inside me," I whine. "I'm so ready for you."

"I love how wet you are for me." He runs his fingers through my center. "And swollen. Your pussy is physically throbbing for me. I can feel it on my fingers."

I nod before reaching down and pushing his tip to my entrance. I try to tilt my hips to get him inside me, but he manages to control his movements, only sliding in an inch or two at a time before withdrawing.

His fingers work my clit while he teases my opening over and over again, never pushing all the way in like I want him to. His teasing is driving me crazy with need. I can feel my juices dripping down my thighs. While I hate how big I am, the one good thing about the pregnancy is how overly sensitive I've become. He barely has to touch me and I orgasm. I think all the blood in my body is down there right now.

He's still teasing me when another orgasm slowly ripples its way through my body. As soon as it hits, he thrusts all the way in to the hilt. "Oh fuck, baby, you're squeezing me so hard."

He grabs one of my nipples with his rough fingers and pinches it, causing another wave to crash down over me. I'm thrashing around, unable to control my movements or my sounds. God, this is so damn good.

As soon as my moans subside, he tilts my head back toward him and brings my lips to his. "I love you."

"I love you too," I mumble back before he kisses me at the same slow pace that he makes love to me. He moves in and out of me methodically, drawing it out so we can stay connected for as long as possible.

We're so in love that it's almost disgusting. The previous me would be appalled by my lovesick behavior, but I can't help it. I'm addicted to him every bit as much as he's addicted to me. We're inseparable. We do everything together, from working out to everyday household chores and baby preparation. I guess they call it nesting, but whatever it is, I can honestly say that I've never been happier in my life. I've never felt so loved, seen, and safe.

We're still as playful as we've always been, and I hope we never lose that, but it's always in good fun. Daylen didn't only become my husband, he became my best friend. Our house is full of laughter and love every single day.

When it's over, we lie in comfortable silence with him remaining inside my body, wrapped around me, neither of us wanting to break the connection. We know it means he'll have to leave.

At some point, I need to be the strong one. "You'd better go before they find out you're missing."

"Hmm, no," he speaks into my neck, "I don't want to. You know I'm a cuddler. I need more cuddling." He squeezes me tight.

"Go cuddle with Champ. He's a cuddler too."

He playfully bites my shoulder before grabbing my breasts with both hands. "His tits aren't as big as yours. I think they got bigger since yesterday."

"No, they didn't, freak." I think he's right. They did. They won't stop growing.

He chuckles as he runs his nose up and down my neck, inhaling me. "I'll miss you today."

"You're playing in the biggest game of your life in front of seventy million people. I think you'll manage a few hours without me."

He holds out his ring finger and slides his wedding band a bit, revealing my name tattooed on it. "You're always with me, no matter what."

"Don't be so damn swoony," I warn. "It's making it hard for me to kick you out."

I can feel him smile into my neck as he kisses it. "You sure you don't want some more #HumbleCock? I guess you're now Mrs. Humblecock."

"That's what it says on my license," I joke. "Kennedy Jeffries Humblecock. You should have seen their faces at the DMV when I went to change it."

He bites me again, and I giggle. "You think you're so funny," he jokes.

"I'm hysterical."

He moans as he continues to fondle my breasts. "Ugh, I guess I should go, funny lady. Everyone will be waking up soon." He gives them one last squeeze. "I'll miss the two of you. Keep growing for me."

"No more growing. I can barely walk without toppling over."

A few minutes later, I'm in my red silk robe that he loves, walking him to the door hand in hand. I hate that he has to leave, but I don't let on because I know this week of separation has been hard on him and today is his big day. I won't do anything to dim his shine. He deserves this spotlight.

When I open the door, he stops in the doorway and turns around, looking so unhappy.

"Why are you sad?" I ask.

He puffs out his lower lip. "Just realizing all my future kids are going to get bullied for having a hot mom. It's tragic."

I roll my eyes. "Nice line, and there's nothing hot about me right now."

"Are you kidding me?" He stares at my chest. "I'm *obsessed* with your body." That's true. He is. "One more good luck kiss? Please?" He gives me his best puppy dog eyes.

Unable to resist him, I grab his face, bring my lips to his, and give him one last long kiss he won't soon forget. When we break, he's in a bit of a daze, but I notice my father opens his hotel room door across the hallway. "Hi, Daddy," I innocently say.

Daylen's face lights up, not realizing my father is standing behind him. Tracing the tops of my breasts with his fingers, he says, "Ooh, I like it when you call me that. I *was* your daddy this morning. Maybe I should take you over my knee and spank you."

I can't help but let out a laugh, but my father grumbles, "Humblecut!"

Daylen immediately pulls his hand away from my body, and his eyes widen in horror, but he doesn't turn around, likely in fear.

Deciding to fuel the flames, I bop him on the nose and say, "You certainly were my daddy this morning, and I would *love* for you to take me over your knee. Maybe after the game tonight. Thanks for all the orgasms, baby." I wink at him with a huge smile on my face. "Good luck. Love you."

His eyes widen further, but I quickly close my door and leave him alone with my father. I happily look out the peephole and listen for voices. Daylen still hasn't moved. My father looks murderous. "Humblecut, I'm going to fucking kill you this time."

Daylen swivels his head from side to side a few times before taking off down the hallway in a dead sprint.

DAYLEN

"When the safety rotates down, rip the seam," Coach yells at me while grabbing the cage of my helmet.

I nod and robotically say, "Yes, Coach." Normally, I would have some silly, perverted response to that command, but in light of this morning's activities, I decide to keep it clean. The Daddy thing was bad enough, but my witch of a wife had to go and fan the flames further. If I wasn't scared for my life, I'd think it was funny, but I thought Coach was actually going to kill me this time around. Beau had to hold him back until he calmed down.

Coach is still grappling with my marriage to Kennedy. He knows I love her beyond comprehension, but I can understand that, as a father, having heard the things I've said and done for the past ten years, he would still struggle with it at times. I appreciate that he doesn't want to hear about all the orgasms I give her.

Although sometimes I think how seamless and fantastic she and I are together freaks him out just as much as the thought of me touching her. Kennedy and I have something very special. We're best friends and lovers. She's my favorite person in the world. My marriage is exactly what I always hoped for. It's the playful, fun, sweet, loving marriage my parents had.

She's not due for another month, but she looks ready to pop. The doctor told us she could go at any time as the baby was quite large at our visit last week. I was torn on whether it was safe for her to come out here, but there was no stopping her. She didn't want to miss my big day. And, honestly, I couldn't be away from her.

I've been so afraid it would happen this week, when I was barely able to be with her due to team obligations and rules. After tonight's game, I'm not leaving her side until that baby is born. I brought the baby's first outfit with me just in case. I'm absolutely convinced I will win the bet. BJ thinks so too.

I run back onto the field to begin the third quarter. The first half saw a lot of offense on both sides for what has turned into a seesaw game.

Vance bangs his helmet with mine. "Let's fucking do this."

I nod. We both want our first Super Bowl ring more than anything. We've worked long and hard to get here. This is our moment.

We're moving down the field, now sitting at our opponent's thirty-five yard line for a third and ten. We need a first down here.

Vance calls the play, an eight-yard slant to me to the right side. The goal is for me to catch the quick, short pass and then muscle myself downfield a few more yards for a first down.

The ball is hiked, and I move across the field to get a step on my defender. Vance throws me the ball, and I catch it. Unfortunately, I've got three defenders hanging off my legs, trying to tackle me. Knowing I'm not going to get any extra yards, I toss the ball backward toward Champ for what is called a hook and ladder. Coach never calls this play because it's risky, and he hates when I do it, but we need this first down.

Champ catches it and dodges defenders, running all the way down the field for a touchdown. I sprint toward him with my hands in the air, screaming in celebration.

He and I do our special handshake before heading off the field toward our sideline. Coach is scowling at me. "That's the second time today you almost gave me a heart attack."

I smile. "Love you too, Coach. I can call you Daddy if you prefer," I offer.

He narrows his eyes at me, but I chuckle. "Too soon?" I ask.

His lips and fingers twitch to beat me senseless, but I know he won't on national television.

The second half progresses similarly to the first, with both sides putting on an offensive display, trading touchdowns on nearly every drive. After a miracle play by Beau on defense, we've got the ball back with less than a minute on the clock, down by three. I can physically see all the pressure Vance is feeling right now. Games tend to fall on the shoulders of the quarterback, but he's having a great game. We just need to finish it with things going our way.

An option play is called, meaning Vance will read the defense and decide which person to throw the ball to. I'll be the downfield, winning touchdown option. The safe play is a short pass to Champ or one of our receivers for a few yards, where we would kick a field goal to tie it, and then head into overtime.

Vance tends to play it safe at times. Too safe in my opinion. I'm going to have multiple defenders covering me, and he's going to be afraid to throw it to me, fearing losing the game.

I look at Coach on the sideline, and he nods at me. He wants us to go for broke. I mouth to Vance, "Just throw it to me." I silently communicate that I don't care what I have to do, I'll catch this ball no matter what.

Vance and I have played together long enough that I know he's reading my mind.

The ball is hiked, and I run my route straight toward the endzone with defenders draped all over me. Peeking back, I see Vance scrambling out of the pocket, away from defenders. I change course a bit to get to myself on the same side of the field as him, making the throw a bit easier. In the process, I shake all but one defender.

I can't tell you how many times my father and I ran this play in our backyard. We'd pretend it was the Super Bowl, and I'd run as far away as I could before he'd throw it as far as he could. I'd catch it and we'd celebrate like it was actually the big game.

I'm now living that moment for real. Vance plants his feet and throws the ball high into the night sky. It's a perfect spiral heading straight for me. The defender and I are shoulder to shoulder as we make our way to the back of the endzone, both with the goal of catching that ball, both with an equal chance of catching it.

As the ball approaches from the sky, we leap into the air for it. Both our hands grab it at the same time, but I muscle it away from him before dragging my toes down and then falling out of bounds. I think I got mine down in bounds, but it's hard to tell. The back judge holds up his arms, indicating a touchdown. We win.

My teammates are all running toward me, but I do a little airplane move to get away from them so I can bust out all my best dance moves. First, I do my little swim move, then the Cabbage Patch, then the Running Man, then the Ted Lasso, all before I rock the baby and point to the suite where I know Kennedy is sitting, making my hands into a heart shape. I can't see her with all the flashes and confetti, but I know she's there smiling at me.

My teammates finally reach me and pile on top of me, blanketing me with their bodies in mere seconds.

Madness ensues as everyone around looks to congratulate me. What I really want is my family, but I know it will take them time to be escorted by security from their suite down to the field.

Given his size, I see my father first. His blue eyes are filled with tears. I know he remembers all the nights we practiced together for this very moment.

He wraps me in a huge bear hug and lifts me off the ground. "I'm so proud of you."

"Thanks, Dad. I wouldn't be here without you."

"I love you, son."

"Love you too, Dad."

Next, Jagger leaps into my waiting arms, screaming and crying tears of joy. Ashleigh follows shortly after, but I can't find my girl. "Where's Kennedy?" I ask them.

There's some commotion with Vance and Sulley. People start to move toward them. When they clear away, that's when I see my wife, standing on the sidelines with tears in her eyes.

She's waiting for me. I start running toward her and smash my lips to hers as soon as we come together. She briefly kisses me back, but then mumbles into my lips, "I'm so sorry."

I jerk my head back in surprise. "Why? What's wrong?"

She looks down at her body. "My water just broke."

EPILOGUE

KENNEDY

I'm sitting in my hospital room watching Daylen hold our daughter. He's so gentle with her. He knows exactly how to hold her and soothe her. It's all so foreign to me. I'm terrified that I'm now responsible for the little being who can't do anything for herself. He's calm as a cucumber, loving every minute of it, unwilling to let anyone else hold her or do anything for her.

The madness of today is running on a loop through my mind. I might still be in shock.

It was an exciting game that I got to watch from a luxury suite purchased by Vance and Daylen. It was filled with our friends and families. I laughed my ass off when we busted Pierce and Jagger locked in the bathroom together. Hank wasn't as amused as I was.

I got to watch my husband be the big hero on what must be one of the greatest catches in Super Bowl history.

I was hanging back to let Daylen have his moment with his father. It was emotional seeing the way they embraced each other. I can almost imagine long nights of the two of them throwing a ball, preparing for this moment. Their bond is so strong. Love and admiration ooze from them when they're together.

I could see him looking for me, loving that he wanted me in his big moment. The second our eyes met, I felt a pop and then liquid running down my legs.

I was frozen in shock, thinking *not now*. Please, *not now*.

As soon as Daylen realized it, he went into full-blown, take-charge, papa bear mode. He did what he's done this entire pregnancy. He took care of me and our baby without an ounce of hesitation. I did nothing but allow myself to be taken care of. I'm not sure he understands how much that means to me.

Given that there's emergency personnel on hand at these events, he had us in the back of an ambulance speeding off the field and toward the hospital within only a few minutes.

Ten minutes later, in the back of that same ambulance, baby Rose came into this world with my husband right by my side, whispering words of love and encouragement.

Less than thirty minutes after her father made a catch that will forever be memorialized in the record books, Rose Cunningham Humblecut decided she wanted to be part of the celebration too.

I have no idea who she looks like—she's a wrinkly mess—but she's the most beautiful wrinkly mess I've ever seen in my life. I'm kind of in shock that we created her.

Our families just left. My dad openly wept when he met Rose. It made me cry to see him so emotional over her. He and Daylen even hugged, no small feat considering how the day started.

Vance and Sulley walk in with huge smiles on their faces. Sulley runs straight to my bedside. "How are you?"

I exhale a long breath, not really knowing the answer. "Well, nine inches went in, but twenty-one came out, so how do you think I feel?"

She bursts out laughing. "I suppose that's one way to look at it."

Daylen mumbles, "I think it's closer to ten inches."

I point to my horrifically aching and sore lower half. "There will be zero inches going in for the foreseeable future."

He deadpans, "Your mouth still works, doesn't it? You know my favorite holiday is Suck a Dick Sunday. Today is Suck a Dick Super Bowl Sunday."

I narrow my eyes at him. "I just pushed your giant, nine-pound baby out of me without any drugs. That little holiday of yours is on hiatus."

He twists his lips. "Hmm, I guess I'm not heartless. We can skip this week. But just one."

Vance and Sulley laugh while I glare at my husband with murderous intent. He smiles and winks at me.

They spend the next ten minutes oohing and ahhing over Rose, but when she begins to get fussy, Daylen kicks them out so I can feed her.

He gently places her in my arms. I look up at him. "I'm scared. What if I hold her wrong?"

"You're doing just fine." He gives me a little demonstration. "Hold her like a football. You need to support her head until her neck muscles develop."

I gasp. "She was born without neck muscles? Is that bad? Should we get the doctor?"

He chuckles. "All babies are born with weak muscles. It takes a few weeks for them to strengthen."

"What if I drop her?"

He raises an eyebrow. "You're one of the best athletes in the world. I don't see it happening." He cups my cheek with his hand. "Babe, you'll be fine."

"*You'll* be fine, you're an expert. *I'm* going to fuck up."

He shakes his head. "We're both going to fuck up. That's normal. I had the benefit of a baby sister when I was sixteen, or I wouldn't know anything either. You'll be up to speed in no time at all."

She starts wiggling in my arms. "She hates me," I pout.

He rolls his eyes. "She's hungry. She just did the same thing in my arms."

I pull out my nipple for her to take into her mouth and wince when she latches on. "Fuck, was she born with razor-blade teeth?"

He shakes his head. "No teeth. Yet."

"Is it normal to not have teeth when you're born?"

He smiles. "Yes. Relax. Look at you two right now. It's the most natural, beautiful thing I've ever seen. Enjoy yourself. Don't worry. Take it all in."

I stare down at her in wonderment as she happily sucks away. It's wacky, but in an amazing way.

He smiles. "See, you gave her exactly what she needed."

I nod with a heavy dose of pride. I suppose I did. "She's good at this. Did you see how quickly she latched on? I read that a lot of babies struggle with that at first."

"I told you, she's going to be a freak athlete."

I look down at her again. "Maybe you're right."

He watches us intently and licks his lips. "Don't take all her milk, baby girl. Leave some for Daddy."

"Are you out of your fucking mind?" I practically shout.

He laughs. "I'm just messing with you. We'll wait a few more weeks for that," he announces with a smirk on his face.

She eats for a while before I motion toward the bathroom. "You should shower and change. Vance brought your bag from the locker room."

He's still in his uniform pants and a T-shirt with my face on it that reads: *My Wife is Hotter Than Your Wife*. He was wearing it under his jersey for the game and planned to show it off in post-game interviews.

A year ago, that would have been a giant red flag. Now I love it. He loves me so openly and proudly.

"Will you be okay?" he asks with concern written all over his face.

I look down at her and nod. "She and I need a little time alone together." Lifting my face so my eyes meet his, I say, "I'm sorry you didn't get to celebrate with your team. I feel like you got deprived of the glory you deserved. If you want to get out of here for a bit, she and I will be fine." I'm not sure that's true, but he got shorted so much today. I can always have a nurse help me if I need it.

He gets down on his knees so our eyes are on the same level. He softly kisses my lips before saying, "I appreciate you saying that, but this has been the best day of my life and football has nothing to do with it. There is nowhere in the world I'd rather be. No one I'd rather be with. You two are my everything, and I will spend every day of my life proving that to you. There is zero chance I will be leaving your side anytime soon, so get used to me being around."

With glassy eyes, I nod. I hit the jackpot with this amazing man.

Five minutes later, I can hear him singing "Waterfalls" in the shower. I look down at Rose, who's somewhere between eating and sleeping, I'm not sure which.

"Daddy loves that ridiculous song. The rap verse will probably be your first words."

She coos in contentment. Damnit, she already loves the song. It's probably because he sang it into my stomach a thousand times over the past few months.

I gently rub her cheek with the backs of my fingers, marveling at the softness of her peaches-and-cream skin. "Look, we both know Daddy is going to be a rock star. I'm going to need you to bear with me. I'm going to mess up, but I promise to try my hardest, and I promise to love you no matter what. Even on my bad days, I won't ever make you feel anything other than loved and prioritized."

"You're going to be a great mom, Kennedy," an intruding, deep voice declares.

I look up and see my father at the door with a few tears trickling down his face. "I'm afraid, Dad," I admit.

He nods. "All parents are. Especially with their first. It's a learning process. I know I wasn't the best father in the world, but I loved you from the second I saw you and every day since. I know the type of woman you are. You're going to be a great mom. You're going to protect and love the hell out of that little girl."

I exhale a long breath. "I hope you're right."

"I know I am." He nods toward one of the chairs next to my bed. "Pierce forgot his hat. Do you mind if I grab it?"

I look down to make sure nothing is showing that a father shouldn't see. When I realize it's not, I nod. "Of course. Daylen is in the shower."

He sighs. "I can hear that. He's always singing."

"Because he's always happy. It's nice to be around, isn't it?"

He offers a small smile as he approaches and grabs the hat. "I suppose it is."

The sound of the shower water goes quiet, but Daylen loudly announces from the bathroom, "There's still a little time left in Suck a Dick Sunday. Are you sure you don't want to imbibe, babe?"

My dad's smile quickly fades as he growls, "Humblecut, I would sleep with one eye open tonight if I were you."

I can't help but laugh, and I think baby Rose does too.

IT'S FINALLY time for us to go home. The Camels sent their team jet back for us so we can fly privately with the baby.

My family went home, but Daylen's family thankfully stayed to help us. I think I want them all to move in. I'm afraid to do this without their help. They've been amazing for the past few days.

Daylen smirks as he dresses Rose while I'm seated in a wheelchair, per hospital regulations. All I can see of her outfit is that it's a pink onesie. "What did you do?" I ask accusatorily.

His smile widens. "Are you ready for the big reveal?" He looks like a kid in a candy store.

I shake my head. "I had the cutest Burberry outfit picked out. Our son would have been stylin'."

"Keep it. Maybe we'll have a son next year."

I stare at him in disbelief. "Umm, no."

"Okay, the princess is ready," he proudly announces before holding her up for me to see.

She's in a pink onesie that reads: *Product of a Beau Fudd Boner Shake.*

I spit in laughter. "Oh my god. Did you seriously put our three-day-old daughter in a shirt with the word *boner* on it? She's going to have this photo for the rest of her life."

He twists his lips. "Hmm, I never thought of it that way. I think you'll be the baby stylist moving forward."

Glad he said that, because, unbeknownst to him, her closet is already full of designer girlie clothes. I've been having a blast shopping for this kid since I found out the sex.

He continues, "I'm sure you'll be introducing her to fashion in no time. Her stroller is going to get some good mileage at the mall." He looks down at her and uses his baby voice. "Right, baby girl? You and Mommy will go on shopping sprees all the time. Mommy is not only a professional athlete, but she's a professional shopper. You're a lucky little girl."

I nod as I realize that when I shop for her now, she'll be with me. Maybe it's something special she and I can do together. Hope blooms in my chest as I begin to imagine it.

Hank knocks on the door and walks in. "The car is here." He looks at Rose and fixes her little hat. "Are you ready to go home, baby doll? Is...*yo mama* ready too?"

Daylen's head snaps toward Hank. I stare at them both and warn, "I love this game, but I'm thinking it's a bit much for Rose's little ears right now."

They grin at each other before Daylen looks down at Rose. "Yo mama is so bold, she's featured on the toolbar of Microsoft Word."

I smile, and Hank nods before saying, "Yo mama's so smart, Google uses *her*, not the other way around."

I giggle. These guys are too much. This is clearly a preplanned routine, and I love it.

Daylen looks at me and gives me the sweetest, most loving smile that has ever existed before looking back down at Rose. "Yo mama is so radiant, when she looks in the mirror, *it* starts glowing."

Cheesy jokes used to be on my red flag list, a list I've since deleted from my phone. I can't help but stare at my little family. All I see now are big green flags.

THE END

If you'd like a glimpse into Kennedy, Daylen, and Rose's future, please enjoy their extended epilogue:

ACKNOWLEDGMENTS

To Kennedy and Daylen: There's just something special about you two. I love your unique, messed-up, out-of-order love story.

To the Queen, TL Swan: This amazing journey would never have begun if not for you and your selfless decision to help hundreds of women. You are a shining example of the girl power quotes I place in each dedication. This crazy and unexpected new path in my life has brought me so much happiness. I owe it all to you. Please know that I try every single day to pay it forward.

To Lakshmi, Thorunn, Mindy, and Brittany: My Beta Bitches are always in my corner, cheering me on. I'm so thankful for your friendships.

To Jade Dollston, Carolina Jax, and L.A. Ferro: You are my bookish besties. Our daily texts are my lifeline. I love the support we have for each other.

To The B!tch Squad Members: Thank you for the support, the messages, the posts, the love. It continues to amaze me that such a wonderful group of women support my books wholeheartedly.

To Chrisandra and K.B. Designs: Chrisandra: Thank you for making me feel illiterate. That's what makes you such a great editor. **Kristin**: Thank you for helping this artistically challenged woman who doesn't know what she wants but does. You know what I mean.

To My Family: I truly feel bad for you. An immature mother and wife can't be easy. To my daughters, thank you for tolerating me (ish). Thank you for telling everyone you know that your mom writes sex books. I appreciate that by the time you were each six, you were more mature than me. To my handsome husband, thank you for your blind support. You never question my sanity, which can't be easy. But let's face it, you do reap the benefits of the fact that I write sex scenes all day long.

ABOUT THE AUTHOR

AK Landow lives in the USA with her husband. Her three daughters have grown into the type of magnificent women she writes about. AK enjoys spending time with her family, reading, writing, drinking copious amounts of vodka, and laughing. She's thrilled to have this crazy avenue to channel her perverted, age-inappropriate sense of humor. She is also of the belief that Beth Dutton is the greatest fictional character ever created, but she thinks Kennedy Jeffries may give Beth a run for her money.

AKLandowAuthor.com

ALSO BY AK LANDOW

The Grand Advantage: Palmer and Beau

Signed Books: aklandowauthor.com

If you'd like to order team jerseys, they can be found here:

Did you enjoy meeting Jordie and Phoenix? Those characters belong to my bestie, Jade Dollston, and their love story can be found in Hale No.

Made in the USA
Coppell, TX
10 February 2026

71723563R10260